ALSO BY DAN FESPERMAN

The Prisoner of Guantánamo
The Warlord's Son
The Small Boat of Great Sorrows
Lie in the Dark

The Amateur Spy

The Amateur Spy

Dan Fesperman

Alfred A. Knopf New York 2008

THIS IS A BORZOI BOOK
PUBLISHED BY ALFRED A. KNOPF

Copyright © 2007 by Dan Fesperman

All rights reserved. Published in the United States by Alfred A.
Knopf, a division of Random House, Inc., New York, and in Canada
by Random House of Canada Limited, Toronto.

www.aaknopf.com

Knopf, Borzoi Books, and the colophon are registered trademarks of
Random House, Inc.

Originally published in Great Britain by Hodder & Stoughton Ltd,
a division of Hodder Headline, London, in 2007.

Library of Congress Cataloging-in-Publication Data
Fesperman, Dan, [date]
The amateur spy / by Dan Fesperman.—1st American ed.
p.   cm.
ISBN 978-1-4000-4467-2 (alk. paper)
1. Arab Americans—Fiction.   2. Amman (Jordan)—Fiction.
3. Washington (D.C.)—Fiction.   I. Title.
PS3556.E778A8 2008
813'.54—dc22   2007047313

Manufactured in the United States of America
First American Edition

The Amateur Spy

1

At our end of the island, far from any noisy taverna or buzzing scooter, two owls hold a nightly conversation in the treetops by the sea. They start around midnight, hooting back and forth like village gossips while the landscape stands at attention. The only interruption is the slap and sigh of the Aegean, a timeless incantation that seems to whisper of myth and fallen heroes.

I like to imagine the owls are offering a sort of predator hotline, with frequent updates on the whereabouts of targets in the shadows below. After all, they're the professionals at that sort of business. Maybe that's why I was listening so closely on the night in question. Break their code and I'd learn which creatures were at risk—Freeman Lockhart, power broker of the local animal kingdom, beneficent warlord of meadow and brook.

Obviously I failed. Because nothing in their tone caused me the slightest alarm, yet shortly after the hooting stopped, three predators in gray tracksuits crept into our bedroom, and later I realized that every creature but me must have detected a warning. Even Mila, shivering at my side until they took me away, bruised and bleeding, had noticed the fellows earlier that day on the ferry from Piraeus.

My only vivid memory of our ocean passage was of Mila herself as she prepared to vomit from the stern. She wasn't prone to seasickness, but there she stood, hands braced against the rail in a swirl of briny mist while gulls hovered just above, awaiting the spoils. Her face was pale, accentuating the underfed look of her sharp features and high cheekbones. She looked as vulnerable as a stowaway, so I took her gently by the shoulders in hopes of steadying her with a little warmth.

"Must be the excitement," she gasped, still holding it inside.

"Probably," I answered, although I suspected trepidation was more to blame. This voyage was our running start to a long-planned leap of faith, our grand exit to a new life. Having given up on the world at large, we had decided to finally get everything right by going it alone. Stakes like those might make anyone queasy.

We had been at sea for several hours, among fifty or so passengers on one of the few remaining smaller boats—or caïques—that still ply these waters. Most people make the crossing to Karos in half the time, on one of the huge hydroplane "fast boats." But Mila and I share an aversion for their towering hulls, wide-body cabins, and churning speed. They are as coldly efficient as 747s. Being a firm believer in clean getaways, I am also unsettled by their tremendous wakes, mile-long stripes of foam across the sea, pointing a giant arrow at your route of escape.

Besides, when you're going somewhere for the duration, you want to be attuned to the passing of every mile. So we opted for the smaller, slower sort of boat we had taken on our first trip to Karos, three years earlier. What we hadn't counted on was the bluster of early autumn, which soon built the Aegean into ten-foot waves as the deck heaved beneath us.

After a few minutes of unproductive gagging, Mila finally cut loose. The waiting gulls cried sharply in triumph, yellow beaks plucking at her discharge as it streamed toward the foaming water. They fought noisily over the bounty.

"You okay?" I asked, massaging her back.

"No."

She barely got the word out. Then she pushed away my hand and thrust her face back toward the water. I made my exit toward the bow, not for lack of empathy but because of the memories she had stirred. The transaction with the gulls reminded me uncomfortably of our recent profession and all its shortcomings. Until a week ago, Mila and I were aid workers for the United Nations, acting as glorified caterers to the world's wars, famines, and disasters. Most recently we had super-vised feeding centers, handing out rations which at times were scarcely more palatable than what Mila had just offered, and usually to an audi-ence every bit as ravenous as the gulls.

Toward the front of the pitching deck, several backpacking young tourists stood with knees flexed and sunburned faces to the wind, riding the rollers like surfers. I grasped the rail, still trying to shake the images that had pursued me from the stern. Closing my eyes, I saw skeletal mobs racing through dust clouds toward air-dropped crates of bottled water. Eager hands tore away plastic before the parachute even had time to settle. In the foamy sizzle of the passing sea I detected the crackle of gunfire, and as I reopened my eyes I imagined the wounded falling by the wayside in the troughs of retreating waves.

The deck bounced as the boat carved another blue swell, and I looked anew at the surroundings, trying to place myself more firmly in the moment. The light was golden, the air mild, and my lips pleasantly salty. The other passengers at the bow seemed to be enjoying themselves, and I should have been, too. Karos was only an hour away.

Just ahead on the horizon lay the isle of Argos. I shielded my eyes for a closer look, but the whitewashed houses seemed to trickle down the island's crags like droplets of spilled milk, yet another reminder of squandered nutrition.

Years ago in Sudan, toward the end of one particularly exhausting day, a village chieftain with arms and legs like pipe cleaners strolled into our makeshift headquarters and, without asking a soul, tacked onto a tent post a little gift from his family. It was an embroidered inscription of the famous biblical passage from Ecclesiastes, the one about casting your bread upon the waters. I had of course heard it repeated many times—one always does in the aid racket—but it was the latter, lesser-known portion that snagged in my memory now: "Give a portion to seven, yes, to eight, for you do not know what disaster may come upon the land."

Indeed you don't. Especially when, thanks to the well-meaning actions of those you hold dearest, you end up with only enough for six. But that is another story, and only I am privy to its deepest secrets.

A huge thump of the prow slapped away the thought with a blast of spray. Foaming water swabbed the deck in a bracing dose of autumn, and I gasped in exhilarated relief. I barely managed to keep my footing, and the bearded passenger to my left roared with laughter.

"Almost got us, that one!" he shouted above the wind, a Scotsman by the sound of his accent.

I made the mistake of agreeing in English, which only encouraged him.

"Here on holiday?" he yelled.

"No. We live here." He leaned closer to hear. "As of today, anyway. I've just retired."

"Congratulations! You look too young for it."

"Maybe I am. I'm fifty-five."

"No, no. Everyone should be so bloody lucky. Give me a place in these isles and I'd quit in a fuckin' minute."

Quit was the word for it, all right. But reborn, too. At least, that was the plan. Time to stand tall in the front lines of self-sufficiency, with a fishing rod in one hand and a shotgun for hunting in the other, while Mila tended to orchard and garden. Henceforth, any bread we tossed upon the waters would be for our own mouths. Let the next disaster proceed without us, because our former selves were finished, dismantled.

Our new hopes were thanks mostly to Mila. She was thirty-seven, a Bosnian whom I met in '92 during her country's civil war. We were living and working in besieged Sarajevo then, a time when the fates seemed to be conspiring against her and her country. I was fortunate enough to be able to help her survive the experience in one piece, both physically and emotionally, and when the war ended she was ready to go with me anywhere as long as it got her out of there for good. The UN, far more nimble at accommodating unofficial requests than official ones, obliged our wishes to travel in tandem even though we weren't yet married, and for several years running we were island hoppers of African famine for the World Food Programme. Mila viewed each stop as yet another chance to remake the planet in a better image, even as she was repairing her own damage. We have always been quick to rise to the defense of ideals. It's one thing that made us such a good match, although she has always been the more tactful practitioner. Cross a line into dangerous misconduct and we will both draw it to your attention, but her gentler voice will be the one you want to heed. I have given some thought to why my tone is more cynical and strident, and I've decided it is due to my higher rank in the aid bureaucracy, which afforded a better view of the way things really work. Lucky her.

"Pretty, isn't it?" The Scotsman pointed back toward Argos, receding in our wake.

I nodded to be friendly, but I had never liked the look of Argos. Too barren. Too brown and imposing. In the afternoon light the villages protruded from its ridgelines like bones through rotting flesh, and I was unable to suppress a shudder.

"If you think *this* water's cold," the grinning Scotsman said, "then don't ever take a dip in the North Sea."

"Good advice. Excuse me. I should go find my wife."

It must have been around then that Mila noticed the three men. She told me later that after a second purging she felt well enough to head back inside, where she cleaned up using sterile wipes that I'd pilfered the last day on the job. While doing so she idly surveyed the aisles of passengers.

They were together on the back row. What caught her attention was that none of the three appeared to be either a Greek or a vacationer. Karos wasn't exactly a business destination, yet their attire of smart slacks and button-down oxford shirts was trademark business casual. Each had a single overnight bag close at hand. It was almost as if they had come straight from Wall Street. She said there was also something odd about the way they were clumped together, like wagons circled for protection. Most of the other passengers paraded to and fro, visiting the snack bar or the wildness of the deck.

No sooner had these thoughts crossed her mind than another wave of nausea sent her running for the stern. A half hour later we were within sight of Karos, and by the time we boarded a taxi for the ride to our house she had rediscovered her smile and forgotten the men on the back row.

Our spirits lifted as the taxi climbed into the hills. The soft island air rushing through the open windows made it easy to focus on renewal and relaxation.

Karos is neither the prettiest nor the ugliest, the barest nor the lushest, the most cosmopolitan nor the most rustic of the Cyclades. Photographers in search of the most stunning expressions of Aegean charm almost never go there, yet it boasts a brooding monastery atop its highest mountain, a walled medieval town that clings to a coastal bluff like a barnacle, and terraced green hillsides where goats wander among olive trees and pine groves. The domes of Orthodox chapels, many long abandoned, sprout in almost every valley like sky-blue mushrooms.

In the past few years the island has been "discovered" by one of the popular guidebooks, and it now draws a fair share of tourists during the high season. One of the better results of this boomlet is some new nightlife in the port town of Emborios, where a string of tavernas and *ouzeris* curls along a shingle beach. But the island's twenty square miles of hill and dale still offer plenty of hiding places, and at night Karos sinks easily into slumber, save for the owls.

Our house is near the southern tip, about a six-mile drive from Emborios. It is fifteen years old—practically brand-new by local standards— and is fairly small, with six whitewashed rooms. Large windows capture the sunlight when the shutters are thrown open, and a cistern in the back collects rain from the roof tiles. Best of all, there is a fieldstone patio with a trellised grape arbor overhead and a commanding view of the sea, which is a mere hundred yards away down a gentle slope of grass and stone. We bought the place two years ago, just before real estate prices went through the roof, and just as we began contemplating how we wanted to spend the balance of our lives.

I hadn't always craved this sort of getaway. For several years, in fact, I resisted the idea of marrying Mila, mostly because I resisted her idea of what our lives should be like in retirement. She wanted seclusion, a safe harbor where no one could reach her. A castle surrounded by a moat would have been just fine. I favored the idea of heading off to a vibrant city in the thick of the action, some capital of high culture in a healthy land of plenty where I could sample all I had missed during our years amid need.

But year by year, as stresses mounted and the lines of starvation lengthened, Mila gradually won me over to her way of thinking. I also wasn't blind to one of the other key virtues of seclusion: Surrounding Mila with her cherished moat would seal her away from other men. It is the perennial concern of the older lover, I suppose, even though the eighteen years between us had mattered little up to now. I confess to being relieved when she turned thirty. It was as if she had finally crossed some invisible line of safety, and from then on would be less likely to stray. Not that she had ever shown signs of doing so.

Like many Balkan women, Mila carries herself with more dignity and composure than the region's menfolk, who by and large seemed either surly or downtrodden throughout the war. This resilience is one of the qualities I treasure most in her. It lends a sturdiness to her delicate beauty, and a pleasing gravity to her wit and intelligence. It is her emotional ballast, and I would do anything to protect it.

Although we had been planning our move to Karos for months, we were keeping our ambitions modest. During a previous trip to the island Mila had bought a potter's wheel. She hoped to become a part of the island's tradition of ceramics, and planned to dig the clay herself from the sediment of the ancients. She also wanted to plant all-season gardens— one for vegetables, one for flowers—and she had already negotiated the purchase of five goats for milk and cheese. We planned to harvest the bounty of our olive and fig trees, and also the grapes from our patio arbor. Someday we might even acquire a press for making oil, plus a barrel or two for fermenting wine.

I would be pitching in on all these endeavors while also occasionally trooping into the hills to shoot rabbit and dove for the table. My other immediate goals were similarly basic—to read, hike, and fish, and to explore some of the island's Iron Age archaeological sites. In the longer term I hoped to build a small wooden boat seaworthy enough for transiting the shoreline. The blueprints were packed in my bag, and the necessary hand tools were stored in our shed along with a pile of milled lumber. I was determined to do it the old way, without electricity.

All of this makes us sound like aging hippies on the lam, although we are anything but. We both grew up in cities—Mila in Sarajevo, of course, I in Boston—and in our long years of service in the field we grew accustomed to the amenities that regularly fall into the laps of aid workers. That's the funny thing about our business. We can go for months putting up with mud, mobs, and disease, while enduring enough shellfire and checkpoint thuggery to fuel a lifetime of nightmares. Yet, relatively speaking, we often live like pashas, almost always served by a cook, a cleaner, a driver, and a laundress, complete with armed guards and the best available housing. There is also sex on demand from any number of eager colleagues, the only craving that outweighs wanderlust among our gypsy tribe of do-gooders.

So it was not as if Mila and I wished to start a commune. Our rustic agenda had two basic goals: One, keep from becoming hostages to the overpriced food supplies shipped from the mainland. Two, stay busy enough to be comfortably weary at the end of each day, if only because exhaustion is the best antidote to memory.

And once we had attained those goals? Ask us later. We would climb to the next plateau as soon as it showed itself through the mist. When your emotions have lived hand to mouth as long as ours had, even the little planning we had done seemed above and beyond the call of duty.

Mila unlocked the house while I counted out a few euros for the driver and unloaded our bags. When I joined her she was just across the threshold, sniffing the air like an animal whose den has been invaded.

"What's wrong?"

"Don't you smell it?"

I sniffed. Nothing but dampness and dust. The cool air felt as if it hadn't stirred in ages.

"Cigarettes," she whispered. "Someone's been smoking."

I leaned toward her and sniffed again.

"It's your clothes. From the ferry. You've been around too many Greeks."

"No. It's the house."

"Probably just Stavros, from the last time he made the rounds."

Stavros was our nearest neighbor and acted as a sort of caretaker in our absence. He had grown up here, and lived in a much older and smaller house on the opposite side of the road, a quarter mile up the slope. We paid a small fee for his vigilance, although neither of us had the slightest idea of what could go wrong in a place as sleepy as Karos.

"What's the matter?" I joked. "Getting a craving?"

She frowned. Like most sons and daughters of the former Yugoslavia, Mila had once been a chain-smoker, maintaining the habit at great expense throughout the war only to quit on the very day of the Dayton Peace Agreement, reasoning that if her leaders could give up their vices, then so could she. Like them, she was forever on the verge of relapse.

"Stavros isn't supposed to come inside," she said.

"But he has a key, remember? C'mon, you don't really expect an old goat farmer like him to resist the temptation to do a little snooping around?"

I certainly didn't. Stavros was the quintessential local, which meant he wanted to know all the doings in his patch of the pasture. His family had been here since Hellenic times, and he maintained the limited viewpoint of the entrenched islander. To hear him speak of people from the neighboring isles you'd have thought they were from another country altogether, so disdainful was he of their seamanship and their farming skills. This outlook made him the perfect watchdog, and he had always seemed friendly enough. Although who knows what he really thought of us, with our hobbyist attitudes toward the sort of chores he had poured his life into.

"Well, at least nothing seems to be missing."

"He's not a thief, Mila. Just a gossip. Remember all the dirt he told us when they were building the DeKuyper place? He probably just needed some new material for his friends at the pub. Maybe he's worried you're secretly a Turk."

That produced a theatrical cold stare. Nothing gets a Serb's back up quicker than calling him a descendant of the Ottomans.

"Relax," I said. "If it'll make you feel better, I'll speak to him tomorrow. Lay down a few ground rules. But he's going to be our neighbor for the rest of our lives, so we might as well get used to him poking around."

"The rest of our lives. I had almost forgotten that part."

Her eyes got a little dreamy, and she moved closer, her hand brushing my cheek before she slipped her arms around me. The top of her head came up to just beneath my nose, and her hair smelled like the sea.

We stood that way a moment, tightening our grip while we got used to the idea of settling in. It was scary and exciting all at once, and I felt her heart beating urgently. I looked over her shoulder through the big window facing the sea, searching for an omen. But there was only enough sunlight to see the faintest glimmer of the waves.

"Why don't we wait 'til tomorrow to round up supplies," I said. "I'll fire up the scooters. We can go back into Emborios for dinner, that fish taverna you like. We'll bring back a jug of retsina."

"Sounds perfect." Her forehead was pressed to my sternum, and I felt the words go straight into my chest. "We'll watch the nine o'clock ferry come in, like we always do. When the wake comes ashore we'll know it's the last thing from the mainland that can bother us."

"Until tomorrow, anyway."

She unpacked our bags while I retrieved our scooters from the locked shed out back. I had left the tanks empty, so I poured in fresh oil and gasoline, cleaned the plugs, and primed the carburetors. Each engine choked to life on a wheezing sputter of blue exhaust, and I let them run a while before shutting off the smaller one. We would take the big one into town, riding double. Mila didn't like riding hers after dark on the island's narrow and twisting climbs.

Our favorite taverna was on the opposite side of the harbor from most of the noise and tourists. This offered more seclusion, and also a pleasant view back across the water. At night you could see the ferries approaching from miles away, lit up like floating Christmas trees.

The evenings were still warm enough to eat comfortably outdoors, so we took a table at the edge of the patio. Wavelets hissed onto the smooth stones of the beach just a few feet away.

As with almost any such place in Greece, cats were underfoot from the moment our food arrived. They were fatter out here in the islands, perhaps from hanging around the fishing docks, demanding their cut of the action as the boats came in. Their overwhelming numbers in Athens were easy enough to explain, with all those alleys and sewers to breed in. Here their presence was more of a riddle, and I liked to joke that they must have been placed by the government's secret police. They certainly made perfect operatives—invisible by day and omnipresent by night, eavesdropping on conversations at virtually every café and taverna.

We dined simply but well on a tomato and cucumber salad, a bowl of olives, a plate of the local goat cheese, and a whole snapper, which had been brushed with oil and grilled until the skin was charred. Mila's stomach was still a little shaky from the ferry, so I ate the lion's share.

We also drained the better part of a small carafe of the taverna's home-made retsina, and then bought a corked jug to take home. We had developed a taste for its sharp, piney flavor, much as the Greeks did under Roman occupation, when the centurions and imperial bureaucrats took all the good stuff for themselves.

The proprietor, a big jolly fellow named Nikos, delivered the jug personally to the table, having remembered us from earlier visits. When we told him we were now here for good, he slapped me heartily on the back and called for complimentary shots of ouzo, beaming all the while. Mila was strangely silent throughout, and seemed relieved when he finally left the table.

"Still queasy? Or are you chilly?"

She shook her head and smiled wanly.

"Sorry. He scares me a little."

"Nikos?"

She nodded, knocking back her ouzo in a single gulp.

"It's the only thing I've never liked about this place."

"He's a big teddy bear."

"I know. But he reminds me of Karadzic."

I turned in my chair just in time to see Nikos disappear through the kitchen door.

"You're right," I said, chuckling at the resemblance. "Especially the hair. A Balkan pompadour."

But a glance at Mila told me this was no laughing matter. For a moment she even seemed to be trembling. Reminders of the war could affect her that way, especially when they triggered one particular memory. And I suppose someone who looked like Radovan Karadzic was as potent a reminder as any. I am referring, of course, to the wartime "president" of the Bosnian Serbs, an accused war criminal still at large. As a Serb, Mila had technically been one of his subjects, but by going to work for the UN as a legal protection clerk she had boldly declared her neutrality. That turned all three warring factions against her, and the Serbian soldiers were especially harsh. Just for laughs one of them fired a shot over her head when she was escorting refugees across a snowy checkpoint.

Throughout the war Mila lived and worked at a UN office in the city's hulking telecommunications headquarters, the PTT Building, which sat within a hundred yards of the siege lines like a giant concrete bunker. She shared space with three other women. They slept on cots next to their desks, then stacked the cots in a corner every morning.

They stored their clothes in a file cabinet and their cosmetics in an abandoned office safe.

We met in that office. It's also where we had our first desperate assignation, right there on her cot, taking advantage of a rare evening when her roommates were away. I still remember the sharp press of my elbows against the aluminum tubing, the eerie red flashes in the darkened office every time a tracer round screamed past the windows, and the rumble of the floor whenever a shell landed nearby. Make love during a firefight and the earth *does* move. Afterward Mila took great pleasure in introducing me to friends and family as "battle-hardened," knowing that only the two of us would get the joke.

Since the end of the war she hadn't once been back to Sarajevo. Whenever she needed to touch base with her family she instead visited her mother's Greek relatives, her aunt Aleksandra's brood in the suburbs of Athens. In fact, it was while staying with them that we had planned our first trip to Karos.

But now, seated there at the taverna on the first night of our future, she looked truly shaken, and I wondered if it had something to do with knowing we were now here for good. On previous trips, any annoyance would soon be left behind. Now it was something she had to endure.

"Don't worry," I said, refilling her glass. "If I see him rounding up any tourists for detention I'll make sure he's arrested."

Mila shook her head, and soon afterward I quietly paid the bill to a crestfallen Nikos, who seemed mystified by the pall that had fallen over our table. We strapped the jug to the back of the scooter and set out for home. By then the last ferry had departed, and from across the water only one bar along the strip in Emborios was still playing music, a blaring chorus of the Who.

These scooter trips could be a little harrowing even by day, and the air had cooled considerably in the hours since sunset. Mila kept my back warm by snuggling close and tucking her arms around my waist, and I soon grew accustomed to negotiating the tight curves. I fell into a rhythm, leaning gently into each turn and accelerating on the inclines, just tipsy enough to be thrilled by fleeting glimpses of dimly lit farmhouses in the ravines below. An oncoming van passed a bit too close for comfort, but that was customary here.

It was only the smaller hazards that made me jumpy. Approaching the crest of a hill, the pale beam of our headlight illuminated a clump of pine needles on the pavement just ahead. I swerved to avoid it, trying not to squeeze the brake, and then accelerated jerkily as the engine coughed. Mila must have felt my racing heartbeat, but she was accustomed to this quirk of mine, this remnant of our past. Having traveled on far too many mined roads, I could no longer bring myself to cross suspicious piles of leaves, mud, or trash on any bike or scooter. I had once assumed the habit would fade over time, but if anything it now came to me naturally, like a feature built into the steering. Mila had learned not to mention it.

If we hadn't left a light on we might not have spotted our house. It was something to keep in mind for future late-night excursions, although I wondered if those would become a rarity as our little homestead developed its own comfortable rhythm. Even the worst places did, and I had developed a knack for learning them, a skill almost as useful as picking up the local language.

The last few hundred yards up our stony driveway were some of the trickiest of the ride, and Mila heaved a sigh of relief when we finally bounced to a stop.

"I'm spent," she said, as breathless as if she had been running.

The silence of the hillside seemed to close in on us.

"It's been a long day. Got enough energy for one last toast?" I lofted the jug from the back of the scooter. "Christen our new life?"

The pale glow from our front window illuminated a weary smile.

"Of course."

We had to search the cabinets for the wineglasses, and if I hadn't known better I'd have sworn Mila was again sniffing the air.

"Here they are," she said. She wiped off the dust with the hem of her skirt while I threw open the doors to the patio. We went to the trestle table outside, and she raised her glass to mine.

"To perfection," she said.

"You think that's what we'll find here?"

"Not all the time. No one does. But sometimes, sure. It's what you deserve. You've earned some perfection."

Doubtful. But I was happy to let Mila believe it, so I tipped my glass to hers and savored a resinous sip. Then, as if by prior signal, we strolled off hand in hand to the bedroom, where she placed her glass on the nightstand and lit a candle. I embraced her from behind, pressing against her buttocks as she sighed and arched her back. She turned to me slowly for a lingering kiss, and we undressed each other as tenderly as if it were our first time. Considering the circumstances, it almost seemed like it was. I suppose we were eager to set just the right tone. No need to rush anymore. No mouths to feed or fears to calm but our own.

With a new and unlimited freedom lying before us, we could achieve frenzy by degrees, which made it all the more tantalizing.

Afterward we lay in bed, relaxed and swapping old stories that had always made us laugh. We had made it, it seemed. One journey completed and another begun. The window was thrown open to the night noises of the sea, with a full view of the stars.

"You see?" she said. "It's not always so hard finding perfection."

"Sure beats making it in a tent out in the middle of nowhere."

"No more of that, I guess. God, when I think of all the strange places we've made love. Maybe we should make a list."

"We could have your aunt Aleksandra put it in needlepoint. Hang it on the wall over there."

She laughed.

"Perfect. That little hooch in Sierra Leone could go right at the top."

"What, because of our audience?"

Several lanky young boys had walked in on us while Mila was seated atop me, breasts dripping sweat onto my chest. Fortunately they had not come to alert us to any emergency. They had simply been on a random prowl, checking out the latest arrivals from the outside world. Mila got flustered and told them she was giving me a massage for a stomachache, a story I promptly ruined by heaving with laughter and making her breasts bounce.

"You think we gave them an education?" I asked.

"I'm sure they'd seen worse. Or better. Family of ten living in the same room. Not much they hadn't seen from Mom and Dad by then."

We recalled other locations—a grass mat beneath the stars in Goma, a hammock slung inside a sweltering tent in Congo that collapsed on us during a cloudburst. Or that night on the edge of a mud desert when Mila got up for a drink of water and nearly stepped on a scorpion that had bedded down in her shoes.

Other places came to mind as well, but some were best not mentioned on this night or any other. Merely thinking of one of them made me want to pull the covers higher over Mila, so dark and powerful were its memories. Fortunately, her imagination must not have strayed there, because when she next spoke she sounded as cheerful as before.

"I do miss the mosquito netting. There was something very sexy about it, having it draped all around us like that."

"The lace canopy bed of the aid worker. Maybe Stavros could lend us one of his fishing nets."

"Stavros." She frowned. "Next time he's in here he better not smoke."

Then she yawned and rolled onto her side, facing me. A lock of hair fell across her mouth, and she was too drowsy to even pull it away, so I did it for her. Within seconds she was asleep. I leaned across her to blow out the candle, then thought better of it. I was still too keyed up to sleep. Part of it was excitement over what lay ahead, but I was also still agitated by the disturbing memory that had crossed my mind moments ago.

I slid out of bed and threw on a robe and slippers. Then I took the candle, refilled my wineglass, and stepped back into the night. The breeze was picking up, and it carried the scent of the fields, a grassy blend with weedy hints of caramel and skunk. Somewhere around the house were guidebooks for the local flora and fauna. I needed to start learning which plants made what smells, and which ones might be useful. This was my universe now, a pleasing thought. In the morning there would be no crowds seeking aid and comfort. Only Stavros, uphill with his goats and his blue bee boxes, out walking terraced groves in the sun.

I searched the sky, which on clear nights here was always brilliant with a milky wash of stars. There was Orion with his belt, standing guard. Above him to the right I spotted Castor and Pollux, twin brothers to Helen of Troy. They always seemed more mysterious and timeless when viewed from the land that named them.

It was around then that the owls started up. They'd done this without fail during our earlier trips, and the sound's familiarity was welcoming. I listened for a while as I savored the last of the wine, vainly trying to decipher their meaning, and I was about to turn in when I heard the boat.

The motor didn't sound like a big one, and a few moments later I spotted red and green running lights passing just offshore, moving slowly north to south. By water, we were only three miles from Emborios. The journey was easy under good conditions, and the sea was still fairly calm despite the freshening breeze. But it seemed odd for such a small craft to be poking around at this hour, and in these waters. The fishermen of Karos sometimes trolled or laid traps in darkness, but that usually happened toward dawn, and I'd never heard that the pickings were particularly good along our stretch of coastline.

The boat continued south, now moving out of sight. The noise was loud enough that the owls halted in mid-sentence, as if annoyed by the interruption. Unless the boat was circling the island—which seemed unlikely—its only possible destination was the southernmost dock, at the DeKuyper villa that Stavros had told us so much about. It was uphill from us, barely visible from our place and perhaps a mile away as the crow flies. It was the only house farther out on the point than ours, except for a few abandoned stone shacks built centuries ago by hunters and herdsmen.

DeKuyper was a Dutch industrialist who had made his fortune in plastics, apparently by winning big contracts with the European Union. According to the locals, he rarely visited, and even then he almost never showed his face in the towns. Stavros had positively gushed with tales of the Italianate marble and custom ironwork that went into the construction of the villa, reputedly the largest on the island. But he always showed a grudging respect whenever he spoke of the man himself, in the way of a serf discussing the lord of the manor.

I had always wondered how much Stavros exaggerated these stories. From our vantage point the house seemed to fit snugly into the hillside. It didn't look any flashier than about half the new places that now towered over Emborios. Perhaps DeKuyper had found one of those architects who is an expert at concealing wealth and ambition. Maybe the house, like an iceberg, kept its bulk out of sight. I walked to the southern edge of the patio and looked uphill. Total darkness. If DeKuyper was home, or receiving visitors by sea, then he hadn't exactly rolled out the welcome mat.

It's hard to say for sure what unsettled me most about the boat. Its apparent stealth, perhaps—the careful speed as it crept down the coastline, even though every craft I'd seen before on such a track had plowed by at breakneck pace, trailing a white rooster tail of spray. Maybe it was also the natural skittishness of anyone trying to settle into a new home, especially one as isolated as ours. In any case, when the boat did not return in the next fifteen minutes I watched the hillside in anticipation, waiting for a light to come on. When none did, I concluded that it had either scooted farther around the island or out to the open sea.

I went back inside and shut the doors against the chill. Then I felt my way down the hallway to a closet where I kept an old shotgun. Its heft and shape were familiar, although it somehow felt heavier in the dark. I smelled gun oil and the metal of the barrel as I carried it to our room, careful not to bump the walls. Then I placed it on the floor just beneath my side of the bed, where I hoped Mila wouldn't notice it in the morning.

Old habits die hard, I suppose. Aid workers for the UN had never been allowed to keep firearms, even though we often paid, and paid dearly, for well-fortified security when we couldn't enlist the help of our blue-helmeted protection forces. Walking around armed to the teeth would have made us look like just another combatant, or so the reasoning went. Good advice in theory but not always in practice, so I had learned to use a wide variety of weapons and, in the worst of places, had always kept one nearby, if out of sight. Mila disapproved of the practice, but even she realized that it had come in handy a few times. And she almost never had to deal directly with many of the scoundrels I had faced almost daily.

Just before sliding between the sheets I remembered that the gun was unloaded, so I went back down the hall to retrieve a box of shells. It was in its usual place, but was empty. I was almost certain that I had left a few in there after my last hunting excursion. Maybe Mila was right after all about Stavros, the old brigand. I made a note to call on him first thing.

The owls resumed their conversation just as I was climbing into bed, and their calls were as comforting as an all-clear signal. My precautions suddenly seemed foolish. Mila breathed softly at my side, her body cooling beneath the sheets. I had shut the window, but the shutters were thrown open to a starlit deep blue. It cast a pale light that made my skin look almost as young as hers. The smell of candle wax mingled with the sour aftertaste of retsina. I listened from the pillow until the owls stopped. Probably the night's final update from the realm of the hunter and the hunted.

Soon afterward I must have drifted off to sleep, because the next thing I remember was a flashlight shining brightly in my face, jarring me awake. I blinked and squinted and bolted upright, thinking for a moment that I must be in a tent on yet another scene of ruination. A hand shoved against my sternum to make sure I went no farther. Then a smooth male voice spoke from out of the glare. In English, with an American accent.

"Time to get up, Freeman Lockhart."

Mila was already sitting, rigid beside me with the sheet pulled to her neck. She said nothing, just stared with wide eyes.

Someone flipped on the ceiling light. In addition to the man at my right, another stood by Mila, and a third was at the foot of the bed. They wore identical gray tracksuits, and smelled like cigarettes.

"You were on the ferry," Mila said.

"Good girl, Mila!"

It was again the man to my right who spoke. He sounded genuinely pleased.

"You're very observant. More so than Freeman, anyway. That will have to change."

I was still too unstrung to be very observant. But it somehow made everything worse that they knew our names. Maybe that's what made me think of the gun, just beneath me on the floor. I reached down for it and had just grasped the stock when a foot planted firmly on my hand while a fist struck sharply across the bridge of my nose. The impact was blinding. I dropped the gun and felt blood ooze up in my nostrils and then drip onto my chest. The man kicked the gun away and let go.

"That's all right," he said, still just as calm as you please. "Wouldn't have done you much good without these, in any event." He pulled a few shells from the pocket of his warm-up jacket.

"Who the hell are you? What do you want?" I tried to snarl it, but sounded more like a man with a cold.

"I'm Mr. Black. And these are my colleagues, Mr. White and Mr. Gray."

Black, White, and Gray. Obviously their idea of a joke, although we were in no mood to laugh. But it's odd how quickly one can grow accustomed to an intrusion like this, or at least calm enough to begin weighing your odds for survival. On the positive side, I had yet to see any gun or weapon other than my own, and in disarming me Black had used no more force than was necessary. He also had maintained his strangely placid demeanor. As he spoke I felt my pulse rate slacken. Just try to think of it as one of those times in the field when you were summoned in the middle of the night to some emergency, I told myself. This, too, shall pass.

"As for your second question, we want *you*, Freeman. For a few hours anyway. You don't mind if we borrow him a while, do you, Mila?"

She answered by lunging for the phone on her side of the bed. The fellow named White reacted with an agility somewhere between that of a cat and an antelope, crossing six feet of space in a fraction of a second. I reached across the bed to protect her, but before I could even slip an arm around her waist White had taken Mila's arm with one hand and the telephone with the other. She cried out in pain and shrank back, whereupon White immediately let go. He accomplished all this without even knocking over her wineglass, and then stepped away from the bed as smoothly as a waiter who had just delivered the check. Mila rubbed her wrist. The skin on her shoulder beneath my fingers was gooseflesh, and I felt her body quivering in rage or fear, perhaps both.

"Please," Black said in mock aggrievement. "That's been temporarily disconnected anyway." He dropped a handkerchief in my lap. "You'd better clean up. Where we're going it won't be good form if you start bleeding all over the carpet."

By then, what was disturbing me most was their skill and polish. Black's response to me, and then White's to Mila, plus whatever stealth they must have employed in making their entry, suggested the sort of deftness that results from years of training and days of planning. In a way it would have been less frightening to be dealing with brutal thugs and a host of heavy weaponry, a gang of robbers who would do the deed and then vanish. The professionalism now on display bespoke a higher authority, some organization with deadlines to meet, goals to achieve, and real staying power.

"Who do you work for?" I asked.

"What is it they say? 'We're from Washington and we're here to help.' We're with a government agency near and dear to your heart. No one you'd be embarrassed to be seen with. Not even on Karos."

"And if I'd prefer not to take you up on the invitation?"

"Then I suppose we'll have to be a little more convincing." His tone remained cheerful, his smile intact, but I got the message.

"So, what do you say, Freeman? Will you be coming with us?"

I looked to Mila for counsel, but her eyes offered only despair. All things considered, I decided that leaving might be the best course of action.

2

It was certainly a low-tech abduction. A single flashlight lit our way as we threaded uphill along a stony path, stepping past brambles and goat droppings. I had not yet explored this part of the hillside, and kept thinking we would soon reach a road where car doors would slam and other figures would emerge from the darkness, well armed and efficient, to bundle me up and drive me away. But we just kept walking, no one saying a word.

After half an hour we finally reached a gravel lane, and I looked around for a truck or van, some vehicle bristling with antennae, or lit from within by the glow of sensitive equipment. But still we walked, having covered at least a mile by now. I was beginning to regain my confidence, and with it, my eagerness to find a way out.

Black led the way. Gray was behind me. White had stayed with Mila, presumably in case she got a notion to run or tried reconnecting the phone. Although at this hour the local constabulary was probably fast asleep in a haze of ouzo. The whole island seemed hushed, the stars immovable. It was so dry up here that there wasn't even dew on the grass, but perspiration soaked my shirt and I was breathing heavily from the climb.

I suppose it should have bothered me that my escorts hadn't covered their faces, or blindfolded me for our journey. Wasn't that supposed to spell doom? Would I end up in a weighted sack at the bottom of the Aegean?

It seemed unlikely, if only because I have never been a keeper of anyone's secrets but my own. While those are dark enough, they would seem to be of little concern to any larger cause or movement. That is almost always the nature of your secrets when you're paid to stay on the sidelines, closely observing the action but only rarely joining in.

Twice we paused while Black spoke into a handheld radio. I couldn't make out the words, and wondered if he was talking to White, making sure everything was okay back at the house.

Under other circumstances the hike might have been enjoyable. It felt good to stretch my legs. The pain in my nose had subsided to a dull throb, and the fresh air cleared my head after our day of travel and all of the wine. A waning crescent moon was suspended above the sea. The night breeze had shifted, and even through the smell of drying blood I caught a whiff of brine.

Black and Gray still hadn't displayed a weapon, and I mulled the possibility of making a run for it. Compared to war, famine, or even some local thug with a private army, taking on a mere pair of unarmed adversaries on a gravel lane in the dark seemed like a tolerable matchup, no matter how well they were trained. The hang-up was Mila, and what might happen to her if I simply bolted. If I could first grab the radio out of Black's hand, then I might make a run for it with a clear conscience, dashing downhill into the brush. Newcomer or not, I knew the island's terrain better than they did, and I could set out quickly for the nearest village, Kastro. The thought of arriving at its crumbling Hellenic watchtowers seemed like salvation itself. Bang on a doorway to awaken some townsman in his nightshirt, a medieval scene where he would hoist a lantern and sound the alarm, alerting his neighbors to the intruders in their midst.

I waited until Black halted and again pulled the radio from his jacket. Before he could make contact I made my move. But as soon as I took my first step, Gray pounced, pulling my wrist behind my back with some deft move he must have learned ages ago and tripping me with his right foot. The next thing I knew I was on my knees, gravel digging into my joints.

"You're not going to be like this all night, are you, Freeman?"

It was Black, lowering the radio. I said nothing in reply.

"Besides, we're almost there. Bear with us a while longer. Show's about to start."

The gravel lane turned out to be a driveway to the DeKuyper place, and after another few hundred yards our little party sauntered up to a huge wooden door. Black produced a jangling set of keys with the assurance of an invited guest. The house was still completely dark, and I counted at least three unlockings before the door swung free. Gray, taking care to stay behind me, didn't switch on a light until he had shut the door.

Stavros had been right. The place was really something. High ceilings and a cavernous great room with floor-to-ceiling windows, which probably overlooked the sea, although right now the curtains were drawn.

The other rooms, what I could see of them, seemed to have been decorated in good but somewhat sterile taste. Maybe DeKuyper had paid someone. Oak floors were covered with thick rugs and colorful throws, all well coordinated even if the overall effect was a trifle lifeless. Heavy beams supported a vaulted ceiling. Shelves in every corner displayed samples of local pottery. Other artwork seemed to have been selected mostly for the colors, which blended with the rugs and curtains. A passing glance at the kitchen revealed gleaming, oversized appliances and black marble countertops.

"This way," Black said, turning down a hallway, flipping on lights as he went.

"Friends of the owner?" I asked. "Or paying customers? Or did you get those keys some other way?"

"We're friends with a lot of people."

We turned down a hallway. A door at the end opened onto a long room with wall-to-wall carpet.

"In here. We'll do our business in the boardroom."

A boardroom was exactly what it resembled—eight sleek leather swivel chairs around a long teak table straight out of Scandinavia. There was a video screen on the far wall, and someone had set up a laptop at the end of the table. The carpet smelled new. Maybe DeKuyper had built the place as a corporate retreat, a tax write-off where he could harbor one of his yachts. I wondered if Black, White, and Gray were staying overnight. Maybe I would be, too.

"Be seated, Freeman."

Black locked the door behind him and gestured to a chair in the middle, where I took a seat. Gray moved down to sit at the laptop and began pecking at the keyboard. The video screen lit up, displaying a field of icons across a wallpaper of fleecy clouds. It looked as if they were going to treat me to a PowerPoint presentation, as if they were selling Amway, or time-shares.

"We're here to make a sales pitch," Black said, as if happy to confirm my suspicions. "Shouldn't take more than an hour, so relax. Try thinking of us as slightly unorthodox corporate headhunters and it will be much easier to take."

I tried placing his accent. I'm usually good at that. Among fellow Americans I can pin down the lilt of Georgia, the pinched vowels of Cleveland, traces of each of the five boroughs of New York, and any hint of a past tie to Europe, Asia, or the Middle East. So far with these fellows, Gray had hardly spoken and White had yet to utter a word. That left Black, whose intonations were wiped clean of identity. He might have been raised by a family of newscasters in Indianapolis.

What else to make of the man? Urbane. An air of competence. Probably someone who found it easy to get comfortable in a tight place. I had come across men just like him out in the field, especially during a brief hitch in Afghanistan, where intelligence people were as thick on the ground as farmers, planting their own exotic seeds for harvest. As with them, I assumed that whatever poses Black showed me probably had nothing to do with the person he really was. It was part of his profession, a performance to divert your view from everything he wished to hide. So go ahead and look at his face all you wanted, he seemed to say, because he had more important things to disguise.

"There's a job we want you to do for us," Black said. "But before getting into specifics I thought we might introduce our package of inducements."

Gray clicked the mouse. Onto the screen flashed a copy of my résumé, or CV, the entire career of Freeman Napier Lockhart encapsulated in forty-five lines of black type. You couldn't have found that just anywhere, and I stirred uneasily.

"Accurate?" Black asked.

"Must be, since I wrote it. Where did you get this?"

"Let's go back a few years. We'll skip the stuff about law school, the public defender's job, the first UN posting to Singapore. Helping with boat people, wasn't it?"

"Coming from Vietnam, yes. Summer of '81." The smell of fish oil and the green glow of the warm Pacific. Stern Singapore policemen who loved nothing better than bashing skulls with billy clubs whenever a loaded sampan came ashore under our so-called protection. Bashed mine once, too, which won me two expense-paid weeks in a hospital along with an insincere apology from the foreign minister.

"What are we playing, 'This Is Your Life'?"

"More like Scrooge's visitation by the spirits, except that I'll be doing the talking for all three spirits. Just a friendly assessment of your past, your present, and—quite possibly—your future."

"Nice to know I have one. Not sure I like the Scrooge comparison, though."

"Oh, it fits. You'll see. But no need to worry. We're here to help you set things right. Rebalance the ledger. Give us the next image, Gray. Our real starting point. Recognize this fellow?"

I did. The picture on the screen was a tanned, smiling man in his late thirties, dressed in khaki pants, a white polo, and a Day-Glo orange vest that made him look like a school crossing guard. Stones lay on the pavement all around him like spent shell casings, an appropriate image because all of them had been thrown in anger. The air was smudged by traces of oily black smoke, which I knew had come from burning tires. The man stood in front of a white Volkswagen Passat station wagon with a large blue "UN" painted on the door.

"It's me. On the West Bank. Nablus, by the look of it. Around nineteen . . ."

"Eighty-eight. June, to be exact. Just as the intifada was hitting its stride. During your one-year posting, riding shotgun for a two-man observer team for UNRWA." He correctly pronounced the acronym "OON-rah," although with a slight note of disdain. It stood for a mouthful, the United Nations Relief and Works Agency for Palestine Refugees in the Near East, an outfit that was still alive, if not exactly kicking. Its mission was to serve the needs of the millions of Arab refugees who had been uprooted during the procession of wars that began with the creation of Israel in 1948. The wars have continued at irregular intervals since—like a comet with an erratic orbit, capable of destroying entire worlds on every return.

"Interesting place to start," I said.

"Why?" Black sounded genuinely curious.

"It was my first taste of war. Or what I thought was war, until I saw the real thing in Bosnia. I'd never been that close to gunfire."

"Did it scar you for life?" Now he was playing with me.

"If anything, I enjoyed it too much. Watching all the dustups and confrontations, then trying to sort them out."

"Boys throwing stones versus soldiers and tanks. Not exactly a great matchup from the fan's point of view."

"No. It never was. It's why we felt like we had to be there."

"Witnessing for the world."

"Make fun of it if you want, but, yes, that's what we were doing."

"Funny how you fellows got out of the witnessing business once the suicide bombers found their way into the mix. Maybe all your good deeds and compassion helped give Hamas a jump start. Either way, you should have no trouble remembering this fellow."

Gray clicked again. The shot was almost identical, except this time the character standing by the UN car was a bronzed young Arab, mid-twenties, black hair askew. The orange vest draped him like a sack, and he seemed to be suppressing a smile. Suppressing all sorts of feelings, in fact, because that had been one of the job requirements.

"Good Lord. It's Omar."

"Omar al-Baroody, your partner in crime. Almost cute the way they paired you up, car by car. One Palestinian for every outsider. Ten little teams patrolling at any one time. Just like Butch and Sundance. Or Starsky and Hutch. You did two hitches with Omar, correct?"

"Yes. We were partners for my second three months, and then for the last three."

Two stints like night and day—the first tense and argumentative, the second loose and harmonious. In between we did a lot of growing up, and we parted as friends.

"Been in touch with Omar lately?"

"Only by letter. Haven't seen him in years. He still sends New Year's cards when he can find me. For a while I kept expecting his name to turn up on one of the parliament lists for the Palestinian Authority. Then he moved to Jordan."

"That's right. To Amman. He's still there, with a new venture in the works."

"Doing what?"

"More on that later."

Was Omar in some sort of trouble? As far as my country's government was concerned, it seemed a likely possibility for any Palestinian male of means and cleverness, and Omar qualified on both counts. But such worries dissolved when Gray put up the next image.

It was the hulking gray PTT Building in Sarajevo, the bunkerlike fortress of offices where Mila and I had worked for three years. Shell damage made it look like someone had dragged a giant rake across the concrete facing.

"Bosnia, '92. Where you met your wife."

I said nothing in reply. The mention of Mila reminded me of the stakes in play. I wondered how she was faring with White, and what would become of her if they kept me much longer.

"If there's a point to all this, will you be making it soon?"

"Patience."

As Black said it, he bunched and steepled the fingers of his right hand, palm up, then waggled them up and down. It was the same sign that every driver in Jerusalem and the West Bank makes when you honk your horn or yell for them to get out of the way. It, too, meant "patience," but its subtext was "Fuck you, asshole." Black's little way of telling me to shut my yap, or of hinting that this whole production was leading up to something concerning the Middle East.

Gray clicked ahead to an image of lanky African boys crowded at the mouth of a dirty white tent.

"Rwanda," he said. Then he named an outpost town where we had set up shop. "Nineteen ninety-six. Toward the end of your time there. And here's where things get interesting. Gray?"

Gray pulled a Tyvek envelope from a briefcase and slid it across the table to Black. We were moving onto dangerous ground. Everything I had eaten at the taverna was astir, coiling in my entrails like a rattler. I took a deep breath, but this only brought on a cramp, so I exhaled loudly.

"What's the matter, Freeman? Don't like where this is headed? Or just worried we'll keep you up too late? What's on your agenda for tomorrow? Goat herding? Chopping firewood? Trimming the grape arbor? Nothing that can't wait—not for this, anyway."

Black plucked a sheet from the envelope and, without missing a beat, began to read aloud.

"August twelve. You're promoted to chief programme officer. Interesting the way they spell 'programme' with the extra 'M' plus the 'E' on the end, like the British. As if they'll do anything possible to distance themselves from the taint of America. Or maybe I'm hypersensitive. One of those knuckle-dragging 'America Firsters.' " He smiled broadly. "On August twenty you make your first big supply requisition, ordering through a contractor in Kigali known as"—he pulled out a second sheet that looked like an old invoice—"Consolidated Aid Enterprises, Mr. M. Charles Mbweli, proprietor. Possibly a front, possibly the real thing."

"More possibly a bloodsucker, in Mbweli's case."

"So you admit that now?"

"Now? I never had any illusions about Mbweli. None of us did. Whether he was stealing from his own people or shooting them in the back."

In a way, it was a shame they didn't have a slide of Mbweli, because he was quite a sight. Piratical beard, huge biceps, big belly. Wore dark green camouflage and an undersized maroon beret, which was always tilted at forty-five degrees. In the wake of the Rwandan genocide he had waded into the local chaos from neighboring tribal lands and carved out a commanding presence as a local supply broker. It was not a matter of serving the public. It merely meant he had seized control of key roads and transport in the supply corridors vital to our mission. A fan of American action movies, Mbweli kept a collection of bootleg Schwarzenegger, Stallone, and Van Damme videos in a huge, clattering pile that he would rummage through noisily whenever he needed a dose of adrenaline. To emulate his heroes he pumped iron and was always in the market for new weaponry. Firearms rode his body like remoras on a shark, a symbiotic relationship that kept him moving through danger-ous waters. That made him pretty much like everyone else of influence at that particular time and place. But it was the gun he had aimed at Mila, figuratively speaking, that I remembered best. Yet another story for later, because it was clear Black wasn't in the mood for excuses.

"Bad apple or not, you chose to do business with him."

"Choice had nothing to do with it."

"In any event, you ordered enough food, tents, plastic sheeting . . ." He paused to consult the paper. "Blankets, water purification chemicals, et cetera, et cetera, to feed and shelter one hundred thousand desperate souls for up to three months. Then, just like that, you let Mbweli raise the bar to one hundred and *twenty* thousand before you forwarded the bill to New York. At fifteen dollars per person, per month, the cost of that extra freight came to a total of . . ."

"Is this really necessary? A litany of UN fuckups and bureaucratic expedience? If we could have shot the bastard, we would have. But in our business we have to play by rules, even when the other side is mak-ing them up. If you've got a problem with that, then maybe I can save everybody a lot of time by pleading guilty on behalf of all of us."

"You know it wasn't that simple."

"Actually, it *was* that simple. You go along with the locals, even the thugs like Mbweli, or no one gets fed. That's how it works in the field, especially when you're up against the deadline of a famine or a flood, or you're facing three divisions of a revolutionary army that's pushing a million head of human cattle before them, right toward a camp where you and maybe a dozen people have to get everything up and running within a few days. Or else. Every day of delay and another hundred peo-ple are going to die. It *is* that simple. And when it's time to requisition supplies there's almost always somebody like Mbweli standing in your way, with one hand out and the other one on an AK-47. It's the same in every country. Warlords and thugs demanding a piece of the action just to get your trucks through. But they make you spread it around, of course. They force you into the system, to buy everyone's silence."

"*Force* you? Like this, you mean?" He slid the Tyvek envelope across the table. "Take a look inside. Then we'll talk about who forced who."

I won't bore you with the gory details. Suffice it to say that the envelope was stuffed with invoices and eyewitness accounts, some of them almost certainly coerced, or otherwise dubious in origin. And none of it came even close to explaining what had really happened in Africa that summer, or in the terrible years since.

Just the thought of that time in our lives could still fry my brain with its flashbacks of horror and exhaustion. Unbearable suffering had unspooled before us like tales from the darkest passages of the Old Testament. Entire towns and provinces felled by plague, famine, and misfortune, and then we watched as the survivors were descended upon by blowflies, opportunists, and more aid workers, the only three species for miles around that managed to stay fully nourished.

For me, all this had come in the wake of four years of war and upheaval, and somewhere inside me the damage must have been accruing like interest due on a delinquent loan. So I suppose I was too worn out to consider the possibility that any fresh mistake could have consequences for anyone but me.

I would have explained all that to Black if I had thought he was in the mood to listen. But he was already off and running, ticking off the highlights of the materials I was viewing and making pointed references to certain authorities in New York and Geneva who he said might be interested in knowing all about it. To my mind it was nonsense, and I decided it was time to force the issue.

"Enough," I said, closing the envelope. "I could offer you the truth about all this, but you've obviously made up your mind. Why don't you just tell me what you're after?"

He seemed almost disappointed it had been this easy.

"Very well. Mr. Gray, skip ahead to slide number seven."

Gray's fingers tap-danced across the keyboard, and Omar al-Baroody reappeared on the screen, except this shot was more recent. Omar sat in a nice restaurant before a linen tablecloth. Smiling and sunlit, a rather posh lunch. He appeared to be speaking to someone out of the frame. The tops of the heads of other diners loomed in the foreground, giving you the distinct impression that Omar hadn't known he was being photographed.

I was momentarily captivated by his changed appearance. A fleshier face, hair receding at the temples and flecked with silver. But the smile remained the same—confident without being cocksure, generous to a fault. Omar always took his time in deciding whether he liked people, but once he made up his mind there was no turning back, and there was probably no sin he wouldn't forgive in the name of loyalty. Judging by the look on his face, whoever was sitting on the other side of the table had definitely made his A-list.

"As I said earlier, he has a new venture now. Humanitarian aid, same game as yours. Only we're not sure how much money is involved, or where it's coming from. More to the point, we don't know where it's going, although we have our suspicions. Which is where you come in. Omar has just posted a job opening. A position you'd be perfect for."

"I'm retired."

"Director of programs. Omar even spells it the American way. And he could really use a Western face to front for him, especially with the Euros, who've gone a little skittish about bankrolling anything Arab, given the climate."

"Or given people like you."

"Valid point. All the more reason he'd happily hire someone with your pedigree."

"If I was in the job market."

"We're only asking for a few months. Three, tops."

"I haven't seen him in years. He'd probably think of me as an old burnout. Which I am. For all you know, he's already got somebody lined up."

"There *is* a preferred candidate, in fact. A fellow who got in touch only yesterday."

Black slid me another sheet of paper. It was a printout of an e-mail from me to Omar, a chatty message saying I'd happened to hear about the opening and, seeing as how I'd quit the UN but wasn't quite ready to hang up my spurs . . . And so on. The eerie part was that the breezy style was just like mine, as were the salutation, sign-off, bad punctuation, and missing capitalizations. They had me cold.

"Pretty good, don't you think? Our man spent the better part of a day studying your technique."

"Has Omar answered?"

"Gray?"

"Coming right up, sir."

Gray fiddled again with the laptop until an e-mail from Omar appeared on the screen. It was his reply. Omar was ecstatic. The job was mine if I wanted it. Come to Amman and we'll "talk turkey," he said. He had always been proud of his mastery of American idioms.

"Would've printed it for you, but it arrived just this afternoon," Black said. "While we were all riding the ferry."

My palms were sweating, so I wiped them on my pants.

"What does he call his organization?"

"The Bakaa Refugee Health Project. Its stated goal is to secure construction of a hospital for the Bakaa refugee camp."

"There are a hundred thousand people at Bakaa. They could use one."

"No doubt. But his NGO won't be building it. He's just trying to squeeze enough juice to get the Jordanian government to do it."

"Is that so bad?"

"It's fine. It's lovely. But it's not where his money's going. Not the big dollars, anyway."

"Omar would never front for anyone. Or not for a bunch of bomb makers."

"Maybe you don't know him as well as you think. He's gotten religion, your old friend."

"Is that why there's a beer bottle on the table in the photo you just showed me? Because he's such a stern and observant Muslim? Too bad he forgot to grow a beard."

"Not that kind of religion. He still eats full-course lunches all through Ramadan as far as we know. Still likes Johnnie Walker Red, too. Maybe you should take him a bottle. I was referring to his politics. His donors. His fellow travelers. All the wrong sort of people. They disturb us, to say the least."

"And you know this how?"

"From a man inside."

"Then you don't need me."

"Our man was director of programs. Omar fired him."

"After catching him spying?"

"Stealing. Once our boy saw how easy it was for Omar to divert money, he figured why not divert a little for himself. Yet another lying Palestinian."

"Then how do you know he wasn't lying to *you*? Telling you what you wanted to hear for a few extra bucks. It wouldn't be the first time you people have been taken in by a bad source, from what I read in the papers."

"This isn't Iraq, and there's no political agenda."

"There never is."

"This operation is being run from the bottom up, not the top down. And none of what we produce will be acted upon without verification."

"Assuming you can get verification."

"That's where you come in. You're going to find out everything for us."

"Spying on an old friend isn't what I had in mind for this month, thank you. And the more I think about this pile of so-called evidence against me, the weaker it looks. It's an indictment of the system, for sure, but I was a pretty small cog in that machine."

"So is 'no' your final answer?"

"Is this a game show now? Do I win a million if I say yes?"

Black sighed.

"I was afraid of this." He turned toward his partner. "Knew we shouldn't have cut short the entertainment portion, Gray. Why don't we return to the previous section. The stunning climax."

Two keystrokes later my image replaced Omar's e-mail on the screen. This time I was standing in a broad plain of red dirt. It was a place I knew all too well and had hoped never to revisit, even though I did so almost daily in my memory.

"Tanzania." Black sounded like a judge pronouncing a death sentence. "July of '99."

"Stop."

"And of course this time you played it on the straight and narrow."

"I said stop."

"Not because you had a sudden pang of conscience, of course, or because everyone had eaten their fill at the trough."

"This really isn't necessary, you know."

"Not necessary? Not even the part about how you might possibly face real legal action, if it were only known that—"

"Enough!"

My shout finally stopped him. Less by its volume than its tone of desperation. Perhaps Black sensed, rightly, that if he pushed me off this precipice I might never climb back. That's certainly how it had almost gone in July of '99.

But what he couldn't have known was that there were secrets that even he and his friends hadn't yet uncovered, items that for me were still worth protecting from prying eyes at almost any price.

For a moment he said nothing. Merely made some marks on his pad, as if tallying the final score. I tried to collect myself while his gaze was averted, but first I dared a last glance at my image on the screen. The man up there was six years and an entire lifetime removed from the one I'd become. Just look at his smile—comfortable and knowing, completely ignorant of what was to come.

Most people go into the aid business because they feel they owe it to the world. After a few years in the field some begin believing that the world owes them—if not its riches, then at least its attention. That's why so many of us are such crashing bores at Stateside parties or weddings, cornering our relatives with horror stories and sneering at everyone's easy comfort. We take old acquaintances by the lapels and implore, "Take heed of the world!" when of course what we're partly saying is "Take heed of me! Noble warrior on the dangerous frontier!"

This attitude makes it all the harder to endure yourself once you've run up a debt greater than your contribution. And that is exactly what happened in Tanzania in July of '99, for reasons that I would never let Black, White, or Gray learn. Lives were lost, quite a few of them, and I indeed played a role.

But when it came time to parcel out the official blame, some was never placed in the correct places. Based on what Black had already said, he was convinced that my greatest fear was further culpability, and I was glad to let him think so. Had he known the real story, he would have had even more leverage. The sooner I got him off this dangerous subject, the better.

"First things first," I said in a low monotone. "Turn that damn thing off."

Black nodded, and Gray complied. Like magic, Tanzania disappeared into the ether.

"If it's any comfort," Black said evenly, "if Tanzania didn't do the trick, we were going to bring your marriage into it next. Threaten possible visa complications for your Balkan wife, that sort of thing."

"Just tell me what you want me to do."

"It's Omar's money we're interested in. Where it's coming from. How much. Where it's going. What it's paying for. Not the donations from the jelly jars, or Queen Alia's charity kitty, or even the World Health Organization grant money. Just the big money."

I considered that a moment while trying to calm myself.

"A WHO grant isn't exactly small money."

Black waved dismissively.

"A hundred thousand. Mere seed capital. He used it to set up the office and it was gone inside a month. I'm talking about donations from Europe. Money from people who would probably rather not be identified, and so far haven't been. And of course, whoever is kicking in cash from the Gulf States. Seven figures at a time, or so we hear, but staying in Omar's accounts barely long enough to accrue a penny of interest before it flows right back out via some back channel we can't seem to locate."

"I thought you shut all the back channels down after 9/11." I tried to sound combative, but it came out halfhearted.

"Some of them we did. But you know what happens when you dam things up in one place. The water backs up for a while and then it flows somewhere else. I'm talking about the sorts of transactions that don't show up in any bank records. The kind that might be detected only by someone on the ground. You're that someone."

"When would I start?"

Black raised his eyebrows.

"Excuse me," I corrected. "When *do* I start?"

"That will be up to Omar and you. You should reply as soon as possible to his e-mail. Better still, give him a call. Tell him you're reserved on a Tuesday nonstop to Amman out of Athens. As long as that suits your schedule, of course."

It was Friday morning. That gave me only four days to prepare.

"Do I really have a choice?"

"You have lots of choices. We know from your track record that you like to operate independently, so from here on out you'll be pretty much in charge. Your choice of tactics, your choice of equipment. We might even be able to supply you with a few necessities. Within reason, of course. Find out what we need to know and you're a free man, even if it only takes a week. Then you can tell Omar the job wasn't your cup of tea and fly home to your rustic paradise on Karos. Like I said, we're running this from the bottom up."

"And if it takes longer than three months?"

"That will mean you're not doing your job. There's a shelf life to this kind of information, and at three months your coach turns back into a pumpkin and your horses become mice. If you need more motivation than we've already supplied, then consider that lives may be at stake. Think of it as your chance to balance the books. Well, sort of. Only if

Western lives are worth more than African ones. But hasn't that always been the going exchange rate? Which reminds me. There is one thing we're *not* asking you to do, Freeman, and that is to be any sort of action figure who takes matters into his own hands. Your role is to provide information, not to act on it, or even to 'notify the authorities.' " Black made quote marks in the air. "From here on out, we are the only authorities you are answerable to, and when the time for action comes, we'll take it. We—not you, not the Jordanians—will stand as judge and jury."

"And executioner?"

"Let us worry about that."

"Great. And what about training?"

"Training?"

"Technique. Tactics. What to do in an emergency."

Black almost laughed.

"The way I see it, you've spent your whole life training for this. Playing at neutrality all over the globe. The aid chameleon, jumping from one tree to the next. Rubbing elbows with scoundrels while pretending to be their friend. Just be yourself, Freeman. As for your means of communication, don't worry. We'll set something up."

"And what am I supposed to tell Mila?"

"Whatever you like. If you've somehow managed to keep all this hidden from her"—he gestured toward the blank screen, little knowing how close he had just come to the truth—"then I'm sure you'll think of something."

3

In the course of my travels, I have mastered three foreign languages—French, Arabic, and Greek. I've picked up enough Spanish, German, and Serbo-Croatian to fend for myself in restaurants and supermarkets, and during my final years in the field I achieved a brisk fluency in "Directorese," a UN dialect of acronyms and officiousness invaluable when confronting the high and mighty.

But as Black and Gray escorted me back to Mila in a red Opel—a car they seemed to produce from out of nowhere—I confronted a new and unexpected gap in my linguistic skills. Namely, my deficiencies in the language of deception. Because that is what I would need to employ with my wife, less for my own good than for hers.

Over the years I've watched less-harmonious couples develop an all-too-easy fluency in this language, and it has never failed to dishearten me. They disguise it sometimes by hiding among crowds of their colleagues, letting their lies blend in with the surrounding babble. If Mila and I were still traveling, perhaps I could have tried something similar. But out here in virtual isolation, only our voices would be heard. In order to describe my current predicament without treading onto dangerous ground, I was going to need a subtle array of half-truths and misdirection.

Yet, as the Opel rounded the final curve I felt as ill-prepared as a lazy exchange student, still fumbling through the phrase book as he approached the host family's doorstep.

Gray was at the wheel, with Black at his side. I was alone in the back. They had secured the child locks just in case. Black slung an arm across the front seat and turned toward me. He looked relaxed, his mission accomplished, and he spoke in an offhand manner.

"We'll set up a way for you to file progress reports from the field, of course. Details to follow. Don't sweat it—we'll be in touch."

"How will I know when I've given you enough information?"

"We'll make our feelings known. In the meantime the best rule of thumb is to tell us anything and everything you learn. Names, numbers, we want it all. You're to go where he goes, see who he sees. If Omar has a meeting, find out who it's with. Crash it if you can, ferret out the details later if you can't. Whatever files he has, you need to see them. And whenever you find a money trail you're to follow wherever it leads, through records if possible, or on foot if necessary. Even if it's someplace you don't particularly care to go."

He glanced forward to check our progress as Gray bumped the car into the rocky driveway. The headlight beams swung across the front of the house.

"The less you can get away with telling your wife, the better, you know. That's the best policy with spouses. It's in their own best interests."

Interesting that he had arrived at the same conclusion as I had, if for different reasons.

"Is this what passes for training?"

"Relax. Amateurs do surprisingly well in this business. All their mistakes look like honest ones. It's the professionals who have to be extra careful. Which only makes them easier to spot for anyone who's watching for them."

"And who will be watching for me?"

"If I told you, you'd just waste all your time looking for them. Nobody you need to worry about."

"Comforting."

"Just concern yourself with Omar."

We pulled to a stop. Gray left the engine running. Black handed an envelope across the seat.

"Here's your plane ticket. Tell White we're waiting outside, if you don't mind."

"You're not leaving him behind to make sure we behave?"

"You'll behave."

"And if I can't make the flight Tuesday?"

"Then trade in the ticket for Thursday."

"What if I'm not on that one?"

"Then Gray and I will be back in touch. Even more up close and personal than this time. I don't think you'd like us very much."

The locks thumped open, and I stepped into the night. White opened the front door of the house before I could even turn the handle, and he passed me without a word. Mila stood behind him in the alcove, still in her robe.

She slumped into my arms as they drove away. We watched until the taillights disappeared on a switchback far above us. I felt the air leave her body in a huge sigh like the beginning of a sob. But when I pulled back for a look, her face was dry.

"Are you all right?" I asked. "Did he . . . ?"

"He was fine. Very polite. Just sat in a corner and made sure I didn't go anywhere. What did they want with you? Where did they take you?"

"Up to the DeKuyper place. They had a key. We went to some kind of boardroom. Why don't we sit down?"

She nodded, and we sleepwalked to the couch, the one with the fine view out the picture window down to the sea, except now the curtains were drawn. After being in DeKuyper's house the room felt tiny.

"They want me to go to work for them. Just for a few months. Then they'll let me go."

"They scared us like this just to make a job offer?"

"I guess they wanted to make an impression. It's secret work. In the Middle East."

She shook her head.

"Why you? Doing what?"

"Remember Omar al-Baroody? From Jordan? They want me to spy on him."

She had met Omar on our honeymoon, when we had toured Cairo, Jerusalem, and much of Jordan. To her Omar was a big smile and a deep, booming laugh. I'm sure she could easily recall our dinner with his family in Amman, at a Chinese restaurant run by an old diplomat from Taiwan, reputedly a retired spy. The image was still vivid in my mind: Omar, his wife, and their three squirming children seated with us around a circular table in the corner, with all the serving dishes on a lazy Susan. We talked about our futures in the relaxed manner of old campaigners who believed that from then on their greatest worries would be cholesterol levels and colorectal exams. Then we swapped stories of our wild old days on the West Bank. As we polished off a second bottle of wine, Omar and I agreed that dangerous living was for young men, and our wives heartily seconded the motion.

"It seems that he's started up an NGO in Amman. Something about health care in the Bakaa refugee camp. But they're worried he's really giving his money to all the wrong people, so they're vetting his operation for security purposes. He's got a job opening, and they want me to fill it. Apparently it's all been arranged. I don't even have to formally apply."

"And you'd do that? Spy on a friend?"

"It's the people around him they're interested in most," I said, fudging it. "Who knows, maybe Omar's been duped. In which case I'll be doing him a favor. Not that I have a choice. They made it clear that it's pretty much mandatory."

"How can they *make* you do it?"

"Oh, you know, the usual threats. Control over visas and passports. Mine and yours."

"That's illegal."

"Not when they're making the rules."

"So we'll move to the U.S., then. We don't need visas for that."

"You might."

"We're married. That makes me a citizen."

"It's not that simple anymore."

After 9/11, I meant, but didn't have to say. We knew enough couples of mixed national origin whose marriages had been called into question, or whose spousal visas had been denied, to realize that the easy ways of the past no longer prevailed.

"Besides," I said, "this is our home now. And if I don't go, they promised they'd be back."

The statement about home echoed a bit loudly off the living room's bare walls. We hadn't done much decorating, and it still had the look of a place where the occupants were determining their style.

"How long did you say?" she asked, with a note of resignation.

"No more than three months, they said. Or as soon as I can find out what they need to know. Then I'll be back."

She sighed, as if she wanted to ask more but couldn't bear it. Or maybe she was too tired, which was how I felt. We said nothing for a while, and then we curled into a tighter ball of silence and fell asleep right there on the couch. I suppose we were too weary to get up, but it was also true that neither of us wanted to face the bedroom just yet. For the moment, Black, White, and Gray had made it their own. For all I knew, the window was still open. Hard to believe that only a few hours ago we had been making love and laughing about old times.

Later we were up with the sun, groggy and stiff, barely saying a word over coffee until Mila asked, "When do you have to start?"

"Tuesday."

She seemed taken aback, but why even mention the possibility of Thursday? I could bring it up later if I changed my mind. For now I only wanted to get everything over with as soon as possible.

"They already bought the ticket."

"I wonder if they're still here."

"I don't know. Why don't we find out?"

The words came out on impulse, but surprisingly Mila was all for the idea. Or maybe it wasn't so surprising. Like me, she had always favored direct action, even when it wasn't necessarily a wise idea. Risk, like urgency, has its own addictive properties, and it had always been a powerful attraction of our work.

So she threw on some jeans and a shirt, and we rode our scooters up to the DeKuyper place through a chill morning breeze. It made me feel better to answer their assault with our own minor incursion. I also wanted to check for any lingering evidence of their presence. Or maybe I just needed reassurance that they had left. Anything was preferable to sitting around the house.

The big place was locked up, with the shades and curtains drawn. The Opel had disappeared. We walked around back to a path that led down to the sea, going just far enough for a view of the dock. The same yacht that was always there bobbed on the incoming waves, but there was no smaller craft like the one they'd used last night. I wondered when they had picked up the Opel. Had there been a fourth man helping out, someone I hadn't seen? A resident of the island, perhaps? Maybe that's where the smell of cigarette smoke had come from in our house, someone local paid to case the place for the easiest points of entry. Meaning they might still have a way to keep an eye on us.

Mila said nothing, just followed in my wake as I doubled back. I tried the sliding doors and window locks at the rear of the house, but they didn't budge. We peered through an opening in the curtains, but you could hardly see a thing. Then Mila touched my shoulder just as a gruff Greek voice spoke up from behind.

"Do you need assistance?"

I turned. A stocky fellow who could have been Stavros's cousin stood with dirt on his pants and a shovel in his hands. He was frowning.

"Oh, hello. No. Just looking for someone."

"There is no one here."

"There was last night. Do you know where they've gone?"

He shook his head, the mute certainty of the villager.

"No one has been here for weeks. Do you know this is private land?"

"Yes," Mila said, trying to sound neighborly. "We're going now. We live near here, just down the road."

"I know. Stavros told me."

The remark was innocent enough, but under the circumstances it stung like a betrayal. That was when I realized that we would always be outsiders here, just like DeKuyper, only with less power and pull, and on a much smaller budget. No matter how many goats we herded or pots we made, we would forever be visitors, even as years gave way to decades. I was reminded of the scrub pines that grew on the island's windward side, with gnarled roots barely clinging to the rocks. Even after a hundred years they scarcely grew taller than eight feet. All that endurance, and so little to show for it.

"Then maybe you could tell Stavros not to smoke so much next time he comes looking for my shotgun shells. Or maybe it was you who did the poking around?"

Mila tugged at my sleeve, and the man with the shovel just stood there, no change in his expression. I reluctantly gave up on the cause, and we walked back to our scooters while he followed like a terrier. As we twisted the handlebar grips to accelerate across the gravel, I felt his eyes on our backs, a sensation that lingered all the way down the hill. For the first time, our plans for making a life here seemed like an empty gesture, an elaborate hoax.

Back at the house, Mila got right to the point.

"Why are you really doing this? What have they done to make you take this job? Because if it's about me, I can take it."

No, actually you couldn't. That's what I wanted to say, but knew better. So I looked into her unwavering gaze and tried to assess how close I could come to leveling with her.

"They seem to think they've cooked up some sort of case against me. From all the deals we had to make with Mbweli."

She shook her head, and seemed to shiver a little. Mbweli had always upset her, and that was without even knowing the worst of what he had threatened.

"But you had no choice," she said, repeating what I had told her long ago. "No one did. It's the same way things worked in Sarajevo. We used to lose twenty percent of every convoy that came across Mount Igman. After a while it was like a regular highway toll."

"Maybe. But they seem to think certain prosecutors might not see it that way. And even if they couldn't make the charges stick, well, you know how those things can go."

"That's ridiculous, especially after what happened in Tanzania. All of the audits cleared you completely."

So she had gone there, anyway, despite all my precautions. And for a harrowing moment I wavered on the precipice, peering down at all those dead faces. They stared up from a great muddy ditch, eye sockets gorged with flies, their mouths gaping, as if daring me to finally tell all.

It took all my restraint to simply shrug and say, "I don't think they found the audits very convincing. Maybe they've bribed someone to make it look worse. Who knows? Either way, going to Jordan seems like the path of least resistance."

I could tell from her eyes she was disappointed. So was I. But she nodded in grudging assent, then put her arms around me and rested her head against my chest. I could feel her support in the gesture, and also her sorrow. What I couldn't determine was whether the latter was empathy or pity.

"I should try calling Omar," I said.

Black had given me the number, but not the country code for Jordan. It had been so long since I'd been there that I had to look it up, which I took as a bad omen. The Middle East wasn't a place for unsure footing. And even though Jordan's relative tranquillity made it seem benign to the untrained eye, I also knew that the kingdom's Mukhabarat, or secret police, would still happily lock you up for the slightest misstep. I couldn't help but remember a UN human rights report that had come across my desk during the last month on the job, mentioning that a third of all the country's prisoners were jailed without ever being charged or tried.

On my first try I reached a secretary, who, even though I asked in Arabic, informed me in flawless English that Omar was away for at least an hour. She would soon be my secretary, too, I supposed. When I mentioned my name she seemed to brighten, and told me Omar would call back.

Mila, keeping up appearances, rode her scooter to Kastro to buy more potters' supplies, and while she was gone I took a walk along the coastal path.

The wind was brisk, bringing with it the earliest trace of what winter might be like, and I zipped up my jacket as shreds of sea foam tore across the thin scalp of grass. A few scrawny goats scurried out of my way, bells clanking, and within half an hour I was chilled to the bone, so I turned away from the breeze and headed for home.

As I neared the door the phone was ringing. I entered in time to see Mila hold out the receiver, a doleful look on her face.

"Omar," she whispered. "Returning your call."

His was the voice of my past, and as I heard his warm greeting I supposed he was now the voice of my future. But I couldn't yet picture him as the well-dressed, graying man in Black's photo, the one stolen from the posh restaurant. Instead, Omar was still the edgy young man of 1988. There is a photo I have somewhere from those days, even better than the one Black and Gray had. It is of Omar seated on the passenger side of our VW Passat patrol car. His eyes are alert, he is gritting his teeth, and, even though we are at a standstill, his hands are pressed against the dashboard. We were parked on an overlook above Nablus, and I remember the moment as clearly as if it were yesterday because it was one of extreme tension. Below us, on converging streets, were two groups of people in motion, each unaware of the other. On one: noisy Palestinian schoolboys laughing among themselves and swinging book bags. Their dark heads bobbed confidently, the swagger of teens certain that the future had a place for them. On the other: an Israeli Army patrol, six soldiers in loose formation, Galil assault rifles at the ready. They stepped carefully and deliberately. An armored personnel carrier rolled slowly in their wake.

You need only to look at the tension in Omar's face to realize what was about to take place. Convergence, surprise, then confrontation. Stones thrown and bullets fired. It was like a nightmare unfolding in slow motion, and we were too far away to do anything but watch and, after it was over, count casualties and write our report.

So now, even as Omar babbled on about his grandiose plans and how well I fit into them, I thought I heard in the static of the overseas connection the faint echoes of past gunfire, and couldn't help but try to decipher whether it was the sound of rubber bullets or of live ammunition.

"So when can I drag you to come here, then? We must talk about this some more, and come to terms."

I realized that we had been holding an actual conversation.

"How about Wednesday morning? I can make it in on a late flight Tuesday, and we can meet the next day."

"Perfect!"

He was genuinely thrilled, which cut me to the bone. As we made arrangements to meet, I detected a new message lurking in the static, and this one was altogether more disturbing. It was the presence of a hidden enemy, holding his fire from a concealed position. Now, instead of Omar and I watching the warriors of '88 move toward an unavoidable collision, we were the ones being observed. And the outcome of this one also seemed inevitable: For a while Omar and I will walk in tandem. Then, perhaps soon, we will collide with someone or something that we have yet to identify. Whatever is approaching, I will be partly responsible for its arrival. But unless I can find some way to change the dynamics, I will be just as powerless as I was in '88 to stop the oncoming collision. And this time both Omar and I will be in the line of fire.

4

Washington

Being a daily player in the high-speed lottery of close calls and near misses known as the Connecticut Avenue morning commute, Aliyah Rahim knew instantly that the Ford pulling out from Morrison Street wasn't going to make it.

It was a towering SUV with one of those names like Extravagance or Exploiter—she could never keep them straight—and it was about to meet its match in the form of an oncoming L4 Metrobus.

Aliyah instinctively placed her hands against the dashboard of their Volvo while her husband, Abbas, shouted, "Oh, my God!" from the driver's seat. It was a Monday, they were just south of Chevy Chase Circle, and they were both running late for work.

The next sound she heard was the hiss and groan of the bus trying to stop. Brake lights flared red all around them. Then came a sharp bang like that of a small explosion, and she watched in horror as a shower of glass, metal, and plastic blew out in all directions. The driver managed to turn the Ford enough to avoid being broadsided, but his truck still took a full hit to the rear.

Abbas swerved deftly around the bus, darted into the left lane, and then accelerated as their tires crunched across the crystals of the Ford's shattered window. Aliyah finally exhaled.

It was fairly predictable what would happen next. The effect of an accident on Washington's commuter stampede is much like that of a lion attack on a herd of wildebeests. Any driver whose car isn't felled in the onslaught does whatever he can to keep moving, even if it means skirting the victim's bumper with scarcely a glance. The survivor assuages his conscience by reporting the matter on his cell phone because, let's face it, his real responsibility is to the drivers in his wake. Strand not, lest ye be stranded.

By scooting past the wreckage, Abbas initially held to form. But Aliyah knew without asking what her husband would do next, and he did not fail her. Abbas pulled the wheel sharply to the right and eased to the curb, stopping only thirty feet beyond the crushed Ford. She watched him glance in the rearview mirror as if already assessing the condition of the driver. He dolefully shook his head and unlatched the seat belt.

"Looks like two of them up front," he said. "God help anyone in the back. Call 911."

Aliyah did as she was told. She usually did, reserving dissent for larger battles with greater stakes, which invariably occurred in the privacy of their home. Abbas may have been raised in America since the age of thirteen—he was now in his fifties—but lately he was resorting more to the old ways of his West Bank hometown of Nablus, where men generally got what they asked as long as they weren't asking Israelis.

When Aliyah didn't want to play along, she countered with holding actions and mute refusals. "Passive-aggressive behavior" was what her office friend Nancy called it. But that was just a new label for a longtime female staple in Arab households. Aliyah had left that world behind at a younger age than her husband had. She was only five when the Six-Day War sent her family fleeing for cover from a small village near Jerusalem in 1967, and in some ways it felt like she had never lived there at all. But if Abbas was going to resort to the old ways, then so would she.

So Aliyah now tallied her moments of obedience on a mental scoreboard on which she continually ran a deficit, even though she knew Abbas was probably doing the same, with the opposite result. This became apparent whenever their tensions erupted into open combat. Each would argue as the aggrieved party, with both claiming unpaid reparations.

Take this episode, for example. Aliyah would record it as a moment of submission. Abbas wouldn't. Not that Aliyah objected to calling 911. Nor did she disagree with her husband's decision to stop. It was his duty as a doctor.

On the other hand, considering all that their family had endured during the past few years—the slights, the humiliations, and, worst of all, the horrible tragedy abroad that might so easily have been averted—she wouldn't have blamed Abbas for driving on. Let the other Americans help their own, because they certainly weren't rushing to her family's aid.

But by stopping, Abbas reassured her that his professional judgment hadn't yet drowned in a simmering pool of resentment. That meant there was still hope for him and, in turn, for them. With enough diligence, she might yet find the old Abbas, hiding in the shadows of his anger.

Aliyah had lived with her own shadows in the months following the family's ordeal, but she chose to return to the light by seeking the solace of worship and prayer, even though she hadn't been a regular at a mosque since childhood.

She was still not a "good" Muslim in the strictest sense, and did not intend to become one. No five prayers a day except when it was convenient. No mandatory this or that. She skimped on ablutions, still had a taste for both bacon and gin, and wore what she pleased. She believed such matters were trifling as long as your faith was strong. Hers was a searching brand of devotion that sought comfort in unanswerable questions, or in the contemplation of her own smallness on the vast blurry map of God's majesty. The ritual of prayer instilled calmness and introspection, and the mosque itself offered the kinship of like-minded women. If diet and head scarves really mattered as much as the hotheads said, well, then, let God sort out the details of her punishment later. Because surely God was wise enough to decide that what really mattered was the thoughts in your heart. Intentions and beliefs. Your eagerness to do good.

For a while she had tried to coax Abbas to attend the men's prayer service on Fridays.

"Please," he had scoffed. "To do what? Bow my head and raise my voice to some vacant room in the heavens? If there was a God to begin with, he checked out of his hotel room long ago."

Maybe his job was partly to blame. As a surgeon, he was far too often powerless to save the righteous, yet many times had easily rescued the obviously unworthy. By clipping and sewing the innards of the nation's top decision makers, he had sliced away the maladies of dozens of unsavory demagogues and liars, many of whom you have probably heard of. By rescuing them, perhaps he now felt complicit in any number of their actions.

Yet he had never lost pride in his handiwork. He still displayed a framed White House letter of appreciation from 1981, when, as a young trauma surgeon of twenty-seven, he was among the doctors who saved the life of President Reagan following an assassination attempt. He was there when the stricken president dropped to one knee in the emergency room and gasped, "I can't breathe!" And he was the doctor who, three hours later, found the bullet lodged in the president's chest, flattened to the size and shape of a dime. Although, now that Aliyah thought of it, she hadn't noticed the White House letter in its customary place the last time she visited his office.

Aliyah punched in the 9-1-1. So much portent to those numbers now, with all they had brought upon this country, this city, her family.

"It's been reported," the operator said brusquely.

The pace of Washington never ceased to astonish her, especially in its recent push to do more with less. Even at her office, a national charity that raised money for the poor, there was a huge effort to cut and streamline.

She unlatched the door of the Volvo, wondering if she would be able to bear the sight of the accident. Blood made her squeamish, but as a doctor's wife she felt obligated to pitch in. The Ford was pinned to a lamppost beneath a huge oak, which was shedding yellow leaves on the wreckage. Abbas had pried open the passenger door and was leaning across someone. Blood dripped onto the pavement.

A police car rolled to the curb between her and the Ford, blue lights strobing. She heard the wail of an ambulance approaching from downtown. Abbas withdrew from the Ford for a second, as if coming up for air. She could never fathom how he stomached all the gore, and she was thankful for the blinding glare of the windshield as the sun emerged from a cloud. Poor Abbas already looked pale and spent, and he still had a long day ahead. She had heard him moving around downstairs very late the night before, the TV droning loudly.

A policeman stepped from the cruiser. He put his hands on his hips and watched Abbas. Next to him was some fellow in a business suit who had drifted down from a Starbucks for a closer look. The drivers still passing on Connecticut Avenue were now at a crawl. The rubbernecking had begun in earnest.

Aliyah was about to volunteer her version of events when the policeman turned toward the man in the suit and asked loudly, "Who's the Arab guy?"

He said it in the tone Aliyah had been hearing for four years running, a goading note of suspicion that demanded to know whose side you were on. This time she boiled over.

"The *Arab* guy is a doctor!" she said, her vehemence taking the officer by surprise. "He is also my husband, and he saves lives for a living. *Saves* lives. Do you understand this? He is trying to *help* those people!"

The cop raised his hands in mock surrender, but didn't back away. Then he smiled, which only made her angrier.

"Easy, lady. Just trying to sort out the players. I'm glad he's here to help. Now if you and this other gentleman could step back, I'll get the scene under control."

Liar. A sassy reply rose in her throat, but she didn't dare. Not after the last time she had talked back to a policeman, two years ago in New York. Their family picture had run on page two of the *Daily News*, a tourist photo filched from the dockside concessionaire of a Circle Line cruise. A bunch of stupid, baseless accusations and a senseless arrest, all because her son, Faris—*a structural engineer*, for God's sake—had dared to shoot video footage as the boat passed beneath the Brooklyn Bridge. Plenty of other tourists had done the same, but none of them was speaking Arabic, as Faris had been doing with a college friend from Cairo, excitedly describing the engineering wonder of the support towers and buttresses.

The police had hauled them in for questioning, and Abbas's name had turned up on some watch list, thanks to a donation he had made six years earlier to a Palestinian charity that had since been deemed a pariah and made off-limits for American dollars. Abbas spent two days in a Manhattan jail before he was released, even though no charges were ever filed. No one ever offered an apology because, well, you just can't be too careful anymore, you know.

Even then Aliyah might have eventually found some way to laugh it off if not for what then happened to their daughter. How horrible to think that the New York photo that brought them such shame was now a cherished relic, because it was the last image of their whole family together, Shereen in the middle, smiling brilliantly into the summer sunlight, the brown waters of the Hudson behind them. Everyone arm in arm.

"I said move back, lady." It was the policeman again, forceful now.

"Yes, I am moving."

He nudged her with his right hand, and she barely fought down an urge to push back. Her breathing was all bottled up in her throat, and she stepped briskly toward the Volvo, tears of anger and frustration springing hotly to her eyes.

Of all places for this to happen. It was a block she knew well, having shopped here frequently, and its very nature had always made her feel good about where they lived. Just around the corner was an ATM equipped for seven languages. There was a package store run by Koreans, a restaurant run by Dominicans, and a barbershop run by a Hungarian. The backdrop to the crushed Ford was a kitschy billboard on the roof of the American City Diner. It depicted a 1950s family seated three abreast in a big sedan, all smiles and all white above the script, "There's no way like the American Way."

Tell it to this smug asshole of a cop, she thought. She purposely avoided looking at him, and instead sought out Abbas, worried that he might have seen the brief confrontation. Another reason to keep holding back her tears.

The ambulance arrived. Paramedics exited in a rush, followed by the aluminum clatter of a gurney. Abbas spoke a few words to a nodding attendant and then wiped bloody hands on a handkerchief.

She saw that the policeman was still sizing up her husband. The officer then moved forward and said something to Abbas while pointing at her. Her husband went rigid, and color rose in his cheeks. Keep your head, she thought. Don't take this an inch farther.

Abbas turned toward her as if he had received her mental warning, and their eyes met. Patience, his expression replied. There was a hint of something else, too. Something new. Was it malice or just determination? Maybe both, almost like he was saying, "Don't worry, I'll deal with this in my own way. You'll see."

Something about it made her go faint for a second, and she put a hand to her chest. Whatever this new emotion of his was, it couldn't possibly be good for either of them.

Or maybe she was still worried because of what she had found in his top dresser drawer the night before. Some antidepressant, with God knows what sort of side effects. She had seen Abbas sneaking a pill in the kitchen and tracked down the vial later. What's more, there was no prescription label from any pharmacy. He must have gotten hold of it himself from the hospital, one way or another.

It was just like him to think he could deal with his feelings like a technician, tweaking his body's chemical supply just as he might repair some patient's veins and arteries. Instead of talking things out with her or anyone else, he would make everything right through medicine. Study the symptoms, consult a manual, perhaps chat with a specialist. Then find the right tool and make the necessary adjustment.

Worrisome. And so was that look on his face. She resolved to start paying closer attention to Abbas. These were dangerous times, and losing one member of her family was quite enough. Losing another would be more than she could bear.

5

I arrived in Amman on the cusp of Ramadan, watching from the window of the plane as the new moon rose over the desert. Like anything that has grown too fast, Amman lacks grace. It slouches across a series of hills in a tumble of pale boxes, slapped together from cinder block and reinforced concrete. The one neighborhood that should be a gem—the aging downtown, with buildings from the 1920s set along wide boulevards, marketplace alleys, and a huge Roman amphitheater—has been smudged beyond recognition by soot and grime.

My destination was Jebel Amman, a hilltop district of old stone villas with gated lawns and scrawny pines. Decades ago it was the preferred neighborhood of royalty, diplomats, and British officers. Now it was home to the city's poshest hotels, although mine was of the smaller, cheaper variety, mostly because I didn't yet know who would be paying the bill.

For forty dollars a night I got a drab but clean room on the third floor, with a dripping sink and a view of the street. Throwing back the curtains, I saw a large mosque just down the block. Big green loudspeakers sprouted from its tall minaret, meaning I could rely on the muezzin for a wake-up call at first light.

I wasn't due to meet Omar until morning, so I decided on a walk to collect my thoughts for the job ahead. The desk clerk smiled dutifully as I crossed the empty lobby. The streets were also deserted. Everything was closed for the beginning of the month-long observance of Ramadan, and the daily fasting would begin at sunrise. The only shopkeeper in evidence was a grocer stringing holiday lights, the ubiquitous crescent and star blinking in red and green like Christmas decorations.

My last time in Amman, King Hussein had smiled down from posters all over town. Now the reigning face belonged to his son and successor, Abdullah, whose pudgy cheeks reminded me of a middle-aged Jerry Mathers. He, too, was everywhere. On a stone wall draped with fragrant jasmine he stood proudly in white flowing robes and a red-and-white kaffiyeh. On a nearby lamppost he marched ramrod straight in full-dress military uniform. I peered into a darkened toy store and spotted him on a wall by the register, this time in a business suit. Three doors down, in an optician's, he relaxed in blue jeans and an oxford shirt alongside his pretty Palestinian wife, Queen Alia. The man of a thousand faces, stalking my progress.

During my first trip to Jordan, when I helped set up tent camps for Gulf War refugees in late 1990, the profusion of royal images had at first seemed sinister. Big Brother is watching. Then I came across a poster that convinced me otherwise. In it, a smiling Hussein in a black leather jacket sat astride a big motorcycle with his ravishing *Vogue* queen, the blond and blue-eyed Noor. Behind them were the red bluffs of Wadi Rum, the spectacular desert backdrop featured in about half of *Lawrence of Arabia*. Hussein was bareheaded, with a trim silvery beard. Noor's long mane was in sensual disarray, as if tousled by the breezes of the open road, or perhaps by the roving hands of her admiring king. The effect was stunning—two parts Brando, one part Ali Baba. It must have appealed deeply to any Jordanian yearning to believe his homeland was a cut above the neighbors in style and substance. Come to think of it, wasn't that Big Brother's strategy? To boost morale with watchful benevolence, reassuring even as he intimidated.

Small nations, like small men, must be resourceful to stand out, especially if they don't offer the oil of a Kuwait or the numbered accounts of a Switzerland. Jordan tries winning you over with heaping doses of Bedouin hospitality. I had been reminded of this earlier, the moment I climbed into the airport taxi.

"Welcome in Jordan," the driver gushed. It is a phrase a visitor hears often, as if everyone is saying, "Don't worry, we're friendly and sane. Not like all the nuts in Syria, Israel, Iraq, and Saudi. So kick back and tell us your troubles."

More often than not, visitors oblige. Thus has Jordan's capital become a city of loose talk and stealthy listeners. In the thermal pool of babble known as the Middle East, Amman is the drain into which anything worth repeating eventually swirls, and the city has become a listening post for every government that is still a player in the games of oil politics and Holy Land intrigue. With that in mind, I decided on dinner at the China Dragon, a known gathering place for chatty foreigners. It also happened to be the place where Mila and I had last met Omar.

Chinese restaurants offer a comfort zone for wandering Americans. I have sought solace beneath their tasseled lanterns in Zagreb, Freetown, Khartoum, and countless other locations. They offer the same dishes, the same teapots, the same plinky music—all the brand familiarity of a McDonald's minus the grease and the corporate stigma.

The China Dragon was a few blocks off the First Circle, the eastern-most of eight traffic roundabouts along Amman's east-west spine. This end of the route follows along Rainbow Street, and its last few blocks were about a mile from my hotel. By the time I reached the red-curtained entrance I had quite an appetite. Although it was the prime dining hour of 9 p.m., the place was so empty that for a moment I worried it had changed hands, but then the familiar face of the proprietor appeared.

He was known to one and all as Mr. Lee, a former military attaché from the Taiwanese embassy. The gossips said his true role was more intriguing. He had opened the restaurant in the late '70s, and had immediately established its credentials by hiring away a pair of embassy chefs.

"Table for one?" he said, picking up a menu. Then he smiled with dawning recognition. "You are old customer, yes? Gulf War?"

I had come here a lot back in '91, part of a regular wartime clientele of aid workers and journalists, but I was surprised he knew my face. A trick of his old trade, perhaps.

"Yes. Freeman Lockhart."

The name didn't register, but he nodded anyway.

"Yes, yes. Where you like to sit?" He gestured toward vacant tables. The only other party was four men in a corner, speaking French. "Business slow. Ramadan. Always like this first few nights. During Gulf War, never empty. Many journalists. You remember?"

"Oh, yes. And I remember you couldn't get a beer during Ramadan. That still the house rule?"

Mr. Lee lowered his eyes, the bearer of bad news.

"Still rule. Out of respect."

"Of course."

He led me to a small table along a near wall. A few minutes later a tall, thin waiter materialized at my side. He was clean-shaven, and his black hair was trimmed short.

"You are ready, sir?"

He was probably in his twenties, and his manner was pleasant enough. But something in the sharpness of his coal-black eyes seemed to be lying in wait for an opportunity to disapprove.

"Hot-sour soup, the crispy chicken, and the stir-fried vegetables."

"And to drink, sir?"

Without beer, I supposed I'd have to wash it down with a soft drink.

"A Coke."

That drew a look, followed by a remark that from him sounded like an admonition.

"There is only Pepsi."

I immediately recalled the old rumor about Coke that had once swept the Arab world, something about the logo saying "No Mohammad, No Mecca" in Arabic if you turned it backward. Coke hired an Egyptian grand mufti to debunk it, but the taint persisted, and I had always noticed lots of Pepsi signs in the city's more benighted quarters.

"Yes, Pepsi would be better."

His departure was a relief. I had forgotten what it was like working in a place where even your most innocent choice might be held against you. In Jerusalem I had once affronted an Israeli scholar by admitting to enjoying the novels of Thomas Wolfe. He assured me in the gravest tones that Wolfe was a raving anti-Semite, but said he would attribute my error to youthful ignorance.

Up to now I had never been overly concerned by such snap judgments, mostly because I had never taken sides. Even while watching Palestinian boys confront tanks with stones, or haggard Bosnian men shuffle out of Serbian concentration camps, I had operated by the rules of official neutrality. Less in the sense of a journalist than in the sense of someone who knew he might well have to tidy up once the shooting stopped, and would need the cooperation of both sides.

Now I no longer had that protection, or dodge, if you prefer. I was taking sides, and against a friend, no less.

Just as the soup arrived, my attention was drawn to a table by the entrance, where a fifty-something American with a gray buzz cut had sat down with his taxi driver to await a take-out order. The American proclaimed loudly that he had just arrived from Baghdad.

"And what is your name?" his driver asked.

"Dick." He held out his right hand for a shake.

"Oh, yes. Like Dick Cheney."

"There you go."

The American seemed pleased by the association, which pegged his politics. I noticed that my waiter had taken up a watchful perch nearby, and from time to time his eyes flicked toward the American. Mr. Lee must have overheard as well, because seconds later he fluttered up to their table.

"You working in Iraq?" Mr. Lee asked.

The big man nodded.

"Contractor for USAID, restoring the electrical grid. Here for some R and R."

"Many Americans coming here from Iraq. Good place to relax. Good place to eat."

"Yeah, they gotta couple Chinese restaurants in Baghdad. Pretty good ones, too, until one of 'em was bombed. Then Mr. Bremer told us, 'No more.' "

Dick then began name-dropping companies whose logos you saw all over the world. Mr. Lee answered by name-dropping his way around the fringes of the royal family. All the while my waiter stood very still, like a signal tower awaiting the next transmission.

Later, returning to the hotel on a full stomach, I detoured to the edge of Jebel Amman and stopped by a concrete stairway that plunged steeply toward the heart of the city. There was a view across the chasm toward some of Amman's poorest neighborhoods on a facing hill to the southeast. On rooftops here and there were TV antennae shaped like miniature Eiffel Towers. It had long been one of Jordan's favorite affectations, although wealthier homes now sported satellite dishes.

Standing out more were rings of green neon marking the minarets of mosques. I counted seven on that hillside alone, just as the night's call to prayer began. I had always enjoyed this moment, thinking of it as a bedtime story with the narration jumping from one muezzin to the next. Not so different from listening to church bells in small-town America, I supposed. Except there the nuts and hotheads shot up high schools, or roughed up a few homosexuals. Here they joined holy wars.

Walking back, I noticed the smell of jasmine, stronger than ever, and my spirits lifted. Perhaps things would go smoothly. With any luck, the suspicions of Black, White, and Gray would prove to be unfounded, and I could give Omar a clean bill of health.

The lobby was still empty. The desk clerk sprang to his feet, holding an envelope in his right hand.

"There was a message for you, sir."

"Someone called?"

"Hand delivery."

Had Omar dropped by? The envelope was sealed.

Inside was a typed message on hotel stationery. No name. No signature: "House for rent just off Rainbow, on Othman Bin Affan Street. Available Thursday. Phone tomorrow to say you are interested." Then there was a phone number, and nothing more.

"Did you see who left this?"

"No, sir. I must have been in the back. I found it on the counter."

"Sealed like this? In a hotel envelope?"

"Yes sir. Is it bad news, sir? Anything we can arrange for you?"

"No. I'm just curious who brought it. I'd like to speak to anyone on your staff who might have gotten a look."

"I will ask, sir."

I had been wondering when and how Black, White, and Gray would get in touch, and I supposed this was my answer. They had said I would be my own boss, the only part of this assignment I liked, but now I wondered. I had a feeling that wherever I went these people would be watching, just like the smiling face of the king.

6

Mila woke me before the muezzin could. I groped for the ring-ing phone in the dark, knocking the receiver off the night-stand. Her voice came up from the floor like a bulletin from a distant radio.

"Freeman? Freeman? Are you there?"

"Yes, I'm here. I was asleep."

"I'm sorry. I know it's early, but I've been up for an hour."

I checked the bedside clock.

"Mila, it's 5 a.m."

"I was worried you'd leave early for breakfast, with Ramadan and all."

"I'm sure they'll still have something for me. You sound upset."

"I've been checking around with people on the island. And making some calls."

"This morning?"

"Yesterday. And last night, while some of the offices in the States were still open."

"Mila, no."

"It's all right. I'm being discreet."

As if such a thing were possible on an international phone line, or in a place as small as Karos. My last worry before dropping off to sleep had been that she would do exactly this, poking around to find out more about what had become of our night visitors. She must have started her inquiries even before my plane left Athens.

"The Opel was rented to someone named Dillon, with an American passport," she said. "The counterman told me, at Emborios Rentals."

"He rented it?"

"No. He found out from their competitor, at Island Rentals."

So that was at least two people on Karos who knew something was up between us and some strangers from America. And you could multiply the number by at least two for each successive day. Within a week everyone on the island would know that I had departed in the wake of some mysterious visitation.

"Mila, you've got to stop. These aren't the kinds of people we're used to dealing with."

"We've dealt with worse."

Yes, and look at what happened, I wanted to say, but didn't dare, because then I might have to explain.

"Worse, but different. These are people who cover their tracks. If they hear you're sniffing around they'll be back."

"It's you they're interested in. You and Omar. They couldn't care less what I'm up to."

"This probably isn't the right forum for discussing this."

"On this line, you mean?"

"On any line. And you should stop. Just let me do what I'm here for, and then we can both try to figure out what's really going on. Okay?"

"I can't just sit here doing nothing while something happens to you."

"Nothing will happen unless you *make* it happen. I'm fine, and I can take care of myself. Just don't stir them up. I'm almost afraid to ask who you called in the States."

"Pretty much who you'd expect. No one had heard of them. Or you, either, of course. I guess they have to say that. I called the embassy, too, in Athens."

"The American embassy?"

"Yes."

"Good Lord. What did you say?"

"I asked for their intelligence liaison. They told me they didn't have one."

"You didn't give your name, I hope?"

"No. But I guess it would be easy enough to get my number."

"Maybe they won't try. They must get plenty of calls like that."

"Cranks, you mean."

"That's not the word I was going to use."

"I'll bet." I knew from her tone of voice she was smiling—a sign of progress. And who knows, maybe the information she had learned on the island would even be useful.

"So tell me about this Dillon fellow."

"From the description it was the one named Black."

"Dillon probably isn't his real name, either."

"No. But I got his passport number. It's—"

"Mila, not now. But hold on to it."

"Right."

"Anything else?"

"No one else seemed to have noticed them. But I don't think it was Stavros who took your shells. He said someone else had been poking around."

"When?"

"Last week. Two days before we got back. He saw one of the windows was ajar, so he went inside to shut it. He said he noticed then that you could easily spring the window locks from the outside."

"So maybe it *was* his cigarettes you smelled."

"He quit smoking in May. Whoever it was must have stayed for a while. Practiced the whole thing."

Some professional advance man, or a well-paid local. DeKuyper's troll with the shovel, perhaps. I imagined him standing in the darkness of our living room, checking all the drawers and cabinets for anything that might have put a crimp in their plans. And for all we knew, Stavros had been aware of everything, no matter what he said now.

"Mila, I think you should arrange to have somebody close at hand, if necessary, and not just Stavros. Someone you can reach in a hurry, if, well . . ."

"If what?"

"If any of them come back."

"You think they will?"

"If you keep asking questions, I know they will."

"Then I'll stop."

"Good."

"And I'm sorry I woke you."

"It's all right. It's not so bad starting the day with your voice. Yours and the muezzin's."

The speakers on the mosque down the street had just begun cranking up. The first morning of Ramadan had begun.

"God, he's loud. I can hear him like he's next door."

"Just wait 'til the midmorning prayers. He'll go on for ages. I'd better see if the kitchen's got anything left for a hungry infidel."

"Say hello to Omar for me."

I experienced a stab of guilt, anticipating the coming charade.

"Will do. And, Mila?"

"Yes?"

"I love you. But, please. No more of this. One sleuth in the household is enough."

"I guess I was thinking of safety in numbers."

"The moment I need reinforcements, you'll be the first to know."

"Take care, love."

"You, too."

I cursed myself for not having warned her off in advance. I suppose I hadn't wanted to spoil my departure, but I knew from experience that Mila wasn't daunted by the idea of tempting fate. It was leaving fate to its own devices that troubled her. Understandably so, given what had happened to her in Sarajevo, an event that forever shaped how she dealt with the world. It also gave us common cause, if only because I happened along at her most vulnerable moment.

She had already caught my eye in that winter of '92, a season of snowfall and shellfire that drove everyone indoors with its grim smell of woodsmoke and carnage. Her looks were the immediate attraction. In that department I am as shallow as the next man. But what held my fascination was her brisk yet caring manner, a rare combination of warmth and efficiency. She was the sort of person you wanted alongside you when tempers were short and everyone was on the verge of breakdown. Yet it was the momentary failure of those good instincts that helped draw us together.

It began when a family of five came to visit her one morning. The father knew he would have to stay behind because he was a male of fighting age. But he was insistent on getting the others out of town in the next refugee convoy, even though they were well down the waiting list. The Serbs besieging the city seldom let convoys leave, and he knew it might be weeks before the next opportunity. But fair was fair, and that's what Mila told him.

"I'm sorry," she said. "But there are so many others who need to leave just as badly. Maybe the next one."

"But my daughter needs medicine for her heart," the father said. "Look."

He held aloft the trump card, a pill bottle that rattled when he shook it, like a piggybank down to its last pennies.

"It will be gone in less than a week." Then he gestured to a pale, drawn girl of perhaps fourteen who stood at his side, mustering her most pathetic expression.

Mila, nobody's fool, had seen this ploy and dozens of others, equally convincing. It was almost always an act. Maybe the medicine wasn't really for her heart. Or they had a few hundred more tablets stashed back at their apartment. The only way to get them aboard would be to knock someone else off the list who might have even greater needs.

I watched the scene unfold from a nearby desk. Mila and I traded conspiratorial glances, although to her credit she neither smiled nor openly played the cynic.

"Have you tried the Red Cross?" she asked. "They have been bringing in emergency medications. Maybe your doctor can help you get more."

"Our doctor was killed by a sniper three weeks ago. We haven't been able to get a thing."

"Then I'm sure they will be happy to deal with you directly. In the meantime, I can do this for you."

She scribbled their names on a pass that would give them priority on the next convoy, whenever that was. Like many of us, Mila sometimes offered a little help even in response to obvious shams, if only to reward the initiative. And, who knows, sometimes the sob stories were true. But in a city of 300,000 there were too many to choose from.

Shortly afterward I left for some errands. When I returned later to meet another colleague, I dropped by her desk hoping to resume my flirtation. I didn't really expect it to go anywhere, but in a war zone you tried when you could.

No sooner had I struck up a conversation than her Motorola squawked and she took it up with a sigh. It was some liaison officer from the UN Protection Force, speaking in an urgent tone that everyone in the room could hear, which only made it more awful to bear. Something about a family who had been hit by mortar fire only moments ago. A pretty nasty business, he said, but perhaps Mila could help with identification, because in one of the victim's pockets they had found a form dated that day with her signature on it. Something to do with priority on the next convoy?

"Describe them," Mila said, sounding as if she had just had the wind knocked out of her. "How many?"

"Five. Two adults, three children. We might save the mother, but I'm afraid the others are dead. They were waiting in line outside one of the med centers. Somebody said they were trying to get a prescription filled."

Almost everyone in the aid business has suffered from guilt of one kind or another over the years. During the most trying times in the field you can never take a nap, a drink, or a moment of peace without wondering whether your indulgence is costing someone his life. But seldom are cause and effect so clearly and devastatingly linked, and no one in the room just then could have failed to note the crushing impact on Mila. She was glassy-eyed, speechless, and couldn't function for the remainder of the afternoon. When it was time for sleep, her friends had to unstack her cot and smooth out her bedroll. They helped her undress as if she were an invalid.

The next day Mila announced her plans to visit the surviving mother, who had been taken to Kosevo Hospital. When I stopped by to check on her, her Bosnian friends were urging her not to go. The deaths were just another stroke of ill fortune, and not her fault, they said. Another blow of nasty luck in a city where death enjoyed all the short odds. They were right, of course, but they didn't detect the need dwelling so deeply in her eyes, so I spoke up.

"You should go if you really want to," I said. "But you shouldn't go alone."

She nodded, and her friends drifted away, too skittish to accompany this new angel of death on such an awkward mission. So I volunteered, and Mila nodded again, as if my assent were the most natural thing in the world.

We arrived after a chilly walk across the city, shellfire pounding as randomly as thunder, to find the woman barely conscious. She lay buried in a welter of bandages, sheets, and IV bags. The more difficult sight was the small shrine of family photographs that some friend or neighbor had arranged on a bedside table. The four faces lined up like accusers waiting to testify, each with a heartbreaking smile. All that was missing was the daughter's bottle of pills.

Mila took a deep breath and leaned low to whisper in the woman's ear. She never told me what she said, and it wasn't the sort of question you would ask. When Mila stood she had tears on both cheeks. I'm not sure the woman heard a word, and she never opened her eyes. Which was a shame, really, because I think what Mila needed most was a tearful denunciation, any act of anger to allow atonement to begin.

We stood there for ten minutes longer, not saying a thing, and when it became apparent that Mila might remain all evening I gently led her away. We crossed back through the city hand in hand. I steered her into a café and bought her a coffee and a pastry—true luxuries in those days. I was gratified to see some color return to her cheeks, and her breathing seemed to steady.

In the weeks that followed we seldom went more than a day without seeing each other. And, as tends to happen between a man and woman of mutual attraction, one thing led to another. We would joke about it later, but there was almost a reverent overtone to our first lovemaking. It felt like a consummation in several senses of the word, a bond that we both sensed went well beyond the usual desperate coupling of people trapped between danger and tedium.

In her work, Mila henceforth became more of a questioner and an advocate. Although she never turned into what you would call a "soft touch," which would have rendered her essentially useless, she was a tigress when it came to righting bureaucratic wrongs or neglect. And, so, when we later began working side by side on our sojourns into Africa, we were seemingly the perfect pairing: She was the outside agitator, always questioning the status quo, while I was the tinkerer within the system, making adjustments here and there. The dynamic served us well and, more important, served those who needed us even better. As we grew closer in love, we grew also in our respect for each other's powers.

Until, of course, our one huge failure in Tanzania, when our dynamic proved to be perfectly engineered for disaster—unbeknownst to Mila, thank God, even to this day. And now here I was in Jordan, tempting fate once more, wondering if our combination of skills might again prove volatile instead of magical. Except this time we and our friends would pay the price.

The muezzin went silent, his prayers complete, and a stillness fell over the hotel room. It was still dark, but my stomach was empty, so I rose to shower, shave, and dress for the day ahead. Time to start searching for answers to all these troublesome questions. Time to do my part, come what may.

7

Ramadan had indeed cast a pall on the buffet efforts of the kitchen staff. I made do with limp toast, watery yogurt, and grainy instant coffee. Previous experience in the Islamic world told me that things weren't likely to get better. By the end of the month nerves would be frayed and tempers short. There were always a few murders attributable to the strain of fasting—a deprivation that didn't even allow for water. As the days wore on, local judges would begin dismissing many a petty charge as the price of doing business during a time of sacrifice. At least this year the holiday was in October. Summer Ramadans were positively brutal.

No such worries for me, of course, although finding lunch might be tricky. I walked to a small market near the hotel for fruit and bread, so I could snack later in the privacy of my room. Then, having put off the moment of truth long enough, I hailed a taxi to Omar's office.

"You are here for long?" the driver asked.

"A few months." Then I considered my cover. "Or maybe for good. I'm taking a new job. We'll see how it goes."

"You are welcome in Jordan." He nodded emphatically.

The closer we came to our destination, the more I worried. Omar and I had been through too much together for me to approach betrayal lightly. But if he *had* gone off the deep end, maybe I would be doing him—and the world—a favor. Black, White, and Gray had offered little to back their suspicions. Their only hard information was a two-page bio, most of which I already knew. I had heard Omar's life story first-hand, back in the wild days of '88.

We never would have met if not for Hans Wolters, a big German with a generous laugh whose life mission was to save the entire Middle East, Jew by Jew, Arab by Arab. Hans had begun his hopeless quest as a twenty-year-old tourist, one of those earnest young backpackers in a sweaty bandanna who sleeps in hostels and rides the same teeming buses as the natives, subsisting on falafel by day and ramen noodles by night.

He had arrived in Jerusalem only months after the Six-Day War, and upon reaching the stone gates of the Old City he found himself in a moral quandary: With whom should he empathize more—the plucky survivors of the death camps or their downtrodden conquests, the West Bank Palestinians? As a descendant of Crusaders and Nazis, Hans felt deeply indebted to both sides. So he volunteered for a summer of labor on a kibbutz, and then enlisted in the UN's effort to feed and clothe the children of the Jabaliya Refugee Camp in benighted Gaza.

Two decades of this evenhanded approach made Hans the perfect choice to run the show once UNRWA began organizing its human rights observer patrols in late '87, shortly after the intifada uprising began.

He found it a trying experience, especially as Palestinian boys began to die in the streets. The hardest part, he told me later, after a fifth bottle of Maccabee beer at the UN's Gaza Beach Club, was to keep from thinking of the harsher officers of the Israel Defense Force as latter-day storm troopers.

"It is the Star of David, not the swastika," he slurred in his Bavarian accent, his face a study in tortured inebriation. "But to see those skinny boys just standing there, waiting for the tanks . . ."

I wondered if the recent legions of Palestinian suicide bombers had brought on another crisis in faith. Or maybe Hans had finally thrown in the towel, after discovering like the rest of us that neutrality only meant you ended up despising both sides.

Yet back then, he had never tired in his role as our matchmaker, pairing the bold young sons and daughters of the Palestinian elite with international partners for each of our daily patrol teams. At any one time, ten pairs were on duty—five in Gaza and five on the West Bank, from Jenin down to Hebron—working almost continuously in a three-day shift while the ten teams of the next shift cooled their heels.

Hans delighted in the matchups that clicked and sulked about the few that didn't, although only one actually ended in divorce, famously so, when a roaring, bearded Belgian earned a quick flight to Brussels by throwing a full pot of steaming coffee at his stubbornly proud consort.

I met Hans in late '87, just as he began rounding up volunteers. I, too, was working at Jabaliya at the time, helping supply a children's clinic for a now-defunct NGO known rather grandiosely as Save the Planet, a mission it tackled largely on the strength of $300-a-week employees like me.

I'd already been knocking around in the aid business for seven years, long enough to realize that Hans offered my best shot yet at true adventure. It was also a way to get my foot in the door of the many-roomed mansion of the United Nations. Once its blue globe adorns your résumé, you're welcome on almost any of the mansion's floors. Play your cards right and you've got a career, as well as a lifetime badge of neutrality, a universal entrée into the wider world of strife.

I joined too late to make the original cast of observers. But in March I got the call, and Hans shipped me off to Vienna, of all places, for a crash course in training.

Five of us took the course together. We were an eclectic bunch: a pipe-smoking Danish military officer in his fifties, an Italian accountant around my age who was always impeccably dressed, a rather hot-looking nurse from London in her twenties with the unlikely name of Antoinette, and a New Zealand PR man who had dropped out of the rat race at age forty-two and was forever declaring that everything was "bloody brilliant," in sincerity when he liked it, in sarcasm when he didn't.

For three days we listened to management trainers spout platitudes about administrative skills and conflict resolution, in the bowels of the Vienna International Centre, a hideous ziggurat of concrete on the Danube. Then, only hours before our departure, our trainers flipped off the lights and said, "We've put together a fifteen-minute video of what a refugee affairs officer does."

It was a horror show of blood, screams, gunshots, and flaming cars. Before we even stopped shaking they shoved us into cars for the airport, and as soon as the wheels left the ground I ordered my first of four martinis. By the time we touched down at Ben-Gurion I was seeing double.

Hans paired me first with Munira Mirza, a prim and proper young woman whose father lectured in history at Al-Quds University. For the Palestinians, the observer jobs offered a certain prestige, mostly because you had to be well connected to land one. And by local standards the pay wasn't bad. That went for me, too. I was finally making enough money to rent a roomy new apartment in an Arab neighborhood on the Mount of Olives, a sunny place with floor-to-ceiling windows overlooking the Old City.

But everyone figured the jobs would be short-lived because we assumed the intifada would soon spend its anger, burning out like a matchstick. Even the worst pessimists among us couldn't imagine it would drag on for six years.

It was strange and stressful work. Much like a beat cop, we spent our days making a rough circuit of our territory. Sometimes the dispatcher called in an incident, and we raced to the scene. But usually we found trouble on our own, and then expended our energies trying to avert more of the same. We engaged daily in dozens of small negotiations, trying our tact on a bewildering variety of officers from the IDF. Some were high, some were scared, and others were alternately bored, angry, nice, brutal, and fair-minded. You had about fifteen seconds to get a read on their mood and motivation, and about fifteen more to establish enough rapport to defuse the situation.

Munira showed me the ropes. She had been on the job since December, and I learned more about what it meant to be a Palestinian in those first three months than I had in a year of working at Jabaliya. She also taught me the finely balanced etiquette of our pairings. None of the Palestinians ever wanted to be patted on the back or shown any sort of familiarity by an Israeli officer, which would brand them forever as a collaborator. None of the army officers ever wanted to lose face by having a Palestinian talk down to them or brandish one of our handheld radios in their presence.

In all our time together, I don't think Munira once opened her mouth in the presence of a soldier, yet she almost always set the tone in our dealings with the vast, restive rabble of Palestinian teenaged boys known on the streets as the *shebab*.

By the time June rolled around, I was beginning to think I knew all there was to know about our odd new profession. Then Hans paired me with a newcomer named Omar al-Baroody, and it was my turn to be the teacher.

Omar was twenty-seven then, a graduate in urban planning from Birzeit University whose father had achieved a certain status and wealth as the owner of a few hotels on the West Bank. Our first week was rocky, the second rockier. I kept having to remind him not to carry the radio when we left the car, and he kept taking it anyway. Whenever we watched the *shebab* creep within stone-throwing range of the tanks, Omar always seemed on the verge of running to join them, balanced on his toes with eagerness burning in his eyes. In meeting army officers he perfected the art of the bristle, head thrown back and chest out, a smoldering glare in his eyes. We talked about it, of course, with Omar always professing ignorance of any attitude problem. Until one day, with only a week left in our hitch, everything boiled over.

It happened during a visit to an IDF central military office near Nablus. The Nablus route was my favorite, partly because of its stark beauty—not only the city, set between steep, barren mountains, but also the rolling landscape, which in the spring bloomed riotously with wild-flowers. It also offered the most action. The Palestinians called Nablus "Jebel Amnar," the Mountain of Fire. The Israelis answered that they would turn it into "Jebel Ramadh," the Mountain of Ash.

Because the city was so far north of our headquarters in Jerusalem, Nablus was the one patrol that required an overnight stay on location, at a UN crash pad, and by the end of each shift in Nablus you were thoroughly wrung out. That was the condition Omar and I were in as we approached the IDF headquarters.

These compounds were scattered around the Occupied Territories. Each was fenced in and heavily fortified, with its own military court, prison, interrogation center, and barracks. We always parked our Passat outside, out of regard for our own image as much as theirs, entered through a revolving barred gate and then crossed the yard to the main building, where a presiding officer monitored the comings and goings much like a police desk sergeant at a precinct house.

On this occasion we were visiting on behalf of a family in Nablus whose son had been detained an hour earlier after some rioting. The soldiers had come to his house. He had never been in trouble before, so his parents were naturally concerned about his fate. As luck would have it, three soldiers brought the boy out the door of headquarters just as we arrived. Luckier still, Captain David Ben-Zohar led the procession. He had one of the better reputations among the officers, and while I would never have called us friends, I liked to think we had a grudging mutual respect. Captain Ben-Zohar always seemed a little regretful about the business of military occupation, but his reputation for occasional leniency had never cost him an ounce of loyalty among his men, who were invariably well disciplined. No high-as-a-kite young recruits in his command.

But this time I was disappointed to see that the boy in custody was bruised and bloody. It looked like he had gotten quite a going-over, and when Ben-Zohar spotted Omar and me he seemed almost sheepish.

"What's happened to him?" I asked. I tried not to sound confrontational, but, as I said, it had been a long day. Perhaps the same was true for Ben-Zohar, judging from what followed.

"He arrived this way," the captain said wearily. "We only picked him up a minute ago."

"We just came from his family, who told us you took him an hour ago. He's been beaten."

"Jews don't torture people."

"Give me a fucking break."

"Sorry. I don't have time for this."

Ben-Zohar shoved me aside.

The next thing I knew Omar was unclipping the handheld radio from my belt. He began hailing our dispatcher in Jerusalem, shouting loudly, "An injustice has been done in Nablus!"

Ben-Zohar exploded.

"What the hell's he doing with that thing?"

Omar answered before I could.

"I am calling in this outrage. You are acting like a Nazi."

"*Nazi?* Did you say *Nazi?*"

The three soldiers surged forward as one. All I remember now is pushing my hands against their chests. It was a bit like fending off a stampede with a cattle prod. Omar at least had the good sense to take shelter behind me instead of striking back. The first blow glanced sharply off my head, and fortunately that was enough to jolt Ben-Zohar back to his senses. He quickly shouted a command in Hebrew to restore order, and it was a testament to his abilities as a commander that his men immediately backed off, even though they were still snarling for a chance to bring down the uppity young Arab.

"Get him out of here! Now! And don't ever bring him back! You're lucky I'm not arresting you both."

Omar was trembling in anger or fear, maybe both, and once we were back in the car with the doors shut I decided to strike while he was still off balance.

"What the hell was that? *Never* do that again! You are never to use the radio in the presence of a soldier, and you are *never* to cause an officer to lose face. You nearly fucked our entire operation. Do you understand?"

He looked at the floor a few seconds before answering in a tone of wounded indignation.

"I cannot stand by in silence when they lie. I am sorry, but there is no way around it. I must be true to my people. I must be true to myself."

I waited to see if he would say anything more. When he didn't, I took a deep breath to collect myself, while trying not to dwell on what a close call we'd just had. Under a lesser commander they would have beaten both of us senseless and locked us away. Then I spoke again, firmly but gently.

"Omar. From now on you must try to practice *taqiyya*."

He looked up in surprise. *Taqiyya* is an Arabic term for an Islamic tradition of behavior in dangerous circumstances. It basically maintains that when your life is threatened, especially in the presence of the enemy, you are allowed to hide the truth, or even lie, in self-protection.

"How do you know of these things?" Omar asked. "From the Holy Quran?"

Clever boy. It was a trick question designed to expose me as a dilettante, which is exactly what I was. But I did know that *taqiyya* hadn't come from the Prophet himself, but instead from the philosophers who parsed his words for deeper meaning.

"Not from the Holy Quran," I said. "Although I have read the Holy Quran."

"Have you, now. All of it?"

Still testing me.

"Well . . . no. Not all of it."

At this he actually grinned, and you could feel the air pressure in the car drop by several notches.

"Neither have I. But don't tell my mother."

A week later, after we had completed our final patrol and I thought I had seen the last of him, I was sitting up late in my apartment on the Mount of Olives, seated by the picture window with its fine view as I filled out Omar's evaluation. The lights of the Old City twinkled against the clear night sky. His future was in my hands, and for a while I considered recommending dismissal. His temper had endangered our safety. But I doubted Hans would have the heart to drop the axe, and Omar had noticeably mellowed after our close call.

Perhaps, if held in check, his passion would be a good thing. And maybe his lack of control had been as much due to my inexperience as his. Endorsing him for further action seemed like a risk worth taking.

Three months later I knew my gamble had paid off when I walked into the office in Jerusalem to begin my last quarterly hitch and found Omar waiting, smiling and patient. He had asked Hans to reunite us, and for the balance of our time together he was steady and communicative, and played the game as well as anyone.

Might that be what he was doing now? Still playing the game, only on a different field, and with new players? Balancing the hotheads against the cooler ones in order to squeeze out a few million for the rabble at their feet? It would certainly explain why he was keeping the sort of company that would make my handlers queasy. If so, then this could be my mission: to save Omar from his own instincts, even if it meant lying about the true nature of my work. Maybe it was my turn to engage in a little *taqiyya*.

And if I failed? Then I suppose I would instead become the agent of his destruction. The writer of the bad recommendation I hadn't been able to muster before. Only this time the penalties might be harsher than mere dismissal.

That was my final, sobering thought as the taxi pulled up outside his office door.

8

Washington

Aliyah sat up from her nightmare and threw back the sheets. Beside her, Abbas mumbled in his sleep. It was a recent habit of his, as if he had at last found someone to confide in, but only by traveling to another plane of existence. Aliyah had sensed for days that he was up to something, so she was all ears. But the words were incomprehensible, neither English nor Arabic. He paused in conversation, uttered a deep sigh, and rolled onto his side.

For a moment all was quiet. Then a distant siren wailed from somewhere across Chevy Chase, a police cruiser, probably headed for the District. She heard a squeal of tires and somehow knew it was the sound of the pursued, not the pursuer, and she surprised herself by offering a brief prayer for escape. A year ago her sympathies would have been with the police. No use trying to sleep now, so she threw on a silk robe and padded downstairs to brew a cup of tea.

The same dream as always had awakened her, the one that invariably followed her weekly visit to the office of Annie Felton, a grief counselor on Wisconsin Avenue. For almost a year now, Aliyah had used her Thursday lunch hour for an appointment with Annie. Then, without fail, every Thursday night she dreamed she was in London searching for their daughter, Shereen. The scene varied slightly from week to week, but the essentials never changed—Aliyah on a restless foot patrol, walking down rows of redbrick homes, knocking at brightly painted doors one after another. Then, bobbies in pursuit, followed by angry red double-decker buses bearing down from all directions. But no sign of Shereen. Not even a thumbprint. When she awakened she always experienced a despairing emptiness.

Aliyah had come to believe that the dream was Shereen's way of urging her to keep trying, to keep searching for some fuller understanding of what had gone wrong. Prayer helped, too, of course. But in navigating the waters of her grief, some channels were so dark that even God couldn't light the way. So she forged onward with Annie's counseling, week after week, talking her way upstream toward the source of her sorrow. If the dream ever stopped, she would know she had reached her destination.

She wished Abbas could accompany her on this journey, but he had always been too preoccupied with his own despair. Her friend Nancy was willing to lend a sympathetic ear, but with regard to Shereen, Aliyah's emotions were often too raw. She wouldn't dare tell Nancy, for example, that sometimes it gave her comfort to see news footage of American mothers grieving for their lost soldier boys, killed in Iraq. It wasn't that she took pleasure in the deaths. It was that she thought her country needed this kind of sorrow to keep it humble, because that was how it worked in the rest of the world. And also because, to Aliyah, Shereen was just as much a victim of the war on terror as anyone in uniform. That was another thought she could never share with Nancy. But Annie only nodded professionally and asked for more, nudging her with gentle questions and calm reassurance.

Sometimes Aliyah got so wound up that she consumed her allotted hour with a single nonstop monologue. Other times she paused for laughter, sweet reminiscence, or calm conversation interspersed by long and tranquil pauses.

Today's session had been a bit out of the ordinary.

"Is it unusual for grief to have colors?" Aliyah had asked.

"Colors?"

"Yes. There are mornings when I wake up, and the day seems to have a certain tone. When I close my eyes that color is wrapped around everything, and it's around all of my thoughts."

"What kinds of colors?"

"Well, there was black at first. I guess that happens with everybody. Everything is black and you can't find your way out of it. And red, too. When I'm angry it's almost like a halo, an aura around everything you look at. Or, no. More like it's burning off of everything, like the corona in a solar eclipse. But the other colors are more interesting."

"What colors are those?"

"Purple's the latest. A very soft purple, almost velvety. Like you could curl up inside it and shut out everything else. But not blinding like the black."

"Is there room for your husband in this place, when things are purple?"

They had discussed Abbas many times—his reticence, and the possibility that he and Aliyah might find some way to reunite with the help of their sorrow.

"I think so. He's never there with me so far, of course. But sometimes I still feel like there's a little space for him. It's like walking into a room with a big plush chair, and you can tell someone's been sitting there because they left an impression on the cushions. Maybe that person will come back, or maybe not."

"Like the space is still waiting for him. On your purple days, at least."

"Yes. Do you think this means he might still come? Or just that I want him to?"

"What do you think?"

"I don't know. Maybe I'll have to bring him there myself. Without him even knowing it."

"And how would you do that?"

"I haven't figured that out."

"It's a good thing to think about, though."

"Yes, it is. I'm worried about him."

"Why is that?"

She told Annie about the accident they had witnessed Monday, her confrontation with the policeman, and the look in Abbas's eyes that she found so disturbing. Then she told her about finding the vial of antidepressants.

"Hmm. Doctor, heal thyself?"

"Yes, I'm afraid that's his approach."

"Do you remember the name of the drug?"

Aliyah did, so she told her.

"Well, it could be worse. But I'd watch for side effects. They can sneak up on you, and sometimes they get worse over time."

"What are they?"

"The worst is suicide, but that's rare, and usually with adolescents. Too many raging hormones. With Abbas it might be violent behavior, or delusions of grandeur, also rare. The most common ones are the kinds of little things you might never notice. Dry mouth, constipation, insomnia."

"He's been up a lot lately in the middle of the night. But so have I, and I'm not taking anything."

"The one you'd probably notice first is sex drive. Sometimes your libido disappears completely."

"Then I might not notice for a while."

"Sorry. So everything's still quiet on that front?"

"Two months now."

"Who is his physician?"

"It used to be Stanley Wilkerson. The one who treats all the congressmen. Unfortunately they had a falling-out, maybe a year ago. Over a stupid political argument."

"Let me guess. The Iraq War."

Aliyah nodded.

"Abbas left the office shouting, still buttoning his shirt. Everyone in the waiting room heard it. There was even a little gossip item about it in the *Post*, that horrid little column in Style."

"Have you asked him about the pills?"

"It would only make him angry that I'd found them. Then that would be yet another wall I'd have to climb next time we talked."

"Sounds like he's building new ones every day."

"Yes."

"And you need him, Aliyah. Especially with Faris off on his own."

"Maybe I should make helping him part of my own therapy."

"Tricky, but possible. As long as you've got a handle on your own emotions. And I'd say you do. You've made real progress. In fact, before you brought up this business I was going to suggest you go without me for a while. Maybe a trial run for a month or so."

"Even if the dream keeps coming?"

"Maybe if you don't see me, the dream will stop. Besides, the way you've described the last ones, it sounds like even that might be easing up. Didn't you used to see everything from Shereen's point of view?"

"Yes, and I was always frightened. Now it's more like I'm seeing it through a camera, and I just wake up sad."

"The sadness you'll always have. The part that will drive you 'round the bend is hanging on to the belief that there's something you could have done to save her."

"I guess that's why I worry so much about Abbas. He's still trying to set things right, as if that's even possible."

"Not healthy, especially with those pills in the mix. He really should talk to someone."

"I guess that's my job. To get him to talk."

"He's liable to be hurtful, you know. He might even blame you. Not because he means it—only because he has to blame anyone but himself."

"Oh, he won't blame me. But blaming other people? That's a different matter."

"Then heaven help them, whoever they are."

Annie said it with a light tone, and they shared a laugh. But in retrospect, as Aliyah dunked a tea bag in steaming water at 3 a.m., it was unsettling. She had to find a way to keep Abbas from drifting farther away, even if it meant being a little pushy, even meddlesome.

She carried the mug into the family room, thinking she might watch some television, perhaps surf for an old movie. But her attention was drawn to the far side of the room, where the door to Abbas's study was ajar. Months ago he had begun locking it, which had disturbed her for reasons she couldn't pin down. It had always been "his" room, so he had a perfect right to lock it. He used it as a refuge whenever he was caught up in an emotionally demanding case at the hospital, and after Shereen's death he spent even more evenings there.

But it was also where he kept the bills and checkbooks, the family correspondence, and his elaborate plans for their annual vacations. So in that sense his recent embargo seemed unwarranted, and even unfair. Maybe that was why her first reaction upon seeing the door open was an urge to enter.

She paused at the threshold to listen for any footfall on the stairs. There was a muffled grunt from up in the bedroom, but nothing more. She opened the door wider, thankful the hinges didn't squeak. Then she slipped inside.

The room's nerve center was an oak desk with a hinged top that folded down to become a writing surface. Abbas had inherited it from his father. Aliyah opened it without hesitation. The first thing she saw was a blue American passport, which sent her heart to her throat. She opened it and saw that it was indeed Shereen's. Beneath it was a torn envelope with a year-old postmark. It had been mailed from the American embassy in London. Abbas must have collected the mail the day it arrived, and thank God he hadn't showed it to her. It was hard enough seeing it now, Shereen's face smiling at her from a photo taken only days before her death.

Here is how Shereen died:

She was in London, a college graduate out on her own at last, touring a few cities in Europe with her two best friends from Stanford. One last dose of the carefree life before they tested the job market. Not that

Shereen had many worries on that score. Corporate recruiters were already in pursuit.

A day before the young women were to fly home, someone broke into their hotel room while they were at breakfast and stole their purses and passports. They raced off in a panic for the American embassy. Not to worry, they were told. Happens all the time. We'll have everything fixed by the close of business.

So the three girls had their photos snapped, filled out the paperwork, and paid the fees. Then they toured the Tower of London before returning at the appointed hour to pick up their new passports.

Sorry, the man said, but there was a complication. Not for Catherine or Jane, but for Shereen Rahim. Nothing serious, just a little further checking required. When Shereen phoned home that night she tried to put a good face on it, covering for her countrymen as if it had all been an honest mistake.

Abbas saw right through it.

"It's your name," he told her. "Your name and your parents' country of origin. It's because your mother and father are Palestinian. That's why they are making you wait, I'm sure of it, for extra security checks. I've heard of these things happening. Just like what happened to us in New York. Ever since 9/11, the consular officers have gone a little crazy."

The next day, a Tuesday, Catherine and Jane flew home as scheduled. Shereen's passport still wasn't ready. Abbas went into his study and placed a call to the embassy in London. Aliyah still remembered how angry he was afterward.

"He wouldn't tell me anything, of course! Just a lot of lame bureaucratic excuses and vague insinuations. I could just imagine him there in his office, some political appointee who contributed a lot of money to someone with all the wrong ideas about the world. Sitting there with his little flag on his desk and an autographed picture of the president up on his fucking wall!"

"Abbas!" He *never* used the F-word.

"It's warranted. Because when I pressed the point he decided to lecture me on what it means to be an American, and not just 'someone who holds an American passport.' "

"Good God."

"You see? And he said that in his position he has to be very careful, and that we have to learn to live with a few extra inconveniences. It's one of the sacrifices we make for living in a safer nation."

"He really said all that?"

"And then, of course, he mentions my little arrest last summer in New York. The same old shit."

"Didn't you tell him she has a job interview on Monday?"

"Oh, he was quite magnanimous about that. He said he would be happy to phone the prospective employer if necessary. But of course he would have to explain that the delay was due to security concerns. Which would make a perfect job reference, don't you think? The stupid bastard! The son of a jackal!"

Wednesday came and went without a passport. Then Thursday. If Friday didn't work out, Shereen would have to wait until Monday, and would miss her interview.

On Friday afternoon, London time, Shereen called from her hotel room with the latest update. Still no luck. Then her cell phone rang.

"Hold on, that might be them!"

It was, but she had to move fast. They had her new passport, but the consular office closed in twenty minutes.

"You mean they can't send it by courier, or at least leave it with the duty officer?" Abbas shouted. "That's outrageous."

"You're probably right, Daddy, but I might just make it. Better run, then. Bye!"

"Good luck!" Aliyah chimed in from the extension.

But Shereen had already hung up. Fifteen minutes later she was dead.

Aliyah took the call from the embassy at 6 a.m. local time on Saturday, 11 a.m. in London. Yes, they waited that long. A kindly voice which accepted no blame announced that their daughter had been reported dead on arrival at a London hospital after an accident the evening before. She had been hit by a London bus at rush hour. Apparently she had stepped right into its path, which can happen when you're a young woman in a great hurry and haven't quite grown accustomed to looking to the right when preparing to cross a busy street in a place where everyone drives on the left.

And then, unbeknownst to Aliyah until now, some fool of a bureaucrat must have slipped Shereen's new passport into the mail. Abbas had never told her, and she quickly saw why. Its issue date was three days prior to Shereen's death. Meaning that it had been printed at the same time as Catherine's and Jane's, but must have then sat in a desk drawer while everyone asked their maddening questions for the sake of national security.

Aliyah didn't want it in her house. But if she threw it out, Abbas would know she had been here. So she carefully drew her hand away from it, as if further contact might burn her skin.

She sat in Abbas's desk chair, drew a deep breath to collect herself, and recited a brief prayer of forbearance from a favorite sura of the Quran, repeating it several times in a slow, passionate whisper. Annie had instructed her to do this whenever a surge of aggrieved anger threatened to overwhelm her, and it usually did the trick. She sat awhile longer in silence, waiting for her heartbeat to slow down. Beginning to calm, she reached for her mug of tea and swallowed deeply. Too much milk and not enough sugar. If she had the wits about her to notice that, then she must be okay.

She reached up to shut the desktop, yet her eyes couldn't resist one last glance at the pile of papers that sat beneath the passport like a funeral pyre, waiting to be ignited.

The item that now drew her attention was a scribbled note. At the top was today's date. Below was an address on Cordell Street, which she wasn't familiar with, next to the name "Melissa," and a time, 6:30 p.m. Aliyah had caught the Metro home from work today instead of riding with Abbas, which happened whenever one of them had to work late. He had phoned her at 6 to say that an emergency had come up with one of his patients. But surely he had meant at the hospital, not on Cordell Street.

Some wives, upon discovering this sort of evidence, would immediately suspect infidelity. A few years ago maybe Aliyah would have done so, too. But the way Abbas had been acting lately made him seem incapable of even beginning an affair, much less managing one. And he certainly wasn't talking in his sleep with some fantasy woman, not in that passionless monologue. His mumblings were more in the tone of a technician, an engineer, the voice she had heard him use when pondering how to fix someone's faulty inner workings.

No, he wasn't being unfaithful. But this didn't make her any less curious about the note. She took a blank sheet of paper and copied the name and address. Then she shut the desk, rinsed her mug, and crept upstairs. When she reached the bed, Abbas was still talking, still working away at whatever problem had recently taken hold of him.

9

I saw Omar before he saw me. At that moment I realized that this was what spying was all about. Catching your subjects unawares, before they had time for any pose or posturing.

He stood at the curb of the busy street in front of his office, shaking hands and saying good-bye to a couple of tall fellows in flowing robes and white burnooses. They might as well have worn signs saying, "Oil Sheikh," and they were climbing into a limo with smoked glass and diplomatic plates. Potential donors, perhaps. Early birds for sure, seeing as how they had finished their business by 8:30.

I felt a surge of goodwill at seeing my old battle companion, looking so assured and in control. But I resisted the urge to call out as he turned to go back inside. This gave me time to write down the tag numbers of the departing limo while my driver watched with undisguised curiosity.

By the time I had paid him a few crumpled dinars, the limo was gone and the sidewalk was empty. The building was typical for this part of town. Four stories of white plaster walls and brown glass. A dirt parking lot in the back with zephyrs of chalky dust. It was only a block off a crowded interchange, and the traffic noise was deafening. The air smelled strongly of burned coffee, an aroma of unknown origin that always seems to pervade Amman by day.

The headquarters of Omar's organization was down a hallway to the left on the ground floor, and the first thing I noticed after stepping through the door was a framed verse from the Quran on the wall behind the receptionist. Maybe he really had gotten religion. My Arabic reading skills were rusty, and it took a few seconds to puzzle out the Prophet's words:

"A person's true wealth comes from the good he does in the world."

So much for piety. Norman Vincent Peale couldn't have said it better.

"May I help you, sir?"

I realized I had been reading aloud, and the receptionist looked at me in apparent suspicion. She was strikingly beautiful, if a bit primly dressed in a blue silk blouse buttoned to the neck. Her huge brown eyes gleamed with unspoken questions. She seemed like the type who missed nothing. Best to be careful around her.

"Yes, I'm expected. Lockhart. Freeman Lockhart. Here to see Omar al-Baroody."

Before she could answer, Omar's voice boomed through the open door behind her.

"Freeman? Is that really you?"

He bounded toward me with a grin, and embraced me in a massive hug. He was heavier than I'd remembered, and I assumed it was the heft of prosperity, although you never would have guessed it from the looks of the office, with its cracked walls, dingy linoleum, and fluorescent tubing. He and the secretary seemed to be the only ones holding the fort. There was a second cubicle, which presumably would soon belong to me.

"You should have seen me when I got your e-mail, running around like I'd won the lottery. Raniya here thought I must be drunk. I take it you've met?"

She nodded briskly, as if to imply she had better things to do.

"Come into my office, where I can tell you what this is all about. And Raniya, could you please make us some coffee?"

"For one?"

"For two. Both with medium sugar." He glanced my way. "Correct?"

"Your memory's perfect. But you're drinking, too?"

"Please. I only fast at my mother's house. You know that."

"People change." I nodded toward the quotation.

"Raniya's idea," he said in a lowered voice. "And I have to say, it works wonders with the Gulfies. They like to see evidence of your devotion, even when it's insincere. Like their own."

I took a seat in a comfortable chair facing his battered gray desk. Somewhat to my surprise, there was a large framed photo of King Abdullah on the facing wall, the one of him in blue jeans, seated next to the queen. It was autographed and personalized in English: "To Omar, with warmest regards."

"Raniya didn't seem too happy about the coffee," I said after he shut the door.

"But she's very happy about her paycheck, so she'll live with it. I know she doesn't like aiding and abetting my little blasphemies, and I'm sorry for that, because she is good at her work." He lowered his voice again. "But I swear, Freeman. Sometimes she is worse than my mother."

"How is your mother, anyway? It's been years."

I had met her often on mornings when we headed up to Nablus, since it was more convenient to pick up Omar at home on the outskirts of East Jerusalem than to meet at headquarters. She was an unwavering domestic presence in the family's modest home, cleaning in the morning, cooking in the afternoon, and sewing around the clock. She always answered the door with a polite but unsmiling nod, and whenever you stayed for more than a millisecond she offered honeyed treats, bowls of almonds and pistachios, and steaming glasses of minty tea. According to Omar, she passed her few moments of leisure glued to the television, watching Mexican soap operas subtitled in Arabic on an ancient black-and-white Philco.

Omar's house was typical of the many middle-class Palestinian homes I entered that year. The furniture was heavy and dark. The walls were decorated with colorful posters of faraway places—outdoor scenery featuring waterfalls, forests, and snowy alpine peaks, and not a single Israeli. A framed photo of Arafat hung in a prominent place in the living room. His image was everywhere then, just as you once found Tito above every mantel in Yugoslavia, or Pope John Paul II's beatific face all across a restive Poland. It was a genuine underdog culture, exhibiting all the usual signs of tenacity and entitlement. Every minor slight became evidence of some larger aggrievement, and every success was tempered by the deepening shadow of military occupation. Against this backdrop, the eldest son was each family's de facto standard-bearer in the continuing struggle, meaning that Omar carried the load for his people.

I wondered how many of those traditions had carried over to his current home, especially now that he was living comfortably in Jordan, with two daughters already in university and his son nearing the age of eighteen.

"My mother is fine," Omar said. "A little slower and quieter, now that all of her children have moved away. But a little angrier, too, ever since the Israelis put up that damned wall. They ran it right through our old neighborhood, you know, just a few months ago. It's fifty meters from our house. She complains that it blocks the sunset."

"I had no idea. I haven't seen it. In fact, I haven't been to Jerusalem since the last time I saw you."

"You should go when you get a chance. Eight meters high. Just like Berlin."

"Are you still allowed to visit?"

"As long as I feel like putting up with body searches and checkpoints. Four hours to make a one-hour trip. You know how it goes."

Raniya brought in our refreshments on a wooden tray. She cast a stern look at Omar, which he chose to ignore. Then she willfully neglected to shut the door behind her.

"But all of that is old business," Omar said, waving dismissively. "Old struggles and old enemies. Onward to the new one, which is why I've recruited you!"

He raised his cup, so I raised mine. We clinked them as if they were filled with champagne. Black would have loved it.

"You are of course invited to our house for dinner tonight, so I hope you don't already have plans. Hanan is very eager to see you."

"Sounds perfect."

"Eight o'clock, then. We both hope Mila will soon join you."

"Not for a few months, I'm afraid. She's got some family business to wrap up in Greece." Now I was lying for two. I doubt Mila would have thanked me.

"Well, you need to find an apartment first, in any case. Which reminds me, I have a few leads. And of course we'll pay your hotel bill in the meantime. So take your time. Get settled into the job first, if you'd like."

"Actually, I already have a lead. A place in Jebel Amman."

"So quickly?"

"It, uh, came from an old UN buddy."

"Perfect, then. You've always been at home in this part of the world. But tell me, Freeman. Can you really be happy working for my shabby little NGO? As grateful as I am to have you, that's the one thing that worries me. Why quit the UN for this? From all I've heard, you are one of their shining stars, yes?"

Black and I had gone over how to answer this kind of question shortly after his slide show. I certainly couldn't tell Omar that I had just retired. Forsaking the easy life on a Greek island made even less sense than quitting gainful employment. So Black had supplied a cover story and said his agency pals would plant rumors to back it up.

"*Fallen* star is more like it. I had a little run-in with a superior. None of what happened was fair, but those things never are. Officially, I've taken early retirement. Unofficially, the prick forced me out. So maybe this wouldn't have been my first choice, but it's my best hope for getting back into the thick of things. As a bonus I get to work with someone I like. Long as you don't mind accepting damaged goods."

"Do not even say that. It's their loss. Besides, Jordan has been accepting damaged goods from the UN for decades. Palestinians have practically built a whole country out of them. I just wanted to make sure you were fully on board. As I said in the e-mail, if you really want this job, it's yours."

At this point Black's script called for me to graciously accept and shake hands. But I was the boss here. Omar knew I had never made a habit of leaping into things, so I decided to play to type.

"I guess that depends on what I'd be doing."

"That's the good part. It's mostly up to you."

Same thing Black had said, and hearing it from Omar would be music to his ears. Who knows, maybe Black was even listening as we spoke. The office had all sorts of hiding places for microphones.

"As you can see," Omar continued, "we aren't exactly overflowing with help. Besides Raniya and me there are only a few volunteers at our field office in Bakaa, and some doctors who have signed on to run clinics on our behalf. But that's it. And for the biggest job, fund-raising, I'm pretty much the whole show. Frankly I could use a white, Christian face with a pedigree like yours. Especially on those rare days when Europeans and Americans come calling. But don't worry—I'm not expecting you to do much on that front. So maybe I should explain what I need most. And if you're comfortable with it, great. If not, that's fine, too, although I hate to think of how hard it would be to find anyone nearly as qualified."

"Or as white and Christian."

"I knew I shouldn't have mentioned that."

"No, I understand. And I'd be happy to help with fund-raising."

Ecstatic, in fact. Show me to the files and I'd begin straightaway. For all I knew, that was where all the answers lay. Omar beamed, taking my eagerness for generosity. Then he described my general duties.

"Until we really get going, you'd be a sort of jack-of-all-trades. Providing a sense of direction to some of the clinics we're setting up, and to our organizers as we put together a field operation, keeping everyone focused."

"I thought your goal was to build a hospital?"

"It is. But instead of just going into the wilderness with a jar and rattling the coins under donors' noses, we're building a track record as we go. That's why we're underwriting clinics, to establish credibility. Right now we're pushing the ball slowly up the hill. The bigger it gets, the faster it will roll once we push it over the top, picking up donors from all walks of the community, local and international. It's all about creating momentum, synergy. We want to become synonymous with providing health care services for the people of Bakaa. We're building a brand."

Goodness, the jargon. It was a spiel you might have heard at a prayer breakfast of the Akron Chamber of Commerce. If Omar was a holy warrior, then his god was Bill Gates.

"And what do you get out of this?"

"Ah, still the heart of a skeptic. Another reason to have you on board. You must have seen a lot of people like me over the years, coming to you with their hands out."

"Mostly in breadlines. But, yes, a few."

"That's why your experience will make us credible. Which is what we need most. Credibility."

"To build the brand."

"Of course."

"With who? People like that tag team of sheikhs I saw outside?"

"You saw them leaving? You should have said something, Freeman. I would have introduced you."

I realized I'd stumbled.

"I wasn't sure you wanted to be interrupted. They looked important."

"Yes, I suppose you might have startled them. But I did tell them all about you. They seemed impressed you were coming aboard. So, you see? You haven't officially started, but already you are having an impact!"

In more ways than one, of course, and to my surprise my little acts of deceit came with a sort of thrill, a forbidden pleasure that made my fingertips tingle, the same way they had whenever danger had showed up at our feeding tents and emergency camps. I could see how this sort of life could become addictive. I decided to probe for more.

Nodding toward the photo of King Abdullah, I asked, "Is he giving you any help?"

"He's been a wonder, in fact. A breath of fresh air."

I raised my eyebrows.

"Didn't you used to call his father the Hashemite Midget?"

Omar laughed—a little uneasily, I thought—and glanced through the open door toward Raniya.

"I suppose I did. I never thought he did enough for the Palestinians."

"Other than provide a home for a few million. Don't you guys make up more than half the population now?"

"More, much more. That was never our gripe. It was the way the palace shut us out of the power structure. All of that Hashemite tribal snobbery. Plenty of room in their desert, but no room in their tent. But with Abdullah, that is changing."

So in addition to becoming a salesman, he was a budding royalist. Something told me that when I saw Omar's house tonight, it was going to be grand and stylish, with a big-screen television, a dish on the roof, and extra cars for the children. But none of this should be cause for alarm for my handlers. King Abdullah was about as cosmopolitan a fellow as you'd want to meet. He had lived abroad for years, had been educated at Oxford and Georgetown, and spoke Arabic with a British accent. If anything, he was too Western for his own good.

"How is he changing things?"

"The royal court is fed up with the cheap politics in the ministries, so now his top people go straight to the business community. The old guard is being frozen out. Any Palestinian with vision is content to leave all the infighting to the Bedouins and just glide above it."

"People like you, you mean?"

"Me and a few hundred others. We intend to be included when decisions are made, and we want to give back something to our people. You'll see, Freeman. The new governor of the central bank is from Nablus. The king's wife is a Palestinian. Everything is different now."

I had heard similar pronouncements in other countries after a new leader had taken over. Then, almost always, the old guard worked its old magic, often with the help of the military and the secret police. I wondered if Omar was underestimating the opposition.

"Why not get the king to pay for your hospital, then?"

"He'll chip in when the time comes. And he has already promised us a site. With the way land prices are going, that means more than you'd think. But all the real money now is in private hands. So that's who we're soliciting first."

"Any names you'd care to drop?"

"Later. We'll cover all that. But it's fertile ground here, now more than ever."

"The city does look wealthy. I saw all kinds of new construction on the ride from the airport."

"Wait 'til you see Abdoun."

"That's where you live?"

He nodded, house-proud and happy, the man who had finally made it.

"It's also where the new American embassy is. Looks just like a resort hotel. Abdoun is Amman's boomtown."

"And you're part of it."

"But I am still a part of places like Bakaa, too. And if it's all right with you, that is where we will go now. To meet your clientele, the people you will be working with. If everything is to your liking, then we will celebrate in style later. So what do you say, Freeman? Shall we get rolling again, you and me, back behind the wheel?"

"Lead the way. But you never did answer my question."

"Which one?"

"What's in it for you?"

He burst into laughter and slapped me on the back.

"Ah, Freeman, you really *haven't* changed. Haven't you been listening to a word I've said?"

I laughed along, while wondering what I had missed.

10

Bakaa is one of those places for which the word "teeming" was invented. Its grimy lanes and alleys course with life like the tunnels of an anthill—never empty, never silent. Intruders are not cast out, they are swarmed under and disappear.

Visitors tend to take one look at the corrugated metal rooftops and hordes of barefoot boys and see only hopelessness. They hear the words "refugee camp" and sense only despair. It takes a more experienced—or jaundiced—eye to detect the almost staged aspect of its shantytown squalor. Palestinians don't want these places looking too permanent, lest anyone think they've given up claims on their former land, and they have built accordingly—floor by floor, room by room. Arab host countries collaborate in this fiction for reasons of their own. Yet in Bakaa the children are mostly literate, nutrition is on a par with the rest of Jordan, and joblessness is no more endemic than in Amman's more populous neighborhoods.

Bakaa sits at the bottom of a deep, dry valley about twenty miles northwest of the capital. It began as a few hundred tents, pitched in 1968 after refugees crossed the River Jordan to escape the Israeli Army. Its original overlords were aid vagabonds like me. But whereas most of my tent-city creations have long since been reclaimed by grassland, dunes, or forest, Bakaa kept growing. Now some 150,000 people live in or around it, making it the largest of Jordan's thirteen camps. It bursts into view as you top a rise from the south, and this time around I was shocked to see that new communities were crawling up the surrounding hillsides. The bowl of the valley was nearly full, and the hillside homes looked modern and new. Many sported garages and picture windows.

"It's grown," I said.

"This part isn't really the camp. These are the people who've gotten out but didn't want to leave their relatives behind."

"You're telling me Bakaa now has suburbs?"

"More or less. They can get up in the morning and see where they came from."

"So it's still about politics."

"Anything to do with refugees is about politics." He pointed across the valley. "See that open tract on the opposite hill? That's our site. Where the hospital will go!"

"As long as the government builds the roads."

"They will." He nodded firmly. "We have assurances."

Omar and I often conversed in English, and that's what we were doing now. But whenever our West Bank patrols had come up against danger or tension, he had inevitably switched to Arabic. The transition never seemed jarring or inappropriate, but despite my fluency it always gave him a subtle advantage. And now, as we eased downhill, he shifted into Arabic. It made me wonder if he was apprehensive. If so, what about? Maybe he just figured I would make a better impression if we arrived speaking the local tongue.

I rolled down my window.

"Smells better," I said, sticking with Arabic. Fourteen years ago sewage had run in open trenches along muddy streets, and the stench clung to you like smoke.

"They've got sewers now. Plumbing, too. No more getting up at dawn to haul water."

Yet Bakaa's illusion of impermanence was intact. In all the chock-ablock construction there wasn't a plumb line or a squared angle to be seen. It was as if Picasso had drawn the blueprints. Metal rebars poked from upper floors, and corrugated sheet metal was still the roofing of choice, even though some of it supported satellite dishes.

"Still the four districts?" I asked. Three of Bakaa's neighborhoods had been named after the West Bank cities most of its residents had come from—Nablus, Hebron, and Al-Quds, the Arabic name for Jerusalem. Then there was Al-Jadeed, the New Camp.

"Yes," Omar said. "And some of them you probably shouldn't visit without an escort."

I laughed.

"What do you think I've been doing the last few years, playing golf in Florida? If I can handle a war zone, I can survive Bakaa."

He gave me a look.

"All the same, try sticking with someone else until you've got a car with our logo, or you're known a little better. Just humor me."

We had reached the valley floor and turned onto Bakaa's main drag, where the heavy traffic lost all rhyme and reason. Cars and people weaved past the open fronts of streetside shops. A butcher shouted prices as he hacked a cleaver down the side of a dangling goat. A small boy rolled an iron canister of propane half as big as he was. Banners strung above us announced political slogans and sporting events. This had all been farmland once, but the only trees left standing were the occasional lonely poplar, palm, or spindly evergreen, and all were powdered with dust.

"Where are we headed?"

"Al-Quds. To Dr. Hassan's clinic."

Rounding a corner, a flood of black-haired schoolboys engulfed the car, spilling into the street like a sackful of onyx marbles.

"They're out already?"

"They go in shifts. Only way to fit them all in. Damn!" A herd of goats had joined the mix. Omar laid on the horn like the other drivers, and the goats bleated in protest. A Bakaa symphony.

A few minutes later Omar parked outside a nondescript storefront.

"You are about to meet Dr. Khalil Hassan," he said. "With any luck, Nabil Mustafa has already joined him. Nabil is on the Camp Improvement Committee, the closest thing to a town council. They are our two biggest organizers."

"I'll try to make a good impression."

"I'm sure you will. On Dr. Hassan, anyway."

I was about to ask what he meant by that, but he had already opened the door to the waiting room. It was gloomy—shades drawn, walls of dark mahogany. A woman in a head scarf sat in a red vinyl chair next to a sniffling daughter. A wheezing old man in a white skullcap sat in another chair, leaning forward on a wooden cane.

A nurse leaned across a blocky reception counter.

"Hello, Mr. al-Baroody. Dr. Hassan is expecting you. This way, please."

I wasn't thrilled about cutting in line, but this wasn't the sort of clinic I was accustomed to, where an extra minute might make the difference between life and death.

When we came through the door two men looked up with an air of having been interrupted in the middle of a serious, even contentious,

conversation. Their body language was all wrong. The doctor, presumably the one in a white coat, sat behind a chrome-edged desk with a
drawn expression and his arms crossed. The other fellow—who I
guessed was Nabil Mustafa—sat on a torn brown couch facing sideways,
as if refusing to look the doctor in the eye.

The doctor stood, then stepped forward with hand outstretched.
By the time I reached him he had managed a smile. Omar did the
introductions.

"Dr. Khalil Hassan, please meet my American friend, Freeman Lockhart, who with any luck will soon be our new director of
programs."

"Asalaam aleykum," the doctor said. Peace be with you.

I responded in kind. He smelled like medicine, and seemed a little
stiff. Maybe he was still bristling from the argument, but my first
impression was of an aloof man long accustomed to regarding himself as
essential. I had seen it occur often enough in the field, among those who
came to believe their welfare was more important than that of the people they served.

"The doctor now keeps his clinic open twenty-four hours, which has
been a great boost to the community." Omar beamed. Nabil didn't seem
nearly as impressed.

"It is only with Omar's help that I have been able to accomplish this,"
Dr. Hassan said. "I have hired two more doctors. Until a few months
ago it was just me, working fourteen-hour days. Now the shifts are more
manageable, and I can spend my spare hours building support for the
hospital."

"Dr. Hassan can tell you all the special needs that make a hospital so
imperative."

"And those are?" I asked.

"Emergency care is the greatest need, of course. Even on a good day
it takes half an hour to reach the nearest hospital. In winter, when the
snows come, it is much longer. Difficult childbirths are the worst. We
lose far too many mothers and infants."

An important issue for sure, although a half-hour delay was hardly
catastrophic. No reason to begrudge Bakaa its hospital, however.

"And, of course, we need improvements in all manner of outpatient
care. Diabetes is increasing. The food that comes from outside aid is not
fresh. It is mostly in cans."

I gathered from the wag of his finger that he knew I had once worked
for the UN.

"Heart disease and high blood pressure are on the rise. Then there are liver and kidney infections, plus asthma and other allergies due to the dust and motor exhaust."

He cleared his throat to drive home the point. Then Omar turned toward the other man and, in a determinedly cheerful tone, announced, "This is Nabil Mustafa, our eyes and ears in the community. Nabil has been in Bakaa from the year of the camp's founding, when he was only nine, so he knows just about everyone. He is responsible for getting the community leadership behind us in full, while making sure that no one feels slighted or overlooked."

"Tough job."

Nabil nodded as if it were all in a day's work, although he made a more favorable impression than the doctor. Misleading or not, his lean face and alert eyes projected a quiet, humble competence. I thought I knew his type from the field, too—the sort who fumed in silence during interminable meetings and discussions, always preferring action to words. Someone a bit like me, in other words. He seemed young for his age, which must have been about forty-six, based on what Omar had said. A youthful appearance was rare in places like this, and that told me something about his hardiness and energy. I wondered if he had political skills to match, because at the moment he wasn't exactly oozing with charm.

"Nabil and I were just speaking of one of those community leaders," Dr. Hassan said, drawing a sharp look from Nabil.

"Not Mumtaz again?" Omar asked.

The doctor nodded grimly. Omar sighed.

"What is it this time? No, don't tell me. No sense in spoiling Freeman's first day on the job. Does it need immediate attention?"

"He'll get over it," Nabil said.

"No. He won't," Dr. Hassan said. "We should see him immediately."

"This morning?" Omar asked.

"That would be best. If you can just wait a moment while I see my next patients, I will accompany you."

"Very well, then. Freeman, I am afraid I will have to leave you for a while, but you will be in good hands with Nabil. He will show you our field office, maybe introduce you to some of the community volunteers. As for me"—Omar sighed theatrically—"I will spend the rest of the morning applying tourniquets. Or maybe performing a little CPR. Metaphorically speaking, of course. And you thought all of our emergencies would be medical."

"Big contributor?"

"Potentially. In one of those nice houses up on the hill. It's like everywhere else, I'm afraid. Egos are more fragile than bodies."

"Do what you have to. I'll let Nabil show me the ropes."

Nabil said almost nothing for the first few blocks. I drew the usual curious stares that a Westerner attracts in places like this, especially from children. Because of Ramadan, the usual street smells of coffeehouses and *shawarma* vendors were absent, although a few curbside cooks were pouring batter for pancakes on open-air griddles. They stuffed the cakes into plastic bags, which would be snapped up by housewives for the nightly feast, and later served with syrup and sugared walnuts. It seemed almost unfair to have to watch them cooking now, when you knew you couldn't eat them for hours.

"Is it making you hungry?" Nabil said, with the hint of a smile.

"Yes. Sometimes I don't know how you stand it."

"Many years of practice."

We were interrupted by an older man who stopped Nabil to complain about one of the banners. To me the slogan seemed harmless, a benign exhortation for everyone to work together for a better future. Maybe it was the name of the organization printed in the corner, the "Popular League of Bakaa," that upset him. The old fellow glanced warily at me and continued on his way.

"You speak Arabic," Nabil said. "That is unusual for an American."

He sounded almost disappointed, as if I had robbed him of an advantage.

"It's a little rusty, but it usually comes back pretty fast. So, tell me, who is this Mumtaz that Omar and the doctor went to visit? I take it you don't think he's worth the trouble."

"You need not concern yourself with him."

"Omar tells me I need to know all the major players, if I'm going to be director of programs."

"And what does that mean, this title? What programs are you directing?"

"You tell me. A little of everything, I guess. Jack-of-all-trades, master of none."

"So you will participate in all aspects of our effort?" Now he sounded wary.

"Omar has known me a long time."

"You are very skilled at not answering questions." He softened the remark with another slight smile.

"Maybe I'm taking my cues from the questioner. I'm not really sure what to say to anyone at this point. Once I've seen how everything works I can give you better answers."

We passed the rest of the walk in silence, dodging cars and children until we reached a narrow alley where every rooftop was anchored with cinder blocks. We approached a two-story building that looked like it had grown not only floor by floor but room by room. Nabil entered without knocking and I followed. Two young men were speaking on telephones, and a third was stacking flyers on a small table in the corner. Propped against a wall nearby was an automatic weapon, some sort of Kalashnikov knockoff.

I raised my eyebrows, but Nabil acted as if nothing were out of the ordinary. The fellow closest to the door eyed me with daggers until he took his cue from Nabil and lowered his eyes back to his work.

The flyers, at least from where I stood, looked like political tracts, although a large poster on the wall was all about the proposed new hospital. Next to it was a map showing the current routes to the nearest hospitals.

The second fellow on the phone was consulting a list of names and numbers. Figuring it might be potential donors, I moved closer for a better look. He responded by hanging up and folding the paper. Then he stood, and left without a word.

"What does he do for the organization?" I asked.

"He is a representative of a local political committee which sometimes uses our phones. The utility charges would be the same regardless. It is another service we can provide for people here while we are waiting for our other efforts to bear fruit."

"And the gun?"

"That belongs to Hakim. You will have to ask him its purpose. But it is often this way with men in this culture. The women have their jewelry, the men have their guns. It is just another adornment, really."

But Hakim, too, was already out the door, and he had taken his "adornment" with him. I was about to ask if this kind of extracurricular activity—the pamphleteering and the politics—was such a good mix with charity when Nabil preempted me with his own question.

"Omar says that for an American you are very fair-minded about the Palestinians. Is this true?"

No smile this time, but no frown, either, so I decided to overlook the backhanded nature of his compliment.

"That tends to happen when you spend a year on the West Bank during the intifada."

"Working with UNRWA."

"Yes."

"And what have you been doing since then?"

"Aid jobs. Humanitarian work. Africa, Asia, the Balkans. All over the place, really."

"The UN," he said, nodding in a way that said he knew all about the UN. After living here thirty-seven years, maybe he did. The UN wasn't always at its best in this part of the world. It was one of the few things the Arabs and Israelis agreed upon. Which is why I was surprised when Nabil suddenly turned nostalgic.

"I remember when the UN set up the first school here. We sat all day with our feet in mud, but we did have desks. The lucky kids had plastic sandals, the rest of us were barefoot. Every morning they gave us a glass of milk, a vitamin pill, and a spoonful of cod-liver oil, but no bread afterward to get the taste out of our mouth." He smiled while his eyes gazed off into his past. "After school every student went to a feeding center. We lined up in a tent. They made *kofta* kebab with tinned beef. That and potatoes, or rice. The same menu every week. But it was hot, and it was filling."

"So you really were one of the first arrivals."

"Oh, yes. There were only a few thousand then. For two years we lived in tents. Seven square meters for each family."

"Sounds awful."

"I guess it was for my parents. I liked it. All my friends were here. Then my father got a plot of land. Ninety-six square meters! He built a first floor. Ten years later he built a second one, with a terrace on the roof."

"Did you ever think then you'd be spending the rest of your life here?"

His expression went solemn, even stern, and I realized too late that I'd stepped on one of the region's political land mines. Never suggest that an uprooted Palestinian will be in exile forever.

"I still don't think that," he said coolly. "My father always said our family would return to Jerusalem, and that is what I tell my daughter. This is not our home. How can it be home? I am half and half, not allowed to be Palestinian and not really allowed to be Jordanian."

It was a standard line, and I'd heard it often enough in '91. But at least he wasn't offering the old song and dance by showing me the keys to the family's old house, or the yellowing deed to their property.

A small voice interrupted us from the doorway.

"Daddy? I have brought this for your guest."

A girl of about ten stood at the entrance. She wore a pink scarf around her head and carried a tray of hammered silver with a steaming cup of Arab coffee and a tall glass of water.

"Come in, sweet one. This is my daughter, Jena."

Her name meant "little bird," and it fit perfectly. She darted from place to place like a sparrow, and her bright little face brimmed with curiosity.

"How did she know that I—"

"Our house is across the street. I had asked my wife to watch for your arrival."

"Ah. Thank you."

"Please. Be seated, so you may drink your coffee."

Nabil did not join me, of course. I sipped while Nabil questioned his daughter about her schoolwork. He listened patiently as she filled him in on the latest news from the playground. It was his softer side, and what was most interesting was that he didn't mind letting me see it. It made me warm up to him a bit, although I was still curious about his politics.

"Tell Mr. Freeman what you like to do at night, on the computer."

"Write short stories." She said it shyly, looking down at her red plastic sandals.

"She writes some very good ones," he said proudly. "She has quite the imagination. Okay, sweet one. Take the tray back to your mother."

She waved good-bye from the door and ran home, raising puffs of dust with every step. Nabil watched until she was safely across the street.

"Maybe she feels the way I did about this place as a boy, and likes it here. But for a father it is very hard. There is no place for our children to play. That is why she is on the computer so much. She goes online to chat with people in other parts of the world. And the stories she writes—they are always beautiful, but they are never set here in Bakaa. It is her way of traveling, I think. The only other time she gets to leave is when I take her to the Hussein Gardens in Amman. We go every month."

We talked a while longer. He was a bit evasive when I asked about his exact duties in the community, but he spoke freely about his background. During his twenties he had dabbled in communism. It had been trendy among young Palestinian firebrands during the Cold War seventies, fostered partly by an infusion of rubles from Moscow. The Soviets deserted the cause once their empire began to totter, and soon afterward Nabil gave up on Lenin. But he had retained some of the revolutionary's blunt way of expression. That was apparent when Omar pulled to the curb in his Mercedes along with Dr. Hassan. Nabil's face darkened, and he said, "Now that the doctor has arrived, I will take my leave. You will find that we don't mix well."

His animosity seemed to go beyond a mere personality clash. That didn't bode well for the charity, but the spy in me stirred with interest. Fault lines were always fruitful sources of information.

But the idea of a rift sent out danger signals, too. The gun in the corner was one warning. The irritation over the political banner was another. Factional tensions always ran deep in places like Bakaa, and I wondered if Omar was mixing a bit too glibly among rivals, and whether he would soon expect me to do the same.

Out in the field I had learned to trust my gut, and on three different occasions my gut had told me something was not quite right. The successive results had been an ambush, a kidnapping, and a violent beating.

Now my gut was once again telling me to beware.

It was also saying that I had better learn as much as possible about Nabil Mustafa and Dr. Hassan, if only for my own protection.

11

You don't expect to see a Hummer in an Arab capital unless an American soldier is at the wheel. But apparently the sons and daughters of Amman's wealthy never got the message, because a bright red Hummer filled with four teens had just rolled by, blaring American hip-hop from speakers that throbbed like the pulse of the earth.

So this was Abdoun. Let the good times roll.

It was certainly a popular place. My taxi was crawling through four lanes of traffic among Mercedes, BMWs, and big SUVs. I was late for the dinner party, but the backup gave me a long look at an Amman I had never seen. So far I had also spotted a two-story Starbucks, a Guy Laroche Paris with valet parking, and nightclubs named Scruples, Mirador, Da Willy, and the Blue Fig. Inside their glass doorways, stylish twentysomethings smoked scented tobacco from tabletop hookah pipes. A few young women wore head scarves, but most were bareheaded and wore short skirts or tight jeans.

From the overflow customers on the sidewalks I heard English phrases like "What's up?" and "How's it going?" interspersed with their Arabic. Others spoke English exclusively. Towering over the tableau like a watchtower was a floodlit billboard for McDonald's, with an apricot pie poking from a red pouch above the words "Sweet Ramadan Treat."

Years ago, Shmeisani had been the neighborhood with all the pretensions, in the city's northwest. Clearly, the social balance of power had shifted south, and Omar was in the heart of it. Not bad for a fellow who made his fortune in the hotel supply business, although lately he was also into stocks and real estate.

I didn't know what to expect at Omar's, but I was hoping for more than just a family dinner. I was ready to get down to business. Time to meet some movers and shakers.

The cab at last pulled up at a magnificent sandstone house. Its two stories were illuminated by floodlights mounted on a lofty palm. Every upstairs window had a stone balcony. Omar's Mercedes was in the driveway next to a Jeep Cherokee. Three more cars were out front.

Omar's wife, Hanan, greeted me warmly. Her kindness had endeared her to Mila, and I liked her, too. She had always struck me as a keen observer, and that meant she would be worth watching with regard to Omar. If he was flirting with any sort of dangerous fringe, it might be evident in her words and actions.

It quickly became clear that I had walked into the middle of a heated discussion between Omar and a young man who must have been his son, Kemal.

"No!" Omar said. "You are *not* to do that. I forbid it!"

Hanan squeezed my arm.

"Omar, Freeman is here."

"Freeman, I am so sorry! You remember Kemal, of course?"

"Not when he was this big."

Oldest line in the book, but it loosened things up. Kemal was taller than his father and had his mother's intense brown eyes. His thin face and cropped hair reminded me of the imperious waiter at the China Dragon. He acknowledged me with a nod.

"You will address him with respect," Omar said.

"I haven't said *anything* yet."

Kemal then had the good sense to look me in the eye and say, quite agreeably, "I apologize, Mr. Lockhart. I should have said hello right away, of course."

"We were having a little disagreement about his cruising habits," Omar said. "His older friends have cars now, but they don't know how to use them properly. Or soberly."

Kemal reddened, offered a clipped, "Pleasure to see you, sir," and bolted out the door.

"Cruising seems to be quite the rage," I said. "The traffic was horrible."

Omar's jaw twitched as Kemal departed, but he held his tongue. Then he threw an arm around my shoulder and walked me toward his guests.

"Ah, Freeman, was it ever really like that between us and our parents? He is seventeen, and already he has forgotten everything I taught him."

"I thought that was mandatory when you're seventeen."

"It's worse now. They're totally irresponsible, driven only by personal objectives. My elders taught me one thing: It's you who will deliver us, you who will go to college and help us live a better life. One of my teachers said that any of us might be the next Saladin, so we had to be prepared to lead. This bunch thinks they're leading if they're first in line at Starbucks. But come meet the others. Everyone here is one of our major backers."

A man in his mid-forties approached as we entered the living room. He was dressed as if he had come straight from the office—crisp gray suit, yellow paisley tie. A wedge of lime perched on the rim of his cocktail glass, and I smelled gin. He addressed me in perfect English.

"You must be the famous Freeman Lockhart. As honored guest, please feel free to tell the host to shut up about today's youth."

Others joined in the laughter, even Omar.

"Speaking of blatant self-interest," Omar said, "this is Rafi Tuqan."

"He is making fun of my chosen profession," Rafi said.

"Which is?"

"Financial adviser. Something that almost didn't exist here twenty years ago. It's another of our growth markets."

"That's why we like having Rafi over," Omar said. "Whenever he gossips, you get a free tip or two."

"Buy low, sell high?" I asked Rafi.

"Don't make it sound so easy. Bad for business. But it's true that in Amman right now even a fool could make a fortune."

There were four other guests. Two were Dr. Hassan and his wife, Rima, a tiny woman with a cackling laugh who was drinking pomegranate juice. There was also an older couple, Sami and Badra Fayez. Sami didn't say what he did for a living, although I gathered from the others that he owned loads of property and had long been a lubricant of Amman's sociopolitical machinery. Over a second round of drinks, Rafi told me that Sami kept a sort of salon in a restored house downtown, where drop-in guests traded rumors and hatched plots over a bottomless supply of coffee and sweets.

"You should go," Rafi said. "A splendid old place, and Sami would enjoy showing you off. Old-school Ammanis, mostly. They're convinced that's where the action is."

"And it isn't?"

"The only real action is at the palace. And in the financial markets, as long as the war in Iraq keeps going."

"The war's good for business?"

"The Iraqis had to put their money somewhere. A lot of the old Baathists came pouring out before the shooting started. Even the people who stayed, hoping to take over, sent their money. Divided in war, united in flight capital. You should see their villas, bigger than the Saudis'. I was in a belly-dancing club the other night where drunken Baathists were singing hymns of praise to Saddam. Everyone booed, of course, but no one came to blows. Nobody wanted to risk slugging his next customer. Throw in the Gulfies and it's one big carnival. Land prices are doubling once a year."

"Maybe that's why everyone thinks Sami has all the answers."

"And maybe he does. Until the bubble bursts. But don't ask me when that will happen. I'm only paid to make it bigger."

"Hard to see how it could get much bigger in Abdoun."

"Omar is right about these young people, you know. They see someone like me and think it's easy money, but none of them realizes what it took to get here."

"A business degree?"

"Earlier. I never would have learned to hustle growing up in Abdoun."

"Spoken like a West Banker. Or someone from the camps."

"The Al-Wihdat camp, here in Amman. You know it?"

"I went there during the Gulf War, years ago. They were hustling, all right. Picked my pockets twice."

Rafi laughed.

"Well, it wasn't me. Too busy doing chores. Fetch the water at five, the bread at six, the lentils at seven. Then school until four. And it wasn't like you could run away. Amman was tiny then. If you wandered a mile from home you saw coyotes."

I suppose he wanted to let me know he was the genuine article, not just a rich guy buying off his conscience. It made me wonder why Nabil Mustafa hadn't been invited. Palestinians here liked to grouse about the snobby Hashemites, but they could snub with the best of them, and maybe Nabil was too rough around the edges for this crowd. I wouldn't have minded seeing him, though. He struck me as the type who didn't waste time with false fronts, whereas these people might need a few drinks to show their true colors.

Rafi went to freshen his gin, so I wandered across the living room to look at a couple of paintings. The most striking was a bold impressionistic landscape, desert mountains in dusky light beneath an afternoon sky. Shadows loomed heavily in thick daubs of dark oil. I had been to places like that, and the artist had caught the lighting perfectly. But the more impressive piece was a small drawing in charcoal. It was another desert scene, from Jordan's eastern stretches of black basalt, a desolate landscape I remembered from my many trips to the Iraqi border in '91. Setting up aid camps there had been like working on the surface of the moon. The artist deftly captured the monochromatic bleakness. In the foreground, some sort of half-buried ruins lent an air of mystery.

"Nice, isn't it?"

It was Sami, the real estate tycoon.

"Haunting. What are the ruins, some kind of fortress?"

"The ancient dam at Jawa, five thousand years old. Some of the world's oldest hydraulic works, in fact. The artist is a friend, Issa Odeh. He did the oils, too. One of Omar's fellow travelers in the quest for all things old."

"Old? Omar? Those two words never used to go together."

"Oh, he has become quite the preservationist. Always telling me not to sell this plot or that because of its historic value."

"And with good reason," Omar said, approaching from behind. "It's our heritage. Sami likes to pretend these old stones have no value whatsoever."

"Old stones can't feed a hungry mouth," Sami said.

"No. But they can conquer a people. Look at what the Jews do with their old stones. The Western Wall. A few ancient foundations. They've turned them into biblical land claims, and in this part of the world that's as good as a deed. Long as you've got an army to back it up."

"Is this the same Omar al-Baroody who used to say the past was worthless?" I asked.

"*Omar* said that?"

"At least once a day."

"This is the problem with old friends." Omar grinned sheepishly. "They know too much."

By now Hanan had joined us.

"Freeman's right," she said. "Tell Sami what you used to say about your parents."

"No one wants to hear all that."

"Then I'll tell him," I said. "Omar used to say his parents spent their whole lives looking backward. That all they ever talked about was 1948, or 1967, and that's why nothing ever got done."

"My parents were the same," said Rafi, the boy of the camps who had struck it rich. "Whenever I asked about fixing our house they said, 'No, no, we are going to return.' It was always an excuse for doing nothing."

By now everyone in the room had been drawn into the conversation. A few drinks more, and they would really open up. I decided to slow down my consumption so I would still be alert when that happened. The odd part was that they were all speaking English, although everyone must have known I was fluent in Arabic. I was reminded of the kids outside the Blue Fig. But I was reminded even more of those Moscow soirees in Tolstoy, where the Russians chat fashionably in French. Not that it stopped them from kicking Napoleon halfway across Europe.

Dr. Hassan put a hand on my shoulder and, in a tone obviously intended to be sage, said, "If you are interested in old things, Mr. Lockhart, then you should visit Petra."

"Oh, please," Rafi said. "Surely he can do better than Petra. Besides, he's probably already been."

"I have, in fact. Not that it isn't worth another visit."

I didn't say that just to placate Dr. Hassan. Petra is breathtaking, an entire city carved out of rocky bluffs, a two-thousand-year-old public works project in bas-relief. And you got there by riding the final kilometers on horseback through a narrow gorge walled by three-hundred-foot cliffs. I suppose that it took a trendy financial hipster such as Rafi Tuqan to conclude that it had somehow become passé.

"Too popular for you?" I asked him.

"The tourists don't bother me. Or even the trinket sellers. Let the Bedouins set up their little ice cream stands if they want. They certainly never made a dinar to compare with those ugly hotels the government built. In fact, maybe it *would* do you good to go back. There's a real lesson for Americans at Petra."

"Is there now?"

"Well, you emerge from your ride down the narrow *siq* and it is beautiful, yes?"

"Spectacular."

"And you think, my goodness, what sort of refined and proud culture could have built this? Surely not Arabs? But, yes, it was. Then you round the corner, and see what?"

"The amphitheater?"

"Exactly. Built later by the Romans, of course. Because when they conquered a place they had to make it their own. Never mind that it was already the most beautiful city in all of Provincia Arabia. They had to put in a theater, a Roman road, a forum. Who knows, maybe someday they'll dig up a stela engraved with 'Billions Sold.' "

I laughed. So did Rafi, which told me his lecture was in good fun. But a few of the guests stared silently at their shoe tops until Omar rode to the rescue.

"Actually, the Romans helped save the place," he said. "Gave it a bit of a renaissance. You've got to take the long view, Rafi, like our archaeologist friends. Besides, the most interesting aspect of the Roman works in Jordan is that none was ever really completed."

"Is that true?" I asked.

"Oh, yes. Even the theater downtown."

It was a bit magical to see that Omar hadn't lost his touch for peacemaking. In easing the awkward moment he reminded me of the times he used to step out of our Passat into the *shebab* and manage to cool tempers with a few well-chosen words.

"Interesting," I said. "Why do you think they stopped?"

"Who knows? Maybe they ran out of money."

"Now there's your American analogy," I said to Rafi. "Some tightwad isolationist in the Senate must have gotten hold of the foreign aid budget."

This time everyone joined in the merriment. Omar nodded to me almost imperceptibly, as if to acknowledge we were still doing our bit for peace and harmony. It brought on a flush of nostalgia, which of course produced an immediate backwash of guilt. Maybe I needed another drink after all.

Soon afterward, Hanan announced that dinner was served, and the gathering sauntered forward. But Dr. Hassan waylaid me before I could reach the dining room.

"A quick word if I may," he said in a guarded tone.

"Yes?"

"I am a little worried for our friend Omar, at least with regard to some of the company he keeps at Bakaa."

"Is this about Nabil?"

The doctor nodded.

"Tell me, when you visited the field office, were any of Nabil's friends there?"

"A few. Making phone calls." I didn't feel like mentioning the gun or the flyers.

"I was afraid of that. It is not our work they are doing, you know. It would be best to keep an eye on that. I am afraid Omar does not always pay attention. He might be shocked if he knew. But he would be more likely to believe it from you."

"I'll keep that in mind."

"Good." He placed a hand on my arm. "We are grateful to have you with us."

I followed him into the dining room. My earlier instinct that this fault line might produce useful information seemed to have been on the mark.

The food was splendid, with literally a dozen dishes to start us off, a fine Middle Eastern *mezze* of olives, savory pastries, eggplant, fava beans, hummus, stuffed peppers, and so on. That was followed by a roast leg of lamb, encrusted with spices, along with huge bowls of rice and plenty of wine. As the last of the meat was carved from the bone, Dr. Hassan rose with a somewhat pompous clearing of the throat to propose a toast to Omar and Hanan. Everyone raised a glass with cries of approval. Omar then offered a toast to me, which under the circumstances made me blush.

But it did offer an opening. Maybe now was the time to stir the pot. By steering the conversation back toward politics, who knew what I might learn. So I stood, raised my glass, and proposed a toast "to Jordan's next generation."

Predictably, there was some wry grumbling.

"No, I'm serious. Maybe they have the right idea after all. Pay enough attention to their own selfish concerns and they'll forget all about 'the cause.' Get enough young Israelis to do the same and, who knows, you could end with something like peace."

They clinked glasses halfheartedly. For a moment I thought the topic would die for lack of a second. Then Sami, voice of experience, obliged me by getting the ball rolling.

"The problem with that idea is that the children of Abdoun or Shmeisani will party on. But out in Zarqa, or in your favorite camp of Bakaa, everyone else's children will still be seething and plotting. Hatred of Israel and, yes, even of America, is still the glue that holds them together. There are many danger spots. Last month, when those fools fired missiles in the Gulf of Aqaba, you know of this?"

I nodded. I had read about it. A couple of locals with al-Qaeda connections had fired a Stinger at a U.S. Navy ship. They missed. Arrests were made. Situation under control. Only it might not have been.

"If they had been successful," Sami continued, "all of us would have suffered, but there would have been celebrations in the streets."

"Surely not among most people," I said, nudging further. Rafi took the bait.

"It is true, what Sami says. For many, Osama bin Laden is Robin Hood. I would go so far as to say there is a small Osama in the heart of every Arab citizen, even at this table. And because of what is happening in Iraq and in Palestine, that small Osama is growing."

Now we were getting somewhere. There were gasps around the table, and Sami reddened in anger. I suppose they thought I was shocked, but I'd grown accustomed to hearing things like that, even from so-called moderate Arabs. It is a mark of their frustration, and speaks to their yearning for heroes, even disreputable ones. How else to explain why Jordanians cheered in '91 when Saddam fired Scuds into Israel, even though they never would have wanted him as their leader. But I decided to say nothing, and waited placidly until Sami roared back into action.

"You would never talk such rubbish, not even in jest, if you had been here in '70, when fanatical idiots nearly tore this country apart."

"I *was* here in '70," Rafi said firmly.

"Only as a boy. A mere boy in the camps."

The word "boy" was spoken with such obvious disdain that Rafi answered in Arabic. They were finally slipping off their party masks.

"Yes, a *boy* in the camps. And not living well like you, perhaps, but—"

"Please! This is not about class or status. I'm talking about public order, about fools who took us to the brink of anarchy! They hijacked four planes in the name of the Palestinian people, and because of that there was war in the streets."

"Black September," Rafi said distastefully.

"That's what people who should know better are stupid enough to call it, only because the king dared to have a country instead of another Beirut. Anarchy is what happens when you let your 'small Osama' grow up."

I only vaguely recalled the episode they were discussing, mostly because it had happened when I was in college and was wholly ignorant of what went on here. I'm sure it struck me then as yet another blowup of desert nuts with towels on their heads.

"No one was killed on those planes," Rafi said. "Not one single hostage."

"But that was the beginning of the stupidity. From then on, someone was always willing to do anything to get the world's attention. And all they bring us is ruin."

Sami had lowered his volume, and things might have cooled off further if Rafi hadn't then tossed gasoline onto the embers.

"They didn't seem to bring *you* much ruin, out there buying their land for a few dinars a dunam. Isn't that when you made your fortune?"

"That is a lie! I've never invested at the expense of the public order!"

Now even Omar seemed powerless to stop the whirlwind. I saw Hanan grip the edge of the table with both hands.

"Please, gentlemen," she said.

But neither Sami nor Rafi seemed ready to back down. The torchlight of old battles was aflame in their eyes. Rafi, gray suit or not, was back among the *shebab*, reaching for a stone. Then, just as quickly, the muscles in his face relaxed. You could almost see the youthful anger give way to the businessman's pragmatism. Say what he would about Sami, Rafi also had a bottom line to protect.

"I am sorry, Sami." He choked out the words in English, then dabbed his mouth with a napkin like someone who had received a blow to the face. "That wasn't warranted." He glanced my way. "In fact, most of what I said wasn't warranted."

Sami responded with a noticeable tremor.

"My apologies as well, to you and to anyone else who may have taken offense."

"Besides," Rafi said, forcing a smile, "next time it may be me that these little Osamas will want to blow up."

That might have ended it if Dr. Hassan had not said, in his usual stiff manner, "Please. It is best not to discuss such things in this way. You never know when our friends on the Eighth Circle will invite one of us in for tea. If they did, we would not want such a conversation on our conscience."

It was an astonishing remark. If I understood correctly, he was referring to Jordan's secret police, which had its headquarters at the Eighth Circle.

"Are you referring to the Mukhabarat?" I asked.

From the embarrassed silence that followed, I realized that my zeal for information had led me into a faux pas. I suppose no one liked being reminded of the one thing that made his country just like Syria, Saudi, or Egypt. Omar gave me the same exasperated look he had used on patrol whenever I'd said something stupid about his people.

Rafi, of all people, then rescued me by raising his glass and announcing lightly, "Let us have a toast, then, to the value of selective silence."

Sami and Dr. Hassan nodded, and afterward the mood eased, even though Hanan still clung to the table as if it were a life raft. When she looked my way I could have sworn she seemed disappointed, which hurt a bit. But my overriding emotion was curiosity. The episode made me wonder how all the factions might shake out among a group like this if push ever came to shove, the way it had years ago. Sami and Rafi would probably be interested mostly in protecting their investments. So would Dr. Hassan. The missing ingredient was the rougher crowd, exemplified by Nabil Mustafa. Would he and his friends in the camps be the only ones still willing to admit they were warriors? Or, more to the point for my purposes, what if the fight was carried out on a more secretive level? If offered the cloak of confidentiality, I supposed that almost anyone here except Sami might offer some degree of aid and comfort to people whom my handlers would consider poisonous. Maybe they were already doing so. That was what I was here to find out.

Later, with a full stomach and a few too many drinks, I rode back to my hotel with Omar. Just the two of us in his Mercedes. Toward the end of the party, I had announced to one and all that I was officially taking the job. It had put him in a jolly mood, and now seemed like a good time to learn a little more about the other guests. Or so I was thinking until Omar put me on notice.

"I see that you are still just as curious as ever," Omar said. "Or maybe more so."

"Sorry. Didn't mean to get them all wound up."

"Didn't you?" He eyed me across the seat, as if weighing my sincerity. "Perhaps so. I guess you *have* been away too long. But you know how things are here."

Maybe it was the alcohol, or the small thrill that comes with pressing your luck, but for whatever reason I couldn't resist a bit more prodding.

"Speaking of which, Dr. Hassan took me aside to tell me to watch your back. He said he was worried about some of the company you're keeping in Bakaa."

"Nabil, he meant. You're only the latest recruit to the doctor's little war with Nabil."

"Who says I've enlisted?"

"Good for you if you haven't. He thinks Nabil and his friends are all wild-eyed bomb throwers. Not that the doctor minds bomb throwers as long as they're from the right organization."

"I have to admit, things were a little, well, interesting over at the field office. One of them was even toting around an automatic weapon."

Omar shook his head, although he hardly seemed alarmed.

"I suppose if you had to put a label on those people it would be Hamas. Unofficially, of course. The palace has banned Hamas, so they go by different names here. Dr. Hassan, on the other hand, is from a PLO family, a Fatah man. So you might say that he and Nabil are predisposed to rivalry."

"Hamas? Doesn't that make Nabil a little worrisome?"

"It would if he had joined for the wrong reasons. Ask Nabil and he'd tell you it's because of the hopeless corruption in Fatah. The cronyism."

"So why put both of them on your team if they're rivals?"

"Political necessity. Street cred, to use an Americanism Kemal is always using when he's speaking that awful hybrid Arabizi. Let's face it, if they can't work together even to build a hospital, then all hope really is lost for Bakaa. For all of us. Someone has to bring them together. Or something. And maybe this is it. If Nabil's friends want to sponge a little off our phone lines, what can it hurt?"

"Unless your European donors find out."

"*Our* European donors, Freeman. You're one of us now. And part of your job is making sure they *don't* find out."

"So I'm just a decoy? That's why you hired me?" It was comforting to be able to muster a little righteous indignation.

"Of course not. Nabil is the decoy. Just don't tell him I said so. He's our face in that part of the community, a link to some of the more 'committed' among the population, to put it nicely."

"It's not as if those people are likely to chip in much money."

"No. But when, for example, one of the more anti-Zionist sheikhs from Dubai comes calling with his checkbook open, Nabil is there to reassure him that we're true believers."

"And while this fun-loving sheikh is in town, does he also make out a few checks for explosives and suicide vests?"

Omar scowled.

"I'd forgotten what a purist you could be."

"Purist? I'm talking about blowing up buses full of women and children."

"I know. It's dreadful. It's inexcusable. But so is firing a missile into a house to kill one old man in a wheelchair even though he's sitting down to dinner with twenty members of his family. The Israelis did that, you know, to kill an old Hamas cripple. It's a war, Freeman. Just because Jordan doesn't participate doesn't mean that some of us don't still cheer from the sidelines."

"As long as you're not buying supplies for the home team."

"Who said I was?"

He glanced toward me and held it a few beats, as if looking for something more. When I didn't answer, he shook his head and swore under his breath.

"That's the same sort of bullshit the Americans have been spreading about us," he said. "If I didn't know better I'd suspect you'd been talking to the resident conspiracy theorists at your embassy."

For the first time since arriving, I felt at risk, a need to cover my tracks. It was strangely exciting. Even more surprising was that I managed to produce my answer in a calm and even tone.

"No one's told me anything. It was a logical guess after what you said about Nabil."

"Like I said, he's a figurehead."

"I'll remind you of that when it turns out your development fund has been paying for Semtex."

"Is that what's bothering you? Our finances? Because we may play fast and loose with our friendships—hiring an American, for example. Believe me, some of our backers won't look kindly on that—but on finances we run a very tight ship. Check for yourself."

"You'd let me see the books? Just like that?"

"You're director of programs, Freeman. Of course you can look. Tomorrow, if you'd like. I'll alert Raniya, so she won't think you're the fox in the henhouse."

Ouch. But now I had my entrée. From a practical point of view, the conversation couldn't have gone better if I'd scripted it.

We said good night at the hotel entrance, where a band was playing loudly to Ramadan revelers in the courtyard. When I got to my room I could hear the lead singer competing with the neighborhood muezzin, who, frankly, had the better voice. Normally I would have been irritated by the noise. But considering my progress, the music was as soothing as a lullaby. The revelers began clapping to the beat, drowning out the muezzin, and the band broke into the disco standby "I Will Survive."

Interesting to think of it as some sort of Palestinian anthem. Or maybe with this crowd it was only about love and heartbreak. Whatever the case, it made me smile, and as I sank into slumber my final thought was that maybe this job wouldn't be so difficult after all.

The sort of mistake any amateur might make, I suppose.

12

Washington

Having slept uneasily after her rummage through Abbas's desk, Aliyah decided to check out the address on Cordell Street during the next day's lunch hour. She might have put off the task a few days if not for an odd episode that very morning.

It occurred on their way to work, with Abbas again at the wheel. He had turned on the NPR station and hadn't said a word since they backed out of the driveway. Aliyah sipped coffee from a travel mug while reading the *Post*, folded in her lap. Big earthquake in Pakistan. Further government bumbling, post-Katrina. More explosions in Iraq.

Then, some fifteen minutes into the trip, Abbas muttered "genius!" right out of the blue. It was the tone that caught her attention—reverent, almost envious, like a scientist who has just watched a colleague transmute lead into gold.

"Sheer genius," he repeated, shaking his head now in admiration.

Was he reacting to something on the radio? A news summary was in progress. All she caught was the tail end of a casualty report. Fifteen dead in Kandahar. No genius in that.

"What's 'sheer genius'?" she asked.

Her question broke his reverie. When he turned toward her she saw the same light in his eyes she had noticed after the bus accident.

"You weren't listening to that?" he asked, his voice conversational again.

"I was reading."

"It was nothing important."

He looked back toward the road, where a car to their right was straying from its lane. "Learn to drive!" he shouted, laying on the horn. "Always the same jerks in their BMWs."

Obviously the moment had passed, so she filed it away uneasily on her growing list of worries, while vowing to take action at noon. When the lunch hour arrived, her friend Nancy wanted to go to the new Afghan restaurant around the corner, and Aliyah found herself lying rather than having to explain her odd little mission.

"I'd love to, but I have some shopping to do."

"I could be talked into that."

"Well, it's more of an appointment, really. Something I've needed to get done for a while, and I'll have to take the Metro."

"Oh. Sounds like a gift. For Abbas?"

"Something like that."

"Maybe Monday, then. By then I'll have a full scouting report on the Kabul Garden."

Aliyah caught a Red Line train from Dupont Circle to Metro Center, where she switched to the Blue Line for the ride out to the Eastern Market stop in Southeast. By Metro and on foot, it took more than half an hour to reach the 1100 block of Cordell Street. It turned out to be in one of the tougher fringe neighborhoods just beyond Capitol Hill.

That part surprised Aliyah. Few of Abbas's patients came from neighborhoods like this. What interest could he possibly have in a block that was so obviously falling apart? Even more surprising, the address he had written down was for a vacant storefront with a padlock on a steel front door. The sign across the top said, "Alighieri's Pizza," but when she peered through the caged grating across the big front window, it seemed clear that no one had twirled any dough here for quite some time, although a hint of garlic odor still clung to the place. Abandoned cooking equipment was piled on a counter, and a black and orange "For Rent" sign was posted on the door.

She stepped back and looked upstairs. It was your standard three-story row house, red brick with two mullioned windows facing the street from each of the two upper floors. Green paint peeled from elaborate woodwork along the roofline. One window was cracked. None had curtains. The building looked empty, and she wondered if the previous proprietor had lived upstairs. She imagined one of those sturdy Korean or Hispanic families so prevalent at storefront businesses like this one, striving for years until they had enough money to move upward and onward.

But what about this place could have drawn Abbas, and why was he keeping it a secret? She wrote down the phone number of the real estate company from the sign on the door, while wondering if it would connect her to the mysterious "Melissa."

Aliyah surveyed the rest of the block. A Chinese takeout, a mini-grocery with bricked-in windows and a prominent sign for the DC Lottery, a pager and cell phone dealer, and a few businesses that, like this one, were padlocked. The building just to the right was boarded up. To the left was an alley that ran alongside the narrow grassy lawn of a hulking Baptist church. It also had seen better days. Decades of soot and auto exhaust had blackened its formidable stone facade, and the masonry needed repointing.

The only sound of life apart from the occasional passing car was the squealing of children. They were at play in an empty lot at the far end of the block, which adjoined a day-care center around the corner.

She had come here for answers but had found only further questions, and she rushed back to the office in hopes of beating Nancy so that she could telephone the real estate office without being overheard.

"Hamilton Properties," a voice answered.

"Yes, is Melissa there?"

"I'll connect you."

A pause, a click, and then a chirpy, "Melissa Beck, how can I help you?"

"I am calling about the rental property on Cordell Street."

"I'm sorry, it's just been rented. Yesterday, in fact. First call we've gotten in months and now of course you're interested, too. Isn't that always the way?"

"Yes, I suppose so."

"But we have plenty of similar locations—better ones, in fact—if you'll tell me what you're looking for."

"Maybe some other time." She was flustered, and on the verge of hanging up before she recovered in time to say, "There is one thing you can tell me. I wonder if you had a contact number for your new tenant. I am assuming that it is Mr. Abbas Rahim?"

"Now how did you— May I ask who's calling?"

"It's not important."

She hung up before Melissa could ask another question.

So he had actually signed a lease without telling her. She supposed she should be angry. Even at a location like that, D.C. real estate wasn't cheap, which meant he must have written a sizable check. Another reversion to the old ways of Palestine, where men did as they pleased on such matters.

Maybe he had signed the lease to help out some Palestinian merchant who, for whatever reason, was struggling to come up with the permits needed to open a business. She knew that such things went on, and that Abbas had always felt obliged to help others from the Diaspora. He was generous that way, and she wasn't.

Aliyah had never dwelled much on her origins, even when it became a trendy thing to do. Maybe it was because her parents had insisted she learn English right away, before she even attended a day of school. For years it was the one language she and her siblings were allowed to speak around the house. Only during the weekly trip to the mosque—there was only one where they grew up, and they had to drive twenty-two miles to reach it—did she ever hear Arabic, and she now spoke the language with a pronounced American accent.

It was her children who had reconnected her to her "identity," as their son, Faris, called it. He was particularly intent on exploring his Arab and Palestinian roots, even though he had been born here and had traveled to the Middle East only twice. She remembered a fall weekend the family spent in Nantucket, for a family friend's wedding. They had settled into a clapboard house for three days amid remote dunes and the crisp breezes of a Yankee autumn, a place about as foreign as you could get in comparison with the orchard village near Jerusalem where she had been born.

Yet every morning after breakfast Faris and Shereen, both in their mid-teens then, brought her an extra cup of coffee and insisted on hearing her memories, such as they were. Once she began to stir them up, she discovered they were quite rich in old sights, sounds, and smells, as if she had uncorked a bottle long hidden. It was stimulating in a way that surprised her. But it also left an odd aftertaste of melancholy, as if she had never quite realized what she lost by moving all those years ago. So, once her children dropped the subject she hadn't pursued it further.

Abbas had no such inhibitions. He stayed in close touch with Arab American business groups, charities, and support networks, even after that became something of a liability in the wake of 9/11. But on the many occasions when he offered donations or otherwise pitched in, he never insisted on taking credit or even receiving a thank-you. Maybe that explained why he was acting in secret now. If she were to dare ask him about it, he would probably shrug it off as some minor favor.

. . .

But as the afternoon wore on, Aliyah couldn't shake her anxiety about Abbas. It was as if a needle on a meter had just jumped into a red zone, except she had no idea what the meter was measuring, or what action she could take to restore conditions to normal. Something told her she had better find out soon.

13

I awakened with a sense of excitement. Was this the allure of spying, then, this sense of starring on your own private stage before an audience of shadows? Fresh from a shower and a quick shave, I bounded down the stairway. The gloom of the hotel dining room wouldn't do this morning, so I headed for Prince Zahran Street and the pricey but sunlit Hotel InterContinental, where one could unroll a starched linen napkin and order eggs, bacon, and Turkish coffee.

I had stayed there during the Gulf War, when it was a hub for media and aid workers. In those days the American embassy was right across the street. Some sort of loud demonstration had almost always been in progress then, usually a small but vocal crowd chanting for Saddam. If you went back farther, to the chaos of 1970 that Sami had talked about, the InterCon had been strafed by gunfire.

For my purposes, its several bars and restaurants offered a secular refuge during Ramadan, and the breakfast further fueled my upbeat mood. I finished with two hours still to kill before meeting the rental agent, so I set out for downtown.

Few people were out this early, due to the altered rhythms imposed by the holiday. As a result, even the merchants seemed behind schedule. Fruit vendors were still rolling their carts into place. A luggage merchant was setting up an old treadle-powered sewing machine on the sidewalk in front of his shop. The center of the action was the checkerboard marble plaza outside the Husseini Mosque, at the end of King Faysal Street. Lottery salesmen already lay in wait, with stapled tickets fluttering from propped signboards.

The only other early birds seemed to be the beggars. On virtually every corner there was a woman dressed in black, sitting cross-legged in hopes of selling from a meager assortment of toothpaste, cigarettes, and playing cards arrayed on sheets and towels. Most had wiry infants at their feet, as if this were part of the standard equipment.

Sami's salon was nearby, but it was too early to drop in, so I stopped at a clothing store where the proprietor was unrolling his awning. It specialized in the colorfully embroidered blouses traditionally favored by Palestinian women, and the alert shopkeeper began his pitch with the line I had heard hundreds of times in Middle East bazaars.

"You are first customer," he said in English. "That is lucky, so I make good price."

"These are nice," I replied in Arabic. "You must sell a lot."

I considered buying one for Mila, imagining she might wear it as an exotic nightshirt. That and nothing else, with the hem reaching just below the waist, her bush visible in brief glimpses as she stepped toward me. An erotic waltz in our great room, on a brisk night when the stars were hanging high in a black sky. A smile on her face as she handed me a smoky glass of port, then curled up next to me on the couch and tucked her toes beneath my thigh.

"For you, I make very special price," the proprietor said, which broke my reverie.

"No, thank you. Not today."

Stepping around the corner I saw a sign across the street for the Shatt-al-Arab Coffee House, upstairs. Sami had recommended it as a great spot for listening in on political discussions, but during Ramadan it would be dead until sunset.

No sooner had I laid eyes on the place than a familiar face bobbed into view. It was Nabil Mustafa, unsmiling and in a hurry. I backed beneath the nearest awning and saw him check his watch. He paused on the threshold of the doorway that led upstairs to the Shatt-al-Arab.

He was well off his turf, and considering that he managed to take his beloved daughter into the city only once per month, this visit must have required a special effort. When he disappeared up the stairway I crossed the street, reaching the doorway just in time to hear his footsteps on the second-floor landing. There was a loud knock, followed by the opening of a door and muttered voices. Then the door shut. Silence.

I stepped back into the street and looked up at the windows. The coffeehouse looked closed. The blades of its ceiling fans were still, and the lights were out. I stole up the stairway. Pausing on the landing, I again heard voices, but they were coming from the doorway opposite the coffeehouse entrance. At least three different men were talking, although the words were too muffled to comprehend. I crept back downstairs to check the name on the mailbox.

WALID KHAMMAR.

I wrote it down, congratulating myself for bringing along a notepad. Then I crossed the street and took up a concealed position to watch for Nabil. To avoid attracting attention to my loitering, I bought one of the embroidered blouses from the eager proprietor, which earned me the right to browse without being bothered. When Nabil emerged I set off behind him, leaving half a block between us. He turned into an alley toward a steep, narrow stairway leading up the stony hillside. There were only a few other people around, so I lagged further, not picking up the pace until I saw him disappear to the left around the corner of a house.

Huffing and puffing, I quickly rounded the corner. He stood there as if he had been waiting, and I nearly ran him over. The heat rose in my face.

"Following me, Freeman Lockhart? Or do you just happen to be going my way?"

The odd thing was that he didn't sound angry or affronted.

"I, uh, saw you up ahead and was going to say hello."

He smiled wearily, then glanced over my shoulder as if others might also be in pursuit.

"In that case, hello. It is a fine morning. Why don't we walk together for a while?"

I made a show of checking my watch.

"Just a few blocks. I have an appointment to see an apartment. That's why I was hurrying."

"Whereabouts?"

"Jebel Amman."

"A nice neighborhood. Very comfortable." Especially compared to Bakaa, I supposed he meant.

"You think I should choose a more humble location?"

"I make no such judgments. That is for others. And for God, of course."

"Wise decision."

"One we could all live by."

I got the hint, but said nothing. After a pause he continued.

"I know you are curious about me, but you should know that you are not the only one."

"What do you mean?"

"There are others, that is all. And they may not think kindly of you trying to do their jobs for them."

"Look, if you think I was following you—"

"It was only an observation." Still no hint of malice. "I am merely saying there are others who have an interest in me, and you should be aware of this. If only for your safety."

"Who?"

"It would do neither of us good for me to say." He glanced behind us again, and this time I couldn't help but look also. Nothing back there but a few boys, arguing over a soccer ball. "Just pay attention. That is my advice. Pay attention to those around you, and do your work for Omar as best you can. Stick to that and you should have no trouble with anyone."

"Like Dr. Hassan, you mean?"

He shrugged.

"I do not always understand Dr. Hassan. Too often he wishes to make a rivalry where there is none."

"Maybe because he is Fatah and you are Hamas?"

If my remark caught him by surprise, he didn't show it.

"I am not affiliated in this way that you say. I have friends who are Hamas, and sometimes I work with them. That is as far as it goes."

"Friends who blow themselves up?"

"Friends who run feeding stations and health clinics. Who work just as hard as Dr. Hassan and expect less in return. I do not believe in killing in the name of God. The Prophet Muhammad, his name be praised, did not believe in it, either."

"What about your friends? Do they believe that?"

For the first time he seemed uncomfortable.

"You will have to ask them."

He stopped. We had reached another set of stairs, and it was obvious he preferred to continue alone. But he was still in the mood to talk, and his next question was a big one.

"Tell me, Mr. Lockhart. What do you believe?"

"What is my faith, you mean?"

"If that defines what you believe, then yes."

I had been asked this question in one form or another many times during my travels. Oddly, it was one of the first things Mila wanted to know. At the time she was wary of anyone with deep religious or nationalist convictions, having seen such passions tear her country apart. The warmed-over Presbyterian faith of my childhood was hardly worth mentioning, and from there I had drifted into halfhearted agnosticism. Mila found that reassuring, and the very nature of my job convinced her I wasn't blinded by patriotism.

Nabil's inquiry seemed more like those I had fielded from devout recipients of aid. They wanted to know what fueled my sense of mission, and whether it involved spirituality. When I was younger, and freshly launched on the world's beaten path, I tended to say, "I believe in salvation."

Christians often took this to mean that I was on their side. Muslims, Hindus, and others took it as reassurance that I was devout but wasn't going to pit my god against theirs. Nabil would probably see right through such vagueness, so I chose levity as a fallback.

"Sometimes I believe in nothing. Other times I believe in God the Father, the Son, and the Holy Ghost, although not necessarily in that order."

"So you make light of your faith?"

"I thought that faith was the light."

He shook his head slowly, with a doleful expression. I felt strangely disappointed that I hadn't measured up.

"You should have more faith in your maker, if only for the protection it offers body and soul. Not just for you, but for everyone you love."

I suppose that comment reads like a lecture when I state it here, but he said it in the gentlest of tones.

"I'll think about it."

He nodded.

"Tell me, Freeman Lockhart. In your work for Omar, will you be spending much time in Bakaa?"

"I should think so."

"Then you should go carefully, and carry a weapon with you. A firearm."

It was about the last thing I expected him to say, and it threw me enough that I again resorted to glibness.

"You mean like the one your friend Hakim carries?"

"A small one. One you can conceal."

Was this some sort of veiled threat? A way of scaring me off his trail? Or was it simply more of his advice, an offshoot of his plainspoken piety.

First God, then a gun. A Palestinian version of "Praise the Lord and pass the ammunition." I was intrigued, but not convinced. Everyone here was treating me as if I would run at the first sign of danger.

"I'm not so sure Omar wants me walking around armed. Might send the wrong message."

"Then maybe Omar is as naive as you about what goes on in Bakaa."

"Maybe. But it would also irritate the authorities. They're not too thrilled about foreigners buying guns."

"There are ways to avoid their interest."

He slipped me a well-worn card, someone's name and cell phone number next to an address in Bakaa.

"You should see this man. Even if you buy nothing, he may teach you something."

"About what?"

"Just go and see him. I will tell him in advance of your interest."

I was on the verge of another question, but Nabil preempted me.

"Good luck in finding an apartment."

He turned to go. Still puzzling over his remarks and his motives, I watched him ascend another set of stairs until he disappeared.

Oddly, the encounter did little to dampen my spirits. If anything, it raised the stakes with a frisson of danger. Who were these other pursuers Nabil had referred to? Who was Walid Khammar? And what was I supposed to learn from some black-market gun dealer, other than the street price of an AK-47? Plenty to keep me busy, in any event. Any contact of Nabil's seemed worth following up if only because, by extension, it was also a contact of Omar's.

I flagged down a taxi and found myself checking to see if anyone was following. There was only the usual traffic, faces hidden behind the glare of windshields, although at moments like this my shortcomings as an amateur seemed painfully apparent.

With some time to kill before my appointment, I dropped off the shopping bag at the hotel and phoned Mila, hoping to reassure her with my upbeat mood.

She picked up on the first ring.

"Greetings from Amman! How are you holding up?"

"Not so well. They came back."

My spirits crashed back to earth.

"Black, White, and Gray?"

"Someone they sent. To work on the phone."

"The one we're speaking on?"

"Yes. Improvements to the line, he said. He told me not to touch any of his work. Not that I could see any difference after he left."

"So they're listening to us right now. Somewhere."

"Everything we say."

I had already assumed a need for discretion whenever I called home. But it seemed worse that they had made a point of letting us know. The international line hissed with malevolent potential.

"I can't stay here," she said suddenly. "I'm leaving for Athens."

"To your aunt's?"

Mila sighed. Perhaps because I'd just revealed her destination.

"Sorry. But they probably already know about that."

"Probably."

"When are you leaving? Or do you not want to say?"

"They'll know when it happens, but I'm not sure. Maybe today. I'm already packed."

I imagined her bags lined up by the door, the house shuttered, appliances unplugged. If I had called tomorrow would she still have been there? I knew she didn't want a confrontation now, with our new audience, but I had to ask.

"Were you planning on telling me sometime?"

"Of course."

I envisioned the color rising in her cheeks, a Balkan cloudburst brewing behind dilating pupils.

"Nice to know," I said, and immediately regretted my sarcasm.

"You're one to talk when it comes to hiding things."

For a second or two I wondered if she had somehow discovered my biggest secret. Then I realized she was only referring to my current assignment.

"Mila, please."

"Don't worry. I won't spill your secrets. How can I when I don't know them?"

"It's for your own good. Trust me."

"I want to trust you. But it's not easy. Not when I know nothing."

"I know. I'm sorry. When I'm done I'll tell you everything."

Or almost everything. There would always be one item to hold back. I wondered how I could have been stupid enough to believe this would go easily, with no cost to either Mila or me. Just look at what had already happened. Karos was to have been our refuge. I had promised her a castle, and then lured the enemy through the gates.

We said good-bye, and I sagged onto the bed. The professionals would call what I was doing the double game. But it wasn't a game at all. It was a dangerous trial, a test requiring balance, skill, and artful deception among people who were all too real. No matter what course of action I took, the consequences would also be real. For all of us.

14

By the time I arrived at the house on Othman Bin Affan Street I was no longer morose. I was steaming. Why were my employers being so heavy-handed? Maybe one of Mila's phone calls had touched a nerve. They probably saw it as a way to keep us on our best behavior. But for the moment all I wanted to do was lash out.

A property manager was waiting on the sidewalk. Or that's what he said he was. He was a meek little fellow with baggy trousers and rolled-up sleeves, already mopping his brow even though the temperature was comfortable. He fingered a set of worry beads.

"Good morning, sir. Welcome in Jordan. I am Ahmed. You are Freeman Lockhart?"

"Yes. I'm here to look at the place."

"Oh." He frowned in apparent confusion. "I was told you were taking possession."

"And who told you that?"

"The owner, sir. I only collect rent and arrange repairs. Have you not signed the lease?"

I was probably supposed to say yes.

"No."

"Perhaps there has been a misunderstanding."

He worked the beads faster.

"Why don't you show me the place? If I like it, I'll take the keys. Maybe my employer has made arrangements they haven't told me about."

"Yes." He seemed relieved. "Please, let us go inside."

It was pleasant enough, a stout and attractive single-story house built in the 1930s. The walls were made of large stones the color of the desert, chiseled in an age when builders still employed artisans. High, arched, mullioned windows let in plenty of light. They had green metal shutters you could close against the heat. Surrounding the house was a walled garden with tall junipers, a palm tree that had seen better days, and a thicket of sweet-smelling jasmine draping across the wall onto the front sidewalk.

The kitchen had been modernized, with propane burners, an oven, and a mid-sized fridge. The bedroom, tucked in the back, had a decent view of a neighbor's garden.

The furnishings were stately—rich Oriental rugs and dark wood—and the location was perfect, near the shops and restaurants on Rainbow Street, with Othman Bin Affan leading straight downhill to the center of town. It would do fine.

"The phone is already connected, sir."

"Of course."

"Actually, sir, that is quite unusual. It often takes weeks."

"But I have important friends."

"Yes, sir."

Ahmed looked apprehensive again, so I decided to ease up on him.

"It's perfectly satisfactory," I said. "If it's all right with you, I'll move in today."

"Yes, sir. Here are your keys, and my number. Please call if there are difficulties."

"I'll speak highly of you to my employers."

"Very good, sir."

He finally let go of his beads.

"And by the way, what contact number do you have for them? My employers, I mean. I'd like to make sure you have the right one."

He reddened, clutching again at his beads as he edged toward the door.

"I'm afraid they always are in touch with me, sir. That is the way we have always dealt with each other."

"Of course." But he was already out the door.

The first thing I did was check every drawer, cabinet, and closet for microphones. After what Mila had told me, I was assuming the worst. My handlers must have anticipated as much, because there was a surprise waiting in the mahogany wardrobe in the bedroom. It was a laptop computer, state of the art. I plugged it in and booted up.

It appeared to have a full complement of standard software, but

I could find no evidence of any messages. Maybe I needed help from a techno geek. Preferably one who wouldn't turn me in to the government.

I shut it off and resumed my search, checking behind every picture frame and mirror, underneath tabletops and carpets, mattresses and cushions. Nothing. By the time I finished it was nearly noon. If I left now for the office I could get a good start on Omar's accounts. I would move my things from the hotel later. Then the phone rang.

"Yes?"

"Mr. Lockhart?"

"Speaking. Who is this?"

"Of Othman Bin Affan Street?"

"You must know that it is."

"I have a DHL delivery for you, sir. I will arrive in ten minutes."

I sat on the stone porch in the shade of the junipers, watching midday traffic pass on its way downtown. A woman's voice called out in English from the house to my right.

"Hello, there. Am I to take it that you're my new neighbor?"

Her accent was British, and she looked around forty. Brown hair streaked prematurely with gray and pinned into a bun. She wore a sleeveless blue blouse buttoned in the front, knee-length shorts, and gardening gloves covered in fresh black dirt.

"I am indeed." I stepped forward. "Freeman Lockhart. I would shake hands, but—"

"Oh, yes. I decided to take this beautiful day off and plant some bulbs. Not sure it's even the right time of year. I'm just now getting the hang of the planting cycles. Fiona Whitt. Are you moving in for good, or just passing through? The tenants always seem to come and go at that house."

Her curiosity was bolder than I was accustomed to from Brits, which made me wonder if she had ever been an aid worker or a correspondent. People who spent years on the move and under duress learned to quickly cut to the essentials.

"Here for the long haul," I said, sticking to cover. "I've gone to work for a little NGO providing refugee aid in Bakaa."

"Omar al-Baroody's new NGO?"

"I didn't think it was that well known."

"I'm not sure it is. A friend told me about it. Sami Fayez."

"The one with the salon downtown."

"Sounds like you're already plugged in."

"You certainly are."

She laughed. A nice laugh. And then she blushed, ever so slightly. She had a pretty face, just beginning to show the sags and creases of aging, which I might not have noticed if I weren't so attuned to my own. Being married to a younger woman does that.

"I ought to be plugged in," she said. "I've been here six years."

"And you're just now learning the planting cycle?"

Her longevity made me wary. I wondered if she worked at one of the embassies.

"I'm new to the gardening part. Been too busy 'til now."

"Diplomatic posting?"

"Just a scribbler, I'm afraid. Came here on holiday and never quite made it back. So I pick up work where I can get it. Travel pieces, mostly. For magazines, some of the guidebooks. With a little photography on the side. Lately I've gotten steadier work from the Ministry of Tourism."

"Nice."

"It seems that the king happened to read one of my pieces. They're very image-conscious here. Very keen on keeping a good rep in the West. So now I don't have to scramble quite so much."

"Looks like you scramble pretty well," I said, nodding toward her house.

"The house is the secret to my success. Rent free. Belongs to a retired British military officer who hasn't been 'round in ages. Old friend of my mum's."

It crossed my mind that someone with her connections might have been asked to keep an eye on me. Was I another job on her freelance menu? Or maybe she was just being friendly. I could already see this was one of the drawbacks of the trade. You couldn't really trust a soul. This morning that had seemed bracing. Now it was maddening.

"What else keeps you here?"

"It's a pleasant way of life, really. The people are friendly and, frankly, it's easy to make your mark. It's one of the appeals of a small country, especially one that hasn't lost all its old charm. Jordan still has plenty of fallow ground. Just look at your friend Omar."

"The West Bank boy with friends in high places."

"Exactly. Even I have some palace contacts. Whenever I need an aerial photo they fly me 'round in a military plane."

"Sounds like you're practically royalty."

She laughed.

"Not exactly. And the bigger attraction is the climate. Especially this time of year. Still plenty of sunshine but some nice cool evenings coming. In fact, you better make sure your heat's working properly. These old places are beautiful, but the stone walls and floors make it chillier than you'd think."

"I'll keep that in mind. Nice meeting you."

"Likewise. Oh, and by the way, there's a lovely flea market just down Rainbow Street every Wednesday. It starts in late afternoon, although I suppose for Ramadan they'll be moving the hours back 'til after sundown."

"Sounds nice."

"Once you're settled, stop by for a drink. Long as you don't mind gin. I'm afraid that and a little wine are all I've got."

She gave me a shy smile before returning to her garden, and I decided she might make a handy ally, after all. My evidence? Gut reaction. Sometimes that's all you've got.

The DHL truck pulled up shortly afterward. The driver left the engine idling and approached with a stiff, flat envelope, light as a feather. Further marching orders? I signed for it and waited for him to drive away. Then I looked around for any evidence of nosy neighbors—Fiona included—and, seeing none, took the package inside.

There was cutlery in a butcher block on the counter, and I slit the edge open with a boning knife. There was no note, no message. Just a single unlabeled CD, which I slipped into the laptop. After a few grinding noises from the hard drive, the screen flashed to life with a message, which lingered only a few seconds:

"E-mail all correspondence to Black. Modem will dial automatically."

I tried it out, plugging the laptop into a phone jack and clicking onto the e-mail icon. The only item that appeared on the screen was a box with an address line and some room for text. Maybe I was just supposed to type in "Black." As soon as I typed the letter "B," the computer supplied the rest of the name.

I wrote a brief message—"Parcel arrived, house fine. This is a test."—clicked on "Send," and watched the whole thing disappear off to who knew where, so apparently the modem had activated automatically. I spent the next five minutes trying every trick in the book to find out what Black's e-mail address was, but there was neither an address book nor any record of what I'd just sent. A decent hacker probably could have pierced this veil of secrecy, but I couldn't. I discovered to my pleasure that I did have Internet access. On second thought, probably every move I made online would be monitored. I'd glimpsed an Internet café at a bookstore not far from here, and I resolved to use it.

Somehow I had expected to receive more. I rechecked the DHL envelope for any notes or instructions I might have overlooked. Empty. Would there be no "dead letter box," then, like the ones you read about in novels? No fallbacks or contact signals? I had been looking forward to learning a few tricks of the trade—chalk marks on a sidewalk cedar to signal for a meeting, perhaps, or a flowerpot on the corner of my porch. As with other aspects of life, technology seemed to have made even the business of espionage more prosaic. It was worrisome, too. Computers crashed. Electricity failed. What would I do in an emergency?

It was nearly 1 p.m. by the time my taxi reached the office, and Omar seemed impatient to get out the door.

"Success with your house hunting?" he asked.

"Yes. It's a very nice place. I'm lucky to get it. Friendly neighbors, too. Someone named Fiona said hello."

"Ah, Fiona Whitt? Lovely woman. And helpful to know. She's become a favorite at the palace."

"I got that idea."

"And now, to set your mind at ease." He handed over two file folders, each no more than an inch thick. "Donations in the blue one. Expenditures in the red one. Summaries only, of course. I wish I could say we had more, but that's part of the reason you're here. To make sure these folders grow fat and multiply. Especially the blue one."

I'd figured on taking the material into my new office, which, like Omar's, was partitioned and offered some privacy. But Raniya, who hadn't said a word since my arrival, quickly set me straight.

"I have cleared some working space for you on the table," she said, pointing to a Formica countertop a mere six feet from her desk. "That way, if you need further details on any of the transactions, I will be able to locate them quickly."

It would have seemed churlish to say no, although I suspected she only wanted to keep an eye on me. If Omar noted the tension between us, he didn't acknowledge it. Or maybe this was his doing.

"And where are you going?" I asked him.

"To Bakaa, with Dr. Hassan. He has arranged a meeting with a hospital architect, to discuss design possibilities. You would be welcome to join us, of course, but—" He gestured toward the folders.

"Absolutely. I'll have plenty to keep me busy."

"Once you've put your mind at ease, tomorrow we will get down to business. And, Freeman?"

"Yes?"

"Aren't you going to ask about salary?"

"I was getting to that."

"Tomorrow. We'll wrap up everything over coffee and sweets in the morning." He glanced guiltily at Raniya, who of course wouldn't be having a daylight snack tomorrow or any other day of Ramadan.

"Splendid."

"I hope you're still saying 'splendid' after you've heard what I can afford to pay you. We'll also provide a car, of course. In the meantime, keep your taxi receipts. Oh, and one last thing."

He ducked into his office and rummaged through a desk drawer. I glanced at Raniya for a hint of what was coming, but she maintained her rigid expression. Omar returned smiling and held out a set of keys.

"These are yours. One to the office, one to your desk, one to the filing cabinets."

It seemed too easy.

"Good luck with your meeting."

"Good luck with your explorations."

He said it with the carefree certainty of a man with nothing to hide.

The moment he was gone I surveyed the field of play, with all its cabinets and drawers, and a copy machine in the corner. Easy pickings if not for the imperious Raniya. If I was the fox in the henhouse, then she was the fighting cockerel with talons of steel. The office was going to be a very icy place while Omar was away. I settled in at the table and opened the blue file.

So far, Omar had managed to bring in about $1.4 million. Not terrible, but nowhere near what would be needed to build a hospital. He had said the night before that more money had been pledged but not yet received. The visitors from the Gulf whom I had seen the other day— from Dubai, it turned out—had promised to pony up $5 million.

What surprised me was the number of smaller donors, checks from here and there for dinar totals amounting to a few hundred dollars apiece. Only a handful of people had kicked in more than $100,000. All had Arabic names except for a professor from George Mason University in northern Virginia, and another at Stanford. I made a note of both, just in case. Some of the Arabic names also had U.S. addresses, even among the smaller donors, and in jotting them down I wondered uncomfortably if they would soon be receiving unwanted scrutiny as a result of my work. If Nabil was funneling some of their proceeds to the wrong places, then maybe they deserved it.

The expenditures were equally unexciting. The only one that seemed curious was an unexplained check for $10,000 to a Mr. Hamdi of Madaba. I asked Raniya if there was a file for him, and she retrieved it without a word, dropping it brusquely on the table. He was a direct-mail consultant who had arranged for mailings to big shots in Amman's business community.

I paused only once in my labors, to walk to a mini-market down the street for bananas, tea biscuits, and a bottle of water, a meal that I ate furtively in my bare little office, shutting the door so Raniya didn't have to watch.

The phone rang a few times with calls for Omar, but otherwise she didn't break her silence until three hours later, when I finally dropped the files back on her desk and announced I was finished.

"Nice to see everything is in tiptop shape," I said. "Obviously you're keeping things very well organized."

"*Mr. al-Baroody* is keeping things well organized."

"Of course."

The ringing of the phone saved me from further scolding. When she answered, her voice rose by an octave to a warble as pleasant as a songbird's.

"Yes, sir," she said cheerily. It must have been Omar calling. I do believe she had a bit of a crush on him. "I will see to that immediately."

I drifted away and pretended to consult my legal pad while listening closely.

"But surely not that weekend, sir. What about your travel plans?"

That got my attention.

"Very good, sir. I will take care of it."

She hung up. I knew better than to expect a straight answer, but asked anyway.

"Omar's going somewhere?"

"Yes."

She said no more. The only sound was the scratching of her pen on a steno pad, which she then shut with a pop. I watched over the edge of my notebook as she swiveled toward her computer and began pecking away. A few moments later the printer sprang to life. I considered sauntering over for a look, but she was there in a flash to retrieve the pages.

"I have some chores to attend to," I announced. "See you in the morning."

"As you wish, sir. The workday begins at 8:30."

On the way to my hotel I detoured to the gigantic Safeway in Shmeisani, legendary for selling almost anything you'd need. I bought groceries and stocked up on bed linens, towels, and washcloths. I had the taxi wait outside the hotel while I quickly packed my clothes back into the suitcase. I arrived at Othman Bin Affan Street looking like a gypsy.

Another parcel was waiting on the porch. At first I assumed the DHL man had returned. But on closer inspection I found it was a bag of fresh dates. A handwritten note from Fiona poked out of the top: "They sell these wonderful things at the flea market. It's the vendor by the dreadful potter's stand, in case you want more. Welcome to our street."

Was I supposed to read a pun into her choice of fruit—dates for a date, perhaps—or was she just being neighborly? Either way, I should mention soon that I was married. I popped a date in my mouth. Delicious.

"You are welcome in Jordan," I said to myself. Fiona had become just like the locals, eager to make outsiders feel at home.

There were no further surprises—just as well after the events of the morning. I considered phoning Karos to see if Mila had left yet, but I couldn't stand the thought of either a ringing telephone in our empty home or another overheard conversation. My guess was that she was on the ferry, watching the island recede in her wake. She might even have chosen a fast boat for a change.

With those anxieties weighing on me, I decided on an early dinner at a modest café a few blocks away. When I returned I settled down at the laptop and dutifully typed in the day's findings on an e-mail to Black.

Supposing that any messages would be automatically encrypted, I decided to send one to my personal e-mail account just to see how it would look. I would try calling it up later at the Internet café. But no matter what letter I typed on the address bar, only the name "Black" appeared on the screen. I guess they didn't want me contacting anyone else on their machine.

Stymied and tired, I called it a night at 10 p.m. Already it was chilly, just as Fiona had warned. I would have to return to Safeway for another blanket. Fall could sneak up on you in this part of the world. I preferred the autumnal explosion of color and crispness from my home state of Massachusetts. It was a clear announcement of change, one last celebration before winter brought everything to a halt. I have always hoped that I will approach death the same way, with one last blaze of brightness and frolic, and a harvest moon to light my exit. Good God, such morbid thoughts, and it was only my second day on the job.

It must have been only a few hours later when I awoke to a scratching noise, like fingernails against a windowsill. Certain that it was an intruder, I sat up with a gasp, heart beating wildly. The gun purchase urged by Nabil suddenly seemed like an excellent idea. Then I realized the noise was coming from behind the baseboard, underneath the bed. It was a mouse, no doubt, prowling for food or seeking shelter as the desert winter approached. I shifted on the bed and the mouse stopped.

A few moments later he began clawing again. His rustling explorations were oddly comforting, and they kept me company as I drifted back to my dreams.

In this house, I suspected, sleep was never going to come easy.

15

I tried out my new key shortly after 7:30 a.m. and then stood in the silent, dark office, contemplating my plan of action. The file cabinets could wait. First I wanted to see Raniya's printout of Omar's travel plans.

Her desk drawer was locked. I stooped beneath the desk to try and jimmy it free. Then it occurred to me that anyone as efficient as Raniya would never leave herself vulnerable to the possibility of a lost key, so I took my own set across the room to the filing cabinets.

I found what I wanted under the heading "Keys," in a small envelope tucked in a green folder. I opened her desk drawer and found the printout right on top, folded like a business letter. There was just enough of a whiff of her perfume to give me the willies. Then I began to read.

Omar was flying to Athens, of all places, leaving on a Sunday afternoon about two weeks from now and returning the following Tuesday. Even more surprising, he was staying both nights at the Grande Bretagne, across from the parliament building and the National Garden. A night there could easily cost you five hundred dollars.

At the sound of footsteps in the hallway, I clumsily shoved the paper into the drawer and locked up, then stood rigid, like a cheater caught stealing the final exam. But the footsteps passed down the corridor, so I retrieved the page and switched on the copy machine. While it was warming up, I scanned the files for any headings related to Greece, Athens, or Europe. Nothing. If Omar was meeting donors, or attending some sort of conference about charities or medical care for the poor, then shouldn't he have told his new director of operations?

Maybe he planned on doing so today. But he might just as easily have mentioned it yesterday. According to the airline information, the flight had been booked sixteen days ago. My inspection of the donor lists hadn't revealed anyone in Greece. Black had said to follow Omar wherever he went, but did that include trips outside of Jordan? I hoped so, even if my motive was selfish. Maybe I could visit Mila at her aunt's.

The copier was ready, so I slipped in the page and the flash lit the room. I turned the machine off, returned the itinerary to Raniya's desk, and locked the drawer. Then I found a key for Omar's office, but none for his desk. The only item of interest on top of his desk was a date book, so I quickly scanned the days covering his trip to Greece. They were blank except for a single notation on his first full day, a Monday: "10 a.m.—Meet K."

Deciding not to press my luck, I relocked his office and put the duplicate keys back. Wise decision. Ten minutes later Raniya arrived a half hour ahead of schedule. By then I was seated at my desk, reading through a folder about the Bakaa field office in search of more information on Nabil and his friends. I'd already seen enough to know there were no references to either Hakim or the gun dealer.

"Looks like everyone wanted to get a head start," she said, with an actual semblance of warmth.

"You know how it goes with eager new employees. I'm sure it will wear off."

"Yes, I am sure."

I flinched when she unlocked her desk, but she didn't react as if anything was out of the ordinary. She took some papers from a side drawer to the copy machine, where she paused before flipping the switch. Frowning, she placed a hand against the side, as if feeling for a pulse in some animal she'd just shot.

"It's warm," she said. "You've been making copies." She flipped opened a small panel where there must have been a counter. "Only one."

"Am I not authorized?"

"Of course. But next time leave the machine on. It's not good for it to keep switching it on and off."

Unless you're trying to keep someone else from finding out you've used it. I knew that's what she was thinking, and realized I'd been overly clever. It crossed my mind that maybe she, too, was working for someone else. Why else would she be so well trained to spot signs of deception?

The door jangled open. Omar was also ahead of schedule, and

seemed surprised to find the two of us already there. It was as if all three of us had planned to beat each other to the punch. After a brief moment of awkwardness he smiled broadly.

"I can see that you are going to keep me on my toes even better than Raniya, Freeman. Just like old times. Do you know that our season on patrol was the first time in my life I had ever been punctual? My mother claims it made me a better man. Have you settled into your new place? Hanan has some things for the kitchen if you need them."

"It's pretty well equipped, actually. They must rent to a lot of businesspeople who come and go."

"Then they're probably glad to have a more stable tenancy."

"Yes."

"And now you can bring the rest of your things. Your wife, too. Do you have a time frame?"

"It might be a few months before Mila can make it." Then I got an inspired idea, in case Black, White, and Gray decided I needed to follow Omar to Athens. "I've got enough of my things here to tide me over a while. So I was thinking I'd pick up the rest in a couple of weeks. I could leave on a Sunday, when the ferry schedules are better. That way I'd be back in Amman by the middle of the week."

Had I again been too clever? Even to my ears it seemed painfully obvious that I had just mentioned dates virtually the same as those of Omar's arrival and departure. I glanced at Raniya, but she was already tapping at her keyboard.

Omar frowned.

"Are those dates a problem?" I asked.

"No. It's just that I'll be out of town, too. I was hoping you'd hold the fort."

"Hmm. I'd switch, but those dates work better for Mila, too."

"Then by all means take that weekend. I'll just shut down the office for a few days. With pay for Raniya, of course."

She didn't even look up. Omar threw me a questioning glance, as if checking to see if the idea met my threshold for fiscal responsibility.

"Of course," I said. "Where will you be going?"

A pause. Maybe he wouldn't say.

"Athens."

"Goodness. What a stroke of luck. Maybe we'll be on the same flight."

He smiled weakly.

"Maybe."

"Meeting donors?"

"Something like that. Potential donors anyway. A European foundation has expressed an interest."

"Great. Sounds big."

"Potentially."

"I don't remember them from the files."

"They're not in there. They're a bit, well, shy about attention."

"Anyone I've heard of?"

"Doubtful. But you will if they come through, of course. For now they'd prefer to remain under the radar. They've asked me not to bandy their name about. At least not for now. I'm sure you can understand, given the climate."

"Certainly."

I assumed he was referring to the general nervousness over anything to do with fund-raising for Palestinian causes. In attempting to shut down terrorist financing pipelines, the U.S. Treasury Department had red-flagged so many Middle Eastern charities that no one was quite sure who was okay to deal with. It was overkill, of course, but try telling that to some nervous banker in Zurich who controlled the purse strings for your philanthropic foundation.

"Good," Omar said, clearly relieved to move on. "Have Raniya book your flights. We'll pick up the tab. And you'll of course give my love to Mila."

"Of course. And thank you."

Generous of him, although on second thought I realized it allowed him to ensure that I didn't end up on his flight. I was already a little queasy about following him. Part of me hoped Black would want someone else to do the job. Then I could go to Athens anyway and just spend time with Mila.

"Oh, one more thing, Freeman. Your car will be delivered tomorrow. A Passat, in fact. And with our logo prominent on the side."

Omar and I then retreated to his office to discuss my salary. It was small, just as he'd hinted, but I assured him it was fine by me. I spent the rest of the morning snooping through the files for more information, but didn't turn up anything of interest. At lunch I caught a cab back to Othman Bin Affan Street, where I spent several minutes at the laptop, e-mailing details of Omar's travel plans and asking for further instructions. As I sent the message it occurred to me that Omar might be having some sort of affair. A weekend fling to the ruins of the Acropolis with a lover, perhaps? It even seemed possible he could be traveling with

Raniya, who would have booked her own ticket separately. Stern or not, she was quite attractive, and I could imagine the two of them in one of the fine rooms of the Grande Bretagne—Raniya flushed and breathless, pulling open the brocaded curtains onto a sunny view of the leafy park scene of the parliament square; her fine features smiling up from the bed, hair unpinned. An affair with the boss would certainly explain her wariness around me better than secretarial zeal. If it was true, then I pitied poor Hanan, who deserved better.

I returned to the office to find that Omar was away, gone to another appointment with Dr. Hassan. He had left the message that I was welcome to join them. But I had another Bakaa destination in mind—the gun seller's address Nabil had given me the previous morning. I was just leaving my cubicle when the phone rang.

"For you, Mr. Lockhart. An American."

A quick response to my e-mail, perhaps? Surely Black wouldn't call here.

"Freeman?" a man's voice said.

Familiar, but I couldn't place it.

"Yes. Who's this?"

"So it's true. You really are in town. Mike Jacoby here."

"Good God. You're with the embassy, aren't you?"

I detected a flicker of interest from Raniya, so I swiveled the chair away from her and lowered my voice. My antenna was on alert. If someone at the embassy had heard I was here, the news must have come through back channels via Black, White, and Gray.

"Yes," Jacoby said. "I'm the press officer. Third year in Amman. Not as exciting as what we used to get up to in Gaza, but it'll do."

Mike Jacoby had started out with the same cheap aid agency as I had. He, too, knew Omar from back in the day. Since then he had taken the Foreign Service exam and joined the diplomatic corps. We hadn't spoken in years.

"Anyway, I heard you were in town."

"I'll bet."

" 'Scuse me?"

So he was going to play dumb. Fine.

"Nothing. Inside joke. It's good to hear from you."

"I was hoping you might want to stop by. See our new digs in the high-rent district."

Was this official? He was certainly convincing at making it sound offhand. Maybe he, too, had learned to play this game. Press officer seemed as decent a cover as any.

"Love to."

"Maybe we can go for a bite afterward."

"Sure. When's a good time?"

"Around seven? That way we beat the crowds. The hottest places are packed by nine."

"Sounds good. See you then."

Interesting. Maybe this was Black's way of relaying some sort of message. And, conveniently, the hour of our appointment still left me with enough time to do a little snooping in Bakaa. I fingered the business card Nabil had given me and headed for the door.

The taxi driver was reluctant to wait for me in that part of Bakaa, but the promise of an extra ten dinars overcame his anxiety. I could understand his concern. This was a district of metalsmiths and welders, of blank storefronts and locked metal security awnings. Instead of pulsing with busy shoppers and playing children, it was sparsely patrolled by watchful young men. A few carried weapons, and all wore an earnest, burning look that said they were out to earn their stripes.

All this tended to make a yellow Mercedes taxi look vulnerably out of place—even more so when an American in khaki slacks and an oxford shirt stepped out from the passenger door and began trying to act like he belonged.

Maybe this was the sort of neighborhood Omar had in mind when he warned me not to travel alone. It also occurred to me that Nabil had arranged a setup, if only to teach me to back off.

The name on the card he gave me was Malik al-Masri, but there was nothing on the rusting gray door to indicate either Malik's presence or that of a gun shop.

I tried the handle. Locked.

Turning around I saw two armed men staring from across the lane.

I knocked, loudly, then heard the scuffle of sandaled feet and the groan of rusty hinges.

A strong smell of hot oil and metal poured from the opening. A bearded man stepped forward. He beheld my presence as incredulously as if I had just descended from the clouds.

"Nabil Mustafa gave me your address," I said in Arabic.

He nodded, puzzle solved, then stood aside for me to enter. It was a dim, windowless room, lit only by a bare forty-watt bulb dangling from a cord above a service counter. The air was dusty, and so were the counters. But all the boxes stacked on shelves that ran the length of the room were quite clean. In a seller's market I suppose they didn't have time to collect dust.

My host said nothing. He shuffled behind the counter while a second man watched from the most distant corner, peering through the gloom without expression. Some sort of big ugly gun was slung across his back. There was an unintelligible shout from somewhere in the back, and a new face appeared behind the counter. It was Hakim, the fellow I'd seen at the field office carrying the AK. No wonder, if he worked here. Maybe he got an employee discount. In his hands was an unmarked white box. Hakim set it on the counter and signaled that it was mine.

Under the circumstances, I supposed I had better buy it. I dug out my wallet, hoping I had enough cash.

"How much?" I asked in Arabic.

"No," Hakim said in English, waving his hand in refusal. "It is gift. Gift from Nabil."

"Gift?"

He nodded.

"In exchange, you must come see. See with me."

"See what?"

"Here. I show you."

He handed over the box, unexpectedly heavy, but guns almost always are. Then he came around the counter and led me to a side door, next to the glaring sentry. It opened onto a smaller room, empty, with yet another door. Hakim opened that, and we entered a world that might as well have been in another dimension, so different was its lighting, atmosphere, cleanliness, and bustle from the one we had just left. Several children played with blocks in a corner. Three more sat in blue plastic chairs alongside their mothers. They looked a little sleepy, maybe sick. The walls were painted bright green, with a quote from the Prophet in shaky Arabic beneath a hand-drawn Palestinian flag. A main entrance opened onto the street just around the corner from the gun shop.

"Clinic," Hakim said. "No price."

"A free clinic, you mean?"

"Yes. Free. With Dr. Hassan, there is price. Bad cold, three dinar. Bad stomach, three dinar. Anything, three dinar."

Or about five bucks a visit. The sort of rates Americans would kill for, but maybe a full day's pay for, say, one of those women in black selling toothpaste downtown.

"Here, no dinar. The guns, they pay."

I switched to Arabic to make sure I had it right.

"You mean, they use the proceeds of the gun shop to keep the clinic going?"

"Yes."

So this was what Nabil had wanted me to see, the secret knowledge he wished to impart. His friends selling guns for butter. Or guns for aspirin, anyway. Of course, with the gun trade there was always an additional price, paid by whoever was on the receiving end of the ammunition. But I doubted Hakim would want to talk about that.

The revelation was a disappointment to my spying side. And it was almost touching in its naïveté, because my handlers would be interested only in the gun running, not the clinic. I doubted Omar's money helped keep supply lines open, but I supposed I was obligated to mention all this in my report.

"Impressive," I said, figuring that was what Hakim needed to hear before concluding our tour.

He nodded. Then he escorted me back the way we had come without a further word of explanation.

"Thank you," I said when we reached the gun shop. "It was interesting."

"You wait," he said, continuing our awkward exchange of him in English, me in Arabic. "Earlier I call Nabil. He comes."

"I'm afraid I can't stay. My driver is waiting."

Hakim nodded again, but looked disappointed.

My driver was indeed anxious to leave by the time I emerged. But I still had one last chore, so I slipped the bag with the gun box through the window along with an extra fiver and said I would be only a few minutes more. I walked 'round the corner to check out the rest of this miniature wonderland, and he nervously followed, driving slowly in my wake as if I might try to get away.

The route took me past an alley leading behind the gun shop just as a truck was backing down it, toward the shop's rear entrance. If this was a delivery, then I supposed it wouldn't hurt to get a tag number, although I certainly wasn't fool enough to take out my notebook.

Word of the big event must have spread, because kids began appearing from nowhere, some with mothers and fathers in tow. A gun truck as

Pied Piper. I recognized two boys from the ones who had been playing with blocks inside the clinic. The sullen men who'd been lurking in the streets also gravitated to the scene, and within minutes there must have been a few dozen people.

Someone threw open the rear door to the shop and another fellow hauled open the truck's louvered cargo door. The truck was half filled with long wooden crates, some of which had Chinese characters stenciled on the side. One fellow was dragging crates to the edge of the cargo bed and another was hefting them into the shop. The next crate that emerged had some sort of shipping manifest on the side, so I eased past a couple of boys for a closer look, hoping to see something I could memorize for my report.

That's when a hand grabbed my shoulder from behind and a stern voice said in Arabic, "Stop him!" Another hand reached out, and between the two of them they nearly wrenched me to the ground. I saw then that the crowd had swelled to more than fifty people.

In the field I long ago learned to trust my gut when it told me that something was not quite right—a road or a village that had grown too eerily quiet, a crowd tipping toward a mob—and belatedly I realized this situation was out of hand. I stepped briskly away from the truck—the taxi was idling at the end of the alley—but the men who had grabbed me followed, and one took hold of me again, pulling roughly.

"Easy," I said in Arabic. "No need for that. I'm leaving."

"He speaks Arabic!" my assailant announced. "He is a spy!"

Lucky guess.

I tried breaking into a run, but the crush of the crowd prevented me, and two more men closed in.

"Jew!" one shouted.

I looked around frantically for Hakim, or the owner, but the men pushed me back, then knocked me down. The last thing I saw before I was submerged beneath them was my driver being pulled from his taxi. My hands broke my fall against the dirty cobbles just as a sneakered foot kicked me sharply in the buttocks, then another kick thudded into my lower back. I tried to rise, but a new set of hands shoved until I was prone, so I rolled onto my stomach and raised my hands around my head for protection. More hands and feet went into action, turning me on my back like some great squirming beetle.

"Help me!" I shouted, but only once, because one look at the surrounding faces and I knew that helping me—or anyone—was the furthest thought from their minds. The odd thing was that no one was shouting now, not in bloodlust or encouragement. It was a workmanlike effort fronted by a handful of men, and the only noise was their grunting as they kicked and flailed, blow after blow into my sides, legs, and arms.

I was panicked, screaming inside, kicking out with my feet and still trying to rise, while certain that any minute a blow would find my head and the world would go dark, lights out on Mila and everything I lived for.

Then a voice raised itself in anger, at first unintelligible, then clearer, shouting, "Stop! You must stop!"

Some of them did. One didn't, and another shoe landed hard against my thigh.

"He is a friend of our people. You must stop!"

Everyone went still. I lay there, breathing heavily, heart beating so wildly it seemed as large as an overripe melon, primed to burst. But I felt joy, too, a giddy release, because I recognized the voice as Nabil's, even though only his sandals had come into view. Then his face leaned down, and he helped me to my feet. Somehow, maybe because so few had been participating, he had stopped them.

I wobbled on my first step, and he steadied me. One of the small boys who had been in the clinic rushed to my other side and took my arm, but everyone else stood back and turned away, refusing to look me in the eye now that everything was over.

"You must go," Nabil whispered tersely in my ear. "Quickly!"

He helped me over to the taxi, where the boy opened the door. I slumped in and found myself sitting on crushed glass. The windows were smashed, and the driver was gone.

"Where are the keys?" Nabil said.

"I don't know." My voice rasped. I was aching, out of breath. "Driver took 'em."

"Then you must walk. But just go, and do it now."

I nodded, climbing stiffly into action. Bruises and welts were already rising, hardening to knots in my sides and rear.

"Here, take this." It was the gun, still in its bag and box. "You see now why you must have it with you, always, when you are in Bakaa."

"Yes. Thank you, Nabil. Thank you."

The acknowledgment seemed to embarrass him, and when I looked in his eyes I could tell we both realized that neither of us would repeat a word of this to Omar. Not Nabil because it would reflect poorly on his clumsy effort to educate me. And not me partly because, yes, I had been spying, just as my accuser claimed. But even more so because I had been a fool. Decades of aid work had wrongly convinced me that my selflessness, not the organizations I represented, had secured a lasting covenant with the wider world, as if my very nature as a do-gooder managed to shine through the surrounding brutality.

In taking this assignment I had crossed all my old boundaries, exceeded my limits, and it had stripped away my immunity. Shorn of the UN's blue globe, or even Omar's logo, I was easily spotted by these rough fellows of Bakaa for what I had become, or perhaps what I had always been—at best a voyeur, at worst a snoop, showing up time and again to feed upon their misery.

"Go," Nabil said. "Go quickly."

Strangely, bizarrely, I simply walked away. First one block, then another. No one followed. No one in the street even wanted to look at me, much less hunt me down. As I neared the end of the second block I heard the *whump* of a small explosion, and turned to see a column of smoke rising. The taxi. A bonfire of my troubles, burning away the last remnants of the incident for the benefit of all concerned.

Eventually I flagged down another cab and rode numbly to my house in Jebel Amman, taking refuge in the driver's silence and the click of his beads on the mirror. I showered, dressed a few cuts and scrapes, and put on fresh clothes. Other than feeling like I had just been tackled by a gang of stevedores, I was surprisingly intact. Nabil had arrived just before the blows began inflicting real damage.

Emotionally the verdict wasn't as clear. Although I wouldn't admit it until much later, some vital part of me was critically wounded that day, not just by the beating but by the experience of having the whole episode watched by a crowd, everyone staring and silent, seemingly impassive as to whether I lived or died. Ask those people about it now and I'm sure they would claim to a man that nothing much happened that afternoon, just a brief flare-up in which they had no role and barely saw a thing. Previous experience had taught me that this was common behavior among most witnesses to thuggery or even genocide, at least for those with no emotional attachment to the victims. They take refuge in what they later decide is their neutrality, and offer themselves the absolution of a faulty memory. A dodge that sounded all too familiar.

That afternoon, however, my most salient emotion was an urge to move on. Buck up, I told myself. You survived, so pull yourself together. I had chosen this path and would follow it to its conclusion, if only because Mila stood waiting at the end with her salvation intact. That was what kept me moving.

But, good Lord, did I ever need a drink, and there was nothing but juice and soda in my Ramadan fridge. A hotel bar would have to do the trick. The InterContinental wasn't even a mile's walk, but I was stiff and sore, and in no mood to navigate sidewalk crowds of Jordanians. So I caught another cab. Toward the bottom of a double gin and tonic I glanced at a clock and remembered I had an appointment in half an hour, at seven.

Had it been anywhere but the embassy I probably would have called to cancel. But, if anything, that location sounded appealing right now. Mega security. A Marine in the lobby. Rub elbows with my own kind for a while, people with the same faults and weaknesses. A chance to lick my wounds without fearing a fresh blow.

There were also practical matters to consider. For all I knew, I was about to receive new marching orders. I swallowed the last of the gin, laid a dinar on the bar, and headed for the door, already back on the beat.

The embassy was rather grandiose—three stories of beautiful sandstone blocks. It squatted in the middle of a walled compound surrounded by palm trees and well-watered grass. If not for the smallish windows—for security reasons, no doubt—it would have looked like a pricey hotel.

As an aid worker I was accustomed to embassies. We occasionally need their help with passports, visas, and the like. In addition, their staffers like to touch base with us now and then because we're decent sources of information. Twice at embassy receptions I've sensed gentle recruitment efforts in progress, veiled suggestions from officials of uncertain pedigree that I might be of service to my country in some unspecified manner, if I were so inclined. Both times I politely demurred, and no one ever took it personally. Which is another reason it was so shocking when Black, White, and Gray bounded through our windows on Karos.

I cleared one security station, then another, relaxing a bit more at each point along the way. A U.S. Marine in dress blues escorted me back to Mike's windowless office.

"I was worried about you," he said in greeting. "Supposedly there was some little dustup out at Bakaa involving an American this afternoon, and it crossed my mind that it might be you."

I searched his face for any sign of irony, but there was none.

"Hadn't heard that," I said warily.

"Oh, yeah. Blew up a cab and everything. But apparently the fellow got away all right, so maybe it's nothing."

"I could always ask around next time I'm out there."

"Could you?" He seemed sincere. "That would be great, especially if we get questions from the press."

It took me aback. But Mike himself was a reassuring presence. Physically he had barely changed. Trim, tan, and with plenty of laugh lines, he still wore the sunny if weather-beaten look of the young vagabond he had been in Gaza, only now his wardrobe included a red tie and blue blazer.

"Nice digs," I said, trying not to wince as I settled gingerly into a chair. "Where's the squash court?"

"Beats the hell out of the old bunker off Second Circle, doesn't it?"

"What became of that building, anyway? I was at the InterCon the other day and didn't even see it."

"Tore it down. Just as well. A bomb trap, really."

"So what's the occasion, Mike?"

"Occasion? None really. Just wanted to say hello. Maybe catch up on old times. And I thought it might be easier meeting here. Or less embarrassing for you, anyway."

"Embarrassing how?"

"Well, given your current position, obviously."

So maybe he was going to be up front about things, after all, although I doubted he would come right out and say "CIA." I've yet to meet any embassy employee who would willingly utter those initials on the premises.

"How do you mean?" I said, expecting him to offer a nod or wink, or some other clue to verify his status. But he disappointed me.

"Working for Omar and his new NGO. Being a local outfit, they've probably got all the local phobias, and we're surely one of them."

"With 'we' meaning exactly who?"

"Americans. I figured that was obvious."

"Okay. Any other reason I should be embarrassed to be seen with you in public?"

He furrowed his brow.

"None I can think of. Can you?"

So he was going to play it coy, after all. Or was it possible he was really in the dark? Either option seemed plausible.

"I guess not," I finally answered.

"How'd you end up climbing aboard with them anyway? Last I heard you were headed off into a Cyclades sunset with the lovely Mila. Did I miss something?"

"Is that a serious question?"

"Why wouldn't it be?"

"C'mon, Mike. Don't tease. What is it you really want?"

Mike frowned, and then shook his head as if to clear the cobwebs.

"I must be missing something. This isn't official, if that's what you're thinking. It's not like I've been asked to debrief you, or that I think you've got something to hide."

"Not from you, anyway."

Mike cocked his head.

"Care to elaborate?"

"This is amazing."

"Okay, forget I said that. But this conversation is damned strange."

Another possibility was that this was a test, a means of finding out how easily I could be goaded into blowing my cover. That would certainly explain why he had invited me inside, since he wouldn't have wanted to try it out in public. So for a moment I said nothing, which only seemed to discombobulate him more.

"I'll start over," he said. "As one old pal to another, why on earth are you doing this gig? Really. I mean, not to pry or anything, but you and Mila are still together, right?"

"Absolutely."

"Then why give up the good life to get back into the aid racket? If anything, I'd heard you were a little burned out."

I decided to stick to cover.

"Maybe I got a second wind. Or maybe I was just burned out on the UN. The whole damned bloat and bureaucracy of it. Some auditor from the Secretariat always asking where you'd stuffed those last hundred tents."

"And you figured Omar knew better how to save the world?"

"Or his little corner of it."

"Quite a corner. And not exactly one that's going hungry, needy or not."

"Which is why he's focusing on the medical side. C'mon, Mike. He's trying."

"Just never had you pegged as the type who'd enlist with an Islamic aid agency. You were always as neutral as they came."

"Now we're getting somewhere. But it's Arab, not Islamic."

"Whatever you say."

"Oh, c'mon. Omar doesn't even fast. He drinks, for Chrissakes. He's no zealot."

"I was referring more to his funding sources."

"Which are?"

"Well, the Gulfies—that's the assumption around here. Oil-rich Saudis buying off their consciences. They've been seen 'round his office, I'm told."

That information might have come straight from my report. In which case Mike was a damned good actor. Or maybe I wasn't the only person watching Omar.

"You know what they say. Don't look a gift horse in the mouth."

Mike grinned uneasily.

"Like I said earlier, this is one of the strangest conversations we've ever had," he said.

"Not counting when we were young, drunk, and foolish in Gaza."

That finally relaxed him a bit. He seemed happy to move to the more comfortable ground of our past.

"And using controlled dangerous substances in uncontrolled dangerous places."

"I guess this really *is* off the record. Or did you turn off the microphone before that last crack?"

He laughed, taking it as a joke.

"Glad to see you returning to form, Freeman. Should we head out, then? Try an Abdoun hot spot? I've even started smoking nargileh. Not bad when you get used to it."

"Maybe your first instincts were right. Maybe it's not such a great idea to be seen together in public. At least until I've settled in."

"Suit yourself." He stood, the smile gone. "You know where to reach me."

Mike and the Marine escorted me to the exit. I handed back the security badge and turned to wave good-bye. He stood with hands in pockets, brow creased, as if he had just spotted a familiar face but couldn't quite place the name. If it was a test, had I passed?

I rode a cab back to the house and spent the first ten minutes sipping bottled water. I was still a little shaky, and when there was a knock at the door I nearly jumped out of my skin. Maybe it was Fiona. I'd be happy to take her up right now on that offer of a drink.

Instead it was the DHL man, the same one as yesterday, with yet another flat envelope. This time there was a note inside, printed on plain white paper: "Check e-mail."

Without an in-box, that might be difficult, but I booted up the computer anyway and clicked for the dial-up connection. The message appeared before I could make a single keystroke. It was from Black.

"Emphatic YES on Athens. Follow closely. Note all contacts. Take laptop. From airport, proceed to this address:" It listed a scooter rental shop in Plaka, in the city center. "Present yourself as Robert Higgins."

A bit odd, I thought, although not as much as the next paragraph.

"Emphatic NO on further prying in all the wrong places."

Was he referring to Mila's recent actions, or to something I had done? Either way, his closing comment was downright alarming, the last in a long day of shocks to the system.

"Need I remind you of the stakes? (1) Tanzania. (2) Mila."

The order of those items made me wonder if they had finally made the connection. If so, then my last and most vital secret was blown, and everything important was in danger.

I took a moment to collect myself. Then with a shaky hand I copied the information about the scooter rental and cover name. It was a good thing I did. When I checked the computer later, the message was gone. They were very thorough, these people. And, like the angry young men of Bakaa, they certainly knew how to keep me in line.

16

Washington

Aliyah was beginning to wonder if her fears about Abbas were unfounded.

It had been a week since she discovered he was secretly renting a vacant storefront downtown, but in a pair of subsequent visits to the site during her lunch hour she saw no sign of occupancy. The "For Rent" sign was still on the door.

Abbas had also exhibited none of the odd euphoria that had so unnerved her—that strange light in his eyes that seemed to promise only trouble—and for five nights running he hadn't talked in his sleep. If he was still taking the bootleg antidepressant, he was hiding it well, because it was no longer in the medicine cabinet. Perhaps the crisis, if there was one to begin with, had passed.

The only recent surprise from Abbas was a pleasant one.

"The Harmons have invited us over for dinner Saturday," he announced on Wednesday during their drive home from work. "Just a small group, if that's all right with you. I assumed you might want to get out of the house."

To say the least.

In the past year Abbas had turned down every social invitation that offered the prospect of intimate conversation. They had attended only a few large fund-raisers or charity functions, mob scenes that allowed him to hide in the crowd. Even at those she noticed him nervously scanning the room for familiar faces. Whenever anyone they knew moved within range, he steered her by the elbow to a remote corner to ride out the storm.

She understood his reticence, and for a few months she shared it. It was a fear that someone might offer their sympathies, or ask too many prying questions, or, heaven forbid, say something awkward about the way Arab Americans were being treated by the government. Any such instance might have offered too great a temptation for Abbas to cut loose. They had worked hard to hold their anger in check.

But their reticence and isolation took their toll. For a while she felt like an over-inflated balloon, and assumed Abbas did as well. One puncture and who knew where they might fly off to?

Besides, people simply had no right to assume kinship with their feelings. Live in a West Bank village for a while and get back to me, she wanted to say. Or have your children manhandled by a policeman because of their surname.

The pressure eased as the months passed, and she found herself craving some of the old evenings they had once spent among friends. Now maybe Abbas was also ready to reemerge into the light. When he announced the dinner invitation, it was like watching him exit from an air-raid shelter and blink into the sun. Aliyah didn't want to startle him back underground by making too big a deal of it, so she swallowed hard and responded matter-of-factly.

"Yes, that sounds like a nice evening. We haven't been out in a while."

Had she been allowed to fashion her own night on the town, her preference would have been a concert or a trip to the theater, followed by a late but leisurely dinner with friends in Georgetown. But for now a dinner party at the Harmons' would do just fine.

As they dressed on Saturday evening, she decided to press her luck.

"What finally changed your mind, Abbas?"

"What do you mean?"

"About getting out of the house. Don't get me wrong, I'm looking forward to it. But you surprised me. I was worried about you, thinking maybe we'd lost you for good."

He shrugged and looked the other way while he pulled on his trousers.

"I don't know. I guess I decided it would be good to see people outside of work again. Maybe it's time."

"Yes, maybe it is."

She smiled, and then glanced toward him as if trying to catch him in the act—of exactly what, she couldn't have said. But he was still facing the other way, a small gesture of concealment that gave her the slightest pause before she concluded she was overreacting. Guarded progress was better than none. She should accept it at face value.

"Who else will be there?" she asked.

"The Harmons. Todd and Maggie Wilkins." Another doctor-and-wife combo. Not exactly a diverse crowd, but the Wilkinses were pleasant enough. "Plus Skip Ellington and his wife. What's her name? Sheila?"

"Sharon. Now that's a surprise."

"What, that I forgot her name?"

"That you still said yes when you heard Skip was coming."

"I don't mind Skip." His tone was defensive.

"You used to."

"No more than any other lobbyist. At least he's on our side."

That, too, was debatable. Skip Ellington had once been an administrator at Abbas's hospital. Ten years ago he became a lobbyist, employed by one of the big law firms in town. His first client was the American Medical Association, but he soon added drug companies and makers of medical hardware to his customer list.

"You used to say that he drove you crazy."

"He can be pretty entertaining if you know how to take him."

"And you do?"

"Of course. He has a lot of good war stories."

"He's certainly a name-dropper, if that's what you mean."

"That's half his charm. Get a few drinks in him and he will even tell you what some of the high and mighty are really like. As long as you're not working for the competition."

She decided not to argue the point. But something about the prospect of Skip's presence made her uneasy. Maybe it was his fondness for steering medical conversations onto awkward ground by posing hypothetical questions, then seeing how far he could push everyone toward their ethical boundaries. He made it all such fun. Even Aliyah found the discussions entertaining. Yet she always sensed an underlying smugness on Skip's part, as if he were proving to himself that these high-minded healers were just as susceptible to a sellout as he was.

But the specific nature of her worries didn't occur to her until they arrived at the Harmons' and she spotted Skip Ellington across the room, drink in hand. His face crinkled into a teasing grin as he said something to Maggie Wilkins. Aliyah could easily imagine him putting that smile to use in the corridors of Congress, killing his audience not with kindness but by feeding its insatiable appetite for gossip about the enemy. Now Skip was laughing archly. That was when Aliyah remembered.

It was a conversation that had taken place years ago, at a gathering like this. Skip had waited until everyone was well into their cups before broaching the subject.

"So tell me something," he had said. "Having worked in a hospital awhile—though never from your side of the bed, of course—one thing I've always wondered is how easy it would be to bump off one of your patients. Not saying you'd ever do that, of course. But let's say you wanted to, and without risking a malpractice suit."

There were a few gasps, as well as a few giggles. That's what made it quintessentially Skip—his usual game of ethical roulette, bumping the stakes higher on every spin, yet smiling all the while because, hey, no one's playing for real money.

Aliyah got just as caught up as the others, alternately fascinated and appalled as the doctors described tweaks and dosages that might cause a borderline patient to quietly slip away, no questions asked. Abbas was the only one who didn't participate, which Aliyah didn't notice until he piped up at the end, a fussy voice of doom.

"This really isn't an appropriate conversation, you know."

"Oh, Abbas, don't be such a prude," she answered, embarrassed. "No one's taking it seriously."

"But that's my point." He plowed on. "Deep down we all know there really are times when we might consider something like this. I mean, let's say that the world's most notorious butcher, someone responsible for the genocide of thousands, suffered some sort of emergency while on a state visit to Washington, then ended up on your operating table with, I don't know, a fifty-fifty chance of survival. Would you really do everything within your power to make sure he could live to kill again?"

"Interesting," said Skip, never one to squander such an opening. "Addition by subtraction, you mean. Save thousands by maybe not doing your best for one."

"You could say that. But to me there is still no question that you would do your best. Or else you're playing God. The Hippocratic oath has to count for something. We can't just rent ourselves out as medical soldiers in someone else's cause. We have to do our duty, no matter how loathsome to others."

"Bravo," Skip had cried. A little too glibly, Aliyah thought. But by then they were on the fourth bottle of wine.

The thought that troubled her now was: What if something like that came up again? Given his current state of mind, Abbas might say anything. And now, as opposed to last time, sensibilities had become far more tender on such topics. After 9/11, you had to be more careful what you said, because word could get around. Especially with a name like Rahim. It sounded so paranoid, but that's how it was.

"Aliyah, how lovely to see you." It was Becky Harmon, the hostess. "Let me take your coat. I'll have Bob get you a drink."

"Please. Something stronger than wine, if you don't mind. Gin and tonic."

"Absolutely. It's been that kind of week for me, too."

Aliyah doubted it. But who cared as long as Bob supplied the proper dosage. Oh, hell, she told herself. Relax and enjoy yourself. All this worrying was exactly why they needed a night out. Let it go. Or save it for your next session with Annie Felton. Becky brought her drink and she swallowed deeply, tasting the sharpness of the juniper berries. Bob Harmon had mixed it too strong, but that was okay. She spotted Abbas across the room nodding pleasantly as he spoke with Maggie Wilkins, and she felt silly for having worried. They would be fine.

It took two hours for her worries to resurface. By that time everyone was on the main course, tucking into slices of a beautiful tenderloin, red in the middle and charred at the edge. Blood crept across the china serving platter like a stain across a tablecloth.

"Abbas, isn't Senator Badgett one of your patients?" Skip asked loudly.

"Yes. For some time now." Abbas sounded wary. He had always been quite scrupulous about protecting his patients' confidentiality.

"I hear the prognosis isn't good."

"That's no secret, I guess. It's been in the news. The family has been quite willing to talk about it."

"So I've noticed. I ran into his wife at a reception the other day. More details than I cared to hear, or would want to repeat over dinner."

Abbas frowned, either at the wife's indiscretion or at the idea of discussing surgical matters over a plate of blood-red beef. Skip took no notice.

"What she didn't mention was all the worry over whether he'll last another thirteen months, until next November."

"The elections, you mean?"

"Yes. I hear the odds aren't so great."

"I couldn't say."

Skip smiled, as if he found Abbas's reluctance quaintly amusing.

Aliyah noticed Drs. Harmon and Wilkins nodding, as if to affirm that her husband had said exactly the right thing. Not that it had any effect on Skip.

"I've been hearing he won't even come close. Which is why his wife has been out and about, showing her face and trying to make an impression. There's talk of appointing her to serve out his term. But if that's the case, they'd prefer he went sooner rather than later, especially if he's terminal anyway. Give her time to make a name so she can hold on to the seat next fall. All the betting is that he'll go pretty soon."

"Simply because they *want* it to happen?" Abbas looked incredulous.

"Well, from what I'm told, it's more because of what people are hearing from the hospital."

"Maybe so."

"But not for certain?"

"As I told you, that's not for me to discuss."

Another round of approving nods. Skip forged on.

"And I wouldn't expect you to, of course. But, theoretically speaking, aren't there certain treatments the family could withhold if they were so inclined? Once things have reached the point of no return, of course."

"Theoretically speaking?" Abbas paused, as if to consult his colleagues. Their faces were blank, so he moved gingerly forward, holding his fork and knife in abeyance. "Only if he was incapable of making the decision for himself, and had some sort of living will."

On this point, Aliyah was better informed than Skip. She had overheard Abbas on the telephone telling the hospital the senator had lost consciousness and was unlikely to regain it. She suspected Skip had heard something similar and wanted to confirm it. But Abbas said nothing more. There was an awkward pause. Then Bob Harmon spoke up.

"You always were one for getting us talking about things we shouldn't, Skip."

The others chuckled while Skip looked chastened, although to Aliyah he already seemed to be angling for another opening.

Sure enough, when everyone later retired to the living room and broke into smaller groups, she saw him huddled in a corner with Abbas. The surprise was that this time it was Abbas, not Skip, who seemed to have initiated the conversation. And now her husband was the one with the eager look, the same expression that had unnerved her at times during the preceding weeks. Both men held cocktails mixed at Bob Harmon strength, and they stood by a table lamp that cast their faces in an unflattering light.

Aliyah excused herself from a chat with Becky about college visits and took up a station at the end of a couch, just within earshot of Abbas. She arrived in time to hear Skip again mention Senator Badgett. To her surprise, Abbas was now the one probing for information, and Skip seemed happy to oblige.

"Oh, yes, when the day comes it will be quite the event," Skip said. "And you're right, the church is very small. Every seat will be at a premium. Think of the most elite of the inaugural balls, then pare it down by a few hundred, and that ought to give you an idea."

"But hasn't he faded from power in recent years? I can't imagine many people of consequence would attend."

When had Abbas become a political gossip? This stuff usually bored him to tears. She glanced at his face and realized he was goading Skip on, a role reversal in which Abbas was playing to the lobbyist's vanity as a so-called insider.

"That's not the point," Skip said. "It's not *his* power they'll be paying court to. It's his wife's. You can bet she'll be a lot more active once she holds the seat. She'll be out to make an impression. Any way you look at it, she's key. Swing vote on an important committee. Plenty of patronage. None of the big names will want to miss it."

"Really? Even the White House?"

"Schedule permitting. Plus Cabinet secretaries, the Supremes. It'll be an A-list event. Sort of a Fortune 400 of Washington, except with room for maybe only half that number. And as attending physician, you'll no doubt be invited. So be prepared to arrive early and give me a full report."

Skip laughed oleaginously and placed a hand on Abbas's shoulder.

"Oh, I never have much use for such events," Abbas said modestly.

"So I've heard. You've never been one to use your position like some of them."

Aliyah could have sworn that Skip then nodded toward Drs. Harmon and Wilkins, who were chatting in other corners. Abbas, to his credit, didn't nod back. But the conversation still bothered her for reasons she couldn't put her finger on. At least Abbas wouldn't be attending the funeral. She could imagine how tempted he might be to climb on his soapbox in such powerful company, lecturing on how they'd led the nation astray. Truth be told, she wouldn't mind the opportunity, either. They could use an earful, all of them. But she could also imagine how that would go over with the Secret Service. An agent might place a hand on her husband's arm, and then he would explode. Or maybe she was thinking back to the cop on Connecticut Avenue and projecting her own reaction. Another topic to raise next week with Annie Felton.

"Dear, are you all right?"

It was Abbas, standing by with her coat. Others were also preparing to leave. She didn't know how much time had passed, just that she was the only one still sitting there at the end of the couch. Maybe she was the one with the problem, jumping to wild conclusions on the scantiest of evidence.

"Yes, I'm fine. Just a little tired."

"Let's get you home, then." He leaned forward as she stood, and whispered into her ear, "Home, and into a nice warm bed."

It was unmistakably an invitation, and she was pleasantly surprised to find that she was receptive. Their eyes met, and she smiled back warmly.

For the first time in months they made love that night, Abbas gentle and solicitous, the nimble compassion of his surgeon's hands gradually giving way to urgency and more emphatic movement. So much for the supposed side effects of his antidepressants. It was the first time in more than a year that the act hadn't seemed fraught with desperation. Perhaps the alcohol helped, but in any event she felt like they had crossed another threshold back toward normalcy.

Afterward, Abbas fell into slumber—a silent one, thank goodness—but Aliyah was wide awake. She lay there replaying the evening's conversations in her head, with a nagging sense that a stray word or phrase had snagged on some troubling event from the past few days. But the connection lay just out of reach, as if hovering above the bed. She gave up and rolled onto her side, and she was about to drift off when the realization hit her. It was that morning in the Volvo on their way to work, when Abbas had muttered, "Sheer genius." Something to do with a radio news report had triggered the remark, and it was now prodding her. All that her conscious mind could recall was a mention of Kandahar and a casualty total, but something more must have also registered.

The broadcast would be archived, she knew. Available online. She need only remember the date and approximate time. She slipped out of bed, put on her robe, and crept downstairs to the computer in their kitchen. The link for NPR's archives was easy enough to find. The page for *Morning Edition* displayed a calendar for the current month, and she clicked on the correct day for the previous week. Then she turned down the volume to keep from waking Abbas and slid the bar across to about where the story should be in the broadcast, based on the approximate time.

A minute or so later it jumped out at her like a voice from a bad dream:

Twenty-three people were killed today in Afghanistan when a suicide bomber struck at a mosque in Kandahar. The blast occurred at the funeral for a prominent Muslim cleric who had been assassinated by pro-Taliban gunmen three days earlier. Authorities said several local leaders were in attendance and are believed to be among the casualties.

"Sheer genius." That's what Abbas had said of this horrible event. And she supposed that it was genius, in its twisted fashion. Kill someone prominent, then wait for his famous friends to gather at the funeral so you could kill them all. Aliyah flushed with horror, thinking of all Abbas's questions about Senator Badgett's funeral. She clicked off the rest of the broadcast before any further such "genius" came blaring from the speakers.

It all added up, yet she couldn't quite accept the conclusion. Everything had come together so fast that it literally made her dizzy, and she placed a hand on the table to stop the spinning. The gin, perhaps. Bob mixed drinks so strong. For a moment she felt as if she might be sick, but she held on. Could Abbas really be planning something so diabolically awful?

She steadied herself and reconsidered. Then she took the mouse and clicked to a search engine. What church had Skip and Abbas been talking about? She couldn't recall a specific name or denomination, so she tried typing in Senator Badgett's name along with the words "church" and "Washington."

The hits were all over the map, mostly having to do with the senator's past comments on the issue of school prayer, so she tried again with just the senator's name. That gave her his Web site, where she clicked on the link "About Senator Badgett." His bio appeared. The last paragraph said he was Baptist but didn't mention a particular church. She searched again, adding "Baptist church" to his name, and this time she got what she needed on the first hit, right there in the summary.

"The Badgetts are members of the United Baptist Church of God in Washington."

She found a Web site for the church. Its address popped onto the screen with the power of an alarm: Cordell Street, in Southeast. The same block as the vacant storefront Abbas had just rented. It was the church across the alley. She gasped out loud.

It was too horrible for words, but now she had to know more. She walked through the family room to try the door of his study, but it was locked. Her heart beating urgently, she tiptoed back upstairs to the threshold of their bedroom, where she stood for a moment as her eyes adjusted to the darkness. Then she got down on her hands and knees and crawled to where Abbas had left his trousers, tossed on the floor as they had undressed each other in their rare moment of passion. She slid her hand into a pocket and withdrew his keys with a small jingle. She clutched them tightly to keep them from ringing further while she rose slowly to her feet. Abbas hadn't moved a muscle, and his breathing was regular.

Aliyah headed back downstairs, unlocked his study, then gently shut the door behind her. Barely able to contain her growing dread, she opened the desk and rooted carefully through the papers and envelopes, hoping she wouldn't again come across Shereen's passport. The note was still there with the address on Cordell Street and the name of the real estate agent. But nothing else seemed to offer a clue.

She tried the rest of the drawers, and in the last one the back cover of a large paperback book caught her eye. White type inside a black box, with the words "Warning! Read this book, but keep in mind that the topics written about here are illegal and constitute a threat."

Aliyah turned the book over and sagged in despair. Her knees were wobbly, so she sat back on the floor while staring at the title stenciled white on black: *The Anarchist Cookbook*. Abbas had folded back the corner of a page for easy reference, and she opened the book to chapter four, "Explosives and Booby Traps."

At that moment the door to the study opened, and Abbas appeared on the threshold.

He, too, had put on a robe.

"Aliyah?" he asked, his voice ever so quiet, as if their children had returned home and he was taking care not to wake them. "What are you doing in here, down there on the floor?"

His expression was neither hostile nor challenging. There even seemed to be a hint of sympathy in his eyes. Or maybe that was wishful thinking, because already he was scanning the evidence of her betrayal—the book in her hands, opened to the damning chapter; the scribbled address on Cordell Street atop the pile of papers on the desk—his deepest secrets, laid bare.

Yet he did not shout, or even frown. That was the oddest and most disturbing thing of all, Aliyah decided. He didn't seem to mind in the least.

17

Most first-time visitors to Athens are disappointed, and I assumed Omar would be no exception. To the untrained eye, the marbled glory of the Acropolis seems to frown down through the haze at the architectural chaos below, as if regretfully surveying Sparta's final triumph. I once felt that way, too, until Mila helped me discover the city's hidden charms. Without her at my side, maybe Athens would again hold me at arm's length.

I had only a few hours to prepare for Omar's arrival. I hadn't yet told Mila I was coming because I didn't know if I would have time to see her. And after Black's last message I didn't want to mix her up in this business more than she already was. We had spoken often by phone, but she was clearly haunted by the thought of eavesdroppers parsing every word. This led to long silences that spooked us as badly as any warning.

"When will it be safe?" she had finally asked, only two days ago.

"Soon, I hope. But until then maybe you'd feel better if we didn't talk for a while. Our conversations don't seem to be making things any better."

"I'll let you decide. You can tell me when it's safe."

I had then vowed to myself to surprise her with a visit if at all possible. It now seemed that the Athens trip might be my only chance to see her for months, since my work in Amman had slowed to a crawl after such a promising start. Following my fruitless search of the files, I settled into a dreary round of meetings with doctors, medical suppliers, and pharmaceutical reps. Omar wanted me to secure pledges of donated drugs and equipment, and that left little time for visiting Bakaa. And when I did go I treaded lightly, still smarting from my close call even after the bruises healed.

Nabil seemed equally wary. I hadn't seen him since the day of the mob scene, which left me instead in the tiresome company of Dr. Hassan. I also hadn't been able to drop by Sami's salon. He was out of the country, destination unknown.

I easily found the scooter shop in Plaka, a onetime slum of cobbled alleys and leaning homes that had recently been gentrified. There was only one fellow on Sunday duty, a gray-haired man reading a sports tabloid at a cluttered desk. The small office was set up like a tiny showroom, with scooters taking most of the floor space.

"Mr. Higgins," he said before I could open my mouth. "I've been expecting you."

A Piaggio Typhoon had been reserved in my name, the same model I drove on Karos. But how would I sign for it without proper identification? The deskman supplied the answer by handing me a slim white envelope. Inside was a U.S. passport and an American driver's license issued in Virginia. Both had my photo and the name Robert Higgins. There was also a Visa card in Higgins's name, along with a strip of paper carrying the name and address of a local hotel.

"Is this where I'm supposed to stay?"

The deskman's frown told me I had strayed from the script, so I took the keys without another word. The Typhoon was gassed to go. I didn't bother mentioning I'd return it on Wednesday. He had already gone back to his newspaper.

The hotel was also in Plaka, and as soon as I'd checked in I set out for a reconnaissance of the Grande Bretagne, which was only five blocks away. The lobby was spacious, but for all the grandeur of its mosaic floors and tall windows, it offered no suitable nooks where I could wait in seclusion yet still have a view of the elevators. I would have to sit in the open, with only a newspaper to hide me. I tried it out, drawing a suspicious glance from a woman speaking French on a cell phone. Uniformed desk clerks scurried back and forth at the far end. Outside there was a host of taxi hailers and liveried doormen. I would have to park my scooter around the corner, which could make for a rough start if Omar took a cab in the opposite direction.

On the way back to my room I withdrew five hundred euros from an ATM with my own card, not theirs. Then I set out to find someplace sunny for a drink to steel myself for Omar's arrival. Plaka's outdoor cafés were already filled with Germans and Japanese, so I wandered farther, working my way around the base of the Acropolis. To my right, young men rolled dice on backgammon tables and sipped chilled Freddocinos from tall glasses. An old man sat at the curb playing a sort of Mediterranean bagpipe. I paused at an iron rail to stare up toward the Acropolis, where the white colonnade of the Propylaia was rosy in afternoon sunlight. Only at the last second did I notice a Greek man approaching in apparent interest.

"You are American?" he asked in English. He looked to be in his sixties.

"Yes."

"Where are you from?"

"Boston." The truth was too complicated. And I was already wondering if this encounter had been arranged. I half expected him to thrust a folded message into my hand, but he kept his distance.

"I live in America fifteen years. Houston. Exxon Corporation. Then Saudi Arabia for last ten."

Right across the desert from Amman. The coincidence seemed too close for comfort.

"Dhahran?" Taking a guess.

"Yes. You know Dhahran?"

"Sure." Another stop along the way during the Gulf War. "Can't get a beer there."

"Yes, no beer." He smiled and nodded. What did he want? "Where you go? You stop, drink a beer?"

He nodded toward the café tables. Was he scrounging for a drink? But he was too well dressed to be a bum.

"Sorry, but I'm on my way somewhere. Have to go."

He nodded again, seeming disappointed. I glanced over my shoulder a block later to see if he was following, or snapping a photo. But he was gone, or at least I couldn't find him. I still craved a drink but was too wary to stop until I wound up back at the hotel, where I took a beer from the minibar. Then I telephoned the Grande Bretagne.

"Mr. Omar al-Baroody, please."

"Yes, sir."

A few clicks, a ring tone, and then Omar's voice.

"Hello?" He had arrived on schedule.

I hung up, walked back to the Grande Bretagne, then spent the next several hours peeking around the edge of a *Herald Tribune*. Either Omar had already gone out or he had decided to eat in his room. At any rate, he was a no-show. At ten I walked to a souvlaki place in Monastiraki, then returned to my room and laid out clothing and supplies for the next morning as if preparing for battle. Then I crawled beneath the sheets and shut my eyes.

An hour later I was still awake, agitated by the idea that Mila was mere minutes away. She was probably drinking coffee after a late dinner with her aunt and cousins. They would be laughing around the table as they passed platters of pastries and fruit.

It took only half an hour to dress and ride the Metro to within a few blocks of her aunt's building. The apartment was on the sixth floor at the far end, and I easily picked out the balcony from my vantage point in the street. A light was on. She was up there—I knew it. My spirits lifted in anticipation, and I set out for the entrance.

I had scarcely stepped into the parking lot when the main door, thirty yards away, opened with a burst of animated conversation. I stopped in the shadows, hesitant, while four people stepped into the glare of an overhanging streetlamp. One was Mila. She spoke Greek, and her fluting voice was quite a contrast to the despairing tones of our last conversation. This was the Mila who could charm your socks off.

I was about to call out her name when I realized that the foursome was actually two couples. Two men, two women. If I hadn't known better I would have guessed from their body language that they were double-dating, headed out for a late night on the town. The second woman was Mila's cousin. The men were strangers. I opened my mouth to speak, but the words dammed up. Not now, something told me. Too awkward. Too much of a surprise in present company.

By the time they had climbed into a car I was regretting my reticence. This was foolish, a product of my old insecurities about marrying a younger woman. For Chrissakes, she was my wife and we were in love. There was no reason she should stay cooped up every night just because I had temporarily deserted her for a nest of Middle Eastern snoops and fanatics.

But it was too late. The doors slammed shut, the engine started, and the car rolled away while I remained in darkness. It turned up the street, taillights receding.

It was about then that an engine started on a dark sedan parked across the street, opposite the parking lot. I hadn't heard its doors shut, and its headlights remained off as it pulled away from the curb. More paranoia on my part? I didn't think so. And at that moment I boiled over. Enough of this meddling in our lives.

I ran into the street, making it just in time to stop the sedan. The driver slammed on the brakes and laid on the horn. I stepped forward, placed both palms on the hood and glared into the smoked windshield. The engine revved, but I didn't budge. When you've been thrown to the cobbles by a mob in Bakaa you develop quite a tolerance for petty threats like this one. I slammed a fist on the hood.

"Open up!"

At first, nothing. Then the window on the driver's side glided down, and a face poked into view. Young fellow. Short dark hair. Stupid sunglasses. He'd probably put them on for my benefit.

"You must be Freeman. Mind getting out of the way?"

The accent was American, right off the Jersey Turnpike.

"Tell Black this has to stop."

"They warned us you might be dropping by."

"Enough! You tell him that. I know the stakes, but I'm doing my job."

"It's like this every night, you know. With your wife and all."

"Did you hear me?"

"Parties. Nightclubs. Same joints all the time. She gets around. Maybe you'd like to read the logs?"

I slammed down a fist again and stepped around the fender toward the driver. As soon as I cleared his path the car roared forward with a screech of rubber. He still hadn't turned on the headlights. I watched, fuming. When he reached the end of the block he turned right, just as Mila's car had done. As if he knew exactly where to go.

18

My life as a full-time stalker began promptly at nine the next morning, when I arrived at the lobby of the Grande Bretagne with a folded newspaper and a foul disposition. It was the day of Omar's appointment with the mysterious K, according to his date book. I had already fortified myself with three cups of Greek coffee and a sugary pastry after not getting to sleep until nearly three. Every time I closed my eyes I imagined the worst possible scenes. In some, Mila was pursued down darkened streets by the asshole from the sedan. In others she was in the arms of a Greek lover, slouched on a leather banquette at some disco bar.

I opened a fresh copy of the *Herald Tribune*. Members of an airline flight crew offered additional camouflage, milling around their luggage by the revolving door.

I kept thinking of the driver from Jersey. A liar, no doubt. Just trying to get my goat, which he had done with ease. He must have laughed for blocks. But what would I say now when I finally saw Mila? Warn her? Scold her? The elevator doors opened, and I glanced over the paper. Another stewardess, carrying a Styrofoam cup of coffee, followed closely by a pilot who wore a smug look that said he had scored. Love was in the air in Athens, and wasn't that just my luck. I shook out my paper and angrily turned the page.

Knowing Omar's penchant for tardiness, I was surprised to see him bound out of the elevator at 9:45 for his 10 a.m. appointment. He carried only a rolled-up magazine—a recognition signal, perhaps?—and headed straight for the exit. I didn't stand until he was pushing through the door. If he hailed a cab I would have to run for my scooter. Instead he turned left, still on foot, toward the five-lane bustle of Vassilissis Amalias Avenue, and by the time I emerged blinking into the sunlight he was crossing toward the parliament building and the National Garden.

I barely beat the light, while fretting over the possibility that he would turn and see me. I had already decided that if he spotted me I would laugh and exclaim loudly at the joyous coincidence. He had always been a great believer in Kismet, and he knew I would also be traveling in Greece. He headed up the crowded gravel sidewalk, and I dropped back long enough to buy a pretzel ring from a street vendor. Was this the right distance, the proper technique? I had no idea. I knew only that I felt a little silly yet also a little scared, as if I should be watching my own flanks as well.

Omar turned left some fifty yards ahead, disappearing through a wrought-iron gate into the green coolness of the National Garden. When I reached the entrance I spotted him receding through the shadows of the trees, and I set off down a gravel path in pursuit.

The park was a calm oasis amid the city's smog and car horns, with a dense canopy of palms and casuarinas, and lush hedgerows. But the isolation made me stand out more. I put on a pair of sunglasses, feeling ridiculous but safer.

Omar took a left fork from the main path. A wooden arrow indicated he was heading for the botanical museum or the park café. He almost never did business without a cup of coffee, so I was betting on the café. A horde of schoolkids approached from the opposite direction, darting and chattering like birds. Once they passed, Omar and I were practically alone, and I felt more exposed than ever. He paused next to a small brick building. Probably the botanical museum. A sign said it was closed for renovation. Omar seemed to be looking for somewhere to sit.

I ducked left down a narrow path through a maze of hedges, while still catching glimpses of him through the foliage. He was lingering by the museum, a tiny brick building with faded green shutters and a terracotta roof. Finally he sat on a bench just to the left, looking nervous, watchful. Or maybe I was projecting my own emotions. The newspaper in my right hand was damp with sweat.

I decided this must be his rendezvous point. It certainly offered seclusion. And with the building closed there was little chance that others would interrupt. The only sounds were the squawks of ducks and geese over at the children's zoo. From where I was now I wouldn't be able to hear a thing, so I looked for a closer position.

In front of Omar's bench was a patch of grass, so you couldn't sneak up from that direction. To the rear of the building were more hedges, so I set out for them, circling Omar until I came up behind the building, just around the corner from him. As I did so, I heard a sudden burst of conversation. His contact must have arrived, but where had he come from? Only now did I bother to wonder if someone had spotted me creeping around.

They were chatting freely. I wasn't yet close enough to make out the words, but oddly enough it sounded like German. I edged behind a large hibiscus toward the corner of the building, angling for a peek. The bench was now about twenty feet away. Yes, the language was definitely German, and Omar had just come into view. He sat beside a stoop-shouldered man with a shock of silver hair and a black wool blazer.

About then, someone fired up a chain saw over toward the zoo, so I had to ease closer to hear. Through the bushes I now spotted another bench that was behind the building, and far enough around the corner from Omar's that they wouldn't be able to see it. I squeezed through an opening in the hedge and took a seat, just as the chain saw went silent.

I was now only about ten feet away from them, but still hidden. My German was rusty, but I made out a few words, especially from Omar, whose diction was painfully slow. He called the man Herr Doktor Rieger. Or Krieger, perhaps, recalling the "K" in the date book. The Herr Doktor's accent was difficult to place. Austrian? Bavarian, maybe, with a few notes picked up from living abroad. Maybe he lived here now.

Krieger said something about a professor, and then mentioned money. Omar clearly said, "Funfzehn Uhr," or 3 p.m. What little I picked up during the next half hour didn't add up to much beyond a vague combination of money, a professor, and another possible appointment. One problem was the German's muffled voice. Was he a donor? If so, this certainly wasn't the optimum place for writing a check.

I slid down the bench to peek around the corner, realizing belatedly that now they would be able to see my shadow. I considered sliding back, but then the shadow would move. So I froze. That meant I was caught a few seconds later when the silver-haired man emerged around the corner and looked at me in surprise.

Omar wasn't with him, fortunately, but I had to restrain a gasp. I looked down at my newspaper and felt his gaze as he shuffled past, footsteps crunching the gravel at the deliberate pace of an old man. He was so close I smelled his aftershave, plus a whiff of wool and cigarettes. Then he cut through the hedge at the same spot I had used moments ago. It was the only way to and from my bench that didn't cross in front of the building—the route of a sneak—and he must have realized I had taken it as well.

Five yards past me, he stopped and turned.

"Wieviel Uhr, bitte?" he asked in German.

I looked up, feigning ignorance, glad that I had put on the sunglasses.

He asked again, this time in halting English as he pointed to his wrist.

"The time, please?"

I tried to give my English a Greek accent.

"Just after ten thirty."

"Danke. Thank you."

I looked back at the paper and listened until I no longer heard his footsteps. Then I took a deep breath, counted slowly to thirty, and stood. I peeked around the corner to make sure Omar was gone and then went looking for the German. At his speed he couldn't have gone far.

When I reached the main path I spotted his silver head moving toward the entrance Omar had used, and I walked briskly to narrow the gap. He turned right, as if heading toward the Grande Bretagne. But instead of crossing the boulevard he walked onto the plaza in front of the parliament building, where he joined a crowd of about a hundred people watching the change of the guard.

I had seen the ceremony before with Mila. The tunics and tasseled caps of the traditional Greek uniforms were mildly interesting, and their high-stepping was mildly comical, like a Monty Python silly walk. But usually only newcomers watched, which told me that either the Herr Doktor wasn't a local or he was waiting to see if I would follow, so I took care to conceal myself in the crowd.

My new vantage point afforded a better look at his face. I guessed he was in his early seventies, and I found myself performing the old Israeli parlor trick of trying to calculate how old this German must have been during the war. Probably too young to have been a soldier. But definitely old enough to remember the postwar years of deprivation. Some of those Germans, I knew, had supported radical Palestinian movements during the 1970s, particularly in East Germany and leftist quarters of West Berlin. Maybe that was this one's game. But why not just mail Omar a check? Why arrange a rendezvous in a city where neither of them seemed at home?

The soldiers finished their business, and the crowd dispersed. The Herr Doktor walked to the curb to hail a taxi. A blue one pulled over almost immediately, and as he climbed inside I scurried across the street, still half a block from my scooter. A red light bought me a few extra seconds, and as I hopped aboard I saw the taxi angling up Panepistimiou.

The best thing about riding a scooter is that you can easily maneuver to the head of traffic at every light. The worst thing is that all the other scooters do the same. Every green signal becomes a noisy scrum, and for the rest of the block it's like traveling with a swarm of angry hornets. But I was able to keep an eye on the blue rooftop of the cab, and I soon moved to within a few car lengths. He continued six more blocks, passing the Court of Appeals and the National Library before veering left. After winding a few more turns the taxi dropped him at the Central Market, which was teeming with shoppers. I locked the scooter while keeping an eye on the Herr Doktor, then followed him inside.

He had entered the butchers' quarter. Although I am an enthusiastic carnivore, I had always been overpowered by this market's smell of hacked flesh and its din of cleavers striking blocked wood. To my relief, he cut through a passageway into the fish market. The crowds made it hard to keep him in sight. Aggressive vendors held aloft huge, gleaming fish and shouted prices, while counter boys dumped new loads of ice.

The Herr Doktor stopped at a table of zebra shrimp and held up two fingers. A boy moved into action, tossing handfuls onto a spring scale and then wrapping the order in white paper. The Herr Doktor couldn't cook in a hotel room, so maybe he was a local after all.

Back outside, he again hailed a cab, and by the time he got one I was ready to roll. He headed north, straight up Athinas through the hellish traffic of Omonias Square before angling right up Marni to the open grounds of the National Archaeological Museum. I shot past while the Herr Doktor paid his fare, then walked the scooter back down the sidewalk as I watched him head up the steps beneath the entrance colonnade. Perhaps he was going to see the handiwork of his countryman, Heinrich Schliemann, who had unearthed the museum's star attraction, the so-called Trojan gold of Mycenae.

I entered the museum in time to see the Herr Doktor disappear up a marble stairway to the left, just past the ticket kiosk. I went that way, too.

"Excuse me, sir," a woman in the kiosk said. "Your ticket?"

I shelled out the requisite price and bolted after him, but again the woman stopped me.

"Sir, the exhibitions are this way. You are not allowed in the offices."

"But I have an appointment." Then why had I bought a ticket? "I, uh, am accompanying the Herr Doktor. Doktor Krieger."

She frowned, but the name got her attention, and she consulted the visitors' ledger, which Krieger must have just signed. I took the opportunity to lean over and double-check the name. Yes, it was Krieger, first name Norbert, although his handwriting was appalling. She snatched the book away, but not before I saw that his destination was room 212. The name of the person he was visiting had been illegible.

"I am sorry. There is no other appointment with the professor listed. Would you like me to call him?"

"No," I said abruptly. "I'll come back later."

I dashed out the door in flustered embarrassment, ticket still in hand, and then ducked behind one of the big columns to wait for Krieger to leave. It took nearly an hour, but he made it worthwhile. He was no longer carrying the bag of shrimp, and as soon as he strode into the sunlight he pulled a fat green envelope from an inside pocket of his jacket. He gave it a glance and thumbed the contents. It was a hefty stack of lavender paper, the shape and color of 500-euro notes. That meant it was an awful lot of money. At the street he hailed another cab, and his final stop came fifteen minutes later at a small hotel in Kolonaki. It was a far more modest place than the Grande Bretagne, and when he stepped out of the taxi I zoomed on past with a roar of the Piaggio.

For the moment my work was done. It was just before one o'clock, and if Omar's next appointment was at three, as his conversation had hinted, I didn't need to return to the Grande Bretagne until two thirty. Of course, he might have gone somewhere else in the meantime, but that was beyond my control. It was early for lunch if you were a Greek, but a nearby taverna was already doing a decent trade among office workers, so I treated myself to a beer and a bowl of pasta, then headed to my own hotel, where I phoned the National Archaeological Museum.

"Good afternoon. I am calling to confirm an appointment with a professor there, but I'm sorry to say that I've misplaced his name. But I do remember that he is in office number 212."

"And your name, sir?"

"Al-Baroody. Omar al-Baroody."

"That would be Professor Yiorgos Soukas. I will connect you."

I hung up and phoned Omar's room. He picked up after the first ring, and from his groggy tone it sounded as if he had been dozing. I hung up and sat on the edge of the bed wondering what the hell I was doing. Making a living, I supposed. Securing a future for Mila and me. The thought of her produced a pang of worry, which I tried unsuccessfully to ignore as I set out again for the Grande Bretagne.

Omar stepped from the elevator promptly at 2:45, once again playing against type. This time a hotel employee hailed a taxi for him. I scrambled to the Piaggio, swerved past a bus, and followed the taxi east along the northern side of the National Garden. Was he headed to Krieger's hotel? I suspected as much when the cab turned north into Kolonaki, whizzing past pricey boutiques and a splendid green square. But we kept on going, straight up an incline to the lower slope of Lycabettus Hill, the city's mightiest summit. The taxi finally ran out of roadway just outside the station for the funicular railcar that climbed the rest of the way to the top. Omar paid the fare and went inside the station.

I parked to the left of the entrance, where the street came to a dead end, and then waited outside a few minutes to give Omar enough time to buy a ticket. I entered just as the cable car was leaving on its uphill journey through an underground tunnel.

"When's the next one?" I asked at the ticket window.

"Fifteen minutes."

Damn. Whoever had planned this rendezvous chose wisely. A pursuer afraid of being spotted would never have boarded the same car, but by the time you got to the top in the next car any meeting might be over. And if Omar made the return journey on foot he might take any of several walkways.

A crowd of Japanese tourists arrived just as my car was about to depart. They bustled past me through the turnstile and crowded into the seats, shooting videos of the dark tunnel as we rose. Halfway up we passed a descending car, lit up like ours. Omar was in it, and I cursed under my breath. He didn't see me, thank goodness. If anything, he seemed preoccupied, and just before he eased out of sight I saw a green parcel beneath his arm. It looked like the envelope Krieger had carried from the museum.

At least now I knew who he had been meeting, unless Professor Yiorgos Soukas was handing out these envelopes all over town. Maybe Omar was now headed to a bank, but I would never catch him in time to find out. Krieger was probably gone, too, so I decided to plan my next move in the café at the summit. I bounded into the sunlight and took the curving walkway at full stride, only to find myself looking straight through the glass doors at Herr Doktor Krieger, who fortunately was reading a menu.

I faltered, then veered quickly to a marble stairway on the right, which circled up to a small white chapel. Flushed and breathless, and not daring to look back, I crossed to the far side of a little terrace outside the chapel and sat down on a low stone wall.

I faced away from the direction I'd come from and looked back across the city. The Acropolis was well below us in the gathering haze of late afternoon. Farther out, sunlight reflected in a blaze of burnt orange on the Aegean. I began to breathe easier, and when I checked behind me there was no sign of Krieger. Maybe he hadn't seen me. Or if he had, maybe he hadn't recognized me. I wasn't wearing sunglasses now.

I passed the next half hour reading my *Herald Tribune* and admiring the view. A distant thunderstorm was skirting the northwest edge of the city. Olympian bolts of lightning crackled in plumy clouds. A falcon flew past just below, searching for dinner. I decided to stride past the café and head quickly downhill. If he followed I could always walk faster.

As I passed the glass doors I saw that he was still at the table, smoking now. He looked right at me. I checked an urge to speed up as I rounded the corner toward the station. A funicular was waiting to depart, thank goodness, so I quickly showed my return ticket and sagged into a seat.

Most people made the return journey on foot, so only four other passengers were in the car. The speakers announced the last call. Just before the doors slid shut, Herr Doktor Krieger stepped aboard.

He took a seat on my row, against the opposite wall. There was nothing else for me to look at except the floor and ceiling, or the tunnel ahead. The only sound was some silly Greek techno music playing from speakers. I glanced in his direction and he nodded in recognition, as if he had been lying in wait.

"Good afternoon," he said in halting Greek.

I responded in kind, hoping to sound like a native. Then I noticed he was looking at my lap, where my *Herald Tribune* was open to the front page, its English headlines announcing me as an impostor.

The car began its slow descent. Did he have a camera, some miniature bit of hardware that even now was taking my picture? Or was he, too, just dabbling at this, making it up as he went along?

The latter possibility calmed me. Maybe he was the one who should be worrying. So I looked over again and took further note of his appearance. His hairstyle and clothing were old-fashioned—wool and tweed and thick white socks. Up close he looked older than before, although still not old enough to have fought in the war. It was easy to picture him behind a university desk, walled in by books. Herr Doktor Professor, perhaps.

He turned away from my stare. Now he was the one getting nervous, looking out his window at the passing wall, where the lights winked slowly past in our descent. He glanced over, then quickly looked away while I held my gaze. He pulled a handkerchief from a trouser pocket to blow his nose. Maybe he was in over his head. I knew I was, even though I currently held the upper hand. I was quite willing to bully while I had the chance, but were reinforcements awaiting him at the bottom? This thought made me waver, and each of us spent the rest of the ride avoiding the other's gaze.

I exited first, and walked quickly to my scooter, exhaling in relief as I twisted the handle to rev the engine. But, of course, with the street at a dead end, I had to pass the station entrance to make my getaway. I took a deep breath and accelerated into a wide U-turn. And there he was, out front on the sidewalk, now holding pen to paper. His right hand worked furiously as he stared at my bike. He was taking down my tag numbers, which was alarming until I remembered I had rented the bike with a fake name. Thank God, at least, for that bit of help from Black, White, and Gray. Trust the professionals to get it right. If Herr Doktor Krieger's employers bothered to track me, they would turn up only some unknown visitor named Robert Higgins.

Relieved, I scooted down the hillside, glad to be rid of the old German. But I needed a drink to calm my nerves, so I crossed town to the Monastiraki district near the city's flea market, took a table in the sun, and ordered a gin. Two drinks later, and feeling tipsy, I remounted the Piaggio. Almost immediately after turning into traffic I was overtaken by two motorcycles, one on either side. I expected them to blow on by. Instead they matched my pace, and squeezed toward me like pincers. Were they trying to force me to the curb, or merely following me? Neither possibility calmed my overactive imagination, which was now primed by alcohol. My palms were slippery on the handlebars. As we throttled down into a curve I braked to let them pass, but to no avail. Then I accelerated, herky-jerky with a flush of blue smoke, but they nimbly matched my every maneuver, herding me along like a pair of border collies. Whenever I dared a glance, they stared impassively at the road ahead. Was it me, or did the faces beneath the Plexiglas shields look Middle Eastern? With Greeks it can be hard to tell the difference. All I knew for sure was that neither was the fellow with the Jersey accent.

We pulled to a stop at a red light, and they sidled up closely, still looking straight ahead. It was as maddening as it was worrisome, and I flashed on a vision of myself riding deep into the suburbs and then onto country lanes, mile after mile with these two at my flanks until I ran out of gas and they beat me to a bloody pulp.

"Why are you doing this?" I shouted, but I was cut short by car horns as the light changed, and they pulled off with me. Finally, a mere block from Nikis Street, they dropped back and peeled away as I turned right toward my hotel. My shirt and trousers were clammy with sweat. I rolled the scooter to the curb and locked it for the night. I had told myself that nothing more of this nature would frighten me. But my legs were so rubbery that even the small g-force of the elevator nearly buckled my knees.

I took a long, slow shower to calm down, then pulled back the bedspread and stretched out naked on the clean sheets. I felt old, past my prime. Cuckolded, too, for all I knew, even as I lay here trying to puzzle things out. What had this latest effort at intimidation been all about? And by whom? Black had already made his point, emphatically. Anything more seemed like clumsy overkill. And I doubted Herr Doktor Krieger could have produced results so fast. If so, then he was probably good enough to figure out my true identity. Maybe Omar would soon know I had been following him, and in that case I might as well not even board the flight back to Amman.

Maybe it was some sort of escort, a bizarre safe passage to protect me against intervening forces I had failed to detect. But if that was my employer's idea of protection, I wanted no further part of it.

I mustered enough nerve to step out for dinner around nine, and chose a small, well-lit taverna only four blocks away. Taking comfort in its clientele of local families and a few quiet Scandinavians, I ate slowly, trying not to dwell on Mila while I sipped my way through a carafe of cheap retsina as a sleeping aid. I wondered how many spies became alcoholics.

Walking back, I glanced over my shoulder several times, but no one seemed to be paying undue interest. I toyed with the idea of another trip to Aunt Aleksandra's but decided I was too exhausted. Why not wait until my work here was done? Yes, that would be better.

All things considered, I slept pretty soundly. By the time I'd had a

morning coffee I was feeling restored enough to entertain the possibility that the young men on scooters had simply been a pair of assholes
who got their jollies scaring slow old farts on Piaggios. I'd certainly seen
worse behavior on the roads of Greece. With my equilibrium nearly
restored, I decided to return to my room to prepare for one last stakeout
at the Grande Bretagne. Omar was due to leave Athens this afternoon.

The desk clerk offered her usual smile, and as I rode the elevator
to the third floor I was more convinced than ever that I had overreacted
the night before. I then threw open the door to find a shambles of
overturned furniture, scattered clothing, and tossed drawers. The place
hadn't merely been searched, it had been turned upside down. And the
worst of it, I quickly discovered, was that my laptop was gone.

The message seemed unmistakable. Someone was telling the fool
Robert Higgins that he had better get the hell out of town.

I began packing, quite happy to oblige.

19

On any country road in Greece, the dead are always with you. They stalk you at every turn, haunting their points of exit from life in the form of tiny memorials that resemble bird boxes. Gathered at blind curves and steep drop-offs, their mournful huddles warn each passing motorist: Beware. Pay attention. Watch your back.

Mila and I once counted 129 of these little shrines on the fifty kilometers between Sparti and Tripoli. At first we laughed as the number quickly mounted, but by the time the toll reached a hundred we were sufficiently spooked never to try it again.

I mention this because I was feeling a particular kinship with the dead just then. I, too, was engineering a sort of departure from life. I was officially on the lam. Absent without leave. Vanished without a trace.

Or so I hoped.

From the moment I viewed the wreckage of my hotel room in Athens I wanted out. That probably accounts for the recklessness of my exit. I dashed down the block, having left behind razor, toothbrush, and scooter. Clothes bulged from my unzipped suitcase as I pushed through the glass doorway of a tiny rental car agency and demanded a car, any car, from a bewildered clerk whose broken Greek had come by way of Albania. He seemed relieved to be able to set me up right away with a cramped Hyundai shaped like a thumb. I paid in cash using my real name. Robert Higgins was dead, slain on the battlefield of intimidation. I had tossed his passport and credit card into a Dumpster.

Without so much as glancing at a map, I folded myself into the cockpit and set out in the general direction of the expressway leading to the

Peloponnese. Why the Peloponnese? Partly because it was close. Partly because I had been there with Mila, and knew its hiding places. Partly because its remote roads would allow me to see any pursuers. But mostly because I was in a raging panic to flee Athens, and I needed someplace, *anyplace*, where I could pause to take stock.

So there I was, on an empty road in a pretty Arcadian valley somewhere between Levidi and Karkalou, at an elevation where the bracing air of autumn had already come to stay and the yellow leaves of hardwoods fluttered into sheep meadows and roadside streams. The road behind me was clear.

With each passing mile my panic eased its grip, and by the time I reached the smoky mountain village of Stemnitsa at midafternoon I was ready for coffee.

I took a seat at a rustic café that offered a view of both the highway and the steep valley below. The only other customers were a young couple with a baby.

A stooped old woman straight out of Grimm poured a muddy cup of Greek coffee from an hourglass pot of hammered brass. The grainy first sip worked its magic, linking this time and place to all the old routes of trade and conquest from centuries past. I experienced an eerie moment of kinship with each soldier and spy who had ever been on the march in these lands. Already I knew enough of the way the game worked to realize that I wouldn't be able to just drop out like this. Sooner or later, someone would find me, and I would have to return to Amman. The question, then, was how to best use my time once I went back. I figured I had a day or two at the most to come up with an answer.

I finished the coffee and felt better. Deep in the valley, a bank of clouds crept across the treetops like the smoke of an advancing wildfire. Two gunshots echoed up the hillside. Hunters, probably, shooting birds. I decided to order lunch even if it meant I would be here another hour. I knew from experience that I had better make the most of every peaceful moment while I had the chance. This was not the first time I had gone on the lam, even if my previous flight had been more of a mental journey, an escape to a place deep within, where only Mila could reach me. She, alone, had been able to lead me back to the surface. It's one reason I vowed never to let her learn her true role in the events that led to my downfall.

But I suppose it is time to come clean on those matters, if only to better explain how Black, White, and Gray were able to coax me into accepting this assignment. As I have hinted, it all goes back to Tanzania in the fall of '99, the misadventure that Black was about to detail—his version, anyway—back at the DeKuyper villa on Karos. But the seeds of that tragedy were planted in the other episode Black dredged up, the one three years earlier in Rwanda.

As you may recall, the instigator was the well-armed thug and scoundrel M. Charles Mbweli, who first approached me in Rwanda with a corrupt proposition. Mbweli controlled the suppliers and transporters for all humanitarian aid in the vicinity. So when he talked, you had to listen.

I remember clearly the first time he walked into my ramshackle headquarters. As usual, he was carrying a gun, an ugly model that he waved like a big stick of candy. He tapped it on the edge of my desk and announced that it was time to negotiate.

His pitch was pretty much as Black described it: Mbweli would be the broker to provide all emergency food, tents, and medical supplies, and in order to guarantee safe and timely delivery we were supposed to order 20 percent more than we needed. He would then pocket the additional money without providing the additional supplies. His means of keeping all of us worker bees from grumbling too loudly would be the forcible injection of some of the nectar into our bank accounts. Yeah, twist my arm, you may well be saying, just like Black did.

But Mbweli did twist my arm, as a matter of fact. Initially I turned down his offer.

"Out of the question," I said. "We don't do business that way."

At first, Mbweli was speechless. He shifted his weight in the squeaking chair and let his camouflage jacket fall open to reveal yet another gun, bulging from a shoulder holster. Then he leaned close enough for me to smell the garlic on his breath from lunch. He liked to dine at a terrible Italian joint where they made pizza crust out of stolen UN flour and used ketchup for the sauce. To his uninformed palate the cuisine was equal to Rome's finest.

"But you must do this!" he finally said, adopting the tone of a spoiled child.

"Sorry. If my requisition exceeds need by 20 percent, the bean counters might cut my next request. I can't operate on that kind of risk."

"You are wrong. No risk. Next time you again ask too much, so you still have enough after they cut it. You see?"

"No. I don't see. I'll lose credibility and maybe my job. No can do."

He rapped the gun barrel twice on my desk.

"You are wrong! Yes can do!"

He never actually pointed the gun at me. For Mbweli it was more of a business tool, his version of a BlackBerry. But it still looked threatening, propped there a foot or two from my face. I mustered the remnants of my dwindling fortitude and said, "I really am sorry, Charles. But this goes higher than me."

Mbweli let out a deep sigh and rose slowly like a boiling thunderhead. For a moment I thought he might shoot me and have his men cart me away on a UN stretcher. But I suppose he realized how bad that would have been for business, so he tried a new approach that showed he had some brains to go with his brutality.

"Then I *no can do* security guarantee for your Feeding Station Blue."

Feeding Station Blue was a magic location on my list of our outposts. Mila ran it, and somehow Mbweli had found out.

"They are on the fringe, you know," he continued. "Bad guerrilla country there. A lot of shooting and raids. No guarantees there. *No can do* for security. You see?"

I could have moved her, of course. I had enough authority to engineer it. But his mind had already considered the same possibility.

"If you move her," he said, "I will find out where. So no tricks with me, you see? You make deal or I make tricks with you and your woman. Station Blue or wherever else. You see?"

Maybe I was tired. Or maybe I thought he just might do something foolish like having one of his men kill or kidnap Mila. Whatever the reason, my resolve crumbled on the spot. Mbweli got his money, we got our supplies, and most everyone who got wind of the shaky arrangement dismissed it as the price of doing business in a landscape of guns and chaos.

Mila eventually heard a few details of the dirty deal—complaints about Mbweli were rampant in those days—but I made sure she never learned of the threat that sealed it. And I figured that with any luck, next time I wouldn't be operating within range of Mbweli.

But three years later there he was, back on my doorstep with his hand out. We had set up shop just down the way from Rwanda in the borderlands of Tanzania, this time to await a surge of refugees fleeing the Republic of Congo.

Frankly, I was surprised to see him so far afield. One's sphere of influence in such matters generally depended on connections with local clan leaders and village elders, and I knew Mbweli had few such contacts in Tanzania. Furthermore, he had a powerful rival in the local marketplace, a fellow named Paul Uwase who was willing to ease the provision and delivery of the goods for only a few small bribes, and nothing even approaching the 20 percent cut demanded by Mbweli. We had also recently fortified security at all our feeding stations.

Yet he demanded the same arrangement as before. So I told him no. He raged for a few minutes, uttered a vague threat or two, and then departed. End of story.

Or it would have been, if not for the well-meaning actions of my wife.

As I mentioned, Mila had been a vigorous interventionist ever since her disaster in Sarajevo. She took advantage of every chance to right bureaucratic wrongs, or tweak the system to ease suffering, even if she had to skirt the rules. This practical brand of zeal was almost always a plus, and whenever we set up shop somewhere new Mila cultivated local sources to help circumvent corrupt officials and opportunistic thugs. She was particularly effective in connecting with women, whose potential influence was often overlooked, and in Tanzania that fall she quickly developed ties with the wives and concubines of the local elders. In fact, Mila was my initial source for the knowledge that Uwase, not Mbweli, was the prevailing local power broker.

So it was that when she heard through her women's grapevine of Mbweli's visit to my office, she set her network into action. I suppose she feared I might cave in otherwise, based on what had happened before, although at the time we never discussed it. We were somewhat out of touch during those crucial few days. The roads were unsafe and in terrible condition, radio communication was patchy, and Mila had been dispatched temporarily to a location several hours away. That meant I didn't hear about her actions until days later, from an indignant Uwase himself, and by then it was far too late to repair the damage.

As best as I've been able to determine, the events unfolded something like this:

Mila, hoping to stop Mbweli in his tracks, spread the word through her network that Mbweli was trying to cut in on Uwase's action. If allowed to succeed, she warned, he would insist on a rapacious 20 percent cut, and everyone would suffer. This news filtered back to Uwase the day after he and I struck a deal. By then, Mbweli was out of the picture.

Given the weird logic that rules in such chaotic locales, I suppose Uwase's reaction was predictable enough. Rather than be grateful that someone had helped block the competition, he felt instead that he had been played for a fool. Outraged at having settled for peanuts when he, too, might have raked in up to 20 percent, Uwase decided to change his terms without telling me or anyone else—meaning that Mila never heard either. So he took the full payment, but when the convoys arrived with our food and supplies, they were 20 percent short of the expected load.

I was stunned, but not overwhelmed. Shortages had occurred before on my watch, and I had always managed to overcome them. Up to that point, refugees had been reaching our area at a manageable rate, and as long as nothing unexpected happened we might still hold out fine until a supplemental order could be filled.

Then the unexpected happened. A sudden flare-up of fighting sent tens of thousands more rushing our way. The first two days were bad enough, when malnourished children bore the brunt of the suffering. To stretch our thin supplies, we weighed all the young arrivals to determine the most urgent cases. I hoisted bony infants and toddlers onto a swing scale one by one, weighing each like some meager offering to be shrink-wrapped for a supermarket on the wrong side of town. They seldom cried. Their mothers, too, were oddly subdued, abiding the long lines with the patience of people who have been waiting all their lives. Flies swarmed every head, seeking entry to cuts, mouths, eyes, nostrils. With their boundless energy and incessant buzzing they were like jazzed electrons orbiting inert nuclei, the quantum mechanics of slow death.

Just as we began thinking we might actually make it through with only hundreds of deaths instead of thousands, the third day brought a measles epidemic. It engulfed everyone rushing toward us and quickly spread into the camps, where, due to our shortage of tents, thousands of people were exposed all day to the brutal sunlight.

By noon of the third day death had gained the upper hand, and by sunset the rout was on. The horror of the days that followed remains with me still, and I doubt that even a thousand sunsets on Karos could diminish its potency.

One of my worst moments occurred when I was pressed into duty on a burial detail. Already worn out from lack of sleep, I was directing a backhoe to the lip of a trench when I stumbled over the edge, and landed with a sickening slap against the cool, soft flesh of two rotting bodies. Too exhausted to climb out unaided, I stood for several dreadful minutes before anyone could lend a hand, my footing unsteady atop flesh and bone. I averted my eyes from what my nose told me was below, but to my fevered mind the maggoty squirm of decomposition seemed palpable through the soles of my shoes, and the stench was so unbearable that I nearly passed out. I strained to raise my face above the edge of the trench as much for a fresh breath of air as to escape what had suddenly become the grave for my sanity.

And that was not all. With food running out at our stations, hundreds of encamped refugees gave up altogether and headed overland through dangerous territory. Around noon the next day a radio flash alerted us to the consequences for one such group, which had been ambushed on a vulnerable stretch of highway.

I arrived with three others in one of our white trucks. The only sound when we reached the carnage was the maddening buzz of the flies in the red stickiness of the butchered corpses. Bodies had been hacked open like sacks of ordure. Slain mothers still held children in their arms. There were probably no more than a few dozen victims, but it might as well have been a million considering my state of mind.

Then came the final blow. A survivor, one of only three, clambered painfully to his knees to tell us that the massacre had been the work of Mbweli's men. The news puzzled my colleagues, but not me. The brigand must have heard that Uwase got the same deal I had refused him, and then decided to take out his frustrations on the helpless.

A colleague told me later that when it came time to leave the scene I just stood on the road with my mouth agape, one foot propped on a corpse. I was unable to utter a word or move a muscle, and the others bundled me into the truck along with the survivors. The doctors called it a combination of exhaustion, sleep deprivation, and dehydration. But it was something else, too, of course—the burden of knowing about the well-meaning deed of Mila's that had helped set the catastrophe in motion. By week's end I had been airlifted to the States and was back in Boston.

In an earlier time people would have called my collapse a nervous breakdown. In today's world it was diagnosed as a severe case of post-traumatic stress disorder, and people were fool enough to feel sorry for me.

Because Mila and I weren't yet married, it took her nearly a week to arrange a visa to be at my side. So for a while I was alone. I spent a few days in a hospital and then moved to my parents' house. In retrospect it is appalling how unhelpful they were initially, although it shouldn't surprise me. They had been deeply disappointed when I gave up a career in law to go gallivanting around the world, and the way they saw it I had now bungled even that modest vocation. The idea of facing not only an in-house audit but also a therapist or two was just the sort of messiness they would never be able to explain to their friends.

Fortunately, Mila's arrival changed everything. She became my ambassador-at-large to my parents, and also to my sisters and cousins, a tireless shuttle diplomacy that eventually yielded love and, almost miraculously, a measure of respect for what I had endured. She then plugged into my old network of friends and wisely spirited me away to a pal's vacation home in upstate New York, where I watched cows graze and leaves fall between lengthy naps and marathon viewings of cable television.

It was during this interlude that she really came into her own. Mila was my nurse, my lover, and my confessor, abidingly ready to hear every thought and doubt—except, of course, the one crucial item that I could never tell her. Having seen how shattered she had been in Sarajevo, I knew that the truth of what had happened in Tanzania might crush her beyond repair.

All the same, there were times when I was tempted to unload the burden, especially when I had to face a UN board of inquiry to explain how we had botched things so badly. I went down to Manhattan to prepare for that fiasco, thinking that I was ready, only to fall asleep in a deputy director's office while waiting for a midday appointment. He found me snoring on a couch, and no one had the heart to wake me until the office closed at five. I went to my hotel room and slept for two days more, until the manager knocked on the door to make sure all was well.

Mila helped me through that spell, too, and when the investigators finally got down to business I might have spilled everything if not for her care and compassion. As it was, I shouldered as much blame as I could. Fortunately some of the paperwork had gone missing, and my cover story was that I had blown it by underestimating our need for supplies, and then Uwase had compounded my error by skimming some of the goods as favors for his warlord allies.

They bought it, for the most part. And at the time they never learned about the earlier irregularities with Mbweli in Rwanda, which planted the seeds for the disaster. It would be left to Black, White, and Gray to make that connection. So I survived with only a demotion.

Besides, the world at large had never come pounding on the UN's door to demand an explanation. Everyone in Europe and the United States had grown so accustomed to grim news out of Africa that no one raised a cry, or even an eyebrow. Hardly surprising, since not a single foreign correspondent had visited our camp during that horrific week. The only filmed record of our catastrophe is the fuzzy one that is forever unspooling in my head.

It was while Mila and I were awaiting reassignment that it occurred to me that perhaps I could give her the life she wanted, after all. I, too, now wanted to wall myself up in some safer location, and what better place to do that than on an island, with an entire sea for a moat?

The ultimate irony was that we were able to afford our house on Karos thanks partly to the money that Mbweli had transferred into my account three years earlier. At the time it occurred it would have been too complicated and would have raised too many questions to simply disburse it elsewhere. My intention had always been to someday dispose of it in a charitable manner. But after Tanzania it seemed almost like justifiable compensation—with "almost" being the key word—for the price of my silence. Protection money to keep Mila's secret safe forever.

After a few more months of filling in at various desk jobs around the UN's warren of Manhattan offices, we both went back into the field. This time I was at a lower pay grade, which I welcomed because it meant I no longer had the burden of responsibility for deciding how much was enough.

A year after that we were married, and began planning our eventual escape. Mila knew it had taken something terrible to change my outlook, but with each passing year I was able to bury the secret that much deeper. And if Black, White, and Gray had not come along, I'm sure it would have been concealed forever.

So now you know my main mission in this assignment. Not just to give my employers the secrets they crave, but to conceal the very ones that could destroy Mila and me. That's why, despite having flown the coop from Athens, I knew I would eventually return to the chase. Come what may, my work had to be completed, if only because the consequences of failure were unthinkable.

My lunch arrived, and I was suddenly ravenous. From my vantage point in the café I saw that the clouds had moved farther down the valley. By now I was the only customer left, and the road was still quiet. I paid my bill and left.

Halfway down the mountain, on the long, narrow downgrade to Megalopoli, I overtook the rain clouds. The downpour slanted into the windshield, and I slowed to a crawl before nearly being blown off the road by a passing dump truck, just as three small memorials beckoned from the right shoulder.

"Next time," they seemed to say.

I pressed the accelerator to the floor and didn't look back.

For the next two hours I fought my way through rush hour around Kalamata and stuck to the coastline. By then the sun was sinking into the hills across the Gulf of Messinia, and I was tiring. That was when I spotted a sign for a small resort along an empty stretch of roadway, and braked just in time to turn left into a broad driveway up the hillside. It was a cluster of new but simple cottages, and the only other car in sight was parked at the office. The innkeeper seemed happy for some off-season business, and we quickly settled on a cut rate of twenty-five euros, plus another euro for a beer from the office fridge. I paid in full, whereupon he announced he was heading home, meaning I would have the place to myself and could leave as early as I liked the next morning.

I parked the car well out of sight of the highway, and after dropping my bag I threw open a shuttered French door onto a stone patio with a stunning view across the bay. The only sound was the chirping of crickets.

I poured the beer into a bathroom glass and slouched into a patio chair. Just as I was entertaining the idea of perhaps holing up here for a day longer, a flicker of movement to my right told me I had company— a cat, of course. Even here there was no escaping them, and he yowled for a handout. I vowed to depart in the morning.

An hour later I, too, was hungry, so I drove toward the nearest lights on the horizon, which turned out to be a coastal village a few miles south. There was a single taverna on a spit of rocky land above the sea. The proprietor had lowered a sheet of clear plastic around the terrace to ward off the chill, but you could still see the bright lights of Kalamata lining the shore to the north.

It was a dreary place, with slow service and a blaring television mounted on the wall next to the register. An older German couple to my right barely made a peep as they ate, and the only other customers were a noisy couple, probably local, who seemed comically mismatched. She was a platinum blonde in her early twenties, wearing a dress with a low neckline. He was at least fifty, with a huge belly and a scratchy but roaring baritone—Don Corleone on steroids. He kept calling the waiter over to refill her wineglass from a large carafe.

As my meal arrived, a tough and stringy cutlet, limp fries, pale tomatoes, and an Amstel—the only warm item among them—the TV blared an ad for an old James Bond film, one of the early ones with Sean Connery. Dubbed clips showed beautiful women in casinos, and then

Connery in a tux uttering his signature line, the same in any language—
"Bond. James Bond"—as he slid a stack of chips across a roulette table.

I smiled, wondering if Bond had ever settled for such a leathery strip
of meat while shivering in his anorak in a drafty off-season café, feeling
lonely and out of sorts. No gorgeous blondes here, unless you counted
the bimbo snuggled with the town blowhard. This was the real life of a
spy, I supposed. Injecting cinematic drama would have required the
Germans at the next table to suddenly leap to their feet and reveal themselves as confederates of Herr Doktor Krieger. They would brandish
their cutlery in a martial arts pose and convey me to a waiting car.

This got me thinking about Krieger. What had passed between him
and Omar? Money, apparently, but had there been something more? A
blueprint of a U.S. military installation, for instance? Marching orders
for some atrocity? I smiled again, this time at the absurdity of such
ideas, which seemed more Bond-like than realistic. The better possibility was that the German had given Omar a few snapshots of his grand-
children.

Yet here I was, in the middle of nowhere, having gone on a one-day
lam after convincing myself the stakes were too high and the players too
lethal. I felt foolish, and I resolved to return to Athens first thing tomorrow. I would visit Mila, put my mind at ease, and set us back on course.
Then I would take the ferry out to Karos to retrieve my things, catch my
scheduled flight back to Amman, and finish the job. Because what was I
really up against, after all, except an elderly German, a genial old friend
from my days on the West Bank, some lowlife from Jersey, and three
blandly efficient Americans who obviously had too much time and government money at their disposal. Young toughs in Bakaa could be
avoided. Hotheads on motorcycles eventually drove in another direction. I would be fine.

I ordered another beer. The big Greek fellow across the room was
now demanding that the channel be changed on the television. The
waiter switched to a show with loud music and dancers in traditional
costumes. That made the young woman giggle until the big guy told her
harshly to shut up.

As I downed the second beer, my confidence continued to grow. Perhaps I was not as powerless in my current arrangement as I thought.
Maybe I, too, had some reinforcements I could call on. The aid business, like the spy trade, is rich in such connections. It, too, is a vast marketplace of privileged information. It's why their world sometimes
recruited from ours, and over the years I had met a few people who had

later crossed over into intelligence work. So, I asked myself, who among past friends and acquaintances might better know the ways of this secret world? Three names came to mind, all of them with experience in the Middle East. I vowed to get in touch as soon as possible. Then I called for the bill.

Outside, the night was quiet. It was so dark I had to let my eyes adjust before groping my way to the car. Halfway there a voice called out.

"You dropped these back in Athens, Freeman."

There was a man by the Hyundai. I couldn't see his face, but he placed something on the roof, then stepped away as I moved closer. I reached atop the car and found the passport and charge card for Robert Higgins.

"Don't miss your flight back to Amman," the voice said. By now he was a good twenty feet away, and I heard his footsteps disappear around the corner. I listened a few moments for a car or motorcycle, but there was nothing. Odder still, the episode barely fazed me. Maybe it was the tranquilizing effect of the beer. But I also credited my newfound resolve. In this business, I supposed, there were always people like that, popping up from nowhere, trying to put you in your place. Well, let them. To survive as an independent operative I would call on sources of my own for help and information. The more I knew, the better off I would be.

It was a good thought to sleep on, and I slept well, stirring only once when a car came prowling through the lot. There was a brief flash of headlights between the shutters, and seconds later I heard the car accelerate down the highway.

I rose early and left before the innkeeper returned. The highway was empty, but I knew better than to be deceived by appearances. Never again would I assume I was unwatched or alone. But before returning to Amman, or even Karos, I needed to see the one person I was doing all this for. It was time to visit Mila.

20

I decided to surprise her. No sense alerting our watchers with a phone call to a monitored line.

But as I knocked on the door after an all-day drive I wondered if it was such a good idea. I didn't know, for instance, what Mila had told Aunt Aleksandra about our present circumstances. This could be awkward.

Mila's cousin Marica opened the door and cried out in happy surprise. I saw her across the room on the couch, wineglass in hand, seated between two men I didn't recognize. Aunt Aleksandra was nowhere to be seen. For all I knew this was the same foursome I'd watched leaving the building for a night on the town.

It seemed to take her a second to register that it was actually me. Her mouth dropped open, then she gave a stifled yelp and broke into a huge grin.

"Freeman!"

She nearly spilled her wine bolting to her feet, and in a moment of endearing comedy she turned to and fro, looking for somewhere to put her glass. It was finally taken off her hands by one of the mystery males, who I must say looked less than thrilled to oblige. I stepped across the room and she rushed into my arms.

"My God, I can't believe it!"

"I wanted it to be a surprise. Glad to see it worked."

"Is it done, then? Are you finished?"

Her happiness had outrun the speed of my explanation, and it felt terrible to have to reel her back to reality.

"No. I can only stay for a while. I'm on my way to Karos to pick up some of my things."

"Oh."

Her embrace lost its urgency, and some of the light went out of her eyes.

"Well, come in, then. Someone get him a drink."

For a moment she seemed a little flustered. Who knows what she'd told the rest of them about the reason for my absence. Maybe by showing up like this I had inadvertently made her look like a fool.

"Can you at least stay the night?"

"I wish. But no. I'm catching the last ferry. Have to make it back tomorrow morning for a noon flight."

"Well, stay for a few drinks, then."

"Here's a glass," Marica said. "We should toast you. Mila says you're doing lots of difficult work. Something about a refugee charity?"

"Yes. Building a hospital." I glanced at Mila, figuring she would signal if I was straying from her script.

"Best of luck, then. Here's to Freeman."

"Thank you."

Mila then introduced me to the men on the couch, which gave me a chance for a closer look. One was Marica's boyfriend, Luka. The other one was Petros, and he looked several years younger than Mila. He was trim and fairly handsome, with dark, curly hair and a thin gold chain around his neck. A prototypical Mediterranean man on the make, in other words. Judging from the amount of sun in his complexion, I guessed that he worked outdoors. Construction, maybe.

"They've all been keeping me entertained," Mila said, gesturing at the others.

"Where's your aunt Aleksandra?"

I immediately felt foolish for asking. The timing made it sound like I thought they needed a chaperone. Maybe I did think that.

"Out with friends," Marica said. "My mother never misses her card night. Have you eaten?"

"No. But please don't go to any trouble. It's early, and I picked up a few things to eat on the ferry."

The five of us chatted a while longer. I say "five" but Petros contributed little more than nods and assents.

Luka asked about my work, and I noticed Mila stiffen. I uttered a few vague phrases about helping Palestinians.

"Do you travel much?" he asked. "What are your duties like?"

Mila leaped in to change the subject.

"Speaking of travels, we're going to Glyfada next week."

Glyfada was a crowded beach resort favored by Athenians. I couldn't help but picture Mila stretched out on the sand, her top removed for sunbathing, with this fellow Petros oiled up on the towel next to her, basting himself an even deeper shade of bronze.

"It's just for the day," she added, which of course made me wonder if the plan was actually to stay overnight.

"All four of you?"

Now she was blushing. Luka jumped back in.

"Well, we're certainly not taking Marica's mother."

This produced some welcome laughter.

"You know, Luka," Marica said, "maybe Freeman and Mila would like some time to themselves before he has to go."

"That would be nice," Mila said.

I thought so, too, given the direction the conversation had taken. We went down the hall to the room Mila shared with Marica. She gently shut the door for privacy, then sat on the end of the bed with her feet tucked beneath her. I leaned back against the headboard.

"Can you at least tell me how things are going?" she asked.

"Slower than I hoped."

I didn't want to get into the details of the past few days, particularly not my little scare with the motorcyclists and having my room trashed. I also didn't want to admit to her that I had been stalking Omar through the streets of Athens.

"But I've got a plan of action worked out," I added. "Maybe now I'll get to the bottom of things quicker."

"And how is Omar?"

"Fine, from what I can tell. They ask about you. Hanan sends her love."

Mila nodded. The subject seemed awkward for her as well. Both of us were probably wondering if Hanan would still be sending her love once my work was done.

"So far I haven't found out anything that Omar should be ashamed of, even by Black, White, and Gray's standards."

"Maybe it will end that way."

"Let's hope."

"And you're safe?"

"Sure. The usual creeps and watchers, of course. Or I guess they're usual in this kind of work. Which reminds me." I had been wondering how to broach this subject without alarming her, but it needed to be addressed. "Do you ever get a sense that anyone is, well, keeping an eye on you here?"

"So it's not just my imagination, then?"

"What do you mean?"

"I'm not sure. Maybe you could tell me."

I couldn't mention the car that was following them the other night without admitting I'd been spying on her as well.

"I guess what I'm trying to say is that you should always assume they're keeping an eye on you. Particularly after some of those phone calls you made. Have you noticed anything?"

"There have been a few times when I've wondered. A face in the street that looks familiar. Maybe a car going by. I'm probably overreacting."

"No. Trust your instincts. Don't let your guard down. I've had a few surprises myself. So stick with your cousin."

"Even if Petros comes along?"

"I'm sorry. I must have sounded like a jealous fool."

"Maybe that's okay, too, in a way. But I wish you wouldn't jump to the worst possible conclusion. You're just going to have to trust me."

"I know. I do know that. Who is he, though?"

She shook her head.

"A friend of Luka's. They work together. He's *their* age, for God's sake. Or closer to theirs than mine. He's just fun to have along."

"As long as that's all it is."

I regretted the words the moment they were out of my mouth, but the vehemence of her response startled me all the same.

"Don't think you can just walk in here and do this, Freeman!"

"Do what?"

"All but accuse me of something, like you expect me to apologize. Especially when you won't even say what it is you're really doing, or why you're really doing it."

"Why should I expect you to apologize? For what?" It was the Jersey boy's words coming out in me. I knew that even as I spoke them but still couldn't help myself.

"Oh, stop. Not now. Not when you're the one who's holding out."

"We've covered this ground before, Mila. There are good reasons I can't tell you more."

"But you won't even tell me the reasons. Look, if you're doing this because you think that, for whatever reason—legal action, publicity, extortion, you name it—those men and whoever they work for could force you to relive all those terrible experiences in Africa again, then okay, I understand. I really do. But you don't need to feel that way, because no matter what happened I would be with you, just like before. I can help you get through all of it again, however they choose to bring it back. I really can."

"It's not that simple."

"But it *can* be."

I shook my head. I could go no further without entering dangerous territory, so I backed away from the edge and sighed deeply. There was no tenable way to keep her from thinking I had sunk into this predicament due to my own weakness, so I just had to live with the idea that she would keep believing it. I suppose that was one reason I had let my jealousy get the best of me. If I could really explain everything, she would thank me. But she might also be destroyed.

"No. It can't be that simple," I finally said. "I'm sorry, but that's how it is. Please just trust me on this, Mila."

"As long as you're willing to do the same."

About Petros, she meant. And she was right, of course.

"Sure. I can do that. Come here. I'm sorry."

We met in the middle of the bed, both in need of comfort and reassurance. The half-light of dusk cast a gloom on the scene, especially since we knew I had to catch the ferry soon. Too much damage from too few words, with too little time to repair it.

We talked for another half hour, mostly low-key. I gave her the e-mail address I'd set up in case she needed to tell me something she didn't feel comfortable discussing over the phone. Then we returned to the living room. This time around, Petros didn't seem half as alluring, so I guess I'd accomplished at least that much for my peace of mind. I just hoped I had done some good for Mila as well, but I wondered. Shortly afterward we said good-bye and I headed for the subway to the ferry port in Piraeus.

On my way out of the parking lot I glanced across the street to where I'd seen the black sedan the other night. It hadn't been there when I arrived, but damned if it wasn't there now. I couldn't see the Jersey boy for the smoked glass, but at that moment a cigarette lighter flared, as if to pointedly let me know that, yes, he was there.

I broke into a run. But before I could even reach the street the engine started and the sedan eased smoothly away. No squeal of tires.

No sign of panic. Just a casual dodge by someone showing me who was in charge.

I tried to swallow my rage. Shouting in anger might bring Mila and the others down to investigate.

"Go ahead and watch her," I wanted to scream. "But keep your distance."

Then, for a fleeting moment, I was back in the role of jealous husband, wondering exactly what this snoop would be seeing in the days ahead.

21

Washington

full minute passed while Aliyah waited for Abbas to speak again. She was still crouched on the floor, knees cramping while she watched his face for any sign of what would come next.

It gave her time to consider every possible consequence, and she was surprised to realize they still had so much to lose. The aftermath of Shereen's death had convinced her that nothing else could ever be so painful or costly, but now she wondered. They still had their son, their home, and their many years together. All were now at risk, awaiting the verdict from her silent husband as he gazed down with eerie calm.

Perhaps a logical explanation was still possible, some strange but reassuring set of circumstances that would add up to something other than a crazy plan to blow up a church. Or maybe it was nothing but an intellectual exercise, an odd form of therapy in which the planning had become an end in itself.

If so, then why sign a lease? Abbas had never been the type to squander money on a mere abstraction.

At last he spoke, in a steady voice that neither scolded nor accused. The coolness made his pronouncement all the more shocking.

"You cannot stop me, Aliyah. You can tell whoever you like—that is out of my hands. Even the police, if you wish. Then someone will come take me away, and nothing will ever happen. But I won't stop voluntarily. Not for you, not for anyone. Because I am doing this for Shereen."

She nodded slowly while wondering what to say. Her response was crucial. Push him away now and he would redouble his efforts at secrecy. Then her only alternative would be to turn him in, as he had suggested. With that in mind, she seized upon a sudden inspiration. She spoke slowly, and tried mightily to match his even tone.

"What makes you think I want to stop you? Don't you think I want the same thing?"

"No. That's not possible. It's not your way. Even if it was, you can't help me. It would complicate everything."

"What choice do you have? I have to help you now."

The pain in her knees had grown sharp enough to bring tears to her eyes. She wanted to cry out, but didn't dare, not while they were out on this ledge where the slightest push might send him to oblivion.

Abbas sighed, in either impatience or exasperation. That was when she knew she had a chance. It was her only alternative—enlist in his mad scheme in hopes of somehow diverting it before it came to fruition or led to his arrest. *Their* arrest, she reminded herself. The stakes couldn't be higher.

"You are certain?" he asked, a note of skepticism in his voice.

She again sensed a need for just the right words. Sound too assured and he wouldn't believe her. Abbas had always mistrusted instant conversions, and Aliyah was the deliberate sort who reached decisions by degrees, after careful consideration. Yet wavering might also be fatal.

"No," she said. "I'm not certain. Although I'm getting there. I think I've been getting there all along, from the time I started to figure out what you were up to. Maybe that's why I haven't said anything 'til now. I can promise you one thing. I won't try to stop you, even if I'm not sure how much I want to help. But I can only keep that promise if you share your thoughts along the way. About everything. So you must tell me about all of this." She held up the awful book, still open to the chapter on bomb making. "And you can start with why you've leased that building across the street from the senator's church."

He seemed taken aback that she had pieced together so many details, but he didn't ask how.

"Fair enough."

He held out a hand to help her up. She suppressed a cry of relief as she stood. Most of the feeling in her legs was gone, and it was all she could do to walk.

"Make some coffee," he said, "and we'll talk. I'll tell you what I can. But first, tell me one more thing."

"Yes?"

"Why? Why would you want to help? And don't say it is because of your grief, or your talks with Annie Felton. You see her to reduce your anger, not to build it up. This will take you in the exact opposite direction. Why, then? Why choose my way?"

She sensed this was the last and most important hurdle. It was like landing in the middle of an ancient myth to face a bridge-keeper's riddle. A lie wouldn't work. He knew her too well. Unless the lie concerned the one part of her life he had studiously avoided, to the point of ridicule. Her religion. He would probably believe that almost anything could have transpired during her journey of faith.

"It is not out of anger," she said slowly, carefully. "It is out of a sense of rightness, of justice. Holy justice. The kind they talk about at the mosque."

Then she quoted a sura from the Quran that she well remembered, not because she had taken it to heart but because she had found it so disturbing. It was like one of those fiery biblical verses the televangelists spouted on late-night cable.

" 'Believers, retaliation is decreed for you in bloodshed.' Those are the words of the Holy Prophet. Annie's words teach me control, but at the mosque I learn about God's power, and how to marshal it and direct it from within."

Abbas nodded slowly, as if taking stock of this new side of his wife's personality. Maybe it frightened him a little.

"Well, this is no jihad for me, I can tell you that," he said at last. "It's strictly personal. To send them all a message."

"Addition by subtraction?" she said, unable to keep a hint of derision from seeping into Skip Ellington's words. "I thought you said it wasn't a doctor's job to play God."

"I'm still keeping all my oaths. I would never betray my role as a healer. This is a job I'm doing as a man, as a father. And, yes, you may call it addition by subtraction if you like. Because I will be doing the world a favor. Righting a wrong, if only by letting them know what they're up against. I will become their worst nightmare, an enemy who is educated, secular, and thoroughly assimilated. One of them. They won't know what to make of *anyone*. So I refuse to make this a godly cause for your benefit, and I will not allow you to make it one. But as long as you can help, and know how to keep a secret, well . . . maybe."

He threw his hands in the air, apparently resigned to her participation, or at least to her knowledge.

Aliyah had to admit there was a terrible brilliance to what he had said. He *would* be their worst nightmare, and for precisely the reasons he outlined. But he was wrong if he thought that would change their behavior for the better. Rather than awakening to reason, they would resort to further insanity and suspicion and would lash out even more. She considered arguing the point, but decided it was too risky. Delusions such as his could never be overcome by mere words. She wondered anew about whatever drug he was taking. In his current state of mind, this plan must seem like the most logical thing in the world. So she nodded, sealing their pact, and then went to the kitchen to make coffee.

By the time she reached the sink her legs were wobbly and she wanted to be sick. The moment's grotesque unreality had unstrung her—the idea that this man she lived with, slept with, and had loved for ages could somehow reconcile a lifetime of saving others with such a hideous plan for murder, and then discuss it with such rational directness. She collected herself for a moment as the water ran into the pot, fighting back tears of fear and disappointment. He was ill, she told herself, ill and in need of her help. And she could provide that only by making the journey with him. Then, at some key moment, she would gently take the wheel and steer him out of harm's way.

"When did you first get the idea?" she called out, laboring to keep her voice from trembling.

"A few weeks ago."

He took a seat at the kitchen table, as if this were just another evening at home together and they were discussing the day's news.

"It was that story on NPR."

"The bombing in Kandahar? The one you thought was such genius?"

"I thought you weren't listening. I was hoping you weren't."

"I wasn't. But it all came back to me tonight, once I started putting the pieces together."

Then she asked the question that scared her most.

"How far along are you?"

"Not far enough."

He creased his brow in worry. Her spirits lifted. There was hope, and with each passing day perhaps there would be more.

"Then you *do* need my help."

"You may be right. Sit down. I'll tell you where I am, and what I need."

She did as he asked, and listened incredulously as he spelled out his plan down to the smallest details. All along she tried to discern points of weakness and vulnerability that she might exploit later. And she was heartened to discover that she had at least one important ally. Time.

"What scares me most," Abbas said, "is that the senator could die any day. One infection, one further complication—just about anything—would be enough to make it a matter of hours, maybe a day or two at the most. That's the point he has reached. So of course I've been doing all I can to make sure that doesn't happen. The family can hardly believe I'm spending so much time on him. They think it's compassion, of course. Or maybe they think the hospital is trying to curry favor. It's always politics with them.

"His wife is the only one who isn't a cynic. She's convinced that somehow the old fool must have won me over, which only shows how blind she is to everything else. So I let her believe it."

Aliyah wondered how he managed to face them day after day while knowing that they would be among his victims. But she supposed that in his twisted new way of seeing the world, his zealous care was yet another affirmation that he was still upholding his professional ethics. Kill as an avenging bomber, but never as a caring doctor.

"My other problem is expertise," he said, "and, frankly, manpower. Getting a tunnel dug properly, underneath the alley to just below the church, then getting the right explosives. The book's a little outdated. It's too hard doing it with fertilizer anymore. Too many controls now on bulk buying. And I think this is where you might be able to help."

"With explosives?"

He shook his head.

"Expertise. Or finding it. Meeting with someone who can help us. I already have a local contact. But he has referred me to someone abroad."

"Where?"

"Jordan. In Amman. They've passed word they're willing to help."

"You're not corresponding by e-mail, I hope. Or by phone?"

"Goodness, no. No one with any brains would try that anymore. Personal contacts. Relayed messages. But they want me to make the next move. I am supposed to demonstrate my commitment, as they put it."

"With money?"

"That, too. But also a visit. To show that I mean business. So I've decided to go there, if only for a day or two. That's where they're supposed to teach me what I need to know."

"In Jordan?"

He nodded. She was astounded.

"Were you going to tell me?"

"Of course. But I was going to say it was for a medical reason. Some special patient who requested my assistance. A prominent Arab. I had already come up with a cover story for both you and the hospital. But that's not my real worry. I'm wondering if I will even be allowed to go. I doubt it will be so easy for me to travel overseas anymore. Not after what happened in New York."

During the Circle Line fiasco, he meant. The stupid misunderstanding that led to their arrest, and then to Abbas's being locked up while clueless authorities debated whether his past donations to Palestinian aid organizations made him a threat to national security.

A few angry letters from his hospital colleagues, plus the discreet pressure applied by a few former patients, had finally freed him, and no charges were filed. But now his name was out there, perhaps still on some watch list. Any trip abroad might bring on renewed scrutiny when he could least afford it, especially if he traveled to a destination such as Jordan.

Aliyah saw her opportunity and seized it.

"Let me go, then. I'm not on anyone's list."

If he assented, then she knew she could stop him, as long as the senator cooperated by not living too long. Once in Jordan, she would do whatever it took to engineer the necessary obstructions. Missed appointments. Delayed flights. Unkept promises. Contacts who failed to show. The possibilities abounded. And while she was at it, she might even learn the best ways to thwart him—which wires to snip, which contacts to loosen to ensure that a bomb couldn't possibly explode. It would probably be far tougher than she envisioned, but anything would be better than just letting events run their course, and this way she could take an active hand in stopping him. It was the best she had felt all morning.

But Abbas frowned. Then he shook his head.

"I can't risk it," he said. "I don't think you realize how dangerous this might be."

Aliyah reached across the table and took his hands in hers. Then she looked him in the eye.

"Don't think of it as *my* risk. Think of it as *ours*. Haven't we always handled our family's biggest challenges together, you and me? Until Shereen died, anyway. Maybe it's time we got that back. It was always our way before, and it should be again. Now more than ever. Let me do this for you."

"Maybe you're right. And they'll be impressed by your faith. That was the one part I was dreading, having to fake that. Although from what I gather, the contact is more the pragmatic type."

"What's his name?"

Abbas retreated to his study for a moment, and she heard him rummaging through his papers. He returned with a single sheet, which he handed to her across the table. She didn't recognize the handwriting, and the information was scant—only a first name and a phone number, and the name of what sounded to her like a charity, and a respectable one at that.

"This is who we're supposed to see?"

"Yes."

"And he wouldn't object to meeting with a woman?"

"I'll check. But I don't think so. Like I said, he is supposedly pious, but also very pragmatic. Whatever gets the job done. He only wants to be assured of my commitment. Maybe sending my wife is all he will need. Then you can find out the information we need and return as soon as possible."

"How long will I have?"

"The senator should last at least another few weeks, assuming nothing unexpected happens. I figure I'll need at least two for the work, even with some help. So you should try to finish up within a week. The visa you can get in a day. The ticket, too. So what do you think? Leave on Wednesday, maybe? Can you get the time off from work?"

"I'll tell them it's a family emergency. But there are some loose ends I'd like to tie up first, so I might need a day or two. Why don't we say Friday?"

He frowned, but nodded. Already she had bargained away two days of his precious time. The moment she hit the ground in Jordan she could begin using up more. It would work—she was sure of it. Unless the senator surprised them all, of course, and kept on living for weeks on end. In which case Aliyah would find some other way out of this mess. If she was expected to gain enough knowledge to help him, perhaps she could also gain enough knowledge to thwart him.

Either way, traveling to Jordan seemed to be her only chance of stopping him, short of turning him in to the police. By succeeding she would save both their lives, and perhaps hundreds of others.

And if she failed? She wasn't yet strong enough to consider the possibility.

She glanced at the clock on the microwave and saw that it was 5 a.m. She was exhausted.

"Let's go back to bed," she said.

Abbas nodded. He, too, looked spent.

She took his hand again, uncertainly now. Hard to believe that only a few hours ago they had been making love and she was thinking their worst days were over. They walked slowly upstairs, the bereaved suburban parents reunited in loss, now beginning their passage to someplace new and frightening.

22

I awoke with a start at sundown, just as the wheels of the jet scorched against the tarmac in a swirl of desert dust.

Somewhere below me in the baggage compartment were two large suitcases stuffed with the items I'd picked up on Karos. But the heavier burden from the visit was the memory of the empty house. It overwhelmed me with its smells of cooking, of Mila's soaps and perfumes, and the ashy taint of cigarettes left behind by the advance man for Black, White, and Gray.

Stavros made an appearance, but hardly said a word as he watched me puttering about the garden and shed, locking everything in sight. I didn't feel like telling him we might never be back. Maybe he thought we had split up. His only real concern was getting paid, and once his euros were in hand he trudged back up the hill to his goats and windswept silence. Watching his retreat, I spied the rooftop of the DeKuyper place, and with an hour to kill before catching the ferry I decided on one last trek to the scene of the crime.

I got no farther than the driveway, where the same fellow who had shooed Mila and me away again stood in my path. This time he held a rush broom instead of a shovel, medieval pikeman on patrol. I surveyed what I could of the scene. Two cars were in the drive—a Mercedes and a Jaguar, but no red Opel. Perhaps the man himself was home. The curtains were open, but there was no other sign of life. I returned to the road and followed it around the hillside to the island's southern tip. From there you could see DeKuyper's big yacht bobbing at the dock. No motor skiffs. If I ever got back here, I was determined to demand entry and an explanation.

Item one on my retooled agenda in Amman was to get in touch with the three contacts I'd thought of at the taverna. Item two was to learn more about Norbert Krieger and Professor Yiorgos Soukas. Maybe Sami would be back by now—a visit to his salon would be item three. I would plug away until I had enough information to either condemn or exonerate Omar. If doing so took longer than I had initially hoped, so be it. One of my earlier mistakes was to assume I could succeed on the cheap. Quick in, quick out. Gather a few raw materials, ship them to Black, then wash my hands of any and all repercussions.

But that course of action left the interpretation of my findings entirely up to my handlers, whose motives I no longer trusted, not after what I'd seen of their tactics. With a little extra effort and risk I might be able to first place the information in context, or sketch out its grand design. If Omar was indeed contributing to harm in this world, then I would help stop him, and do us both a favor. If not, I would clear his name. For once I would leave behind nothing to atone for.

I doubted a professional would have considered such a strategy. From what I gathered, pros didn't want to know anything beyond what was necessary to complete their assignment, in case they were caught or interrogated. But I cared little about protecting my employer's secrets. Amateur status has its advantages.

No sooner had I entered the little stone house on Othman Bin Affan Street than I was greeted by a laptop computer on the kitchen table—the very one stolen from my hotel room in Athens. Impressive, I guess. But I wasn't as rattled as I would have been even a few days ago. I headed out for groceries, and then got down to business, strolling to the Internet café I had chosen as the base for my online research.

An English-language bookstore on a neighborhood street, it kept late hours. I was the only customer, with my pick of five desktops just around the corner from the bored cashier.

I set up a Hotmail account for e-mail, then proceeded to Google. I doubt even the pros would have had such an amazing wealth of data at their fingertips fifteen years ago. The world at large was now better equipped for freelance snooping than at any time in history.

Or so I was thinking until the search for "Norbert Krieger" produced a mere five hits.

Only one seemed plausibly connected to the man I'd seen with Omar in Athens. It was an August 2002 newsletter for the Islamic Association of Germany, and listed a Norbert Krieger among several dozen guests at a fund-raising dinner. The event had been held in Munich.

Perhaps that was where he lived. I did a quick search for the Islamic organization, found its sketchy Web site, wrote down a few names and numbers, and tucked them away.

Professor Yiorgos Soukas turned up most prominently on the staff of the National Archaeological Museum in Athens, where Krieger had gone to meet him. The museum's Web site helpfully provided a link to the professor's CV. He was a specialist in Iron Age archaeological sites and had participated in two digs in the Middle East—one at Jericho, another at a site in Jordan called Wadi Fidan. Nothing about either suggested any reason he would want to contribute to a hospital for Palestinian refugees or the region's more radical activities.

The next order of business was to get in touch with my chosen contacts.

The first was Hans Wolters, my old boss from intifada days. Last I'd heard he was still somewhere across the River Jordan, although no longer on the UN payroll. He was said to be working for some peace group that preferred operating behind the scenes, functioning as middleman between parties who wouldn't be caught dead in the same room. Hans had gone deeper into the morass while most of us had deserted it altogether.

A search of his name turned up a few quotes in an eight-year-old Reuters account of a Palestinian retribution killing in Jenin, but nothing more recent. I supposed I would simply have to ask around, and the best person to start with was next on my list.

That would be Chris Boylan, the former Aussie soldier and sheep farmer who had also patrolled the mean streets for Hans and UNRWA. A mutual friend had mentioned a few years ago that Chris was leading a UN disarmament team in Afghanistan, a role in which he worked hand in glove with intelligence operatives. Later he supposedly wound up in Iraq, working for a private security contractor. If he was still there, then he and I were practically in the same neighborhood.

Sure enough, his name showed up in a *Guardian* piece from the UK, only five months old. He was quoted as a consultant for a London-based outfit called Near East Security Ltd. The firm's Web site was predictably tight-lipped but did offer an e-mail address for inquiries. Hoping for the best, I fired off a brief, general message asking if Mr. Boylan could please get in touch with his old friend, Freeman Lockhart, who was now working for an NGO in Amman.

The third name on my list might be described as a former adversary, although I had always respected his talents and his restraint. During the intifada I knew him as a patrol leader for the Israel Defense Force. Captain David Ben-Zohar was the one who figured so prominently in the famous blowup with Omar and me, when we were inquiring aggressively about the well-being of a Palestinian captive. For the most part he had treated us fairly, considering the circumstances, and had often been willing to barter information. With any luck, he still would be.

Supposedly he had been promoted up the ranks, all the way to brigadier general, before he took an early pension and formed his own security consulting business in Jerusalem for corporate clients. Yes, that line of work again—one of the world's growth industries.

Both he and his company were easy to find, although I was a bit queasy searching for them on a Jordanian computer network. A new customer sat down two seats to my left just as the logo of Ben-Zohar's company popped onto the screen in English and Hebrew, so I shifted in the chair to block his view. A moment later someone else began browsing the paperback shelves behind me. I minimized the screen and waited him out.

When the coast was clear, I clicked on an e-mail link, offered a bland hello and mentioned I was now in Amman, teamed with my old UNRWA partner, Omar al-Baroody. That alone would get his attention. Then I asked, as casually as possible, if we might meet the next time I happened to be over his way.

That was about all I could do for now. Send up a few flares and wait for help. The rest of my work was out at Bakaa, where, whether it was hazardous or not, I needed to probe deeper into the background of Nabil Mustafa and friends. Maybe that gun would be of some use after all. It was back at the house, in the same dresser drawer where I had stashed it the day I got it.

The bookstore was about to close, so I clicked on the history folder and erased the record of the sites I'd visited. I paid a few dinars and walked back to the house, and considered it a minor triumph when no message was waiting on the doorstep. After cooking up a light, simple dinner, I crawled into bed, tired yet oddly exhilarated by my small declaration of independence. The last thing I heard before falling asleep was my fellow lodger, the mouse, rising to resume his endless task of gnawing behind the baseboard.

I arrived early the next morning at the office, where the iron maiden Raniya curtly informed me that Omar was not yet back from Greece. He was two days overdue.

"Is he all right?"

Raniya seemed unmoved by my concern.

"His business took longer than expected. He asked that I tell you to take the rest of the week off. So that you may be better settled in by the time he returns."

It was an odd request, as if he knew I might snoop around in his absence.

"When will that be?"

"He will see you here on Monday."

Not exactly an answer to my question, but maybe Omar preferred it that way. Had he spotted me in Athens? Or maybe Krieger found some way to identify me. I had the whole weekend to stew about it.

"I've got some paperwork to do first," I said, unwilling to give in so easily.

I checked the files—fruitlessly—for anything under the heading of "Krieger" or "Soukas." Each time I opened a drawer Raniya sighed as if I had just stolen another dinar from the coffee fund. Two hours of this festive atmosphere was all I could stand. I decided to put off visiting Bakaa until Monday. No sense checking further on Nabil until I'd run his name by at least one of my contacts.

On my way home I stopped by the bookstore to check my Hotmail account and got a pleasant surprise. Chris Boylan had answered. Good news, if a bit cryptic.

"Freeman! Blast from the past! Yes, am still in the region. As luck would have it will soon pass your way for r&r. Can meet Tuesday if u like. Noon, courtyard Husseini Mosque? Yes-no only, pls. Regards, CB."

He was in Iraq, by the sound of it, but apparently not in the mood to reveal much by e-mail. Maybe his employer often checked over his shoulder. I fired off a quick "Yes" and continued home, where I celebrated that little success with a late lunch.

I threw open the kitchen window to the afternoon air and chopped tomatoes and peppers on a board while garlic simmered in an oiled skillet. Birds chirped and flitted in the jasmine bush outside, and I began to relax.

A pleasant voice piped up, startling me.

"Whatever you're cooking smells lovely."

It was Fiona, calling out from her garden, where she was again on her knees in the dirt, planting and pruning. She stood gracefully, thigh-high shorts showing off attractive legs, her face shaded by a straw hat. The wide brim reminded me of the one Ingrid Bergman wore in the closing scene of *Casablanca*. Or maybe Fiona's brown eyes brought the image to mind.

"You're welcome to join me," I shouted through the window. "There's more than enough."

"Only if I can bring the wine."

"Perfect. There's not a drop in the house."

"I thought that might be the case. It can be hard finding it this month."

She seemed to pointedly avoid saying "Ramadan," as if that would have been singling out Islam for blame.

The wine was already chilled.

"I'm not even sure I have a corkscrew," I said, still busy at the stove.

"Brought that, too. The glasses are up to you, I'm afraid."

"Upper right cabinet."

I glanced over my shoulder at the label as she poured, and was surprised to see it had come from Israel.

"Wouldn't have expected to see that here."

"Actually I bought this during a photo shoot in Galilee. But you can find it in Jordan if you look hard enough. Israel's doing quite a bit of business here these days. Not just selling, either."

"Investing in the boom?"

"Buying land, even."

I raised an eyebrow.

"Not always in the open, of course. But they find their ways."

I worried for a moment that she was about to remark on the shrewdness of the wily Jew, but perhaps I'd misinterpreted the tenor of her remark.

"How so? Silent partners?"

"Or very noisy partners, ones who'll go around proclaiming their pan-Arab brotherhood before handing over the deed to some consortium in Tel Aviv."

"That must go over well."

"The people making a killing from it don't seem to mind."

"Like Sami Fayez?"

"Far from it. Sami's one of the holdouts."

"Maybe he's waiting for the price to go higher."

"That's what the cynics say. Sami does have his doubters, even his enemies. But I don't think so. I've done some work for him, writing about a few heritage sites he owns. Places he wants the palace to protect before some foreigner gets hold of them."

"Is the palace receptive?"

"More often than you'd think. When half the king's friends are striking it rich, it isn't always easy saying yes to the preservationists. Of course, it isn't easy saying no to Sami, either. Just ask your friend Omar."

"Omar's been cashing in?"

"For a while he was. Then Sami made sure he got religion. Now he's on the side of the angels, supposedly. Protect everything before it's gone."

"I had no idea."

"It's not exactly a secret. Ask him. You might even get a free weekend in the desert into the bargain. Omar takes little expeditions to collect artifacts and botanical samples, he and his artist friend. They're a regular Stanley and Livingstone."

"Issa Odeh, you mean? The painter?"

"Yes. You've met him?"

"No. Saw his work in Omar's dining room. Very nice. He sounds like quite the Renaissance man."

"Or a big fish in a small pond. In Jordan you can be out on the cutting edge in about three places at once."

"You're pretty fond of this place."

She smiled shyly, and turned away with what might have been a blush. The gesture was appealing, and I found myself again wondering how to gracefully mention I was married. The optimum moment had passed, and I guiltily realized I was glad. My answer to Petros, I suppose. No harm in a little flirting.

"By the way, there was a woman who came calling for you while you were away."

"A woman?"

"Yes. Quite attractive, too. Her name was Nura. I don't remember the last name."

"I'm not sure I know any Nuras."

"She said you were old friends. Or old colleagues, anyway. From some aid organization. She still does contract work for Save the Children."

A face from my past slowly came into focus.

"Nura Habash, maybe?"

"That sounds right. She said to tell you she'll be back in touch."

Now I remembered her well. Cute and full of energy. We had worked together during those frantic days on the Iraqi border in '91, a few years before I met Mila. The sort of woman who in a crowd seems to dart from person to person, sipping conversations like a hummingbird set loose in a field of blossoms. I wondered how she had known I was in town and, more to the point, how she found me.

"Did she leave a number?"

"Now you don't think I would have helped her with that, do you?"

The remark was coy enough that I was on the verge of asking her over for dinner on Saturday, before a small inner voice told me not to cross that line. Later I was grateful for my caution, when Fiona told me she was heading into the desert the next morning for a weekend photo shoot. Another archaeological site, she said, one of Sami's acquisitions. She would be photographing it from the air, hitching a free ride in a Jordanian military helicopter.

I wondered anew at her closeness to the palace. So many tight little orbits here, all of which seemed to spin perilously near to the center of power. A small country, indeed. Say the wrong thing to one person and someone clear across the kingdom might have heard it by the following morning.

The wine was cool and crisp, and Fiona was pleasant company, but as an amateur I supposed I had best take care in my friendships.

23

New women seemed to be walking into my life from every direction.

The latest arrival, on Monday, was an American—an Arab American, to be precise, even if she had spent only the first five years of her life on the West Bank. Our introduction provided an appropriately awkward ending to a day of uncomfortable events, odd happenings that made me question my chances for success.

The strange doings began in early morning with Omar's return. Instead of greeting me with his usual bear hug, he offered a pained smile and seemed to edit his remarks for the hovering Raniya, who as usual was strategically placed between us, listening intently from her desk.

"Welcome back," I shouted across the office as he came through the door.

"A relief to be back, after everything that happened."

He paused at the threshold of his cubicle, looking as weary as if he had returned by camel caravan.

"Bad news?" I asked.

He glanced at Raniya. Her eyes were locked on the computer screen, but her hands were motionless above the keyboard.

"Somewhat. In fact, there is some business we should get to right away, if you have a minute."

"Sure."

When he asked me to shut the door, I experienced a sense of dread. I wouldn't have been surprised if he had then produced a Tyvek envelope just like Black, White, and Gray's, only this time stuffed with incriminating photos of Freeman Lockhart in the National Garden of Athens,

Freeman Lockhart riding the funicular up Lycabettus Hill, Freeman Lockhart ducking into a dark taverna in the Peloponnese. I imagined how I must have looked through a long lens as I went about my duties, lurking at park benches and peeping through hedgerows, as tawdry as a flasher.

Omar drew a deep breath, and in my growing anxiety I couldn't help but do the same. Was he about to fire me?

"From now on," he said, "I must ask you to take special care wherever you go. Particularly when you leave the country, but also in Jordan."

"Yes?"

"I say this because I recently learned that while I was in Athens I was observed—perhaps even photographed—by agents of the Mossad. Some of their men out of Europe, I am told."

I suppose my jaw must have dropped. Omar nodded as if he understood.

"I know," he said. "I couldn't believe it either. I seriously considered not telling you. But I decided that I owe it to you, if only to let you know the stakes of what we're playing for, the odds we're up against. I suppose I also wanted to offer you a graceful way out, before you get in any deeper. Work for me long enough, and in some quarters you might never be trusted again. Maybe that is already the case. If so, my apologies."

"No need to apologize. And I'm not quitting. But thank you all the same."

He nodded resolutely, as if to say he had expected nothing less than steadfast loyalty from his old friend and fellow warrior. The ashiness on my tongue was the taste of betrayal, but Omar misread my expression of self-loathing.

"You don't look too pleased with me," he said. "Can't say that I blame you."

"It's not you I'm angry with. I would hope that's obvious. Any idea why they were targeting you?"

"None at all."

A disingenuous answer, I thought. It occurred to me later that I should have asked then and there about the source of his information, even though I doubt he would have told me. Maybe it was Norbert Krieger. Or someone he had met after I left Athens.

"None whatsoever?"

"I'm afraid it's just an occupational hazard of doing business as a

Palestinian. Give an Arab from the West Bank some money and a tiny bit of influence, and suddenly he is seen as a threat, even on the streets of Athens."

That sounded like a weak rationale, even for the Mossad. Perhaps they were probing for the same connections I was. Maybe they had even found them. They must have picked up my trail as well. In fact, the two intimidating fellows on motorbikes suddenly made a lot more sense, even if some of the other pieces still didn't fit. Whatever the case, yet another player was now on the board in what was rapidly becoming a crowded field. I would wager that by now the Mossad had found out more about Norbert Krieger than I had. Maybe I should just tell my handlers to ask their friends in Tel Aviv for help. Everything that had happened in Athens now seemed like a comedy of errors for both of us. Me trailing him, and God knows how many others trailing the two of us—a grimy kite's tail of watchers and confidence men, with me as the loosest knot.

"Is this why you were gone longer than expected?"

Omar shrugged.

"Did they threaten you?"

He shook his head.

"I didn't even know they were there at first. Too naive, I guess."

"Then how do you know it was Mossad?"

"Certain information I received later. And I wouldn't be doing you any favors by telling you what. The less said about it here, the better." He nodded toward Raniya, visible through the glass, still bent over her keyboard. "Suffice it to say that I was convinced."

"How did it go otherwise?"

He frowned, seemingly lost in thought.

"The fund-raising," I prodded. "In Athens."

"Oh, that." He waggled a hand in midair, a gesture of ambiguity. "Okay, I guess. Nothing concrete. I may have planted the seeds for future success. But after this news, who knows. Just about any potential donor might be scared away by this kind of attention."

"Anyone I need to follow up with?"

The question seemed to annoy him.

"Not for the moment. I will keep you posted, of course."

"Of course."

He wasn't a convincing liar. It was the worst I'd felt about Omar and his enterprise since coming aboard. For all I knew, the Mossad had good reason to be interested.

"Thanks for the warning," I said. "I'll watch my back."

Omar nodded blankly, again lost in thought.

I decided to head out to Bakaa. I had put the gun in my satchel, although I had yet to buy any ammunition. I supposed that simply waving it around might offer some protection, if the need arose. But the phone rang before I could leave.

"For you, Mr. Lockhart," Raniya said. "It is a woman."

Mila, perhaps? That would be a pleasant surprise.

"Hello?"

"Freeman?" The voice wasn't familiar. "I don't know if your neighbor mentioned I dropped by the other day, but . . ."

"Oh, yes. Nura Habash?"

"Yes. You remembered!"

"It's been what, fourteen years? How are you?"

"Holding up. Still in the aid racket. Working mostly with Bedouin women and children, so I'm out in the desert a lot. You'll be able to tell from the tan."

"But still living in Amman?"

"Oh, yes. And I heard you were back. Maybe for good this time."

"News travels fast."

"You might say I had an unfair advantage. You got the job I wanted!"

"Oh. Sorry."

She laughed.

"It's all right. I didn't have your qualifications. I figured if Omar got desperate enough, maybe I could end up as Plan B. Lucky for him, Plan A came through. You're the perfect choice."

"Probably not, but thanks for saying so. So tell me what you've been doing. Do you keep up with any of our old crew from '91? I figure half of them must be in Iraq by now."

"About half of them were, me included. But it got too dangerous. Most of us ended up here. Which is why I'm calling. A few of us are meeting for drinks this Thursday, if you can make it."

"Thursday? Isn't that the last day of Ramadan?"

"All the more reason to celebrate."

"I'd have thought everyone would want to be with their families for Eid."

"Oh, we will be for the big feast day on Friday morning. But my family lives right in town, so I don't need to travel. I'll have to help my mother Thursday with the shopping, but by that night I'll be ready to blow off a little steam."

"In that case, count me in. Where are you meeting?"

"The InterCon. Just like old times."

"I was there the other day. Saw they'd remodeled, but didn't make it to the bar. Still a good one?"

"They've got a Mexican place, Cinco de Mayo, with a bar we like. The drinks are a little pricey, but the snacks are free. Sometimes from there we go to dinner. Plenty of places right in the neighborhood. So we'll see you, then?"

"Absolutely. What time?"

"How 'bout seven?"

"Perfect. See you there."

It was surprising how good it felt to be in demand again by females, even if just for a drink at a casual mini-reunion. Between Nura and Fiona, I supposed I wouldn't be lacking for company.

My reception at the field office in Bakaa was considerably chillier. As before, two men who seemed to have nothing to do with fund-raising for a hospital were holding down the fort, pecking away at manual type-writers, although Hakim and his cut-rate automatic rifle were nowhere to be seen. The men briefly looked up when I entered, then resumed their typing. One was close enough that I could see he was working on a flyer announcing a political rally. I made a note to get a copy before I left. Maybe I would attend the event. It might be instructive to see who came.

"Is Nabil around?" I asked in Arabic.

Neither said a word, but at least they stopped typing. They exchanged glances before the second one mumbled something in street dialect about Nabil's being "on a tour."

"You will have to come back," the first one said. "This afternoon."

"Maybe Nabil is at home. Doesn't he live right across the street?"

My knowledge seemed to surprise them, and they exchanged another glance.

"He is not home," the first one said. "It is just as Mohammed said. Nabil is escorting a guest through the camp. It is a tour."

"Who's he showing around, someone from the government?"

"No. An American."

That got my attention.

"A guest of the charity's?"

"Yes. A donor."

"Then if you don't mind, I'll just wait here."

Apparently they did mind. Both of them left within minutes. Each heaved a great sigh, as if my lingering presence was the rudest sort of imposition. Unfortunately they took their work with them, so I never got a chance to read their creations. I checked around the office for anything more, but there was only a stack of pamphlets promoting the charity.

I tried to imagine how an American had arranged to visit without Omar telling me. And why would Nabil be leading the tour? If the object was to impress a Westerner, a staff member with possible ties to Hamas seemed like a shaky choice, especially when Dr. Hassan offered the pedantic self-importance that overseas benefactors had come to expect in places like this. Maybe he was too busy seeing patients, although even then I found it hard to believe that Omar would leave an American in Nabil's care.

I took a seat allowing a decent view into the street through the open door, and a half hour later I spotted Nabil walking slowly toward the office alongside a sturdily attractive middle-aged woman. She wore stylish yet modest Western clothing, with a jade silk scarf covering her hair. As they moved closer I realized they were speaking Arabic, and the woman seemed entranced.

Maybe the choice of Nabil made sense, after all. I can't imagine any woman who would have preferred Dr. Hassan's stuffy company, while Nabil was the prototypical tall, dark, and handsome man. He carried himself with confident grace. You might even have called him dashing, and, as I had discovered during our conversation downtown, he could be quite engaging when he turned on the charm.

"Hello," I announced in English.

Nabil stopped speaking in midsentence. I was able to pick up only the cryptic phrase "It mostly depends on how you're wired" before he looked up in surprise. Intriguing choice of words, I thought.

Nabil immediately switched to English, perhaps to let his guest know where I was from, although in short order his decision would prove to be a tactical error.

"No one told me you were coming," he said.

"I wasn't aware I was supposed to give advance warning, seeing as how I work here."

"Does he know why I'm here?" the woman asked in Arabic. Her tone sounded worried. She probably assumed I didn't speak the language.

I replied in Arabic.

"No," I said, "I don't. But that was my next question."

She blushed and turned to Nabil.

"You must be tired from all your traveling," he told her calmly. "Don't worry, he is not here to pressure you for an immediate donation. All in good time."

"I'm sorry," I said. "I'm being impolite. I should have introduced myself right away. Freeman Lockhart, Omar's director of programs. You've met Omar?"

She again turned to Nabil for help.

"That introduction has been delayed due to Omar's absence abroad. As I said. All in good time."

"Of course. In the meantime, maybe I could offer some assistance, Ms. . . . ?"

"Mrs. Aliyah Rahim," Nabil said. "From Washington. Although she was born near Jerusalem."

"Washington? Are you with the government?"

This time she spoke for herself.

"Oh, no. Nothing like that."

"An NGO, then?"

"Just an interested citizen. I haven't lived in Palestine since I was five, and I've come to see the sights of Jordan." Her Arabic was rusty, with a pronounced American accent.

Often when two Americans meet abroad in a benighted place like Bakaa there is a brief flare of kinship, usually marked by an exchange of information about hometowns and occupations, followed by the obligatory session of "Do You Know?" Then someone might offer a light remark about the state of affairs back home, or commiserate about how long it took to get there. Mrs. Rahim offered nothing of the sort, and seemed quite willing to let the conversation die. But I wasn't, so I lobbed her another question.

"How did you hear about us?"

Another glance toward Nabil, who supplied yet another answer.

"There was some literature about our organization at her hotel."

"The InterContinental," she added.

"Nice place. How long are you staying?"

"A week or so."

"And now," Nabil said, "I am afraid we must keep moving. Dr. Hassan is expecting us. Unless, of course, you needed to see me about something urgent?"

"Nothing that can't wait. Obviously you're busy."

He led her gently toward the door.

"Pleasure meeting you," I said. I then took one of the business cards that Omar had printed for me and pushed it into her hand. "Hope to see you again before you leave, Mrs. Rahim."

She smiled wanly, then disappeared into the crowded street.

Well, now. What was that all about? I somehow doubted she had really heard about us in town. I decided to check later with Dr. Hassan. Maybe he knew more.

By then it was well past noon. What I would have liked to do next was to visit a falafel stand for a fat, overstuffed sandwich. But during Ramadan that was out of the question, so I settled for yet another visit to a market for fruit and bread to eat in the office.

I was just finishing when a blare of loudspeakers caught my attention, and I threw open the door in time to see a Toyota truck rolling by with hand-painted banners on its sides and a young fellow in a red-checked kaffiyeh leaning out the passenger window. He held an electric megaphone, barking out announcements over the heads of the midday throngs. In the truck's wake were a few dozen schoolboys, who seemed to be following for lack of anything better to do.

It wasn't easy deciphering the message through the fuzz and burn of feedback, but as best I could tell he was urging everyone to attend a rally that weekend. Maybe it was the same event Nabil's friends were promoting. For all I knew, the pamphlets being scattered like flower petals from the back of the Toyota had been printed in this very office.

It was the usual junk and glory of Palestinian activism. The rally, the fellow on the megaphone said, was going to offer everyone who attended a chance "to show them all up." Whoever "them" was. On the West Bank, "them" always meant the Israelis, the armed occupiers of the IDF. Here it could be referring to local political rivals or the Jordanian government, and I had little doubt that such processions attracted their share of Mukhabarat operatives or informants. By later this afternoon, a full report would probably be on someone's desk at the big building off the Eighth Circle.

The noise faded as the parade rounded a far corner, and I decided to check in at Dr. Hassan's. A twenty-minute stroll brought me to the crowded waiting room, where I asked the receptionist to tell him I had arrived.

"I am sorry, sir, but Dr. Hassan is away."

"Then maybe you know where Nabil and his guest have gone."

She regarded me with puzzlement.

"Nabil Mustafa, I mean. Wasn't he here earlier? With a Palestinian woman from America?"

Her puzzlement turned to amazement.

"He would never come here uninvited, sir. He is not welcome."

I left a bit sheepishly, feeling as if I had been made the butt of a practical joke. As I went out the door the little political procession passed my way again. It had picked up more followers, and now there were about fifty chanting males in its wake.

I wondered again about the mysterious Mrs. Rahim. Whose rallying cry, if any, was she marching to? Maybe, as she said, she was simply a tourist on a sentimental journey. It wasn't unusual for wealthy Palestinians of the Diaspora to want to see how the less fortunate were faring. That could account for why she seemed embarrassed once I showed up. A fellow American had caught her in the act of slumming.

But there were other possibilities, too, involving more secretive and even alarming motives. Nabil's cryptic phrase, "It mostly depends on how you're wired," certainly covered some interesting territory.

I added the name of Aliyah Rahim to the list of those worthy of further scrutiny.

24

The surreal nature of Aliyah's mission didn't sink in until she landed in Frankfurt for a six-hour layover.

She hadn't slept a wink on the overnight crossing. Instead she squirmed her way through a dreary movie, three European sitcoms, and a chilly breakfast served in the blinding glare of sunrise over the North Atlantic. By the time she finally slumped into a cushioned chair along one of the terminal's busiest thoroughfares she was too dazed to do anything but stare at the passing crowds with eyes that felt sanded and buffed.

That was when it hit her: In a matter of hours she would be meeting with plotters and bomb makers, the very people she had always scorned as a hurt and hindrance to her family. In trying to imagine the days ahead, she envisioned hooded men bristling with weapons. They would blindfold her and bundle her into the trunks of cars to drive to their hidden lairs and safe houses, where bearded men would sit cross-legged on threadbare carpets beneath posters of Mecca and Jerusalem's Dome of the Rock. She would drink tea served on brass trays in between discussions of bomb placement and wiring, and she would endure endless diatribes against infidel Americans. Arab or not, she supposed she had been influenced by Hollywood as much as any American.

She shifted uncomfortably in the airport chair. Next to her, an Asian man in a business suit began snoring. How had matters come to this? Could she really pull it off? Suddenly it seemed like a terrible idea to have left Abbas to his own devices in Washington. He might get it in his head to try anything. Thank goodness they had never owned firearms.

Their parting had been awkward. Abbas drove her to Dulles with quiet solicitude, but his farewell at the security barrier unnerved her.

"Remember," he said, reaching up to lightly stroke her cheek, "you are doing this for our children."

The gesture was touching, the words chilling. Carrying out his plan would damn their children's names forever, and his words rendered her speechless. She only nodded in reply, and then held him tightly as she wondered what other thoughts and secrets were adrift in his mind.

Then she reminded herself that, under her agenda, this trip really was for the children. And for Abbas, too. But what if she were caught by local authorities? A day earlier she had read a story in the *Post* about how the Jordanian government was cracking down on young jihadists as they straggled back across the border from Iraq. Maybe she would wind up in the net also. And even if she had the best of intentions, her actions could land her in jail back in the United States if American authorities ever got wind of what she was up to.

Such thoughts continued to trouble her in Frankfurt, so she went to an airport café in search of relief. A strong cup of coffee and a four-euro pastry revived her spirits. She watched with envy as a young mother at the next table tended to a drowsy pair of twins in a double stroller.

In a surge of optimism she bought a *Herald Tribune*. Perhaps there would be a late bulletin of the senator's death, making a shambles of Abbas's plans. Instead there was only more news from Iraq, with its bombings and failures. She shoved the paper into an overflowing trash bin as bile rose in her throat, tasting of burned coffee. No more looking back, she told herself. No more hoping for an easy way out.

The burst of resolve calmed her, and by the time her plane took off for Amman she was relaxed enough to sleep.

No one met her at the airport, thank goodness. The only information she had to go on was the contact name and number from Abbas. He had insisted that she stay in first-class accommodations, and had booked her a room at the InterContinental. She reached the hotel in late afternoon. The bellhop threw open the curtains onto a street scene of heavy traffic and long shadows. Just one more hour of daylight, she told herself. Wait it out, drink a bottle of water, and then sleep. She would telephone the contact number in the morning. That way she would have already put one day behind her without having advanced Abbas's cause.

For security reasons, Abbas and she had agreed not to be in touch until the day before her departure, when she would send an e-mail detailing her flight plans. She believed this isolation would work to her advantage. He would have no way of knowing how little she was doing, or what sort of questions she was asking. Her plan, apart from her delaying tactics, was to learn more about disarming bombs than making them. But she also realized the potential disadvantages. What if Abbas did something rash in her absence? Or, worse, what if he grew impatient and found some way to carry it off without any help from abroad? Teamwork had always been a hallmark of how they dealt with important family matters, and she was counting on that to prevent him from acting alone. But she worried that in his current state of mind, if he was pushed for time, his resourcefulness might overcome his spirit of cooperation. That, and his vial of little pills.

Aliyah slid open the door to the balcony and stepped outside. The crisp evening air felt perfect. It was her first time in Amman, and she hadn't expected all the hills, with their crowded, blocky architecture, everything rendered in watercolor shades of tan and off-white. Or so it seemed in the slanting light. The air had a strange smell, which stirred a vague familiarity. It was the dry, smoky character, she supposed, which took her back to distant times she hadn't revisited in ages.

She recalled in particular a walk she had taken with her brothers between West Bank villages high in the crags above the Jordan River's valley. They had been visiting relatives at the time, and she must have been only five, just before the '67 war. Her brothers grew impatient with her slow pace and told her to wait for them to collect her on their return journey. She was tired, and happy to oblige, so she stretched out on her back on a barren hilltop, feeling the warm ground against the back of her cotton dress as she stared up into the sharp blue sky. The noise of her brothers' chatter receded until she was blanketed by a thrilling silence.

A few minutes later, as she still gazed skyward, there was movement in the corner of her eye, followed by a light wisping sound from above. It was a stork, she saw. No, three of them, now hundreds, maybe thousands. They were far overhead, like a great mass of white confetti, blowing south toward the Sinai. Then they paused as if the wind had stopped them, and the white particles began to circle. It took a few moments before she realized they were moving closer, easing lower with each revolution. Maybe they were coming to say hello, or just to find out who she was, what she was up to. She never felt threatened, only thrilled, as if at any moment one of the storks might cry out, try to speak to her. Soon they were close enough for Aliyah to hear every wingbeat, a thousand whispers like a roomful of gossips. By then they were no more than a few hundred feet above her, casting shadows where she lay. Then, as if following some silent command, they suddenly began to rise, until they were high enough to continue southward. She was so spellbound by the experience that when her brothers returned they were certain she had been bewitched by a jinn, some rogue spirit loose on the landscape.

Now where had that memory come from? She looked across the city, certain that deep within her there were plenty of other connections to this land. It might do her some good to acknowledge that more often. She knew it was what their son, Faris, wanted from his parents. He yearned for touchstones.

Aliyah hadn't been to this part of the world in nine years, and even that visit had been a sad journey to Nablus for the funeral of Abbas's mother, a trip that had turned tense and ugly when an Israeli soldier was shot in the town. They spent most of the week indoors or waiting at checkpoints.

She yawned. The hours of travel were catching up to her, so she stepped back inside and slid the door shut. The hum of the air conditioner beckoned her to bed.

At 10 the next morning, after a leisurely breakfast in the lobby café, she reluctantly got down to business by punching in the phone number. As the line rang she prayed for a tape-recorded answer, hoping against hope that the number had been disconnected. Instead, a woman picked up on the second ring. Aliyah asked to speak to Khalid. It was the only name she had.

"Just a moment."

The line crackled with static as the phone changed hands. Then a male voice said, "Call my mobile instead."

He gave her the number and hung up. Aliyah scrambled to find a pen before she forgot it. Then she calmed herself and dialed again. Khalid answered right away but still wasn't ready to do business.

"Where are you?" he said.

"My hotel. The InterContinental."

"Those lines aren't so good. Please try me on *your* mobile."

"I don't think my cell phone will work here."

"There are some shops down the street where you can buy one. I will be here all morning."

He hung up. A matter of security, she supposed. Just as well, because it was another delay, and she would make the most of it.

She spent two hours finding the right shop and settling on a phone. Then she ordered a room service lunch, ate at a snail's pace, and shoved the tray and its clattering silver lids into the hallway before calling back. With any luck, Khalid would have given up.

He again answered right away, with no hint of impatience.

"We need to meet," he said. "Preferably at a café, someplace in public. After sundown, of course." Because it was Ramadan, he meant. She hadn't been at all vigilant about her holiday fasting back in the U.S., but supposed that she should take more care here. "I must break fast first, and then I will see you. Eight o'clock. The Al Khabar Café, in Shmeisani. Any taxi driver will know it."

The more she saw of the city on the ride across town, the less it impressed her. It was a sprawl with no center, and everything had been built in a hurry. Each successive boulevard looked like the one before it, with the same billboards and banks. Clean enough, she supposed, and some of the new hotels begged spectacularly for attention. But there was little of the concentrated bustle that she had always found so stimulating in other Arab cities, such as Cairo or Damascus.

When she arrived at the Al Khabar she wondered if the taxi had taken her to the wrong place. The clientele and atmosphere wouldn't have been out of place on Dupont Circle in Washington. Subdued track lighting beamed onto leather-backed stools and black circular tables with chrome edging. Wall-mounted speakers pulsed with a driving beat. Was that Madonna singing? Anticipating something far different, Aliyah had dressed conservatively and covered her head with a scarf. Only one other woman here was similarly attired, and even she wore a scarlet silk blouse and tight jeans. Half the customers were smoking cigarettes, which took some getting used to. Others puffed at hookah pipes of flavored tobacco.

Shortly after entering she noticed a small man with a trim salt-and-pepper beard nodding to her from across the room. She nodded back and approached his table.

"Khalid?"

"Yes."

"Is that your real name?"

"Of course."

As if he would have said otherwise. He signaled to the waitress, and Aliyah ordered coffee. Then, perhaps to set the tone, Khalid began tossing out the euphemisms they were presumably supposed to use from then on.

"I understand you are looking for investment expertise to help in your acquisition project."

"Yes. We need lots of advice."

He nodded, as if to affirm she had answered in just the right way.

"What is the timing of your acquisition?"

"That depends."

"On executive health issues, correct?"

"Yes."

"Then we will try to act as expeditiously as possible."

"All right."

She felt supremely ridiculous, and could hardly believe the conversation was taking place. Between jet lag and nervousness, she wanted to burst out laughing. It was like a school play, and her pose as a willing participant made it a sham within a sham. Nor did it help that Khalid cut a ridiculous figure. His short legs didn't even reach the floor from the stool, which made him look like a boy with a fake beard. At least no one else seemed to be paying them any attention.

Her coffee arrived, hot and strong. She sipped and looked down at the table while trying to forget where she was. Khalid leaned across the table and spoke up to be heard over the music.

"I am going to put you in touch with two people, both of them in the Bakaa camp. The first will advise you on technical matters. His name is also Khalid."

"Are all of you named Khalid?"

"Don't ask those kinds of questions, please."

She searched his face for any hint of amusement, and found none.

"You will meet him tomorrow. A driver will come to your hotel at noon. We will reveal the name of the second contact only when we have decided you are ready."

"You mean I have to prove myself?"

"There is no need to burden you with too much information until you are fully prepared for the next step."

"And how long will that take?"

"Not so long. After you meet your contact tomorrow you will receive a call on your mobile with further instructions. Always use your mobile. And, Aliyah?"

It was the first time anyone had used her name since she left Washington, and it was jarring. It told her this wasn't playacting after all.

"Yes?"

"Do not create any further delays. I understand why you might have some reluctance. You are taking an important step. But it should not have taken you two hours to buy a phone and return my call."

His tone wasn't angry and his expression didn't change, but she got the message all the same. They were watching closely, and wanted to see a more convincing performance.

"Tell me one more thing," she said.

"If I can."

"Why am I using my real name when no one else is?"

"Because your name is one of your advantages. In Jordan, where many names automatically attract attention and suspicion, yours is a good name, beyond reproach."

Tell that to the authorities in London, she thought, or in New York. Maybe she should even say that out loud. It was why she was here, after all, the mere fact of their name and the consequences it had produced. But Khalid had already hopped down from the stool and was dropping dinars on the table. He then headed for the door without a further word. Aliyah followed a few seconds later. By the time she reached the sidewalk he was gone.

As promised, the taxi came for her the next day at noon. At first she wondered if the driver himself was the contact. Five minutes of small talk convinced her he wasn't. And when they reached Bakaa he had trouble finding their destination. It didn't exactly seem like a smooth operation. Encouraging.

Bakaa, at least, was more in line with her expectations than the Al Khabar Café. The cab dropped her off on a narrow lane strewn with garbage, which had attracted a flock of foraging goats.

"That is the building you want," the driver said. "The one with the blue sign."

He motioned toward an auto repair shop across the street.

"Are you sure?"

"I am positive. You see?"

He showed the directions he had scribbled on a spare receipt, a series of twists and turns ending with the name of the garage.

"Thank you."

The taxi departed in a zephyr of grit, and she stood uncertainly at the curb. Once again she had dressed all wrong. This time she had chosen not to cover her head, so now, of course, all the women walking by had covered theirs. Aliyah stood out as an obvious visitor. All the more reason to get off the street as quickly as possible. But who was she supposed to meet?

In the garage bay, a man covered head to toe in grease had just disappeared beneath a truck, and a second stood at a workbench, welding something in a shower of sparks.

A voice spoke up from behind, making her jump.

"Are you Aliyah?"

"Goodness. Yes, I am."

"I am sorry. I didn't mean to frighten you. But I believe you are here to meet me. I am Khalid."

He was tall, a striking man dressed all in white, with intense but kindly eyes. Just as he spoke again, a pneumatic drill shrieked into action, rattling like a machine gun, but she understood enough to realize she was supposed to follow him. When they had put some distance between themselves and the garage, he said, "I have been asked to help you."

"So I'm told. Is there someplace we should go to talk?"

"Walking may be best for now. Then it is less likely we will be overheard."

"You have to worry about that here?"

"Especially here."

She took a closer look. He was probably in his mid-forties, with a calmness to his movements that helped put her at ease. He said nothing for a moment, as if waiting for her to start things off.

"Well?" Aliyah prompted.

"We are supposed to talk about explosives, I think," he said.

"You think?"

"Is this not the case?"

"Yes, this is the case."

"Very well. The problem is that I don't know very much about the subject. So I am guessing that I am supposed to find someone for you who does."

"You're guessing?"

"Yes. I am afraid that they did not tell me much more. You see, I am not accustomed to this sort of work."

"I can see that, Khalid."

Her emphasis on the name seemed to make him uneasy. Or maybe he was embarrassed. She supposed it was also possible he didn't trust Americans, even if they were Arabs. Or perhaps he was an uptight young religious conservative, an Islamic fundamentalist who wasn't comfortable addressing a woman as an equal, especially a bareheaded woman. But that reaction would probably have produced scorn, not shyness.

"Well, there are several ways we can approach this," he said.

"Perhaps you should start with the easiest."

"As you wish."

He began to speak calmly, if somewhat distractedly, of people who knew of detonators and circuitry, and of others who might know about the maximum poundage that a woman of her size might reasonably wear beneath her clothing. He didn't seem at all comfortable talking about it. But he said he knew of such people if they were the types of people she truly wanted to see. That's when she realized, to her horror, that he must believe she wanted to wire herself for a suicide bomb.

"They say that it depends greatly on your strength," he said. "Do you have much stamina?"

Had no one told him her actual plans? For the first time, she seriously doubted the soundness of having come here. Far from being scarily competent, these people seemed like a loose collection of misfits. It was time to put an immediate stop to this terrifying nonsense. She stopped in her tracks and turned sharply toward Khalid—or Khalid II, as she already thought of him.

"I am not aware of what anyone may have told you about me, but I really am not planning to blow myself up. Not here, not anywhere."

"Oh."

Was it her imagination, or did he seem relieved?

"I had not been told fully of your intentions, you see."

Yes, he was definitely relieved. Color was returning to his face.

"As I said," he continued, "I am only acting as a favor to someone else."

"I can tell."

"You can?"

"Yes. Because this is new for me, too. I know exactly how you feel."

"Ah."

"And although I am interested in learning about explosives"—mostly in learning how to ensure that they *won't* go off, she thought—"I definitely don't plan on this being my last act in life."

He smiled a bit nervously, as if waiting for her to explain further. His awkwardness was appealing, and she realized now that he reminded her a bit of her son, Faris—an older version with the same eagerness to please, the same courtly manner.

"I really don't know what else to tell you," he said finally.

"Then maybe you should refer me to someone else. In the meantime you can call me a taxi."

"Yes. We can do that at my office. Please, it is this way."

They turned up a long alley, and for a while they said nothing more. But as the shock of the misunderstanding wore off, Aliyah decided that she wanted to know more about this seemingly reasonable man and how he had ended up in such an appalling line of work. Because if he was truly as reluctant as she was, maybe he could help her after all.

"What else did they tell you about me?" she asked.

"Only that you were an American from Washington who was interested in bomb making. And that you would be arriving in Rashid's taxi."

"You know my driver?"

"Yes."

"Interesting. He played it pretty cool."

"As I said, this work is new to me."

She smiled.

"And what were we supposed to do, once we met?"

"I was told to let you set the tone."

"I had the opposite understanding. Sounds like someone screwed up."

"Yes."

Then he, too, smiled, and she felt better until reminding herself that only moments ago he had been advising her on the best ways to blow oneself up. The thought made her shiver, because for a moment she could almost imagine the horrible feeling of carrying out such an order. It was bad enough contemplating the heat and pressure of the heavy vest beneath your blouse, or the moment when you would pull the lanyard to vaporize yourself. Still worse was the idea of strolling into some crowded shop and scanning the faces of everyone you were about to kill. Hearing their laughter and conversation, getting a brief glimpse into their lives. She remembered the mom at the airport café, tending to her twins, one last act of love before the descent of death and chaos.

"Are you all right?" Khalid II asked. "You seem very tired."

She looked at him again, wanting to believe that he would have been unable to complete his instructions. Right now she needed a kindred spirit, and Khalid II was the only possibility at hand.

"Tell me one more thing," she said. "Where was I supposed to have been blowing myself up?"

He shrugged and looked away.

"They didn't say. I assumed it was somewhere across the river."

"The West Bank?"

"Or Jerusalem. Tel Aviv. No one would have told me that, of course."

"So if I really had wanted that kind of advice, what were you going to tell me to do? How does one prepare for that? Mentally, I mean."

"I don't know."

"What about physically?"

"I am not so sure about that, either." He pointed toward an open doorway just ahead, presumably their destination. "I only know some of the basic things that others have mentioned, but I know little about the technical part. I think it has to do partly with the configuration of the explosive. They say it mostly depends on how you're wired."

He stopped abruptly just after crossing the threshold, and when Aliyah went inside she saw why. There was a man in the room—a Westerner, judging by his appearance. Khalid II seemed to know him.

"No one told me you were coming," Khalid II said in English.

"I wasn't aware I was supposed to give advance warning," the man answered, "seeing as how I work here."

Good God. He sounded American. And in her momentary panic Aliyah assumed the man didn't speak Arabic, or else she never would have spoken up in the local tongue. But she did, asking abruptly, "Does he know why I'm here?"

Things quickly went downhill from there. Not only did the man speak Arabic, he even introduced himself, and Khalid II was fool enough to give her name. Then he handed her a business card, which made matters stranger still, because the charity he worked for was the same one Abbas had mentioned in reference to his contact.

She was sick to her stomach with fear until Khalid II finally extracted them by saying they had another appointment. They left at a brisk walk, and for a few blocks neither of them said a word.

"I am sorry," Khalid II said. "If I had known, I never would have taken you there."

"You work with that man?"

"Not directly. He helps run the hospital charity I do some political work for."

"Is it really a charity, or a front for something else?"

"A charity. Without a doubt."

"Do you think he overheard us?"

"I don't know. Even if he did, he wouldn't know your purpose here."

"Let's hope not."

"Yes. For both of us."

She reached into her pocket and felt the man's calling card. She was about to throw it into the street, but decided to keep it. Maybe Khalid II believed the charity was on the level, but she wasn't yet convinced. She would check later to see if his phone number matched the one Abbas had given her.

"So who can help me?" she asked. "Who do you know who can teach me what I need to learn?"

He frowned and shook his head. He, too, seemed rattled by the encounter at the office, and before he answered he looked up and down the street in both directions.

"I will find someone," he said.

"Or maybe you could find out what I need to know, and tell me yourself."

"Maybe." He didn't seem happy about it.

"What's wrong?"

He shrugged.

"Is it because I am a woman?"

"No. It's because, well . . ."

"Yes?"

"I'm not sure I am comfortable teaching you these things, even if I learn them correctly from someone else. I was asked to meet you today, so I have. But still . . ."

"Are you not certain of the cause?"

"I am very certain. The cause is just."

"But you disagree with the means? This need for killing people?"

He sighed and looked at her intently, as if wondering whether to trust her.

"We should not be speaking in this way."

"I won't report you, if that's what's worrying you. I'm not so certain about the means myself. In fact, what if I were to tell you a great secret. Do you think you could keep it, especially if you thought it might save lives?"

"Of course."

"Then find out for me what I need to know. How to wire and put together a bomb, and, just as important, how to take one apart without setting it off. Can you do that, and then meet me again?"

"I don't think this is a safe place to talk about these things. Maybe somewhere else, and in a few more days."

"Should we set up another appointment, then? What about Thursday, three days from now?"

"I will try. But aren't you in a hurry?"

"Did someone tell you that?"

He shrugged, seemingly uncomfortable about answering. Either he didn't know or he was hiding something. Maybe Khalid II wasn't so easy to read after all. In that case, she had probably said too much. But at this point he seemed to be her best hope.

"Let's say four o'clock. Just tell me where. Preferably not at your office. I don't want to bump into the American again."

"My house, then. Across from the office, but a few doors down. Just ask for me by name. People will know."

"Even if I ask for Khalid?"

He reddened. Such inexperience. If she had really wanted help in a hurry she would have been furious by now.

"I will be looking for you," he said. "No need for you to ask anyone."

"Very good. I'm at the InterContinental if you need to reach me. How can I reach you if there is a change in plans?"

"I am probably not supposed to tell you that."

"Probably. But you took me to your office and told me where your house is. So I already know at least two ways."

He again seemed flustered.

"I'll give you my number."

She took out a pen to write it down, but he stopped her.

"Probably better not to put it on a piece of paper. In Bakaa, no one's secrets are safe."

"Not even yours?"

She said it as a tease, to lighten the mood, but his face was deadly serious, and his next words surprised her.

"Especially not mine."

Yes, he might well be more complicated than she had thought. But she would just as soon see Khalid II as anyone else, at least until she had a better idea of what they had planned for her. She then recalled that the next contact was due to get in touch shortly after this appointment. So during the taxi ride back to Amman she switched off her cell phone, and when she reached the hotel she asked the desk clerk to block all calls to her room.

That ought to hold them at bay for a while, she thought. At least until Thursday.

25

On my way to meet Chris Boylan I finally got to see Sami Fayez's salon. It was up a musty stairwell, and the moment he opened the door I knew I'd come to the right place for informed gossip. Several conversations were going at once, and the portly Sami roamed the sunlit floor between them, an impresario of gab as played by Sydney Greenstreet, minus the fez and flyswatter.

I was mildly surprised to see that a few of his guests were drinking Turkish coffee, and Sami noted my reaction.

"They are Christians," he explained. "So of course you will have coffee, too."

He snapped his fingers toward the doorway of a small kitchen. Instantly a pot clattered, followed by the sound of gushing water.

There were three rooms across the front of the house, all with high ceilings, tall arched windows decorated with panels of stained glass, and sluggish ceiling fans that looked as if they had been spinning since the 1930s.

Rather than spruce up the space, as someone in Manhattan or Paris might have done, Sami let the old cracks and blemishes speak for themselves. The only lighting was a bare bulb dangling from the ceiling of each room on a long, frayed cord. Yet there was almost a stagy feel to the place. It was more restoration than relic, a living museum. Maybe that's why some of the conversations sounded almost scripted, like role-players at a tourist site. At Colonial Williamsburg you got powdered wigs and tricornered hats. Here the players came outfitted with worry beads and olive-wood canes.

Most of the guests were older than me. At the end of a long couch was the curmudgeonly Ali, in a brown sweater vest that smelled strongly of tobacco. He thumped a cane against the floor to punctuate a diatribe against government intransigence.

"No one at that stupid ministry ever returns my calls!"

"That is the most hopeful sign of progress I have heard in years," rejoined the smiling Shakeel, in the role of agent provocateur.

A while later they moved to the topic of loose women, loudly speculating on whether the parliamentary prudes of the Muslim Brotherhood would try to ban a singer named Topaz from the next Shubaib Festival. The consensus was that they certainly hoped not. If she was the enemy, then bring on the attack, in all its fleshpot glory.

"You see," Sami told me, "it is the same with men everywhere. As soon as we tire of politics, we talk only of women and football. But what are your interests these days? You've had time to settle in—how do you see things here in Jordan?"

"I'm surprised at how little it's changed since '91. Nice to see the king still has some popularity."

"Yes. I worried for a while that Abdullah would not be able to keep a lid on things. He has made mistakes, of course. That is the way of any young man in a hurry. But the people have accepted him. The fact that everyone is making money helps, of course."

"I noticed. All your friends seem to be doing all right. Omar, for one."

"You sound as if that is not necessarily a good thing."

"Do I? I don't mean to. Omar deserves to live well, and he's obviously trying to give some of it back. But I do worry about some of the people he has surrounded himself with. I wonder what they're in it for. Present company excluded, of course."

"He has little choice. Politics in Bakaa is a blood sport, so you have to have contacts on all sides unless you wish to be seen as a partisan. And of course when someone like Omar comes along in Bakaa, offering his friendship, it is not only his checkbook they're interested in. They want part of his reputation, because they know that the security services are always looking over their shoulders. That's one reason I avoid the place. Too many informers out there for my taste. Rivals reporting on rivals. But I shouldn't worry about Omar. He knows what he's doing."

"Maybe."

"Who in particular worries you? No, let me guess. Nabil Mustafa?"

"Sounds like you've been listening to Dr. Hassan."

"Who is probably the second name on your worry list."

"Dr. Hassan?"

"Of course. An old hand with Fatah. If you say his name to anyone with the Muslim Brotherhood, be sure to stand back so the spit will not land on your shoes."

"But he's so . . ."

"Stodgy? Arrogant? Yes, he's a regular old snob. He discovered long ago that it allowed him to mix well in polite society. He has even been invited to the palace. It was a party for more than a thousand guests, but still. If there's anyone Omar keeps a close eye on, it's probably Dr. Hassan."

I filed that away, then moved on to the name I'd seen on the downtown mailbox where Nabil had paid a visit.

"What can you tell me about a fellow named Walid Khammar?"

"What of him? Is he also a new associate of Omar's?"

"I'm not sure. It's one reason I'm asking."

Sami stole a glance toward his other guests, and then lowered his voice.

"Let's go into my study."

We walked to an office in the back. The only window was a small, cracked pane of glass overlooking an alley. A huge oak desk faced the doorway, but Sami sat instead on an overstuffed couch in front of a battered coffee table, and directed me to a wing chair on the opposite side. An older woman followed us in with a tray. Sami watched in silence as she poured syrupy coffee from an hourglass pot, and then she left without a word.

This was probably where Sami did his thinking and planning, moving the pieces of his real estate chess game. On the wall behind the desk was a framed, yellowed map of Amman in the 1920s. Propped on the desk were several photos of Sami with the late King Hussein. Everybody who was anybody in Jordan prominently displayed such snapshots in their homes and offices, but his were less formal than most. In one, the king wore the same black leather jacket that he had worn in the motorcycle poster, and he looked genuinely relaxed. Sami's photos with Abdullah, on the other hand, looked like everyone else's—Sami in a suit at a royal birthday celebration. Sami with a cocktail glass at some charity gala.

"What makes you think Omar is involved with Walid Khammar? You have seen them together?"

"Not exactly." I certainly wasn't going to admit to spying on Nabil, so I improvised. "Someone at Bakaa mentioned him in the same breath as Nabil."

"May I ask the context?"

"I'm not sure I understood the conversation well enough to say."

Sami inspected me closer.

"You're very good at this."

"At what?"

"Trying to get something for nothing. You should use those skills down in the bazaar. Buy something nice for your wife. But seeing as how this is your first time as my guest, perhaps I should respond with more generosity. Tell me, though, is this purely for your own use?"

"I can't think of anyone else who'd want to know."

"Oh, I can. Walid Khammar is the sort of fellow who . . . well, let's just say that whenever something disturbing happens—the errant missile down in Aqaba, for example, or those idiots caught sneaking into Israel with a grenade launcher—he often gets a call from our friends on the Eighth Circle."

"You mean the—"

"No need to say it aloud. Not when all we're doing is engaging in a little friendly conversation. You might alarm the guests. Speaking of which, will you please shut that door behind you?"

I did as he asked. Then he paused, listening for any breaks in the murmuring conversations beyond the door.

"No one thinks Walid would actually get up to something like that. But he might know people who would."

"Someone like Nabil?"

Sami tilted his head like a dog who'd heard a strange noise.

"I doubt that's Nabil's style. That's why I'm surprised to hear he has been associating with—excuse me, 'mentioned in the same breath as'—Walid Khammar. Although Nabil is certainly a pious young man, to hear Omar tell it. And Walid has been known to seek the company of pious young men, of a certain political stripe."

"Hamas, you mean?"

"You *have* been snooping around, haven't you? Maybe I'm the one who should be asking questions."

"I'm just repeating what Omar told me. Or what Dr. Hassan told Omar."

"Dr. Hassan again. As you said, he certainly thinks highly of himself. But I suppose he has earned that, after twenty years of working in the trenches. Playing doctor to all those thousands."

"I doubt his patients would call it playing."

"You're absolutely right. I should be more charitable. Please, drink your coffee. Fatima will be serving juice in a minute, so you might as well empty the cup or you'll hurt her feelings. By the time you've left she'll have made sure your bladder is ready to burst."

I sipped down to the gritty mud.

"What more do you know about the doctor?"

"Nothing of interest, really."

I suppose I had reached the limits of Sami's generosity, unless I had something to offer in return. A dismissal seemed at hand.

"I should return to my other guests," he said. "And didn't you say something about another appointment?"

"Yes. I'm meeting an old colleague downtown."

"Care to share his name? Perhaps he is an acquaintance of mine?"

"I doubt you've met."

"Very good, Freeman. Very frugal of you. And please do come again."

Although next time I'm sure he would expect me to bring more to the table. In Sami's information bazaar, my introductory offer had just expired.

It was a short walk to the Husseini Mosque, but with fifteen minutes to kill I took my time, heading slowly around the corner to King Faysal Street. Only two days remained before Ramadan's last sundown, the market crowds were growing larger as families began stocking up for Friday's Eid al-Fitr celebration.

The beggar women sat at their usual corners. I stopped to buy toothpaste from one, drawing a mute nod of appreciation from a black-veiled head. Crossing the street toward the checkerboard marble plaza of the mosque, I spotted the wavy blond hair of Chris Boylan, who easily stood out in the crowd. He had yet to see me coming.

Even from afar he looked careworn and distracted. He was deeply tanned, but had lost weight, and his shoulders sagged. A war zone can do that to you. It was probably a relief for him to be somewhere he didn't have to worry about kidnappers or bombs.

"Chris!"

He smiled broadly and called out in his Kiwi accent.

"Bloody long time, mate. Thought you'd given up on the charms of the Near East."

"I had. Our old pal Omar brought me back."

"I'd heard you two were back in tandem. Is he coming, too?"

" 'Fraid not. Maybe next time."

"If there is one. Never thought I'd say it, but I might have finally had my fill of the Orient. One more tour of duty and I'm cooked."

"Iraq?"

"Belly of the beast. And the beast gets hungrier by the day."

"You look it."

"And you don't. I hear you married well. She the one who keeps you looking like this?"

Maybe I blushed, or maybe he knew it was the sort of remark that always got my goat. In any case, he laughed.

"I take it this isn't just a social call," he said.

"Not strictly. How'd you guess?"

"It's the same way I work whenever I'm starting fresh some-where. Look up a few old hands and assorted spooks to see what they're hearing."

"Which are you, old hand or assorted spook?"

"Little o' both, mate." He gripped my arm and nudged me into motion. "Let's walk, long as we're talking shop. This isn't Baghdad, but it's not Manhattan, either."

"Tell me what you're up to."

"Keeping my head down. Not much to tell otherwise. Or so my employer would have me say."

"Sounds like you're in deep."

"Got the bug in Afghanistan. Spent a year helping the UN look for where the warlords had stashed their guns, and ended up working with a lot of Humint operatives, army and otherwise."

I didn't need to ask what he meant by "otherwise."

"Some don't know their ass from a hole in the ground. They show up in khakis and aviator glasses at the wheel of a big Chevy and can't figure why they're not blending into the scenery. But the good ones are a real trip. Helpful, too. And once you're splashing around in the same tub, the water gets comfortable. So you sign on with somebody, and they send you someplace where you might actually know a thing or two. Which for me means this part of the world. How 'bout you? Is this char-ity of Omar's on the level?"

"Why do you ask?"

"Because you've got the look of somebody who just got his member-ship card but is still wondering whether he joined the right club."

Chris was good that way. But I didn't want to open up too much, if only because I wasn't all that sure about his club.

"Seems to be on the level. I'm still doing background checks on some of the players."

"And you want my help."

"Yes."

"Depends on what you want to know, I guess. Where do you want to start?"

"Hans Wolters. Any idea where our old boss is?"

"Hans is keeping himself under wraps, although he'd probably come out of hiding for you."

"Under wraps how?"

"Dug in on the West Bank. Doing his version of shuttle diplomacy between local factions."

"Which ones?"

"You name it. Hamas, Fatah, right-wing settler groups, the non-affiliated. People who would never talk to each other, but who might let Hans do the talking for them. Which is why he lays low. Steers clear of all police, and certainly avoids any sort of official-looking American. Except you, of course."

"Am I official-looking?"

"Nothing personal. After a few months in Baghdad every American starts to look official."

"How would I reach him?"

"Drop an e-mail to his sponsors. Keep it brief and noncommittal. They'll forward it."

"Got a name?"

"I'm trying to remember. One of those pie-in-the-sky outfits. The West Bank Peace Network, that's it."

"Talk about an oxymoron."

"Try 'WBPeace dot org.' And if your message ends up at Warner Brothers, then you'll know my memory's gone to hell. He'll probably be thrilled to hear from somebody who isn't insane."

"Is that the way you feel?"

"Been here twenty-four hours and I'm still getting used to the idea I'm not about to be blown to pieces. I'm good for another six months, tops."

"And then?"

"Maybe someplace comparatively sane. Like Afghanistan. Not that Afghanistan will be any better in another six months."

"Why don't you come here? Plenty of professionals in Jordan, from what I hear."

"Jordan's no given, either, you know. Never has been. Lately it's trickier than ever. Lots of funny business spilling over the border from Loonyland in Iraq."

"Anything I should know about?"

"Nothing specific. Just general bad vibes. Creeps with nothing better to do. Maybe you've met some and don't even know it. Got any names to run past me?"

"Heard of a Nabil Mustafa? Or a Walid Khammar?"

"The last one's familiar, but, hell, they all sound the same after a while. Ten Ahmeds and fifty Mohammeds. Who else?"

"An American. Woman, late middle-aged. Aliyah Rahim."

"Sorry. That one's a blank."

"How are you on out-of-towners? A Greek, in fact."

Chris raised his eyebrows.

"Living here, you mean?"

"No. But he may have contacts here. A professor. Yiorgos Soukas."

"Spell it."

I did.

Chris shook his head.

"Nope. Another blank."

I was beginning to think this was a waste of time. Maybe I should have stuck to chatting about old times.

"C'mon, don't be shy."

"Another out-of-towner. A German, Norbert Krieger."

Chris stopped in his tracks, and I nearly walked past him. We became an island in a jostling current of shoppers.

"From Munich?"

"I think so."

"You're joking, right?"

"No. Why?"

"How did his name come up?"

I wondered how specific I could be.

"He was seen in Athens. Supposedly handing over a pile of money to someone from here."

"Handing it to Omar?"

"Uh, no. Someone I'm not familiar with. I'm not at liberty to say."

I wasn't sure he bought it, but it didn't dampen his interest.

"Whoever it was, keep an eye on him."

"Why?"

He looked around. We stood between a butcher shop and an incense dealer, and the crowds were elbowing past. A slightly fevered expression crossed his face, as if he were suddenly back on duty in Baghdad. Then he grasped my shoulders and spoke into my ear.

"Not here. The Roman Theatre. Twenty minutes. Buy a ticket and meet me inside, I'll be up near the top."

He then darted into the crowd with the swiftness of a small fish that has spotted a shark. I whirled 'round as if I, too, might need to fend off a predator, but there was only the usual array of grim faces and dour looks. I drew a deep breath, nearly choking on a cloud of sweet gray smoke from the incense shop. Then I set out slowly for the theater, which was only a few blocks away. It was going to be a long twenty minutes.

The theater, probably Amman's best-known attraction, looks pretty much like the Roman amphitheaters you see everywhere, as if they were all built by the same franchisee. Or maybe I'd been swayed by Rafi Tuqan's lecture. It was hard not to think of them now as some ancient chain, like Starbucks, still serving lattes after 1,800 years.

It cost only a dinar to get inside. Then I began the long trudge up the steps. Squinting into the sun, I scanned the top rows for Chris. He was up to the right in the shade. I waved, but he didn't wave back. The steep climb made it easy to imagine Romans gasping in their togas as they cursed the summer heat in this forlorn imperial outpost.

Breathing heavily, I sagged onto the stones a few feet from Chris, who had yet to acknowledge me. As I was about to speak, three boys ran behind us. A man, presumably their father, called out from the stage below as they lit firecrackers and tossed them high in the air, sending their little bomblets toward a scattering of helpless people in the lower rows.

"Damn kids," Chris said. "Wait until they've passed."

"You're actually worried they'll hear us?"

"What's the expression? Little pitchers have big ears?"

"You've been in Baghdad too long."

"You may be right." A firecracker popped loudly a few rows below. "All the same . . ."

We waited until the little terrors had run past us to the bottom, scampering after their father. No one was within fifty feet of us. Chris spoke first.

"The Romans built these places so that the acoustics would carry even a whisper all the way up here from the stage. Did you know that?"

"What about the reverse?"

"Doesn't work that way, fortunately. The actors never would have wanted to hear all the catcalls."

"Then no one down there will hear us if you tell me who Norbert Krieger is."

"My sources aren't exactly up to date."

"Does that mean they're not reliable?"

"It means I haven't talked to them in ages. Five, maybe six years. And even then Krieger was supposedly no longer a player. It was just one of those names you were told to keep an ear out for, in case he ever got back in business. Not that there weren't hundreds of others like him. But still."

"What kind of business?"

"Oddball philanthropist, that's probably the best way to put it. Going back maybe twenty years. Before you, Hans, Omar, and I were all doing our good deeds during the intifada. He was known as a soft touch for underdog Arab causes. Well and good, I suppose, until he started bankrolling shady imams in Cairo. Turned out he was helping to keep the Muslim Brotherhood in business."

"The precursors to al-Qaeda, weren't they?"

"Something like that. In Cairo, anyway."

"Can't imagine that went over too well back in Germany."

"Got that right, mate. This was still during the Cold War, remember, when being pro-Arab could also look pro-Soviet. It cost him a professorship at some university in Munich. Not to mention no small amount of embarrassment for the West Germans. In those days they liked promoting the idea that only East Germans were still making trouble for Jews."

"What was he, some kind of unreconstructed Nazi?"

"Not really. Too young to have been in the war, or even Hitler Youth. And not one of those Auschwitz deniers, or anything like that. Although some of his crowd didn't always have the best reputation in that department."

"Such as?"

"Some outfit calling itself the Islamic Association of Germany. Originally started by some SS officers to rally Soviet-bloc Muslims to take up arms against Stalin. Worked, too, which meant that after the war a lot of

Muslims needed to get the hell out of the USSR. So they wound up in Bavaria. Presumably some of them met good old Norbert and won him over to the cause, which by then was anti-Israel. For a while he was one of their biggest contributors. Old family money, some of it. He was also a conduit for others. People who didn't want their names turning up on any contributor lists, so they let Norbert give on their behalf. Nowadays, of course, half of Europe speaks out on behalf of the Palestinians. Maybe that's what brought old Norbert out of the woodwork."

"How long's he been out of circulation?"

"Losing his university post pretty much put him out of business, and that must have been around '90. Except for a few sightings in maybe '93 he hasn't been heard from since."

"Why '93?"

"The Oslo Agreement. Who knows, maybe he was actually hopeful for peace. A lot of us were."

"Me, too. But that hardly makes him a candidate for underwriting bombers and hijackers."

"No one ever said he was. It was more the company he kept. Of course, people who lose their jobs sometimes change for the worse. And there's a lot more anger out there now than twelve years ago."

"Still, from what you're saying, it doesn't fit his profile."

"Unless he's been duped."

"What do you mean?"

"Told he was contributing to something peaceful when it was anything but."

Like Omar's charity, I thought. Maybe that's what Chris was thinking, too, but he had the good taste not to say it. He had known Omar almost as well as I had and would have been appalled by the possibility.

"But if that were the case," I said, thinking out loud, "then why keep it a secret?"

"Is that what Krieger's doing? Donating on the sly?"

"That's what it looked like in Athens, apparently."

"Care to elaborate on your sources?"

"Not really."

"Meaning that maybe you're not exactly on the level, either. Somehow I doubt it's Omar who has you sniffing around on this. Who's paying for the moonlighting, Freeman?"

"It's not that simple."

"It never is. It's just that you never struck me as the type."

"I'm not."

"I'll have to take your word for that, I guess."

"Suppose so."

He snickered, as if enjoying our little back-and-forth.

"Well, this sure beats what I've been up to. Kind of a relief to talk about something as simple as a money trail. But if Krieger is back on the board, plenty of people are going to want to know. And as possessor of this information, you should know that things could get a little dicey for you."

"You think?"

"Absolutely. You want my recommendation?"

"You're the pro."

"Forward whatever you've got to your sponsors, your handlers, whatever it is you want to call them, including anything I've just told you—minus my name, of course."

"And then?"

"Let it go. They'll know what to do, if anything."

"Thanks."

"Doesn't sound like you're going to follow my advice."

I shrugged, noncommittal.

"Then maybe I'll do a little asking around, if you don't mind. And if I hear anything more, I'll pass it along."

"I'd appreciate that."

"Just do me one favor in return."

"Okay."

"Don't get back in touch. Not even by e-mail. My employers might frown on it. If you hear from me, don't answer."

"Fair enough."

He nodded and stood. It seemed clear I wasn't supposed to follow. Then he walked slowly down the steps, back toward his life on the front lines. Or maybe I was the one now heading in that direction, just on another front of the war.

26

So here's what I knew: Omar was taking money—perhaps a lot of it—from an old German once infamous for contributing to radical Arab causes and mixing with questionable characters. Maybe this time the cause was just, but the secrecy of their handoff in Athens, not to mention the Mossad's possible interest, seemed to argue against it. At the very least, Omar would have mentioned the donation by now if it were on the up-and-up or was intended for the hospital.

Exactly where a Greek professor of archaeology fit in was another matter. Maybe Omar had met him while visiting a dig in Jordan. But plenty of people from all walks of life in Europe these days were sympathetic to the Palestinian cause, and surely not all of them were discriminating when deciding where to donate money.

At the Amman end of the chain there was Nabil Mustafa, who not only had a connection to Hamas but broke bread with gunrunners and visited the likes of Walid Khammar, a figure of interest to local security officials. Then there was his prosperous-looking visitor from America, Aliyah Rahim. I had Googled her in a spare moment, but found nothing of interest except that she might have a role in a Washington charity that seemed to have nothing to do with the Middle East. There was also a curious factoid about a man who might or might not be her husband, a Dr. Abbas Rahim. He was one of the surgeons who had saved the life of Ronald Reagan after the assassination attempt by John Hinckley. Hardly the stuff of wild-eyed radicalism. But if that was her, then how come she had lied to me about what Nabil and she were up to at Bakaa?

From all these threads I suppose it would be easy enough to weave a loose fabric connecting Krieger to the bomb makers of Hamas, with

Omar functioning as some sort of conduit. And if I were to turn over my findings to Black, White, and Gray, that's probably exactly what would happen.

Here was my problem with that conclusion. In my travels over the years I have seen scoundrels of every possible stripe. Warlords and gunrunners. Smugglers and racketeers. Mercenaries and true believers. And, of course, there was the pirate king Charles Mbweli, who would forever stalk the darkest fields of my imagination.

I suppose that Nabil might be shoehorned into one of those roles, humble family man or not. His piety alone made him potentially vulnerable to hothead meddlers in Bakaa. With a little scholarly coaching from some radical holy man, he might be coaxed to justify any manner of frightening actions. But I had my doubts.

Omar was an even poorer fit. In my sketching out of possible conspiracies, he was where the lines ran crooked. You needed only to look at the life he had built, and how he had built it, or at his secular lifestyle, his pragmatic wife. Even his grasping son, tooling around Abdoun's cafés and hookah bars, argued against Omar's participation. Why risk losing everything over a few bombs, especially when even the palace was smiling on your good fortune?

Unless, of course, there had always been a different Omar behind the facade, one I had never really known. If such a man existed, Jerusalem offered my best hope for finding out. Hans Wolters had known us both for as long as anyone else. And there was also David Ben-Zohar to consult, the old soldier and patrol commander now working in the security business. As a onetime adversary, he would view Omar with skepticism, and in his line of work he might even know why the Mossad had taken an interest.

Luckily, Hans responded promptly to my e-mail. I opened his answer Wednesday morning:

"Come over anytime. Shabbat is always a good day to try me, since both sides tend to stay quiet. But later is fine, too. Just name the date."

We set up a rendezvous for the following Monday afternoon at an Arab home on the Mount of Olives.

Ben-Zohar also answered, and in his curt, close-to-the-vest manner he suggested I call when I reached Jerusalem. Maybe he would have time for lunch. Perhaps meeting someone like me was bad for business.

I decided to cross the border next Monday morning to meet Hans, then try to catch up with Ben-Zohar the following day. I freed up the time by telling Omar I had further personal business.

And if Hans and Ben-Zohar couldn't help? Then I supposed that I would steal into the office late one night for a final, exhaustive sweep of the files, page by page, pulling an all-nighter if that was what it took to wrap up my business. One way or another, the end of the trail was in sight.

In the evening I phoned Mila. By now I no longer cared if our calls were monitored, as long as I got to hear her voice. Or maybe I still felt a need to atone for some of the stupid things I'd said in Athens.

There was no answer. Then I remembered that this was the day of their beach getaway to Glyfada. It was only seven, and they were probably fighting heavy traffic on the return trip.

But later calls were also unsuccessful. At 10 p.m. her aunt finally answered.

"They are not here," she said. A bit curtly, I thought.

"Didn't they go to Glyfada today?"

"Yes. I am sure they will be back soon."

"All right. I'll try again."

"Must you? I am going to sleep now. I will leave a message that you called."

My patience ran out at midnight, and I called again.

In a beleaguered and drowsy monotone, Aunt Aleksandra repeated what she had said at 10.

"They are not here. I do not know when they will return. I have left her a message."

"Tell her it doesn't matter how late. And please make sure she sees it."

"Yes, she will have your message. She will have *all* of your messages." Click.

When yet another hour passed I resigned myself to the idea that Mila wasn't coming back to Athens tonight. I then recalled the taunts of the watcher in the dark sedan and the cozy scene I'd witnessed from the shadows on that first night outside the apartment. Four heads in one small car, two up front and two in the back. And by now, of course, the fellow named Petros had grown even more handsome than I remembered, and was somewhere on a darkened beach, or a shuttered room by the sea, speaking endearments in Mila's ear in flawless Athenian Greek, offering her cigarettes and shots of ouzo as he slid closer, reaching for the buttons of her blouse.

At some point later I fell asleep, once again to the sound of the mouse, which was back on duty with renewed fury. By now I considered him both companion and intruder, a status akin to mine. Maybe that explains my dreams that night. In one, it was me down there behind the baseboard, scrabbling to get out even as I paused to eavesdrop. In another, Black, White, and Gray took the place of the mouse. They were in hiding, shrunken to the size of microdots while awaiting the right moment to emerge. Then I dreamed of Mila. She was back in her cousin's car with Petros, except now Black was at the wheel, showing the ravenous teeth of a rodent.

In the morning I brewed a pot of coffee, made some toast, and fried an egg. Then I tossed the food into the garbage uneaten. The phone had yet to ring. So much for all our talk of trust. So much for hefting this burden of secrets all these years on Mila's behalf. Or maybe Aunt Aleksandra hadn't left a message after all. I tried the number in Athens. This time not even Aleksandra answered.

I bolted from the house in a rage, and by late afternoon I was furious at everyone. At Black, White, and Gray. At Mila. And of course at Petros. It was with all that stewing in my mind that I resolved to enjoy myself with my old colleague Nura and whoever else she brought along. At worst I now had an excuse to drink heavily.

I was supposed to meet Nura at the InterContinental, and I arrived early. Walking into the posh lobby I was reminded of Aliyah Rahim. According to Nabil, this was where she had heard about our charity, by spotting some literature about us. With time to kill, I decided to check out his story.

Over by the concierge's desk was a small stand displaying pamphlets for nearby tourist sites and local shops. The only one hinting at any charitable connection was a flyer for Bani Hamida's craft and carpet store, which benefited the Bedouin women who made the products. The concierge noted my interest.

"Anything I can help you find, sir?"

"Yes. Do you have any information on the Bakaa Refugee Health Project?"

She creased her brow.

"And what is the nature of this organization, sir?"

"I'm told it's a charity. Raising money for a new hospital. I've heard the hotel might have some literature available."

"A hospital for Bakaa?"

"Yes."

"Then perhaps the organization is located there."

"Apparently it has an Amman office as well."

"I am sorry, I am not familiar with this organization. But I can refer you to the local offices of the United Nations. Perhaps they will know it. Would you like me to place the call for you?"

"No, thank you. I'm familiar with that number." I turned to go.

"Perhaps Save the Children would know."

"Yes. I'll try them. Thank you."

I asked at the front desk for Aliyah Rahim. Was she still registered?

"Yes, sir. You may call her room on the courtesy phone." He pointed across the lobby. "Dial zero and the hotel operator will connect you."

There was no answer, so I scribbled a note on hotel stationery asking her to call, and handed it to the desk clerk.

"Could you place this in her mailbox, please?"

"Absolutely, sir. I will make sure she receives it."

Whether she would call was another matter.

The Cinco de Mayo's bar was just down a corridor from the lobby, a cozy spot with few customers. Nura and the others hadn't arrived, so I took a seat on a cushioned bench at a trestle table. The place was lit dimly by flames hissing from gas jets lined up behind a pane of glass along the far wall. There were bowls filled with pistachios. I grabbed a handful and ordered a gin and tonic to wash them down. The subdued sound system was playing salsa, and the decor featured enough exposed wood and tasteful earth tones to offer the illusion that you were in, say, L.A. instead of the Middle East, especially if you'd downed a few drinks at the long polished-oak bar.

I cracked open the tough little pistachios and dropped the shells into the ashtray. A waiter attired just like the bartender, in black slacks and a sky-blue shirt, swooped in at regular intervals to empty the ashtray and replenish the nuts. As the gin kicked in I tried to think about anything except Mila, and wound up contemplating all the people of my ilk who must have passed this way since I had last been here. I had arrived in the summer of '90, along with a huge first wave of aid workers and reporters. Our two tribes were like rival theater troupes, our tours crossing paths in places like this as we put on one show after another. Some of the faces I remembered from them were now dead—an Irish aid worker who had been ambushed in Liberia, a Swiss nurse who took to drinking and plunged a van off a road in the Pyrenees, an American scribbler sawed in half by an Afghan desperado—all of them casualties of this itinerant lifestyle.

"Freeman?"

I looked up to see Nura Habash. It had been fourteen years, and she had aged gracefully, even admirably. Her years in the desert sun, rather than drying her up like a raisin as happened with most people, had winnowed her down to the essentials, which in her case were striking. She was deeply tanned, with dark brown hair pulled back in a bun and matching brown eyes that lit up when she smiled. Or maybe it was a reflection of the tiny flames along the wall. As I stood to greet her I caught a cinnamon whiff of her perfume and experienced a mild and somewhat vengeful thrill of arousal. This one's for Petros, I thought, as I offered to buy the first round.

Two others were with her, and only one was at all familiar, a woman who looked to be in her sixties.

"Rasheeda?" I said, taking a stab at it as I offered my hand. "From the Red Crescent?"

"Yes. But I am retired now. It was that or go to Iraq. Somehow I didn't feel up to it."

"I understand completely."

The other person turned out to be her old boss, a fellow named Tariq who now worked for the Ministry of Health.

With Ramadan having officially ended at sundown, all of them were in a jubilant mood, a welcome contrast to the gloom of my own day. The first topic of conversation was how they were spending tomorrow's celebratory feast day of Eid al-Fitr.

"I will have to leave here early, I am sorry to say," Rasheeda said. "Or else I'll never finish getting ready. Ten relatives are coming to our house after morning prayers."

"Only ten?" Tariq said. "My wife is cooking for seventeen! I've packed away enough fireworks for the children to start World War III."

"Remind me to avoid your block," I said, intending it as a jest.

But Tariq, seeming worried that I'd meant it literally, hastened to add, "Oh, it is really quite harmless. Mostly sparklers and little poppers. Not to worry."

"I'm sure it is." Did he really believe Americans had become that paranoid?

We talked of old times, of course. Tariq claimed to actually remember me, so I nodded and said that he, too, looked familiar. He had visited one of the tent cities that Nura and I helped set up in the blistering heat of August 1990, after Iraq's invasion of Kuwait. We were there on into early '91.

Rasheeda was almost nostalgic in recounting how innocent the subsequent war had been by comparison to the present one.

"It was over in just seconds," she said.

"A hundred hours," I added, remembering how the U.S. commanders had liked the tidy sound of that number when they picked a time for the cease-fire. As if that might tie up all the loose ends for future years.

From there we eased into shop talk, with its usual doses of rumor and gossip, and sprinkled with the requisite acronyms of our trade. Our set can be every bit as exclusionary and snobbish as the habitués of Monte Carlo or Capri, because deep in our hearts we're convinced that only we are on the side of the angels. The problem with that point of view is that we can never seem to find the actual angels as we make our way around the globe. So we anoint ourselves as their proxies, excusing our excesses and failures as the fair-market value of our services.

After only two rounds and barely half an hour, Rasheeda and Tariq rose to offer fond farewells, which left only Nura and me. We were seated on the same bench.

"Nice to see them," I said, at a loss for words now that the evening had suddenly turned into something resembling a date. The only other people left in the place were four British tourists with three children who were tearing around the room. So there we sat, Nura and me, a little closer than before in a firelit world of possibility, while the Latin brass blew sweetly and the congas kept pace with my pulse. She devoured the last of the nuts, seemingly ravenous. I realized she must have been fasting all day and probably could use some dinner. She was one of those Muslims who fasts but also drinks, sort of like a Baptist who likes bourbon but won't dance.

She ordered her third drink, a gin like mine. Perhaps, like me, she was merely lonely.

A waiter approached. He carried a small wicker basket, which he thrust beneath our noses. It was filled with foil-wrapped chocolates.

"Please, take a sweet," he said with a smile.

"He is getting married," Nura said.

The waiter nodded in reply, grinning from ear to ear. She took a chocolate to let him spread his cheer. I considered doing the same, even though the flavor would be a poor mix with the gin, and the waiter's visit already seemed like an intrusion.

But I had noticed the Brits turning him down earlier. Perhaps they suspected some sort of fee or obligation. And I felt a sudden urge to make a good showing for the West, to let him know—and Nura as well—that we were not all so clumsily reserved or stodgy. So I smiled and reached into the basket.

"Congratulations," I said.

Nura gave my other hand a squeeze. Did she know I was married? Should I tell her? For an uneasy second or two I flashed on my wedding in a Christian Orthodox chapel, the priest in his severe getup and menacing beard. The somber drone of biblical verses in Serbo-Croatian, followed by a joyous feast and lots of dancing. My young country bride and me, the toast of the town. That marriage had become the main pillar of stability in my life, but in my current embittered mood it felt wobbly, a mockery to my years of vigilance.

"Are you all right?" Nura asked.

"Just tired. It's been a long week."

Her hand alighted on my thigh, softly as a sparrow. My erection was almost instantaneous, even though I couldn't quite shake the disapproving stare of the bearded priest, still gazing from the altar.

Our waiter reappeared.

"Do you want another?"

The music had switched to a mild version of hip-hop in Arabic.

"Why don't we leave?" Nura suggested.

I nodded for the check.

"Would you like to have dinner?" I asked.

"I would. But I should call my mother first. She will be wondering where I am."

"Does she live with you?" Something about the possibility disappointed me.

"Next door. So she keeps a close watch. Sometimes too close. It will be nice to have an evening out."

As we crossed the lobby on our way out of the InterCon, Nura stepped away for a moment to make her call. That was when I glanced across the room toward the lobby bar and saw the American, Aliyah Rahim. She was having drinks at a far table, and seated with her was none other than Dr. Hassan. What's more, she looked uncomfortable, like a woman being taken advantage of by an overbearing date. Or maybe that was a reflection of my own situation.

Dr. Hassan's manner didn't seem as stuffy as it usually did, and he certainly wasn't employing his doctorly gestures, with their vague air of brusque disdain. Predatory, that was the word for it. He looked poised to strike at any moment.

If I'd had nothing better to do, I might have approached them, or at least waited around to see what they did next. But Nura returned on a cloud of her cinnamon scent, and by then I was too preoccupied to really care. If I was still curious later, I could always ask Dr. Hassan.

It did make me wonder if maybe Nabil had been telling the truth after all. Maybe he really had intended to take the American to see Dr. Hassan but never made it to the office. Perhaps the Rahim woman really was interested in the charity.

Nura took my hand as we dashed recklessly across the street, dodging screaming cabs and *serveece* vans, to a trendy restaurant called the Living Room. Every table was taken, so we wound up at the sushi bar. A loud sound system was playing hip-hop and techno. Another place with seemingly no connection to its locale. From L.A. to Manhattan in only half a block, yet still in the heart of Amman.

An Asian sushi chef offered a minor floor show as he worked in front of us, attired in a white judo robe with the unlikely name "Mario" stitched in blue. We ordered more drinks with our food. The music was so loud we had to lean into each other's faces to hear ourselves above the din. That gave her words a feathery edge, and I felt the warmth of each syllable against my lips.

When the check arrived, she suggested that we share a taxi. I offered to accompany her home.

"You can walk me to my door, then."

"Won't your mother see me?"

"You mean if I invite you inside?"

"Well, yes, I suppose."

She smiled, and placed a hand on the back of my neck to draw my face closer.

"Perhaps. This is why sometimes I leave the light off on my porch. Like tonight."

That was the moment, I suppose, when guilt needed to give a mighty heave in the game of tug-of-war that it had been playing all night against jealousy. But by then lust had joined the match as well, and between it, the drinks, and Nura's perfume, I found myself climbing into the back of a cab while Nura squeezed my hand. The taxi took us west through the city, all the way to the Seventh Circle before turning north. She had the driver drop us off on a main drag that looked like so many other main drags in Amman, a commercial street four lanes wide, only a block from her apartment. This was no Abdoun, yet nascent prosperity loomed on every corner. Young men were lined up outside food shops. Others were still at work, long after dark and on the eve of a holiday, no less, putting the finishing touches on a new storefront that looked only days away from opening. We rounded a corner and stepped up a flight of stairs into a stucco apartment building. Nura put a finger to her lips and smiled as we approached a darkened doorway. She pointed next door, presumably her mother's place. Then she unlocked the door as quietly as possible before we practically tiptoed across the threshold.

Once inside, she slipped her arms around me, and there was no longer room for second thoughts. She tilted her face to mine for a kiss, and I greedily obliged. Then her warmth and softness overwhelmed me, and from that moment on it was all about forward motion, and how to best maintain it. Her hands reached for my belt, slipping it from the loop. A quick zip and a gentle tug. My trousers tumbled to my ankles. Moments later we made our way down a hallway to her bedroom, stopping only to remove one item or another of our clothing. Then she lit a candelabra on a table by her bed, which cast us in a bright soft glow of amber. For the next half hour I celebrated the end of Ramadan in her arms, breaking fast as it were, in a deliciously secular feast of desire.

Immediately afterward, of course, guilt rejoined the match with the sharpest of tugs. And that wasn't the only feeling that made me sad. If I had tripped across the line so easily, then perhaps Mila had as well. But did I really believe that this was what my wife had been up to with Petros? A few hours ago I would have offered an emphatic yes, but now my gut told me otherwise. Then why hadn't she called?

Nura didn't seem to notice my sudden moodiness. She fetched a bottle of brandy and lit a cigarette, and to my relief she carried the load of conversation, picking up where we had left off earlier in our rundown of old friends and colleagues.

"Do you ever wonder where they will all end up, all of those people in our business? Not just the ones who used to hang out in Amman, but over on the West Bank, too? Fighting all the old struggles, over and over."

"Sometimes. Were you over there much? On that side of the river, I mean."

"Oh, yes. Not so much during the intifada, like you. But later, after Oslo. During the thaw."

"Or what we thought was the thaw."

"Yes. Terrible seeing what's become of it. That idiot Sharon, just walking up to the Temple Mount, swaggering like he owned it, with all his soldiers. What did he expect, that everyone would just take it lying down?"

I had participated in this argument on one side or another for years, usually playing devil's advocate for whichever side needed one. And even that night in Nura's bed I couldn't leave a one-sided version standing unopposed.

"Hardly seems enough provocation to start all that's happened since, though. It's probably exactly the reaction he wanted, and they were fool enough to oblige him."

"Same as always."

"Yes. Same as always."

We swapped a few more memories and a few more names. I wasn't much interested in further affection, and hoped she wouldn't notice. Fortunately Mila's name never came up as we rummaged further through our past—I don't think the two of them had ever met—but Chris Boylan's name did.

"You knew him?" I asked.

"Of course. I thought everyone here in the business knew him."

"Well, he wasn't around during the Gulf War."

"No. But later. On the West Bank. He used to tell all your war stories from the intifada. About you and Omar, all of you out there in your VW Passats, like cowboys in the Wild West."

I smiled in the dark. We really had been foolhardy. But in those days the risks had seemed worth it, even if our results never amounted to much.

"I ran into Chris the other day."

"In Amman? When?"

"On Tuesday. Downtown. He seemed tired."

"I didn't know he was living here."

"He's not. He's in Iraq."

"No wonder he's tired. What was he doing here?"

"Just passing through."

"To visit you?"

I had already said more than I should have. Chris probably wouldn't have appreciated being the subject of pillow talk, given his skittishness.

"No, no. Just happened to bump into him down at the Roman Theatre. Didn't have time for much more than a hello and a good-bye."

"Who's he working for now?"

"Some consultant. He didn't really say."

"Oh."

And then, dead air, the unfinished topic hanging between us like the afterimage of a photo flash. Something about it made me mildly uneasy, or maybe it was just the guilt, peeking again over my shoulder. So I got up to take a leak, and brought back a glass of water. When I climbed into bed, Nura snuggled against my back and said no more. A few minutes later she was asleep, leaving me alone with troubled thoughts of Mila.

In the morning, Nura invited me to stay for coffee, but I begged off by claiming an early social appointment across town. Omar had indeed invited me to spend the holiday with his family, offering to let me share in everything from the morning prayer service to the festive dinner and fireworks afterward. But I had begged off from that invitation, too, with yet another manufactured excuse. I was lying to a lot of people lately. I suppose the necessities of the spy business were partly to blame. But that seemed like scant justification as I quietly rode a taxi to Othman Bin Affan Street, perhaps because I knew Mila was next on the list of those to be deceived.

Her time came sooner than expected. The phone was ringing as I unlocked the door, even though it was only seven. I could tell she was upset by the tone of her voice.

"Where were you?"

The question I least wanted to answer. Not that I didn't handle it like a professional.

"Out at Bakaa. What's wrong? And where were *you* the other night?"

"Oh, Freeman, stop it! I've needed you. It was horrible."

"What was?"

"The entire evening, after our trip to Glyfada."

"What do you mean?"

"On the way back. We were out on the highway. They could have killed us, and it was all my fault. Then when we finally made it back, I kept calling and couldn't reach you for two days, so of course I was expecting the worst. You don't know how close I came to just hopping on a plane for Amman."

"Jesus, what's happened? Some kind of accident?"

"Anything but, although I guess that's how they wanted it to look. It's these people you're working for. I'm sure of it."

"I'm okay, so stop worrying about me. Just slow down and tell me what happened, from the beginning. And why are you to blame?"

She took a deep breath, and the most frantic part of her eruption seemed to subside. Her next words came out slower, and with a more measured tone.

"I'm not even sure I should tell you. You'll be so angry. They're probably listening anyway. Don't you hear it, all the popping and clicking?"

The line was indeed bad, although such noise was a mandatory accessory of Greek phone service.

"We'll just have to live with that, I guess. Besides, from what you're saying they already know what's happened."

"True enough." She took another deep breath. "It started after you left, really. I guess I was still upset there were things you weren't telling me, so I decided to call some of our old friends, from our time in Africa."

"Mila, no."

"I know. I'm sorry. They weren't much help, either, not for what I wanted. But they did say some people had been asking about you, about a month ago. Some kind of security background check, that's how it was presented. So that's when I lost it and called the embassy back again."

"Jesus, Mila."

"They didn't tell me anything, either, of course. I guess I just needed to vent. And I have to admit, it made me feel pretty good. Or it did until we were riding back from Glyfada. That's when they came after us."

"On the highway?"

"Yes. Four of them. They were on motorcycles."

I thought immediately of the two riders who had nearly run me down in the streets of Athens.

"Two came up from behind. One got in front and slowed down. The other came in from the side and wouldn't let us over. We were in the far right lane and they kept swerving closer until they forced us onto the shoulder. The men on the bikes didn't even look at us. They weren't smiling or laughing, so it was no joke. And when Petros honked his horn, they flashed a gun. There was a truck broken down on the shoulder ahead of us, and we almost hit it. When we stopped, they pulled away from us. Then Petros went after them, so of course when the police saw the chase they stopped us because we were the trailing car. They did nothing to catch the others."

"My God. It sounds horrible."

"That wasn't even the worst part. The police held us all night."

So that's why she hadn't been there when I phoned. And I, of course, had assumed the worst and then recklessly acted upon it, taking Nura to bed.

"They wouldn't believe our story," Mila went on. "We gave them tag numbers and everything, but they did nothing to check it out. Just kept us waiting, and asked us the same stupid questions again and again. They said we must have all been drunk, but they wouldn't give us any tests. They didn't let us go until eight the next morning, and when we finally got back to my aunt's she said you had called over and over, and that it was urgent, so of course I thought something terrible must have happened. Then when I couldn't reach you . . ."

"Really, I'm fine. I was just out doing . . . fieldwork." Another wince.

"You weren't the only one who'd left a message."

"Black, White, and Gray?"

"They didn't leave a name. All they said was, 'Tell Mila to stop.' Then they hung up. So you see?"

Just like Mbweli would have done it. I was furious more than intimidated, because once upon a time I had caved in to that kind of threat, and look what happened. Not that I could say that to Mila. Not now or ever, which brought us back to the same impasse as always.

My inclination was to offer yet another lecture on trust, while urging her to hold out a while longer. But under the circumstances I didn't have the nerve for it, and I could never have made it sound convincing. So I resorted to a lame pep talk.

"Look, all I can offer is the news that I'm nearly done, or hope I am. And as terrible as all of this is, it only makes me want to push harder to finish up. But you really do need to sit tight and stop trying to get answers. That's all they want you to do anyway. Then they'll back off. Just be careful. Stick with your cousin and Luka and Petros and anyone else who's available whenever you go out. I'm pretty sure they've got someone watching the apartment, so be aware of that as well, and keep a low profile. Then when I'm done I'll come get you and take you out of there. If we can't go back to Karos, or you don't want to, then okay, we'll live with that. But we'll find someplace where we can make things work, and we'll put all of this behind us. Okay?"

"I hope so. But someday you're going to have to tell me everything."

"Sure. Whatever you want."

I would do nothing of the sort, of course. But a cad like me would be able to come up with something.

"I want to believe you. But you don't make it easy. You should have seen us. We were scared to death. We started to wonder if the police would ever let us go. If you had been there . . .”

“I know. I understand. But I’ll make it stop as soon as I can. I promise.”

We said good-bye. Mila was as calm as I could have expected, and seemed resigned to the idea of waiting it out in relative submission. Quite a concession for her.

Her news heightened my sense of urgency. If my employers had joined forces in Greece with the Mossad, then who knew what that would mean for me in Jerusalem. Yet another reason to watch my step. And if they were going to get rough, then I had to be prepared to do the same. Taking the gun to Jerusalem was out of the question, given all the security at the border. But I was wary of simply leaving it in a dresser drawer. I could imagine how the authorities would react to finding an illegal weapon in the possession of someone who had just slipped across the river to Israel.

I decided to bury it out back before leaving. To keep the disturbed earth from arousing suspicion I drove to the Safeway on Sunday after all the shops had reopened and bought an outdoor plant and a gardening spade. On the morning of my departure I sealed the gun in a plastic bag. Then I dug a hole in the corner of my small yard and dropped the gun in, followed by the plant. As I was patting the soil back into place, Fiona called out from next door. I flinched and nearly dropped the spade.

“That’s not a bad little tree you’ve chosen. Not sure about the placement, though. A little shady, perhaps?”

“How long have you been standing there?”

“Sorry. I’m very nosy when it comes to gardening. Did you fertilize it?”

“Maybe later.”

“I could give you some.”

“Thanks. I’ll keep that in mind.”

I wiped the dirt from my hands and disappeared indoors before she could quiz me further. Had she seen the gun? If so, would she tell her friends at the palace? But that was all the worrying I had time for. Jerusalem beckoned, and I was eager to make the most of it.

27

For three days Aliyah had managed to accomplish absolutely nothing. She spent the rest of Monday shopping. On Tuesday she toured Petra. Then on Wednesday she rode a bus north to the Roman ruins of Jerash. All the while she kept her cell phone switched off.

She knew that her ad-libbing was risky, and that the next scheduled contact might well take matters into his own hands and confront her somewhere when she least expected it. Perhaps they would even relay word to Abbas that she was being uncooperative. But she couldn't resist the temptation for delay, because each day without progress was a further handicap to disaster. Haphazard or not, perhaps her plan to stall things out would succeed. The senator would die, the funeral would come and go without incident, and she would return home to a thwarted but safe Abbas. Eventually he would realize it was for the best.

At breakfast on Thursday, which was the day of her scheduled appointment at Bakaa with Khalid II, she switched her phone back on. It rang before she had finished her second cup of coffee.

A voice she didn't recognize instructed her to meet another contact that very night in the lobby bar of the InterContinental. At least this one wasn't also named Khalid. But of the three operatives she had met so far, he was easily the most disturbing, and so was his news.

Well before that meeting ever took place there was another discouraging development. Khalid II never showed up for their 4 p.m. appointment.

She got there in plenty of time, just as they had arranged. The streets of Bakaa were packed with people, cars, and motorcycles. Everyone seemed to be shopping for Eid al-Fitr, and the taxi had to fight its way slowly down narrow lanes of corrugated metal buildings. She nonetheless managed to reach Khalid II's house promptly at 4 p.m., only to learn that she had been stood up.

A thin, soft-spoken woman who must have been his wife met her on the doorstep. She spoke before Aliyah even gave her name.

"He said to tell you he is sorry, but he had to leave. He will not be back today."

A young girl stood behind the woman in the shadows of the room. Aliyah wondered if Khalid II might even be in there.

"He should have phoned to tell me," she said loudly, in case he was listening.

"He said to tell you that would not have been a wise decision. It was not possible for him. It may not be possible for quite a while."

The choice of words was disturbing. If she wanted to learn how to dismantle a bomb, Khalid II might be her only hope.

"Is Khalid—" She felt ridiculous using the code name. "Is your husband in some kind of trouble?"

The woman's face fell. She seemed on the verge of tears.

"I do not know. But he is very worried."

"Worried about what? Did someone find out about our meeting?"

Perhaps the American had reported it to the authorities. The wrong kind of attention might be ruinous for a young man with a family to support. But it might be a disaster for her, too.

"Please, you should go now. There are other people to consider."

The woman looked up and down the street, as if someone might be coming. Aliyah turned, but saw only the steady stream of shoppers.

"Other people?"

"Please. You must go."

"Let me leave a message." Aliyah reached in her purse for a pen.

"Please go now. I will tell him that you wish him to call."

"But—"

The woman shut the door with an almost frantic heave. It was a little frightening, but it also angered her. So much for her tutorial. If Abbas figured out how to rig up a bomb on his own, she wouldn't have the first idea of how to disarm it. And given Khalid II's sudden disappearance, she supposed she now had to worry about getting in trouble here.

If the authorities wanted to arrest her, Bakaa would probably be the perfect place to close in. Not back at the hotel, where the scene could become an embarrassment, or upsetting for the paying guests. And if she disappeared into some ministry van out here, who would ever pass the word to Abbas?

It made her want to leave in a hurry, but there were no taxis in sight. She tried calling for one on her cell phone, but dispatchers for the first two companies refused to send anyone to Bakaa. The third one gave in, but only after she promised to meet the taxi at a major intersection at the edge of the camp.

The rendezvous point was more than a mile away, and she had to stop several times for directions. Even then, there was no taxi waiting at the appointed spot. She waited another half hour in mounting frustration, feeling dusty and angry, and a little dizzy. A swallow of water would have helped, but she didn't dare drink it in public during the month's final hour of fasting.

As Ramadan's last seconds ticked away, the bustle of the crowd took on a frenzied edge. Compared to the previous days, when nearly everyone was indoors by sundown in order to break fast as soon as possible, here in Bakaa there were still plenty of people in the streets. Their mood was celebratory, an almost manic glee sharpened by their day-long hunger. When the call to prayer finally announced the setting of the sun from the crackling loudspeaker of a nearby mosque, she heard an ungodly squeal from around the corner, followed by the sound of grunting and scuffling. She walked a short distance to investigate and saw a man in a bloodied apron butchering a goat, right on his doorstep. A little farther down the alley, two more men were doing the same thing. The whole neighborhood seemed to be erupting in a frenzy of butchery in preparation for tomorrow's midday feast. Looking into the faces of passersby she saw smiles of anticipation and relief. The long month of self-denial was over, and the animal screams echoed like a signal of primal urgency.

While she could certainly appreciate such emotions, her own weariness and worries left her feeling mostly revulsion. The smell of the blood was strong. It pooled in bright red splotches on the dust and against the curb. She fought down an impulse to retch and turned away, feeling foolish and weak. This was certainly no more barbaric than lopping the heads off millions of turkeys for Thanksgiving, and at least on these humble streets they didn't leave the dirty work for processing plants and supermarkets. Nonetheless, she was physically overwhelmed, and wanted only to get out of there as quickly as possible.

She walked unsteadily up the main drag toward the entrance to the camp, jostling men and women who were carting home sacks and boxes bulging with the fruits of their shopping. It took another half hour, but she finally found a driver who would take her back to Amman. She spent the next forty minutes slumped in the backseat with the windows down, letting the wind off the darkening hillsides blast against her face.

Back at the hotel room, her message light was flashing. The desk clerk told her there was a handwritten message waiting downstairs. She unfolded it as she stood at the front desk.

"Please call," was all it said. It was signed by Freeman Lockhart. The American again. Maybe he was even some kind of operative or agent. For all she knew, he was sitting in a windowless room with Khalid II, interrogating the poor fellow. She crumpled the message and tossed it into an ashtray on her way back upstairs.

After a quick shower, she returned to the lobby just in time for her 8 p.m. appointment. The noon phone call had instructed her to address this latest contact simply as "the doctor."

Whoever he was, he seemed to recognize her right away. She saw someone waving from the far side of the tables, and he crossed the room to meet her. He looked to be in his late fifties, with a mannered patrician air. Aliyah knew a thing or two about doctors, and after only a few minutes of conversation she pegged this one as the sort who would talk down to his patients and hold himself loftily above his staff. Something about his voice, his mannerisms, even the way he dealt with their waiter, marked him as one of those surrogate gods convinced of his own infallibility. Under his rules, she guessed, mistakes were made by nurses, administrators, or assistants. Any patient who died had failed him, not vice versa. Or maybe she reacted so adversely because of what he told her. In any event, they quickly got off on the wrong foot, and things went downhill from there.

"You must be Mrs. Aliyah Rahim?" he said, as if relishing possession of her full name.

"Yes. And you are the doctor?"

"I am indeed. Please, I have taken a table for us. One of the better ones, where we are less likely to be disturbed."

It looked like the rest of the tables to Aliyah, except it was against the back wall. All around them people were in a festive mood, gearing up for tomorrow.

"My favorite time of year," the doctor said, gesturing grandly with his hands. "And how will you be celebrating, being so far from home?"

"Dinner in my room, I suppose."

"How unfortunate. Under more favorable circumstances I would of course invite you to our home, but my wife's family from Madaba has quite filled the place up."

"Of course you would invite me, especially when I don't even know your real name." She had held her fire with these bumblers long enough. "As long as you're extending empty hospitality, *doctor*, perhaps you could diagnose why everyone knows and uses my correct name while I am only told pseudonyms, like Khalid I, or Khalid II, or the doctor."

Her rebuke didn't make the slightest dent in his expression. If anything, his smile widened.

"I am afraid there is no other way. Not if you really want our help."

"I think the question is not whether I want it, but whether I will ever get it."

"So am I to take it that your meeting with Khalid did not go well?"

"Which Khalid? The café one or the Bakaa one?"

"I was told Bakaa was where the more important matters were to be discussed. Am I correct, Mrs. Rahim?"

She wished he would stop announcing her name to everyone within earshot. He wasn't even attempting to keep his voice down.

"Correct."

"So was he satisfactory?"

Had he really not heard?

"He was very kind. Very solicitous." No sense letting them make Khalid II the scapegoat. The young man seemed to be in enough trouble already.

"Kindness is commendable. But was he able to answer your technical inquiries?"

"Truthfully?"

"I deal only in truthfulness, Mrs. Rahim."

"He was a little sketchy on details. I got the idea no one had correctly informed him of my purpose." She leaned across the table so no one else could hear her next words. The doctor leaned forward as well, and she was nearly overpowered by the scent of his cologne. "Someone had led him to believe I was a suicide bomber."

She half expected the doctor to fly into a rage. Instead he smiled smugly, as if she had just told an amusing anecdote.

"Ah. A mix-up, then. Not to worry. I am sure we can find someone else to offer more precise instructions."

"In his defense, he said that he might be able to do that. He was going to try, anyway. But he didn't strike me as very experienced in these matters."

"Oh, but he is experienced now, of course. Thanks to you."

"I don't follow your meaning."

"You don't need to. It is a local matter. But we thank you for your role in it. In return we will do what we can to assist you. Although our services may not be quite as vital as you think. Not with the headway that your husband has made in your absence. I am told that some sort of excavation is involved in his work, correct? And that he has already made substantial progress."

"Substantial progress?"

Her mouth went dry. If the doctor had been wearing a stethoscope she might have asked him to listen for a pulse, because suddenly she barely seemed to have one.

"Why, yes." The doctor took an obvious pleasure in his revelations. "It has been our understanding all along that time was short. So, no matter how slowly you have chosen to move, and no matter how many days you have turned off your mobile phone, it has not stopped us from taking measures to assist him as much as possible."

"What do you mean? I thought you were supposed to assist him by helping me."

"I am aware that is what you thought. But mostly what we sought from you and your husband was evidence of your commitment. Abbas demonstrated that to our satisfaction merely by sending you to Amman. So, once our representatives observed that you were safely aboard the plane at Dulles, we extended an offer of immediate help to your husband."

"Immediate help?" She felt like someone had just knocked the wind out of her.

"Technical expertise. And, when necessary, manual labor. So you should not concern yourself too greatly over your failures with Khalid in Bakaa. As I said earlier, you have served our own interests on that count. In return we are serving your interests in Washington. I am told the work is nearly complete. Meaning that any sort of, well, reluctance on your part has been very ably overcome by others. So you see? Everything is well in hand."

Aliyah felt queasy. Her nausea resurrected the images from a few hours ago at Bakaa, with their animal screams and the letting of blood. The smell of slaughter seemed to emanate from her clothes and skin, as if she had never showered.

"Are you all right, my dear? Can I order you something? I am told that you drink alcohol. Perhaps a gin would help."

"No."

She gripped the bottom of the table and looked him in the eye, determined not to exhibit any further sign of weakness. He was already enjoying her discomfort far too much. As well he might, having played her for a fool. Then she thought of something that might make his smile disappear.

"This all comes as something of a surprise, but I will be fine. There is one possible complication, though."

"Yes?"

"An American. He observed Khalid and me together at Bakaa. He may even have overheard our conversation. His name is Freeman Lockhart. He gave me his card."

Her news did not have the desired effect. The doctor only smiled, broader than ever.

"I am familiar with Mr. Lockhart. There is no way possible that he could know of your plans, so I would not trouble myself worrying about him."

"But what about Khalid? He may have been compromised."

"Precisely. As I said before, that is a local matter. Your news only makes me more certain it will be handled satisfactorily."

Aliyah couldn't take his smugness a moment longer. She pushed back her chair with a noisy scrape and stood so suddenly that she felt a bit wobbly. She had to get out of here—this bar, this hotel, this country. She had to reach Abbas.

"You will please excuse me."

Her intention was to turn and walk away before the doctor could reply. But he stood, too, then reached across the table and gripped her tightly by the forearm. His smile didn't waver, but there was no hint of amusement in his eyes.

"Our business is not yet finished, Mrs. Rahim."

With his free hand he pulled an envelope from an inside pocket of his jacket.

"To show our good intentions, here is some cash to help finance the remaining days of your stay in Amman."

Aliyah ignored the envelope and tugged at her arm, but his grip was firm.

"Thank you, but I don't need your money. I plan on leaving as soon as I can."

"I'm afraid that won't be possible."

He tightened his grip. Now it hurt. She tried to twist away, but to no effect.

"Not possible?"

"We would ask that you remain in Jordan a while longer, so as to prevent any complications in Washington. Given the behavior we have witnessed here, we worry that your sudden arrival there might cause, well, too much of a distraction."

"You're *forcing* me to stay?"

Several people at the next table looked over in apparent concern, then looked away when the doctor smiled back, as if to say, "Women—what can you do with them?"

He lowered his voice and leaned closer.

"Of course we are not forcing you. We only wish to do what is best for your husband. And we will do all in our power to make your stay comfortable. Do you see those men over there, Mrs. Rahim? The ones in brown suits?"

It wasn't so easy turning around with the doctor holding her forearm, but she saw two rather large fellows dressed in brown. One stood near the elevators. The other was by the hotel's main entrance.

"They will be available to you for whatever you need," the doctor said smoothly. "They can escort you on walks. Drive you downtown. Even drive you back up to Jerash, if that is the way you would continue to pass your time. Then, when the time is right, we will arrange return transportation for you to Washington. You may try to leave earlier, of course. But I think you will find that due to the holiday all flights are quite booked up for the next several days. And beyond the weekend, there is the matter of how you will reach the airport. Your two escorts may not be able to arrange transportation for a while, and they will be greatly offended if you attempt to choose other means. Things will go much better for you if you just leave matters to them. Then, when all plans have been carried out to everyone's satisfaction, you may return. In the meantime, I will of course be at your disposal. Just let those gentlemen know if you wish to see me. Farewell, Mrs. Rahim."

He released her arm, dropped the envelope on the table, and walked away. She was furious, and a little frightened as well. She watched the doctor cross the room, half hoping that the men in brown would follow him out the door. Instead, they nodded as he passed and held their stations.

What an idiot she had been, placing so much hope in a passive strategy of avoidance and delay. Tiptoe off to Jordan rather than deal with Abbas directly, as if the whole foolish scheme might rot and decay in her absence. For all she had done to retake control of her life through grief counseling and prayer, she realized now that Abbas was the one who had seized the wheel of their fate, and he was steering them toward disaster.

She walked briskly toward the elevators, not even daring to glance at the posted "escort" as she pressed the button for her floor. Fortunately he did not board with her. Her mind was a jumble of wild thoughts as she rode to her floor. But she was not ready to quit, not nearly. And by the time she reached her door she knew that only two plausible courses of action remained.

One, no matter how many people the doctor had assigned to watch her, she had to get back to Washington as soon as possible, by any means necessary.

Two, even if she was delayed several days, she should make one last attempt to reach Khalid II. In trouble or not, he was her only hope for acquiring quick and dirty knowledge on dismantling a bomb. Perhaps before dropping out of sight he had found out what she needed to know. It was a scant hope, but as long as she was going to be trapped here for a while, sneaking out to Bakaa for one last visit was the only alternative worth pursuing. All her other contacts, she realized now, had been interested only in using her for some other purpose, and in the process they had made a fool of her.

The possibility that upset her most was that this was the way Abbas had planned things from the beginning. Maybe her treatment had been part of his agreement with the Jordanians: Keep my wife out of my hair while you send help. In exchange, you may employ her in whatever petty scheme you wish.

The thought made her so flustered that she had to slide her key card three times before the lock clicked open to her room. She heaved herself onto the bed with a groan of outraged agony.

She picked up the phone, then realized that at this hour all the travel agencies and local airline offices would already be closed for the holiday and might not reopen for several days. Officially, Eid al-Fitr was a three-day celebration. But she'd be damned if she would simply take the doctor's word on how difficult it would be to get a quick flight home. For starters, she might be able to secure a ticket online through the computers in the hotel's business center. With any luck it would still be open.

She made it as far as the elevator, then realized that the man downstairs would follow her. So she ran down the hall to a stairway at the far end. Maybe he wouldn't see her emerge, and she could reach the business center, which was tucked into a back office in the opposite direction.

Aliyah got there just in time, and no one followed. The clerk on duty seemed anxious to leave for the holiday, but Aliyah had the advantage of being a regular visitor. She had been checking daily on the computer terminals for local news from back home, in case the senator died or took a sudden turn for the worse.

Soon after logging on, however, she discovered that the doctor had been correct. Every flight out of Amman was booked solid for the next several days. She vowed to try again later, in case something opened up. But for the near term she was stuck.

Aliyah then checked for any news update on the senator. Thankfully, there was nothing. As long as he held on, she would be all right. For now, then, her only option was to find some way to arrange another audience with Khalid II. Her efforts might well be fruitless, but she had to try, if only to do *something*. Her entire world was on the verge of being consumed by a needless act of vengeance, and she was five thousand miles away from being able to stop it.

28

Peace between Jordan and Israel was supposed to bring harmony to their border.

It didn't. Crossing from Amman to Jerusalem is still a three-hour ordeal of overpriced taxis, flyblown buses, and meticulous body searches. A trip that should be a leisurely one-hour drive through the desert is instead an armed transit between warring tribes, especially in the tender zone astride the River Jordan, with its coiled razor wire, tank traps, and helmeted soldiers peering from the slits of bunkers.

Somewhere in the middle of this ride, the tires of your bus thump briefly on a tiny bridge, and the more vigilant passengers glimpse a narrow brown creek as it passes fleetingly below. This is the River Jordan, the most overrated body of water in the history of time.

Officials on the Jordanian side always seem more relaxed, probably because a lot fewer people are trying to blow them up. They never do much searching or scanning, and the customs men are as bored as tollbooth attendants. Just keep the line moving.

This time they weren't quite so accommodating. Of the twenty people on my bus, I was the only one whose passport prompted the attendant behind the glass to place a phone call. It caught me by surprise, so I wasn't paying close enough attention to see if he had checked my name against any sort of watch list. He punched in a number with the Amman city code. Then he nodded, said a few words I couldn't hear through the glass, and summoned a supervisor from out front who had been relaxing in the shade with an orange soda.

The boss took the receiver. Then he, too, spoke and nodded while writing something in a large black notebook, which he had pulled from a locked drawer. He glanced my way a few times, causing the people in line behind me to shuffle nervously and turn away. He hung up, walked to the window, and briskly stamped my passport as if nothing were out of the ordinary.

"Everything all right?" I asked.

"Yes," he said curtly, already nodding past me toward the next customer.

The security regime on the Israeli side was as elaborate as ever, presided over by young men and women equipped with a dazzling variety of sidearms and big automatics, which they had stuffed into their belts and slung across their backs. Like everyone else, I slipped into bovine submissiveness as I stepped through blowers, scanners, detectors, and dust analyzers, as if being processed for some terrible fate.

Everyone's luggage disappeared into a back room and emerged on the other side, presumably having been searched and x-rayed.

I breezed through passport control while the Palestinians from our bus inched along in a long line reserved just for them. A pretty young woman asked me a few intrusive questions before she sent me along.

At last I was on my way out the door through a cloud of flies toward the taxi stand, where I slumped into the front seat for the half-hour ride to Jerusalem.

We climbed into the bleached Judean hills. Here and there were still the occasional Bedouin tents with their goats and their inevitable Toyota trucks, although far fewer than I remembered from previous years. Where had the others gone, and what had driven them away?

I soon got my answer when I spotted the newest fringes of the Israeli settler exurbs, impressive neighborhoods that gleamed atop ridgelines. Like burbs the world over, these were growing fast, and each new rooftop was a further claim on disputed land.

None of that prepared me for the shock of the wall. We topped a rise overlooking several Arab villages and the distant outskirts of Jerusalem, and there it was, running across the undulating countryside. I had seen Berlin's infamous wall before it came down. In many ways this one wasn't nearly as imposing, but on the barren landscape it stood out like a line of stitching on a fresh wound. And for all its forbidding appearance, what it conveyed most powerfully was the fear within.

The fear was contagious. A few miles later, well inside the barrier, I flinched noticeably when a small boy ran toward our taxi at a stoplight. I was momentarily convinced he was about to throw a bomb or pull a knife. Instead he held out an empty hand, begging.

Hans had asked me to meet him at a friend's place in an Arab neighborhood on the Mount of Olives, just around the corner from the apartment I'd had during the intifada. I had fond memories of the place, having rented from a garrulous Palestinian who didn't care who his tenants were as long as they paid on time. After I moved out, the place was taken over by a sect of Christian evangelicals from Indiana, who prized its picture-window view of the walled Old City. They flew in true believers from America whose only job was to watch the skies above the Old City for signs of the Second Coming. That was Jerusalem for you, a religious shopping mall where every vendor, large and small, had its own sturdy kiosk of faith.

Hans spotted me from an upstairs window and called out as the taxi pulled away.

"Good God, man. Come on up!"

I climbed the stairs to a whitewashed room furnished traditionally, with colorfully embroidered cushions thrown on the floor around a large Oriental rug. A brass pot of coffee was steaming on a tray, and there was a plateful of pastries and a bowl of almonds.

Hans grabbed me by the hand and pounded my back.

"You're still skin and bones!" he shouted, the Bavarian accent as pronounced as ever. "Thank God Ramadan is over so we can actually be civilized. Sit down and eat!"

He had always been a big fellow, and at first glance he had changed as little as any of us. But on closer inspection I saw that all the years in the sun had given his skin a look of desiccation. It was as if he had been covered in parchment and might crumble beneath your fingers.

But the bigger changes were inside, as I was soon to discover. Hans had once been almost unbearably upbeat, ever ready to counter any sign of brooding darkness in his colleagues. Now he more often resorted to a mordant wit tinged by hopelessness.

"So you're still in the business of trying to patch things up?" I said.

"With the same old lousy results. You know how it goes. They killed three, so we must kill six. You've been to places like that. It's just that everybody else finally gets it out of their system. Even the Bosnians gave it a rest. But these people?" He sighed and threw up his hands. "The engine doesn't always overheat, but it never stops running."

"Why don't you leave?"

"Too many of them still want to make it work. Besides, I don't know Europe anymore, especially not Germany. What would I do, work for Siemens? But what about you, working for Omar? Can't say I would have predicted that."

"His charity for Bakaa. It's why I wanted to talk to you. I'm interested in seeing how he's thought of around here. His reputation on the street, assuming he has one."

"Does he know you're doing this? Asking about him?"

"No."

"Then who are you working for?"

"He calls it the Bakaa Refugee Health Project."

"No. Who *else* are you working for? Why all the questions?"

"What if I said it was to satisfy my own curiosity?"

He laughed.

"That answer is not even worth a nod and a wink. There are two types of people around here, Freeman. Ones who ask questions and ones who simply let events roll by as they will, *inshallah*, and take each day as it comes. Nine times out of ten the ones who ask questions are working for someone other than who they say they are."

"So you don't want to help me?"

"I just want you to level with me. Within reason, of course."

"There are some interested Americans who want to know."

"That's all I needed to hear."

"And that's acceptable?"

"It's neither here nor there. It simply is. I only wanted to know your perspective. If you were working for the Israelis, for example, or Hamas—not that I'd expect you to work for either—then I would have had a problem. I have to stay out of those kinds of partisan matters, as you can well understand."

"The Americans aren't partisan?"

"Of course they are. But their interest is once removed. They're the rich uncle who sends gifts to one nephew and only scorn to the other. Which earns him resentment from both, if for different reasons. But any way you look at it, he's still just a rich uncle. So what's your worry about Omar? He hasn't gone radical on us?"

"Not in my opinion. I'm not so sure about some of his friends, though."

"You could say the same thing about me. It's one reason to be careful while you're in Jerusalem, especially if anyone knows you're seeing me. And believe me, someone will know."

"They watch you that closely?"

"That's the nature of being an underground peacemaker. I'm a go-between, which makes me useful to both sides. It means almost anyone will talk to me. Which, of course, makes everyone all the more determined to find out who I've been meeting. So here's hoping you haven't made yourself radioactive before coming here. The last thing I need is to have some of that poison rub off on me."

"What about Omar? What kind of a jolt would he put into an Israeli Geiger counter?"

"Not much, I'd imagine. His friends over here aren't particularly dangerous. Just nuisances."

"How so?"

"In legal ways. Telling their poor illiterate brethren all about their property rights, and then helping stand up for them."

"His friends are lawyers?"

"Property people, actually. Diggers and designers. Archaeologists and architects. Like Basma Shaheed. Omar is supposedly one of her patrons."

"Never heard of her."

"She'd like that. She works quietly. Goes into homes in the Muslim Quarter of the Old City whenever someone is thinking about moving out, or giving up, or just can't keep their place in repair. She shows them how to shore up the walls or the ceiling and hold their ground, then finds them help, so they can stay. That way, no Jewish settler moves in to paint a blue Star of David on the door."

"Sounds benign enough."

"Nothing here is benign when it involves land. She has begun to attract the attention of the authorities."

"So you think her days are numbered?"

"That's where it gets interesting. Apparently she's about to go public. Open an office, hire a staff. Expand her base of operations beyond the walls of the Old City. The Palestinian Authority is going to come up with some sort of award for her, and she suddenly seems to be spending a lot of money."

"I thought she liked secrecy."

"You know how it goes. Start getting some heat and maybe you'd be better off out in the open. That way if anyone tries to take you down, the whole world will know it."

"And Omar is a patron?"

"Him and a few others, mostly Jordanians. Some sort of property baron named Sami Fayez, too. There's also a stockbroker, Rafi Tuqan. People who've scored big in the recent boom."

"Good Lord, the whole crowd."

"You know them?"

"Met them all. At Omar's house, in fact."

Hans grinned.

"Well, there you are. Right under your nose, and you didn't even know it."

"Hardly sounds like anything illegal."

"Just because it's legal doesn't mean it doesn't make people nervous. Especially if the latest is true. She supposedly has a new base of operations right by an archaeological site, a very sensitive one. Next to the City of David dig, outside the Dung Gate. One of the biblical diggers on the Israeli side is convinced he's found the wall to King David's palace. His answer to all those people who've been saying for years that the Old Testament is just glorified mythology."

"Exactly the sort of claim that drives the Arab archaeologists crazy, I gather."

"Of course. Which brings us back to the age-old struggle. If the Israeli right can show that Jerusalem in fourteenth-century B.C. was the glorious metropolis the Bible says it was, then they're that much closer to claiming the West Bank as part of the Promised Land."

"Only in their own minds."

"When five percent of the vote can swing an election, their own minds are all that matters. And who knows, put another hard-liner in office and you push the Palestinians that much closer to Hamas. Believe me, people are going to be shocked next time the Palestinians vote."

"What's all that have to do with this dig?"

"Because if a few Arabs on the edge of the property hold on to their homes, they could stop the dig in its tracks."

"Well, if that's what Omar is up to, backing a few homeowner hold-outs, why hide it?"

"Who says he's hiding it? Unless he's helping on a scale that no one can even imagine."

I thought of the envelope Norbert Krieger gave Omar in Athens, and the archaeological connections of Yiorgos Soukas.

"Maybe he *is* helping on that kind of scale."

Hans eyed me carefully.

"In that case, he's being more than just a philanthropist. Underwrite an entire movement and you've become an agitator, a political force."

"An enemy?"

"Do you really have to ask?"

So, just when I was beginning to put my mind at ease on Omar's motivations, now I was worried again. Could this be what the Americans really wanted to know—the depth of Omar's involvement in a scheme to help Arab homeowners? And if he was using the hospital charity as cover, then wasn't he duping me in the bargain?

"Tell me, has the name Norbert Krieger ever come up in any of this?"

Hans laughed.

"Never."

"What's so funny?"

"Norbert Krieger of Munich? He must be in his sixties by now."

"You've heard of him?"

"He was once a patron of mine. A real peacenik. Ten, eleven years ago. A little too pro-Arab for my tastes."

"You've hung out with worse."

"Not when they're German. With any German that pro-Arab you've always got to assume he's more of an anti-Jew."

"Spoken like a truly guilty German. Still worried if you're *betroffen* enough?"

"That's part of it. But I haven't heard from him in years. I think he knew I didn't trust him. Why? Is he another friend of Omar's?"

"Possibly."

"Well, he's no bomb thrower. That much I know. Unless he has gone off the deep end. But I wouldn't be tossing his name around if I were you, even now. Remember, Freeman, people here take *everything* seriously, no matter how small or insignificant. Be careful who you talk to, and what you ask. Not everyone keeps a secret as well as me."

I didn't feel like telling him that my next appointment was with a former general of the Israeli Army. Maybe because I was already second-guessing my decision to meet with David Ben-Zohar.

Later that day I checked into the American Colony Hotel. Ben-Zohar then telephoned. My first instinct was to cancel, but he was not to be put off so easily.

"Oh, no, Freeman. We must meet. I insist. And if you can't do it tomorrow, I will gladly reschedule."

What must he have heard about me since the lukewarm response in his first e-mail? I chalked it up as yet another lesson learned as an amateur, and I wondered how many more mistakes I'd be allowed before I started paying the penalties of a professional.

29

Career military men never stop looking like soldiers, even when they've been mustered out of the army. So when David Ben-Zohar, private citizen, stood to offer his hand at a sunny outdoor table at a café on Yoel Salomon Street, everything from his posture to the set of his jaw said he might just as easily be leading a patrol as ordering lunch. His eyes particularly demanded attention, cool wells of reserve flanked not by laugh lines but creases of careworn deliberation. It was a face that had turned a thousand corners without knowing who or what awaited, and I suspected he still had a high threshold for shock and awe.

The site he chose for our rendezvous told me a thing or two. Yoel Salomon Street was among the trendiest of pedestrian thoroughfares in the center of modern Jerusalem. That, plus its attractive storefronts of chiseled Jerusalem stone, with arched doorways and seawater-blue trim, made it a magnet for midday crowds of shoppers and diners. To take up such a prominent position in this busy area was to announce boldly that you didn't care who saw you, or whom you were seen with. From a more suspicious point of view you might even say he was inviting surveillance.

This part of town was very much home ground for any Israeli, a safe distance from the shrinking Arab neighborhoods of the east side and the Old City's Muslim Quarter.

Knowing his reputation for punctuality, I hailed a taxi at the American Colony with plenty of time to spare. When it dropped me off at Jaffa and Ben Yehuda streets in the heart of downtown I still had time to kill, so I wandered up the block. A poster on a jeweler's doorway caught my eye, less for the big art exhibit it was promoting than for the name of the exhibit's philanthropic sponsor: the DeKuyper Foundation. So, not only did DeKuyper own a Greek island villa and a big yacht—now he was underwriting an art exhibit in Israel. It made me curious about how else he might be spending his money in this part of the world. Up to now I had assumed that Black, White, and Gray had simply paid off the caretaker, figuring that was why the fellow was so zealous in shooing Mila and me away. Now I wondered.

Ben-Zohar rose from the table as I approached. He looked me in the eye and extended his hand in greeting. As I've said, he still seemed very much the soldier, even in his business grays. Like Omar, he had gained a few pounds but wore them comfortably.

As in many non-kosher restaurants in this part of town, the menu bent over backward to offer forbidden combinations of dairy and meat, so I ordered the first cheeseburger I'd had in ages plus a pint of Maccabee to wash it down. We exchanged small talk for a while. Ben-Zohar described his security consulting business in the vaguest of terms, and I told him about my brilliant career in the aid industry. My worry over whether he would be reluctant to discuss Omar proved groundless. I didn't even have to bring up the subject.

"So how's my old sparring partner, Mr. al-Baroody?" he said.

"Very much like you, from the look of things. Prosperous."

"I always thought he would amount to something. As long as no one shot him first."

"Once he survived your men there wasn't much chance of that. He lives in a big place in Abdoun with a Mercedes in the garage."

Ben-Zohar seemed to enjoy the news immensely.

"So we all ended up with the same thing, I guess. Assuming that you're now feeding at his trough."

"I'm not sure I'd refer to his charity as a trough. It's certainly no horn of plenty."

"Oh, of course not. I was just assuming Omar wouldn't exactly underpay his top staff. Or not an old comrade like you. Do you two still share the same worldview?"

"As much as we ever did. Meaning, less than you probably think."

Ben-Zohar smiled.

"This is beginning to sound like one of our old conversations. Next you'll pull a radio out of your pocket and call for reinforcements."

"Omar might have a little trouble crossing the river."

I hadn't meant the remark to put a damper on the good cheer, but Ben-Zohar seemed to take it that way, because his face turned somber.

"Yes, unfortunately you are right. Those times back in '90 were so innocent, to look at them now."

"Maybe from your perspective."

His smile returned.

"Very good, Freeman. Still sticking up for the *shebab*. You know, in my work today I see some of the old names popping up from time to time. The same boys I used to haul in for questioning, only they're all grown up now. I'm sorry to say that about half of them I never should have let go."

"Or maybe by hauling them in you only hardened them for the next level."

"You may be right," he said, sipping his Maccabee with a solemn nod. "But it is easy to second-guess. Do you think their side does much of that?"

"I suppose every side does. In any conflict."

"Perhaps. I guess I've never known them to admit mistakes. But among themselves, well, who can say? How much do you know about what Omar is doing over here in Jerusalem?"

It was exactly the question I was about to ask.

"You mean with his patronage of people like Basma Shadeed?"

"So he talks about it openly, then?"

"Not really. Or not with me. But word gets around. I was hoping maybe you had some insight."

"Then it looks as if we've both brought empty pails to the same well, and will come away dry. I take it that this dalliance of his worries you."

"Not if it's a dalliance. Does it worry you?"

"Oh, nothing worries me anymore, as long as my wife and children stay off the exploding buses and out of the exploding cafés. I'm no longer employed by the arbiters of public worry." He paused, sipping his beer again. "But some of my clients wouldn't mind knowing a bit more about what Omar is up to."

"What sort of clients?"

"We don't publish a list, and I wouldn't be doing them much of a service if I told you their names."

"What about the name DeKuyper?"

"What about it?" There had been no discernible reaction on his part.

"Is he a client?"

"I should be so lucky. He would pay a nice shekel or two. And by the way, I won't answer in either the affirmative or the negative to any such inquiries, so you can stop fishing. But now I'm curious. What made you ask about DeKuyper?"

"Nothing earth-shattering. I just saw his name on a poster up the street for an art exhibit. Said his foundation was sponsoring it, so I figured he might be backing other local projects. You know, the usual big-time Jewish philanthropist from Europe, kicking in another two bits for the cause."

Ben-Zohar smiled as if he didn't buy that explanation at all, but he said nothing, so I prodded further.

"Would DeKuyper have any reason to be concerned about what Omar is up to?"

"That would depend on his investment portfolio."

"In real estate, you mean?" Was that what Ben-Zohar's clients were fretting about with regard to Omar?

He grimaced.

"I've probably said enough already. I guess I was assuming that if anyone as filthy rich as DeKuyper was worried, it would be because of some financial implication."

It sounded like misdirection, so I decided I must have struck a little too close to the truth. I tried approaching the subject from a different angle.

"Tell me what you know about this archaeological site everyone is in a tizzy about. This new dig at the City of David."

"Are you saying Omar is interested in that, too?"

His apparent ignorance of the matter seemed genuine. Now I was the one who had said too much. Maybe Ben-Zohar's clients were worried only about property inside the Old City. That would be especially true if they were buying up Arab homes, whether their motivations were territorial or financial.

"I'm not sure," I answered. "But maybe I should go have a look at the dig, just to see what all the fuss is about."

"You should stick your head inside Hezekiah's Tunnel while you're there. Especially if you've never been before."

"Why the tunnel?"

"It's convenient, for one thing. The entrance is on the back side of the dig. It's also quite an experience. King Hezekiah built it twenty-seven hundred years ago to supply the city with water from beyond its walls in case of a siege. Half a mile long, straight through the bedrock, and definitely not for the faint of heart."

He said it like a challenge, a double dare.

"So you think I'm not man enough?"

He laughed.

"Anyone who'd try to break up a fight between boys and tanks definitely won't be scared by a tunnel, even if it is kind of spooky. I think it would appeal to you, in fact. Let's just say that it offers an acute taste of this land's deepest fears and desperations." I raised an eyebrow. "No, I'm serious. It's nothing I can adequately explain up here in the light of day while we're drinking a cold beer and watching pretty women walk by. You have to experience it for yourself. An old hand like you will definitely know what I'm talking about once you're down there."

"Interesting. Maybe I'll give it a try."

Not long afterward, he paid the bill, over my protests, and then announced he was overdue for another appointment. Our destinations were in opposite directions, so we shook hands and said good-bye. As I turned to leave, he called out a final time.

"Oh, and Freeman—"

"Yes?"

"DeKuyper's not Jewish."

"No?"

"So if he's part of this game you're interested in, it's for reasons other than heart and homeland."

"What kind of reasons?"

"You'll have to ask him. Like I said, he's not a client."

Then he offered his inscrutable soldier's smile and marched off into the midday glare.

I decided to take the leisurely route to the dig at the City of David by crossing through the Old City. By entering at the New Gate I would be traversing the serpentine warrens of three faiths—crossing the paths of Jesus on his way to the cross, of Muhammad on his way to the Seventh Heaven, and of King David on his way to the throne. A pretty tidy accomplishment for a jaded old infidel like me.

The old routes down the alleys of polished stone were still familiar. The only disturbing change was the prevalence of spray-painted Stars of David, graffitied crudely upon Arab doorways and storefronts here and there, a stamp of political branding that staked a claim wherever it appeared.

Emerging through the Dung Gate, I tried to ford an incoming group of schoolchildren who barely reached my waist, only to stop in my tracks when none of them made the slightest move to let me pass. For a few annoying moments I stood like a piece of driftwood snagged in a raging current. Then I remembered that it had always been like this with Jerusalem's children, Arab and Jew alike. Growing up on such bitterly contested ground they learned early to give no quarter, especially to strangers.

The City of David was now in sight. It supposedly marked the spot where the conquering young king, long after slaying Goliath, established his capital more than three thousand years ago. Revisionist archaeologists now view the enterprise with skepticism, arguing that, at best, the Jerusalem of that era was a modest hill town of Canaanite farmers. I suppose that's why the new dig was such a sensation. It was the latest shot fired in a long and bitter war within the war.

At the moment, no one was at work. The dig was surrounded by chain-link fencing covered with battered tarpaulins and bamboo screening. I climbed onto a large stone to peek through a tear in the plastic. Most of the work was covered by black blankets. In the few bare spots all you could see was an uneven line of huge stones. It was disappointing. Was this really all that remained of a once glorious palace? No wonder the skeptics were in full cry, although I was certainly not qualified to judge. Maybe if Omar could see this place, he, too, would no longer be upset enough to pour money into opposing it. Assuming that was even what he was up to. And if that was his great, dark secret, I wondered if Black, White, and Gray would be disappointed.

The ticket office for Hezekiah's Tunnel was just around the corner, and when I saw there was no line I decided to follow Ben-Zohar's advice and check it out. The brusque vendor told me I had to buy a flashlight because the tunnel wasn't lit.

"You will need sandals, too," he said. "Water runs along the entire route, sometimes knee-deep, and the footing is not so good."

I tied my shoes together by the laces and draped them around my neck, with the socks stuffed inside. Then I plunked down a pile of shekels for the cheapest flip-flops and one of the sturdier flashlights.

I made my way to the entrance, a steep stairway down through a shaft in the rock that led to the Gihon Spring. Then I rolled up my trousers above the knees. Already I could hear the echoing voices of children and the sounds of splashing fluting up through the mouth of the tunnel. I stepped into the water—clear and cold, but not unbearable. The current was surprisingly strong, but at least it was headed in the same direction, tugging the cheap rubber sandals forward with every step. I rounded a corner into total darkness and turned on the flashlight, and the water almost immediately went from ankle-deep to knee-deep. Unable to see the bottom, I stepped awkwardly on the uneven surface and almost fell. I splashed the bottom roll of my trousers, and cursed lightly. Already the walls had narrowed until the passage was barely the width of my shoulders. There were only a few inches to spare overhead. The stone walls were cool and slick, and the sounds coming from ahead were an incoherent tumble of voices. But when I shone the light, there was no one within fifty yards.

At times all of the splashing from ahead sounded like a waterfall, and I experienced a momentary feeling of panic, remembering the clouds I had seen on the horizon and contemplating the possibility of a flash flood. Then I slogged on, continuing around the first of several bends. Any hope of rushing the pace had been dashed by the uncertain footing, and I had to stop several times when one of my sandals came off and floated forward in the current. It didn't help that the ceiling was now even lower than before. I had to bend my neck and also my knees. The water was still knee-deep. My breathing was labored, and I realized it was due mostly to discomfort and a mild spell of claustrophobia. So I stopped for a moment to try and relax. I tried switching off the light and was cast into perfect blackness, which softened the sounds from up ahead. It was oddly peaceful, and the tension in my chest muscles eased. No one seemed to be near me either forward or behind, or I would have seen at least a glimmer of flashlights.

Breathing easier, I flipped on the light and continued on my way. No sense in trying to rush. At the end of a long straightaway I stopped again before making the next turn, wondering if anyone had yet entered the tunnel behind me and was now gaining ground. I again turned off my light and peered back into the darkness. By resting a hip against the wall to my left I could slouch more comfortably as I paused, although I still had to stoop to keep from bumping my head against the ceiling.

It was during this moment of repose that the magnitude of the effort to build the tunnel became evident. Down here it was easy to imagine the arduous and harrowing labor as men hammered their way through the stone. All that strain and bother just to reach a water supply in case of a siege. The same mentality had prevailed ever since—everything for defense, for insulation and separation. And such a fitting symbolic result, too—a deep seam through intransigent stone, set in eternal darkness. Ben-Zohar was right. It perfectly summed up the region's hopes and fears. I was about to enjoy a small laugh on his behalf when a voice called out from behind with the suddenness of a gunshot.

"Freeman!"

I bumped my head in startled reaction, and nearly dropped the flashlight in my haste to switch it on. The beam showed no one at the far end of the straightaway. But the voice nonetheless called out again, this time with a hint of impatience.

"Freeman!"

Was it Ben-Zohar? Had he followed me here like a prankster, just to give me a scare?"

"David?" I called out. "Is that you?"

"No!"

"Who is it, then?"

Our echoing voices seemed to have taken over the confined space. The splashing from up ahead was now faint, as if it had advanced around several curves.

"No one you need to know. I am a messenger."

"Messenger?"

"You must leave Israel. This is not the concern of your work."

Odd phrasing, I thought.

"How do you know that?"

"You must leave. Today. Before the border closes."

"Who are you? Who are you working for?"

Then there was nothing. Only the sound of someone sloshing against the current, a figure working alone in the darkness. He seemed to be receding, going the wrong way, and for a moment I was tempted to follow. But what would I say? And if I caught him, might he carry out the threat implicit in his warning?

I turned and resumed my progress forward, trying to go faster now. The next time a sandal slipped off I let it go, and then kicked off the second one. The rocks on the bottom were sharp, but it was easier to keep my footing. All I wanted now was to get out of here. But the roaring of voices and splashing from up ahead grew louder, and as I rounded yet another curve I spied someone just ahead in the beam of my light.

The first thing I saw was a Galil assault rifle slung across someone's back. It was not a soldier, but a civilian in a red polo. He turned and grinned into my light, a bearded face, middle-aged. He was probably the chaperone of the loud boys ahead. He resumed walking, and the barrel and butt of his rifle bumped the walls with every step. At first it was a relief to have company, even if the gun was a little unnerving, banging around like that. But then the man stopped, and the noise from ahead rose to a din. It was almost unbearable, and after a few seconds it became clear we were making no further progress. I shone my light around the bearded man and saw that the boys had all turned out their flashlights. They were in their teens, maybe sixteen or seventeen, and they scowled and shouted angrily in Hebrew at the probing beam of my light. I then saw that several of them were turned sideways toward the walls, bobbing and bowing in prayer—as much as one could in this confined space—and chanting loudly. In the section where they stood, the ceiling rose much higher, to about twenty feet above their heads. We must be near the end of the tunnel, and they had stopped for devotionals. Some were reaching as high as they could stretch up the walls. I turned out my light to give them the atmosphere they wanted, and the chanting and sloshing continued. Looking behind me, I noticed the flicker of an approaching light. Thinking it must be the man who had warned me earlier, I panicked.

"Move!" I shouted in English to the praying boys. "Move it now!"

I turned on my light again, and they were still at it, calling out to their God from deep in this shaft dug by their ancestral king. Is that the connection they must feel with this place? A sense of doing whatever it takes to survive, to outwit the enemy?

From behind me came a burst of laughter and more sloshing. It was a family, a younger couple with two kids in their early teens. All four were speaking German. I tried asking in their language if they had passed anyone going in the opposite direction, but in my haste I mangled it.

"Hast ein Mann du passiert?"

"Ein Mann?" the daughter asked.

"Nein," the son said. "Kein Mann."

"Was ist los?" the father asked. He gestured with his flashlight toward the bottleneck of boys just ahead.

"They're praying," I said in English. "Religious students, probably."

The father translated for his family, and everyone nodded respectfully. They wouldn't have dared shout "Move it!" as I had just done, especially not in German, down here where the tunnel would make their voices sound like bullhorns, orders shouted by guards along a fenceline.

Eventually the boys moved on, a sluggish procession that soon found its way to the light. They stood off to the side of the Siloam Pool at the mouth of the entrance, putting their shoes back on and drying their legs. I blinked against the sudden glare and kept going, leaving wet footprints on the warm stone walkway. I expended the last reserves of my nervous energy in making the long, steep climb back toward the visitors' center.

I finally sat down to calm myself at an overlook, just as the midafternoon call to prayer began from the speakers of Al-Aqsa Mosque in the Old City, droning out across the ravine. Answering in short order were two mosques on the Mount of Olives, one in a younger voice, the other almost wheezy. It left me at the center of a triangulation of prayer in an auditory target zone.

There was just no getting away from it here, this assault by faith. First I was besieged by prayer in the tunnel. Now I was taking Muslim fire from three sides. In Jerusalem, belief as a form of aggression achieved near perfection. Whether you went deep in the earth or climbed the highest hill, someone's faith would track you down, catch you in its sights, and demand that you choose sides.

I waited a while and watched the people who had been behind me in the tunnel straggle past. No likely suspect emerged, not that I expected him to. I slipped on my shoes, deciding I had better leave soon for the border before someone else opened fire. Next time the ammunition might be more lethal than prayer.

30

Washington

In a smaller, newer tunnel in another part of the world, a tunnel not known to tourists, historians, or government officials, Abbas Rahim crouched with a small shovel in his hands at 5 a.m., digging the last three yards of the necessary twenty.

He had put away the power tools yesterday, and the Arab man who had flown in to help had departed the day before that.

Just as well on both counts, Abbas thought. The power tools, while essential, had been noisy. They risked attracting unwanted attention from above, even though almost no one ever inhabited the church sanctuary or its basement during the week.

The man, too, had seemed like an unwarranted risk, although his expertise in certain matters had admittedly been invaluable. All technical questions were now answered. The proper materials were in place.

But it wasn't as if Abbas needed any company. He found it far easier to concentrate when working alone, same as when he was at the hospital. The nurses were always necessary, of course, but he never would have wanted an extra surgeon at his side. And that's how he thought of this job, as a sort of macro-level surgery. He was performing a public service on behalf of the world's greatest medical emergency, a case of geopolitical addition by subtraction. He was excising a spreading tumor from America's body politic. The malignant hubris had to be removed before it metastasized further and killed more of the innocent.

The beauty of it all was that he could accomplish this without doing a single unethical thing. He was still holding to his oath in treating the senator. If anything, he was keeping the man alive with more zeal than ever, knowing that preparations here were not yet complete. But soon enough, God—if there were such a thing—could have his way and take the man. And then the real work could begin.

The final action would, admittedly, be a bit blunt. That's the way it could go with large tumors. You had to destroy good and healthy tissue along with the insidious stuff. That was where your medical judgment entered into it, making those big decisions that affected lives. Sacrificing the few to save the many.

So he worked away as hard as he could, arriving at 2 a.m. in the darkened neighborhood of rats and ne'er-do-wells, descending into his locked underground chamber to lay out his tools and prepare the patient. Five hours later he emerged at first light, tired and grimy. Then he drove home to shower and shave before a day at the hospital. A grinding schedule, made possible only by getting to sleep every night at 7 p.m.

Every day he awoke in the darkness of the bedroom at 1:20 a.m., always his lowest moment until he swallowed the pill from the orange plastic vial, which was right there on his dresser top now that he no longer had to hide it from his wife. Aliyah had been effectively removed from the operating theater, because even though she may have meant well he had worried that she would eventually have second thoughts. That could have been disastrous. He knew because he had seen it happen before—a squeamish rookie nurse in attendance, not yet accustomed to all the blood, disrupting everything and endangering the patient.

At times Abbas wondered how she must be faring over in Jordan. Their radio silence stood like a wall between them, between past and present, too. He experienced a vague ripple of unease on her behalf as he began to contemplate what their life would be like after he completed this surgery. Mustn't think of that. It led in too many directions he didn't want to go. It led only to more blackness and worry. So he swallowed a second pill while still on the job, because these darkest of thoughts would only stand in his way, unless he pushed harder. Then within an hour or so he felt better, and life continued according to plan.

Keep pushing, he told himself. Just keep pushing, and complete the job. It's all for the best. A service to mankind. Addition by subtraction.

And genius, sheer genius.

31

I awoke late that night to the sound of the mouse behind the baseboard.

Already my sleep had been troubled by dreams of falling—into wells, down staircases, over the sides of high stone parapets—long and heart-stopping plunges that inevitably deposited me at the bottom of some deep pit of darkness, where I scratched and clawed as the walls closed in.

No mystery where any of that came from, I suppose. The scare in Hezekiah's Tunnel shook me up more than I had wanted to admit. Then the mouse provided the sound track.

I threw back the covers. They were soaked with sweat. I stood barefoot on the chilly stone floor and decided to make a cup of tea.

The border crossing had taken even longer than usual, and the atmosphere on both sides had been akin to the electric crackle in the air before a cloudburst, a whiff of something disastrous. Or maybe I was hypersensitive because the Jordanians again phoned Amman while inspecting my passport. As a result, I had arrived back on Othman Bin Affan Street well after dark, and too weary to go out for dinner. So I had scraped together a meal from what was in the refrigerator. Then, just before bed, I padded onto the dark lawn with a flashlight to dig up the gun. I could have sworn the spot looked different, but the gun was there, so I wrote it off to an overactive imagination. Then I caught up on the daily papers and went to bed, only to be troubled by my dreams.

I took the steaming mug of tea back to the bedroom. Just as I came through the doorway there was a popping noise, and immediately afterward the lights went out. Silence followed. Even the mouse was still. I set the mug on the floor and groped my way back to the kitchen, where, as luck would have it, the light switch still worked. The fuse box was just around the corner, and I saw that one of them was blown. But the replacement also burned out with a tiny burst of light only seconds after I screwed it in.

I dug out a candle from a drawer and stepped back down the hall to investigate. As soon as I entered the bedroom I smelled something burning, and not just the candle wax. Stooping to investigate, I saw a tiny wisp of smoke issuing from a seam in the baseboard. I was alarmed. The wiring in some of these older houses was notoriously unreliable, and for all I knew a short circuit was about to burn the place down. I quickly retrieved a stout, sharp knife from the kitchen, wrapped the handle in a sock for insulation, and began prying back the baseboard, working from the seam. A six-inch section snapped off, which surprised me until I saw how chewed it was in the back, presumably from the mouse. Then I saw the body, small and gray and singed. The tiny head was still smoldering, and there was a sickening stench of burned fur.

For a moment I actually felt sorry for my little housemate. The mouse had bitten into a wire, and from what I could tell it wasn't entirely his fault, because the wire never should have been there to begin with. It was attached to a small plastic box, which I unscrewed from its place by using the knife blade. Then I placed the candle on the bedside table and forced open the box on the bed.

I am no expert on surveillance electronics, but it seemed quite obvious that this was some sort of microphone and transmitter. Who knows what its broadcast range was, or where the listeners might be? The manufacturer's name, however, was printed clearly—it was straight out of the U. S. of A. At the sight of it my temper flared.

If this was supposed to demoralize me, it had just the opposite effect. I was more determined than ever to get things moving. In fact, it was time for the next step in the advancement of my autonomy. I vowed then and there to confront my employers. In the morning I would take this item straight to the American embassy and demand an audience. Better to assert myself now, when the only casualty was a mouse.

With that course of action settled, I was finally able to sleep soundly, and didn't wake until after nine. I buried the mouse beneath a jasmine bush at the base of the wall along the front walkway, my fallen comrade in espionage, then washed the dirt from my hands and walked into town to buy supplies for a big breakfast to steel myself for the confrontation at the embassy. After showering and eating, I put the offending bugging device in my pocket, grabbed my car keys, and stepped out the door. Fiona stood in her front garden as if she had been waiting for me to appear.

"Another trip into the hinterlands?" she asked brightly.

The question seemed innocent enough, but I was in no mood for curiosity.

"What do you mean?"

"Well, you were away for a few days, weren't you? I was wondering if you'd been out exploring."

"Jerusalem," I said tersely.

"How lovely." Her tone remained sweet, which softened me a bit.

"I would have been better off staying. We could have had dinner."

"We still can, you know."

"Maybe. I'm not sure how much longer I'll be around."

"Oh. I'm sorry to hear that."

She sounded as if she meant it. But there was an edge of uncertainty in her voice, too.

"You had more visitors while you were away. A couple of rather quiet men."

"Quiet?"

"Mysterious, even. And, well . . ."

She paused, flustered.

"Yes?"

"I've a slight confession to make." She said it haltingly, but her next words came out in a torrent. "I'm afraid that while you were gone I decided to do a good-neighborly deed and fertilize that plant you put in. Which of course required that I do some digging around, and, well . . ."

"You found the gun."

"And put it right back."

"I know. It was there last night when I got home. Did you tell anyone?"

"Certainly not. But when those two men came 'round looking for you, well, naturally I wondered if . . ."

"Yes?"

"You're not just working for a charity while you're here, are you?"

"The answer's a bit complicated."

"I'm sure it is."

"Tell me about the two men."

"They were driving a black Mercedes." She gasped and pointed toward the street. "Like the one that just pulled up next door."

I turned and saw it idling at the curb. The windows were smoked so you couldn't see inside.

"When did they come before?" I asked quickly.

"Both days you were away." She was whispering now. "Usually around this time of morning. They tried your door. I asked if I could help, but they just shook their heads and drove away. I thought you might want fair warning, considering, well, whatever it is you're up to."

"Thank you."

I considered going back inside, but for what? The gun? So I watched their windshield with arms crossed and waited, while Fiona did the same. Then both doors opened, and out stepped two men, presumably Jordanians, dressed in almost identical suits of charcoal gray. They were in no hurry, so I tried not to act impatient. They came up the sidewalk and stopped just short of the porch. The first one did the talking.

"Mr. Lockhart?"

"Yes. Who are you?"

"A representative of the General Intelligence Department," he said in English.

"The Dairat al-Mukhabarat, you mean?"

He nodded, and I thought I heard Fiona gasp again, although no one looked in her direction. It seemed that I had mistakenly identified the source of the bugging device in my bedroom. I suppose I should have known better.

"You will come with us, please. I was told to reassure you that the appointment will not take long. And we will of course provide you with return transportation once it is concluded."

"How long do you mean by 'not long'?"

He shrugged. The man behind him hadn't moved a muscle since they came up the walk. I supposed it was his job to make sure I cooperated.

"All right, then."

"Be careful," Fiona hissed. She had gone pale.

"I'm told these little visits aren't that uncommon." I tried to sound unconcerned.

"So I've heard."

Neither gentleman seemed to mind that she watched my departure. Maybe that was a good sign. Or maybe they didn't give a damn, which could mean anything. I wondered for a moment if I should leave behind the bugging device, but reaching into my pocket seemed like a bad idea with these fellows watching, although I found it curious that they hadn't frisked me for weapons.

"Good luck," Fiona said.

I nodded, stepped into the car, and disappeared behind the smoked glass. She was still watching as we rounded the corner.

The building didn't look much different from any other office block in Amman, and the security, as with all government buildings, didn't seem all that imposing. Either the Mukhabarat's threatening reputation did part of the job for them or they were good at concealing their strength. I had little doubt that if I were to create some sort of scene in the lobby it would be dealt with briskly and forcefully.

My escorts, flanking me like stout gray bookends, took me upstairs on a clanking, narrow elevator, then walked me down an empty white hallway across a linoleum floor to an unmarked office. The door opened to a heavyset, fiftyish man who might have been a banker, although not a particularly successful one. He had thinning gray hair that needed combing, and wore a dark suit that was at least a size too small. He offered his hand, smiled almost shyly, and gestured for me to sit in a cushioned chair that was far more comfortable than I would have expected. A steaming teapot sat on a desktop tray, which had been painted luridly with a scene from Petra. He did the pouring.

"Milk or sugar, Mr. Lockhart?"

"Both, if it's black tea. I'll help myself."

"As you wish."

He sounded neither stern, rushed, nor upset. He might have been about to offer a job promotion, for all you could tell from his tone. It was a strange sensation, sipping the hot, sweet tea as he beamed approvingly from his chair by the window. The blinds were open onto a view of the Eighth Circle, where traffic was in lazy motion in the midday sun. Photos of King Hussein and King Abdullah joined in the smile-fest. The intended effect, I suppose, was to encourage conversation, perhaps even glibness. For the moment I was willing to oblige, if only out of nervousness. My fingers were moist against the teacup.

"I've heard about these little visits," I said.

"Have you? Then you'll know there's nothing to fear."

"Depending on what you want, of course."

"I hope you understand, Mr. Lockhart, that you aren't under any obligation to answer my questions."

"Just as I was under no obligation to get into the Mercedes?"

"Correct."

"So I can just get up and walk out?"

"Of course. We're not detaining you. This is strictly voluntary."

"And if I leave, what happens then?"

"These things are not under my control." Still the benign smile. "I do not have that kind of authority, and thus cannot say."

"So, if my visa was revoked tomorrow, it would have nothing to do with you?"

"I'm glad you grasp the situation so readily."

"Yes. Well, I hope you won't be too disappointed in me, then. I really don't know very much about what goes on in your country."

"We don't expect that you possess any state secrets. We're simply curious about some of your recent activities. What you've been doing, who you've been speaking with. You keep some interesting company, don't you?"

"Depends on what you mean by 'interesting.'"

"Well, your employer, to begin with. Omar al-Baroody."

Was his own government suspicious of Omar? For what? Dealing with people like Nabil, or plotting to protect Arab landholdings in Jerusalem? Hard to believe the Mukhabarat would be too worried about the latter.

"His charity, you mean?"

"Or this, perhaps."

He picked up a glossy black-and-white photo and placed it by my teacup. Everyone who abducted me seemed to have photos of Omar, and this one was an eight-by-ten of him coming out the doorway of a dingy two-story stone building just off the Third Circle, maybe a block down from the InterContinental on Zahran Street. A sign above the arched front entrance said it was the Amman office for the Department of Antiquities, in the Ministry of Tourism and Antiquities.

"Have you ever accompanied your friend on one of these visits?"

"No."

"Do you know how often he is spending time there lately?"

"I wasn't aware he was spending *any* time there. But he has mentioned this as one of his hobbies."

"Is this, in fact, one of the pursuits he is spending his charity's hard-earned money on?"

"Not that I'm aware of."

"And you would be aware, wouldn't you, since you're his second-in-command?"

"As a matter of fact, yes. I would be."

"How much access do you have to his books?"

"The charity's account books? Complete access. I reviewed them a week ago. Nothing out of the ordinary."

"What about contributions from his two friends, Rafi Tuqan and Sami Fayez?"

"A thousand dinars apiece, if memory serves. But I'd have to double-check."

He frowned.

"That's all? Only a thousand apiece?"

"Yes."

"I thought you said you had reviewed Omar's books?"

"I have."

"*Both* sets?"

Well, at least one of us was learning something new.

"I was aware of only one."

"He said that, did he? To his trusted old friend? He told you that with a straight face? 'Here, Freeman, here are our books,' and then let you believe those were the only ones?"

"Maybe because they are."

"Or maybe because you're covering for him."

"I'm telling you what I know, and what I've seen. If you know more than I do, that's not my problem."

"Have you accompanied Omar yet on any of his weekend expeditions into the desert?"

"No."

"No?" He sounded surprised. "Has he invited you?"

"No."

"He will. Soon, I would imagine. Then you'll get the sales pitch. Maybe then you'll learn about the second set of books."

"What sales pitch?"

"Has he ever mentioned a place near Madaba called Hesban?"

"No. What sales pitch?"

"What about Qesir?"

"No."

"Has he ever mentioned something called the Wadi Terrace Project?"

"No."

"None of them has? Not Sami or Rafi or any of that crew?"

"I don't even know where those places are, or what you're talking about. Maybe you could tell me."

"What about the Wadi Fidan site?"

That one did ring a bell, and I couldn't help but pause before I again said, "No." Then I remembered. It was one of the digs that had showed up on the CV of Professor Yiorgos Soukas. My inquisitor noted my momentary indecision, and he stared as if waiting for me to come clean. When I said nothing more, he made a note on a pad. Judging from his expression when he looked back up, he seemed to have reappraised the situation.

"What were you doing in Jerusalem for the last two days, Mr. Lockhart?"

Interesting that he specifically said Jerusalem, not just Israel. It suggested they either had assistance from across the border or their own set of eyes. Or maybe they were just reading my e-mails.

"Visiting friends."

"Old friends of yours and Omar's? From intifada days?"

"Maybe one or two. Anything wrong with that?"

"Nothing at all. Pleased to hear it, in fact. I was beginning to think you were totally clueless. And what are they up to these days, these old friends of yours?"

"This and that. Eating and sleeping. Living and dying."

"What about with regard to Omar?"

"They haven't seen him in years."

"You're sure about that?" His previous tone of certainty seemed to wane a bit.

"Quite sure."

"Maybe we're thinking of different people. This one, for instance."

He held up a photo of an Arab woman. Judging by the scenery, it appeared to have been shot on a narrow street of the Old City. She was fairly young, late twenties perhaps, and pretty in a harried sort of way, with her hair out of place and her clothes rumpled. She was talking to a young man who had his back to the camera. I didn't recognize her, and I didn't recognize the young man. He was too small to have been Hans Wolters, and he definitely wasn't Omar.

I shook my head.

"You're telling me you've never met?"

"Yes."

"Have you ever heard the name Basma Shaheed?"

"I have." It was the woman who was helping secure houses and properties in Jerusalem. "Is that her?"

"Possibly."

"You don't know?"

"We do. But apparently you don't. In what connection have you heard her name?"

"I'm told she is a friend of Omar's."

"But you're certain you've never met her?"

"Positive."

"And you've never seen a second set of account books, apart from those officially presented as those of the charity?"

"Correct."

He took on a bemused look and shook his head.

"My problem with all this, Mr. Lockhart, is that I believe you're telling the truth. Especially since you apparently brought back no appreciable amounts of cash from Jerusalem. Frankly, that surprised us."

So was that what the customs people had been looking for in my luggage?

"I told you, it was strictly a social visit."

"Names, please?"

I decided to mention Hans, if only because it almost certainly wouldn't get him in trouble—as a matter of course, he talked to people who were far more dangerous than me. But I wasn't going to mention David Ben-Zohar if I could help it.

"Hans Wolters was the only one who knows Omar. He was our old boss with UNRWA. He's a peace activist now. Some sort of background negotiator."

"Yes, we're aware of him. And had he met recently with Miss Shaheed?"

"If he had, he didn't tell me."

"You're sure of that?"

"Yes. And I believe he would have said so."

"What about Mr. Chris Boylan? Tell me about your meeting with him."

Now this was a surprise.

"He wasn't in Jerusalem."

"I didn't say that he was. In fact, you saw him in Amman last . . ." He consulted his notebook. "Last Tuesday. At the Roman Theatre."

Had they been following me? Surely Chris, being a professional, would have noticed, particularly since he was being so careful at the time. I decided to test the detail of their knowledge.

"Yes. I met him outside. But he didn't want to pay, so we never went in. We walked down to the Agora and talked there."

"Of course. We're aware of that. So why were you seeing Chris Boylan?"

He hadn't challenged my error. Maybe because he was testing me. Or maybe because his information was secondhand. If so, there was only one other person in Amman who knew I had met Chris. All the questions Nura had asked so tenderly in her bedroom now came back to me. One prod after another, designed to elicit information. What a vain fool I had been, risking what I valued most for a vengeful roll in the hay. And look what it had brought me. Paid in full with another betrayal to match my own. I suppose I'd earned it, but my nervousness nonetheless began giving way to anger.

"I was seeing him because he's another old friend. I have lots of them around here, as you seem to be well aware."

"You haven't seen him in what, sixteen years?"

"Something like that."

"So why the sudden need to see him now?"

"I was back in the region for the first time in a while and heard he was, too. So, naturally, I looked him up."

"Naturally." He pushed my teacup closer. "Here. If that's the best story you can come up with, you obviously need more refreshment."

I looked down at it with suspicion.

"What did you do, put something in it?"

He chuckled.

"Of course we did. Black tea and sugar and milk. There is no such thing as truth serum, Mr. Lockhart. And as I said earlier, we would never hold you here against your will. Your participation continues to be strictly voluntary."

"In that case, maybe I'll go now."

I stood.

"Splendid. I will have the driver take you directly to the airport. And I can assure you with complete confidence that all your personal belongings will be shipped to your forwarding address within a day of your departure."

"And my departure will be strictly voluntary."

"Naturally."

I sat back down, chastened but still angry.

"Look, it was really all quite innocent. Why don't you ask Chris?"

"I don't think his employer would be very happy about that. He's in a rather sensitive line of work, you know."

"We didn't talk about his work."

"What did you talk about?"

"Old times."

"Old times with Omar?"

"Old times with everybody. Just like I did with Hans Wolters. The Israelis and the West Bankers. The bullets versus the stones. The lions versus the Christians. A jolly good time for one and all." My voice was rising. "Chris and I probably would have had a beer together, but seeing how it was Ramadan and we were downtown—"

"No need to get upset, Mr. Lockhart."

"No need? Who else do you have spying on me?"

"Pardon?"

"My neighbor Fiona? Omar's secretary? Or is it just Nura?"

"Please, Mr. Lockhart. Your little infidelities are of no concern to us. We talk to a lot of people as a matter of routine. No need to single out anyone."

"You think you're being clever, but you're really quite clumsy." To my mind, there was now no secret about who had been bugging my house. Not the Americans, but these people. And when the realization hit home, I let my anger get the best of me. I reached into my pocket and slammed the small plastic box onto his desk, rattling the tea tray. "The way you left this behind, for instance. I found it this morning when a mouse gnawed through the wire."

He seemed genuinely surprised, but not at all embarrassed. He picked up the box and slowly turned it over in his hands, inspecting it with apparent curiosity. It was a bit like watching a jeweler admiring a nicely done setting.

"This is an interesting piece of hardware, Mr. Lockhart. Mind if I hang on to it for a while?"

"Keep it, if you like. Replenish your inventory."

"Oh, I don't deny we do these sorts of things from time to time. But this item here"—he turned it over again in his hands—"it definitely never belonged to us. And while I gladly accept your donation, I think now that it is you who are being clumsy when you think you are being clever. Tell me, Mr. Lockhart, how many deliveries from DHL have you taken lately?"

"What do you mean?"

"One of their trucks was seen around your house."

"Why don't you check with DHL?"

"I'm sure we will. It's just that they're known to be a favored courier of an organization we have a certain interest in. You haven't been free-lancing for any other employer, officially or otherwise, have you?"

"Of course not." Now I was on shaky ground, and for the first time felt a hint of genuine fear. "I quit the UN quite a while ago."

He smiled.

"I was not referring to the United Nations, as I'm sure you know. For your sake I hope you are telling the truth. Because the punishment for the sort of illegal employment I'm referring to is quite serious in this country. If you should ever come back to this office for that reason, I can assure you I won't be serving tea."

"And I can assure you that I don't know what you're talking about."

"Just as you don't know about Omar's second set of books. Tell me, what do you make of the people Omar generally associates with? His donors, I mean."

"The oil sheikhs from Saudi or the rich investors from Abdoun?" I tried to keep my expression neutral, but I was so relieved he had moved on to another topic that it must have shown on my face. Being outed as an American spy was hardly the way I wanted to end my stay in Jordan. Assuming they would even let me leave. "I suppose if they're offering what he needs, Omar doesn't have much choice but to associate with them."

"Yes. But do these donors always show up in the books?"

"If they give money they do." Unless their name was Norbert Krieger, of course, not that I was volunteering that bit of information. I was surprised he hadn't asked me about my trip to Athens, especially since it occurred the same weekend as Omar's. Maybe there were gaps in their knowledge. Or maybe they hadn't taken much of an interest in me until recently.

"Even the donors in Bakaa?"

"I wasn't aware we had any donors of substance in Bakaa, apart from Dr. Hassan. It's one reason they need a hospital. Although I am a little surprised you haven't asked anything about some of the other people out there."

"The usual rabble of amateur radicals, you mean?"

"Yes, as long you're bringing them up." I wasn't going to mention Nabil by name, even though he was the one I was most curious about.

"You needn't worry about them. There are always certain people out in Bakaa that we keep an eye on. Just as there are in Zarqa, or anywhere else electronic bullhorns are in excessive supply. In those situations there are usually so many people eager to inform on their rivals that we hardly have to lift a finger. That is one place, I assure you, that is well under control. But you know of no larger donors from that area?"

"No."

"Very well, then, Mr. Lockhart." He surprised me by standing abruptly. Our chat was over. Maybe he had learned whatever else he needed to know about me from Nura. "I doubt that we will see each other again, *inshallah*. But please don't be alarmed or upset if, when you next choose to leave the country, you are asked a few debriefing questions. I suggest you allow an extra hour or two at the airport for your departure."

"What happens if I don't exit via the airport?"

"You may find that difficult. Particularly for certain destinations to the west of here."

And if I were reluctant to answer any future questions, I suspected I knew exactly how they would choose to overcome my resistance. There would be photos available, more of those handy eight-by-tens, except these would show Nura and me. Maybe Jordanian equipment wasn't quite up to the technological level of Black, White, and Gray, so maybe the photos would be grainy, a trifle dark. But effective enough, especially with all the nice lighting Nura had provided with her candelabra, the one that had seemed so sexy at the time. And was my imagination now running wild, or had she gently steered me toward that side of the bed? I remember how smugly triumphant I had felt at the moment, thinking I was getting my just reward. *You still have it, old boy.* Yes, I had it, all right—just enough ignorant vanity to do myself in, perhaps Omar as well, and, who knows, maybe even my marriage, the one item I had always worked hardest to protect.

"You are free to go, Mr. Lockhart."

And I knew right where I was going, with a full head of steam.

32

The way I saw it, two people owed me immediate explanations. One was the resident spook at the American embassy, who for all I knew might even be Black, White, or Gray.

The other was Omar. If he truly kept two sets of books, then he had hidden almost as much from me as I had from him. All along we had been sneaking around behind each other's backs, like two unfaithful lovers.

"Drop me at the American embassy, please."

The Mukhabarat's driver seemed taken aback. He and his gray-clad twin exchanged puzzled glances across the front seat. The second one got on his cell phone, muttered a few words, nodded, and hung up. He turned my way.

"The boss says okay. But he said you may be in for a surprise."

"From him or from the Americans?"

Neither answered the question. In fact, neither said a word for the rest of the ride, not even when they popped the locks to let me out.

I breezed through the first security portal and then phoned Mike Jacoby from the second. Fortunately he was in.

"This is kind of short notice, Freeman. Could you come back in an hour? I'll treat you to lunch at the Blue Fig."

"This can't wait, Mike. Believe me, you'll want to hear what I have to say. Several people will."

A pause, followed by a sigh. If he thought I was troublesome now, he didn't know the half of it.

"Give me ten minutes. Put the Marine on, will ya?"

Fifteen minutes later I was at his desk.

"I need to see your intelligence person, Mike."

"We don't have an—"

"Don't give me any official bullshit, Mike. Just call him. Tell him I just spent the last hour and a half being shepherded around by the Mukhabarat. That ought to get his attention."

"It certainly got mine." He was already punching in the number on his phone.

"Yeah, Carl? Someone here to see you. An American. Says he's been spending his day on the Eighth Circle and wants to tell you all about it . . . Yeah . . . Yeah . . . I think so . . . Sure, I'll vouch for him." He looked over, as if to size me up. "To a point, anyway. Good enough. We'll wait here."

He hung up.

"To a point?"

"Even that offer's null and void if you piss Carl off. We're not exactly supposed to call him unless there's an emergency."

"Is Carl his real name?"

There was a knock at the door before Mike could answer. I half expected "Carl" to be my old friend Mr. Black, but they were nothing alike. Carl was tall, bald, and preternaturally thin, with his elbows angled outward and a permanent squint, as if he spent far too much time peering at reports. Hardly the image of a professional spook that we've come to expect.

"Is this the guy?"

"His name's Freeman Lockhart. He's all yours. Let me know when you're done and I'll escort him out."

"No need. I'll do the honors." Carl's way of saying this was his baby now, come what may.

He led me down a corridor to a locked glass door with a keypad entrance. Inside were four more offices, and Carl's was the last one on the left. No window. I suspected that was true of all of them. He settled me into a chair but remained standing.

"What's your story?"

The brusque tone signaled low expectations. So did the way he glanced at his watch. I started by complaining about the bug I'd found last night in my bedroom. He stopped me when I got to the part about the dead mouse.

"Sorry, not us. Is that why you called the Mukhabarat?"

"They called me. Came to my house, in fact."

"Not our concern, believe it or not, unless you're detained or charged with a crime. I assume they characterized the visit as voluntary?"

"Of course, but—"

"Nothing we can do for you." He rose from his desk and reached for the doorknob. "But that would at least explain the bug."

"It wasn't theirs."

"Or so they told you."

"Which makes their denial about as believable as yours. I guess you'll also claim you don't know anything about Black, White, and Gray."

"What?"

"Who, you mean. Three of your people, or their cover names, anyway. They broke into our house on Karos in the middle of the night. They're the ones who put me up to all this. Spying on my friend Omar, not that he hasn't earned it. And now I'm in hot water with the Mukhabarat and God knows who else. So stop playing dumb with me, and don't pretend you've never heard of this operation. Maybe it would just save time if I made my final report orally, then got out of your hair and out of the country. Good riddance for both of us."

His squint deepened until a bemused smile played at the edges of his mouth. For a moment I thought he was going to laugh, and I was poised to explode. Then he eased away from the door and sat down.

"Good thing Mike vouched for you, or you'd have been out on your ass the moment you accused us of bugging your house. Although I'm beginning to wonder about Mike. But I have to say, that's the oddest little outburst from a supposedly sane person that I've heard in quite a while."

"Is this part of standard operating procedure, denying you ever hired me?"

"Mister, I've never seen you in my life."

"Not you. The fucking Agency."

"So you're saying the Agency hired you? Came to your house in the middle of the night somewhere on . . . where was it?"

"Karos."

"That's an island, right? And they said, 'Hi, Mr. Lockhart, we're with the CIA and we want to send you to Jordan.' "

"Not in so many words."

"Ah. Now we're making progress. Unless you tell me the next thing they did was climb into a little spaceship and fly away."

"Laugh all you want, because if this really wasn't official, then, believe me, you've got a trio of rogue agents on your hands. Or worse."

"Okay, but take it slow. And start at the beginning. Back on Karos."

So I did, and to his credit he listened carefully. I referred to the debacle in Africa in only the sketchiest of terms, with me as the primary scapegoat. I included pretty much everything that had happened since, except the part about Nura.

About halfway through my account his expression began to change, and his squint relaxed into a dawning of revelation, or so it seemed. When I mentioned DeKuyper's name I thought his cheek might even have twitched, but he never said a word until I finished.

At the end he stood and strolled to a stout file cabinet, which he unlocked with yet another keypad. Then he withdrew a manila folder and put it facedown on the desk before I had a chance to read the label. From inside it he pulled out a stack of perhaps a dozen glossy photographs, turning them away from me.

"These people who broke into your house. Describe them again."

I did. He sorted through the pile like a poker player looking for the right discard. Finally he handed me one across the desk.

"Was this one of them?"

I had Black's face in mind when I looked, and it wasn't a match. So I was already shaking my head by the time the features registered as vaguely familiar. I put out a hand to stop Carl from snatching back the photo.

"Wait."

Carl raised an eyebrow.

"I think this might be the sidekick. The one named Gray."

"Sidekick?"

"Yes. Black did all the talking. He seemed to be the leader."

Carl smiled in apparent appreciation.

"That would just about cinch it, then. It's how they always do it. Let some drone be the spokesman so you'll remember his face, his voice. That way the real star gets to sit there observing you undistracted."

I remembered how Gray had almost hid behind his laptop, over in the corner.

"So you know who they are?" I felt a flush of vindication.

"How sure are you on the ID?"

I looked again.

"That's him, all right. That's Gray."

Carl took the photo and slipped it back into the folder. Then he smiled, as if the joke was on me.

"His real name is Bruce Fleischer. Born 1966, Shaker Heights, Ohio, and based in Washington. He's known in the trade as a *katsa*."

"A *katsa*?"

"Hebrew for 'field agent,' or 'case officer.' He's Mossad."

"Mossad?"

Carl could have punched me in the face and made less of an impact. I wasn't sure whether to feel foolish, outraged, or threatened, so I settled for a shocked blend of all three. Carl, watching me closely, broadened his smile.

"But in Athens they—"

"Followed you? Yes. Probably just making sure you were doing your job. In Jordan they didn't have that luxury, but in Athens they'd have all sorts of opportunities."

"Then why not just do the surveillance there on Omar themselves?"

"I'm sure they did. But it gave them a great opportunity to check up on you. Make sure you weren't just going through the motions. And you were an extra set of eyes. Never hurts in this business."

"Where does that leave me?"

"All alone, I'm afraid."

"You mean you can't—"

"Help you out?"

He said it as if I had just asked him to loan me a million dollars.

"Well, I am an American citizen."

"Who is currently employed by the Mossad. If we were in America I'd have to turn you in as an unregistered foreign agent. At the very least, you'd be facing espionage charges. And for an American living in Jordan, well, 'foolhardy' is putting it mildly. So I don't think so. Unless—"

"Unless what?"

The squint returned, and his next words emerged slowly.

"You could always work for us. Keep playing them. Let us in on your means of contact, maybe ask for an emergency meeting on neutral ground. And so on. It might be a real opportunity."

"For what?"

"For learning. Fleischer's one of their better field men, and something about this operation suggests he's engaging in a little freelance. With a bit more leverage, who knows. We might turn him as well."

"I thought they were our allies."

"Usually. All the more reason to know what they're up to. Besides, if you do us a favor, we'll do one for you. We could chalk up your indiscretion to naïveté and call it even. Who knows, we might even be able to make your little track record down in Africa disappear."

All of that appealed to me immensely. Erasing my fingerprints from the events in Tanzania would mean that Mila's would never be found. But I was wary of such an easy solution. Or maybe it was just that my nerves were shot. The events of the past few days had shaken my confidence.

Still, there seemed to be no alternative. And I needed a powerful ally.

"How long would it take?"

"Short and sweet. The longer we string it out, the likelier they'll know something's up, so we'd want you to move fast. I'd say a week. Two at the most."

I sensed a weight lifting from my shoulders. With any luck I'd soon be back in Greece. Get to Athens and spirit Mila away.

"So you'll help us?" Carl said.

"Do I really have any choice?"

"Not one that wouldn't involve lawyers. Although we certainly wouldn't leave you at the mercy of the Jordanians. Not if we could help it."

"Gracious of you."

"Oh, it is, believe me."

So, for the next several hours, Carl and I talked. He told me his last name was Cummings, which was probably about as credible as Black, White, and Gray. We made a few plans, exchanged a few telephone numbers, and then he led me toward the security door. He had decided it would be best if he escorted me from the building without either of us saying good-bye to Mike Jacoby. Especially now that he was my new boss.

Did this mean I had attained professional status?

I might have left feeling pretty smug about that if Carl hadn't offered a dose of reality as he was punching in the key code.

"By the way, Freeman. Do you have family?"

His squint had returned, and for the first time in our conversation he seemed worried about someone's welfare other than his own.

"My wife. She was with me on Karos."

"Is she somewhere safe?"

"Her aunt's house in Athens."

Carl frowned.

"That's hardly what I'd call safe. You saw what they did in Athens."

And I hadn't even told him about Mila's episode on the highway from Glyfada.

"What are you saying?"

"That as soon as you show up as a foreign object on the Mossad's radar, they're not going to be happy. And if this is a freelance job, as I suspect, then none of the usual rules will apply. They can play as rough as they like. You should get her out of harm's way."

"Where?"

"The States, if you can."

"But her visa—what if—"

"She's your wife, right?"

"Yes."

"Then she'll get in fine."

He took me to the main entrance while I absorbed the news. A blow in one sense, a relief in another. I was about to ask for more advice when his beeper went off, and when he checked the message his expression changed completely. Suddenly my problems seemed to be the furthest thing from his mind.

"I have to go," he said quickly, shoving open the door. "The Marine will see you out."

The soldier hustled over while Carl headed briskly in the other direction.

"What about my wife?" I shouted.

But the door had shut behind him.

I wandered outdoors in a daze. Up to now, every move I had made to shield Mila and me had only seemed to push us farther into the open. Maybe I was still making the wrong decisions, but Cummings had at least seemed to offer a quick way to safety for Mila.

I was surprised to discover it was now dark. The night air was fresh and cool, but sirens wailed in the distance. Lots of them. I needed to phone Mila right away, and find some way to convince her to travel to my parents' house without raising too many alarms among our eaves-droppers. Everything else could wait. Once that was done, I could act with more autonomy. I flagged down a taxi that had just dropped off a fare, and gave my address on Othman Bin Affan Street.

We had gone only a few blocks through Abdoun when an ambulance with a red crescent raced past, lights flashing and horn blaring. Outside a crowded café, men and women were running for the parking lot, a pal-pable sense of urgency etched on their faces. I hadn't seen this much commotion in the streets since Eid al-Fitr, but this time the mood was altogether different. Something ugly was unfolding, or maybe that was just a reflection of my own precarious condition.

"Can you go a little faster?" I shouted to the driver.

Mila needed to pack and get moving, the sooner the better, even though she and my parents had never really hit it off. To my folks, Mila was still the quiet Balkan girl whose family had made such an unseemly ruckus at our wedding. But for now they offered the safest possible refuge. I would phone them as well. It had been months since we spoke, so I owed them a call anyway.

We crested the hill onto Jebel Amman and were approaching the Third Circle on Zahran Street when the driver slammed on his brakes. A policeman signaled for us to halt while two more pulled a wooden barrier into the street to block traffic.

"What's going on? What is this?"

For a moment I was certain I was about to be arrested, the whole plot uncovered from top to bottom in a night of intense questioning on the Eighth Circle. But the policemen had no further interest in us, and the traffic piled up behind us. Drivers honked horns and shouted questions out their windows.

"What's happening?" I asked again.

My driver shook his head in consternation and turned on the radio. Another ambulance raced by, and the police pulled the barricade aside to let it pass. The radio jolted to life, but the Arabic was so frantic and the reception so staticky that at first I couldn't make sense of it. The driver went very still and clutched his worry beads.

"A bomb," he said. "No, two of them. Maybe three."

"Where?"

"The Hyatt. Three bombs at the Hyatt."

Now I began getting a sense of the radio report as well.

"Bombs at two other hotels as well," I said. "The Radisson and the Days Inn. My God, is anyone . . ."

"Yes. Many dead. Very many. I am sorry, but I do not think we will reach your house anytime soon."

I pulled a ten-dinar note out of my wallet, double what I owed, and placed it in the driver's palm with a sympathetic pat of his hand. He nodded as if he understood. This was not about generosity. It was about shock and compassion. The machinery of terror had finally gone off right here in Amman. I thought immediately of the people on the fringes of Omar's organization, of Nabil and his shadowy contacts, and even the woman from America, Aliyah Rahim. Everyone was so quick to dismiss the doings out in Bakaa as harmless political maneuverings, but now I wondered. And of the many questions barreling through my mind, the most disturbing was this: Had I done anything that, inadvertently or not, might have tripped one of the switches to set things in motion?

I stepped away from the taxi and began to run.

33

Aliyah heard the terrible news only four hours before her scheduled flight to Washington, and once again her best-laid plans began to fall apart. How horribly ironic, she thought, if a bombing in Amman made it impossible for her to stop a bombing in Washington.

Just before hearing of the disaster, she was sitting at the house of Khalid II—or Nabil, as she now knew him—having eluded the doctor's watchers in the hotel lobby after days of careful planning. She had come to regard the two men as "the shepherds." She had even told them about her nickname, eliciting a smile from the larger one.

For several days she had let them believe she was entirely at their mercy. They drove her to restaurants, to shops, and to the Roman Theatre downtown, even buying her admission ticket and then fending off the predatory "guides" before dropping back a respectful distance to let her enjoy the site in relative solitude.

Having won their trust, she then set out to deceive them. On the final day of Eid al-Fitr, a Sunday, she announced after returning from an escorted walk that she wished to take a nap and watch televsion. She switched on the TV in her room to a volume that could be heard outside her door, tucked her hair beneath a scarf, put on a raincoat and a pair of sunglasses, and then slipped down an emergency stairwell to a rear entrance that led to the hotel pool, where she strolled past puzzled sunbathers to an outdoor stairway that led into the rear parking lot. She walked to the back of the lot, cut through an alley, and emerged on a side street, where she ducked into a café and phoned for a taxi to take her to Khalid II's house in Bakaa.

Once again he was gone, and once again his wisp of a wife was reluctant to speak. But the woman did agree to pass along Aliyah's handwritten message. Aliyah then returned to her room by the same circuitous route. Khalid II phoned her that night. He told her his real name and said that he was in hiding. The details were too complicated to discuss over the phone, he said, but perhaps in a few days the danger would pass. He reluctantly agreed to meet her at his house on Wednesday evening, just after dark. More important, he promised to do what he could to find out the information she needed. He also agreed to arrange for a neighbor who drove a taxi to take her to the airport later that night, after their rendezvous.

Aliyah then sneaked downstairs by her secret route to the hotel business center, which had resumed its non-holiday hours after sundown. She arranged an online flight reservation for late Wednesday night, on a connecting flight via Frankfurt that would depart after midnight.

And then, there she was, seated in Nabil's house, not yet aware of the news that would change everything. She was watching television. It was an aging Philips model, a black-and-white with rabbit ears and fuzzy reception. Her viewing companion was Nabil's young daughter, Jena, who was tucked against her knees while coloring the faces of tigers onto scrap paper by the pale glow of the screen.

Nabil's wife, who had yet to give her name and had blushed when Jena gave hers, flitted from chore to chore in the background like an agitated bird, washing dishes and tidying cushions, and obviously hoping that her husband would arrive soon. He was already more than two hours late.

The TV viewing was downright bizarre—Martha Stewart demonstrating how to make dishes she had cooked in prison. It would have been strange even at home, but watching it here with Arabic subtitles, while seated on the cool slab floor of a shack home in a refugee camp, made it seem like one of those surreal dreams she would have described to Annie Felton. "Perhaps you fear losing your domesticity," Annie might have said. "Maybe you think your actions are endangering your family."

Aliyah checked her watch while Martha popped a cookie sheet into the oven. It was 9:30 p.m. Her flight would depart at 1:30 a.m. Her bags were packed and had already been taken to the home of the neighbor in the next block who would drive her to the airport. She had told her two watchers back at the InterContinental that she was tired and wanted to eat in her room. She had then called room service. When the food was delivered, she dumped the contents into a trash can and placed the tray outside her door. Then she switched on her television and departed down the back stairwell.

But now she was wondering if she was cutting things too close. It would take at least an hour to reach the airport from here. And even if Nabil were to show up now, she supposed he would need at least half an hour to teach the necessary lesson on how to disarm a bomb.

Airport security and customs would mean further delays, and this was a flight she couldn't afford to miss. The senator, so far as she could tell from news accounts she had been monitoring several times a day, was still alive. But you never knew when your luck might run out. She decided to wait another twenty minutes.

That was when the TV announcer broke in with an urgent bulletin: Bombs at three hotels. Scores dead. Through the blue fuzz she watched a chaotic scene of ambulance crews rushing bodies to the curb. My God, was that someone's arm on a table? She wanted to cover Jena's eyes. The announcer said something about a wedding party, how awful. Then they cut away to grim-faced policemen with berets and machine guns, setting up a barricade. She wondered if the airport would remain open, or if she would even be able to get there. After 9/11 some of their friends had been stranded for days in other cities without a way home.

A few minutes later she got her answer. The borders were closed and so was the airport. A curfew was in effect. Aliyah's heart sank. A bombing tonight, and who knew, perhaps another bombing in a few days in Washington, and then her husband's face would be the one on everyone's TV screen.

The image flickered to another hotel. More bodies. A woman's voice shrieked incoherently in the background. A pushy policeman shouted for everyone to move back. The announcer said something about suicide bombers. "They are almost certainly to blame."

Behind her, Nabil's wife dropped a bowl to the floor with a thundering crash.

Aliyah looked again at the screen, this time with a new sense of horror. Could that be where Nabil really was, piled among the dead, his body torn to pieces by an explosion from his chest? No, Aliyah thought. It wasn't possible. Why would he have scheduled their appointment for tonight if he knew he was doing this? Unless that was simply part of his cover. But surely he wasn't the type, was he?

Aliyah placed a hand protectively on Jena's small, warm back. The girl was still coloring happily, oblivious to the television. Nabil's wife swooped in to pick up the girl and cradled the thin body to her breast in a deep and despairing hug.

"Mommy, I was coloring!"

"It's all right, dear. It's all right. Your father will be home soon."

Then, like an answer to their prayers, the door opened. But the sight that greeted them was not at all what they had hoped for.

34

I trotted from the Third Circle toward the Hyatt, which loomed in the darkness like an upended cruise ship in a wash of bright lights, strobed by flashes of red. Sounds of moaning and sobbing were everywhere, and as I approached I saw a hotel luggage trolley—the fancy kind with a big brass bar across the top—being wheeled to the curb like a hospital gurney, piled with victims.

People wrapped in white blankets straggled out of an emergency door to the side. Just in front of me stood a man talking on a cell phone. He seemed to be intact, but his suit looked as if someone had hurled a bucket of red paint on it. Without warning he dropped to his knees and wailed in grief. I stepped forward to help but was preempted by two women who seemed to know him.

On one of the luggage carts I saw a body, barely recognizable as human except for the bright shards of clothing and a shock of dark hair at one end. Wisps of smoke rose from its smoldering flesh like steam off a roast.

I had come here hoping to help, but the scene had overwhelmed even my capacity for macabre chaos. It was clear there was little to be done except get out of the way for the ambulance crews, which were still arriving. So I headed back toward the Third Circle. I was a little more than a mile from home, and decided to walk there as fast as I could.

A black Mercedes pulled to the curb, and out stepped four men dressed much like the two who had escorted me earlier that day to the Eighth Circle. They passed without a glance. My little chat over tea already seemed like an event from another era, but the scene reminded me that soon the security roundups would begin, if they hadn't already.

I reached the house in fifteen minutes. All the lights were off at Fiona's, and I wondered if she was okay. The Hyatt and Radisson were popular for events that attracted foreigners and expats.

I dialed the number for Athens. Mila answered on the first ring, as if she had been waiting by the phone.

"Freeman, are you all right?"

"So you've heard?"

"It was just on TV. It's horrible. This can't be connected with your work, can it?"

Leave it to her to intuitively zero in on my greatest fear. For all my anxiety over our separation, it was a fresh reminder that she still knew me better than anyone, perhaps because she had seen me at my lowest and weakest moments.

"No, of course not. But listen to me, Mila. You have to get out of there. It has nothing to do with tonight, but you need to leave Greece as soon as you can."

"But, Freeman—"

"I'm serious. Those people who ran you down the other day, there will be others just like them. So go. As soon as you can get a flight."

"To where?"

"America. My parents' house in Massachusetts. Any way possible."

"But my visa. You said that—"

"It's not the Americans who are doing this. It's—" I hesitated to say the word on this line, especially with all that was unfolding across the city tonight.

"It's what?"

"Other people. I can't say more about it now, and I'm sure you know why. But you should leave. By air, land, or sea. However you can do it. Then stay with my parents until I can join you. Because this time I can't do anything to protect you."

"This time?"

Shit. How had that slipped into the conversation?

"Or anytime. I'm babbling. Just go. Tell me that you'll leave, that you'll get out of there as soon as you can."

"Yes, I'll try."

"Trying's not enough, Mila!"

"All right, then." A pause, two beats. "I'll do it."

"Good. I love you."

"And I love you. It's not too late, is it?"

Did she mean too late for her escape or for our future?

"No, there's still time."

"I hope you're right."

"I am. See you in Massachusetts."

"Good luck, Freeman. God be with you."

Yes, but whose God? Everyone here would soon be calling on one God or another for either aid or vengeance.

As soon as we hung up, I switched on the television just as another ambulance flashed across the screen, this time in front of the Days Inn. The body count had begun. Thirty and rising. I picked up the phone to call Omar's house.

Hanan was frantic. She said he had gone to Bakaa hours ago, after speaking with Dr. Hassan. He had been angry and upset. Something to do with Nabil. She hadn't heard from him since.

"Nabil?"

"Yes. Nabil was in some sort of trouble. Omar had to find him before it was too late. Then I heard about the bombs and now I can't reach him. Either his phone is off or—oh, my God, I don't know what to think. He could be anywhere. He could even be—"

"It's all right, Hanan. If Omar said he was going to Bakaa, then that's where he is, okay? Cell phones don't always work out there."

"It's just that, well, you've been around him. You must have noticed."

"Noticed what?"

"Omar. The way he's been acting. Not that he would ever tell me what's going on. Has he told you?"

"No."

"But you've noticed it, too, haven't you?"

"Maybe. I don't know. It's Nabil who has me worried right now, considering what's happened."

"You don't think that—"

She didn't dare finish the sentence.

"I don't know. But I'm going to find out. I'm going out there."

"To Bakaa?"

"I'll let you know as soon as I know anything about Omar."

"This can't be a good time to be moving around the city."

"Probably not. Call if you get any news."

"Be careful."

The first thing I did was retrieve the gun from the dresser drawer. No ammo, of course, but sometimes just showing the barrel was enough. I then raced across Jebel Amman in the Passat to the Internet café to tie up a few loose ends, in case I ended up stranded in Bakaa without access to either the Internet or an international phone.

The owner was locking up early, but grudgingly let me in when I pleaded that it was an emergency.

"The whole night is an emergency," he said, shaking his head in despair. "Ten minutes. Then you must go."

I booted up one of the desktops while he stood at the darkened register, his face ashen. To my relief, Mila had fired off a message only moments earlier, with the good news that she had already booked a flight to Boston. She would depart in the morning.

I sent a quick e-mail to Massachusetts with the details, asking my mom and dad to meet her at the airport. I was about to log off when I saw that a new message had arrived that very morning from Chris Boylan, titled simply "Update." I felt a stab of worry. Had he, too, paid a price for my indiscretion?

His message consisted only of two words, "Interesting timing," followed by an Internet link highlighted in blue, which I clicked on immediately. A brief article from a newspaper Web site in Munich popped onto the screen. It was dated yesterday, and Norbert Krieger's name was in the first line. My German was rusty, so it took a few seconds to make sense of the rest. Then I gasped in disbelief.

It was an obituary.

Krieger had been found dead at his office. Not murdered, just dead. Or so the story said. Then again, my employers were extremely talented, so who could say for sure. Black magic, I thought, and I was the apprentice wizard recklessly casting spells. I had conjured up the name of a man in Munich, bandied it about in a few incantations, and then—presto—he turned up dead a thousand miles away.

The shopkeeper cleared his throat, impatient to leave, so I logged off. He waved away my dinar and I climbed back into the Passat, still in shock. What an evening. And who knew what bad news awaited in Bakaa. I had to get moving.

I ran into two roadblocks before even making it out of Jebel Amman. Finally I escaped the hilltop via a steep, narrow alley that cut across to a side street through the edge of downtown. From there I twisted downhill and gradually made my way out of the city like a mouse through a maze, turning around and starting over each time my way was blocked. Eventually I slipped onto the highway to Bakaa well past a cordon of barricades that the police had set up around the rim of the city.

Bakaa was in chaos. The main drag was impenetrable, which meant reaching Dr. Hassan's office was out of the question. By using side streets and alleys I was able to drive within a few blocks of the field office. I parked the car and set out on foot.

At the office there was a commotion outside the doorway, although everyone in the crowd was looking back across the street. I pushed through, barely able to open the door against the crush of bystanders. I flipped a light switch, but the power had been cut. Then I saw Omar, seated in the darkness next to a typewriter. He wasn't making a sound.

"Where have you been?" I said. "Hanan is worried sick."

"I just reached her. She's fine now."

His voice was a monotone, the flat register of utter defeat.

"What is it?" I asked. "Where's Nabil?"

Omar slowly shook his head.

"I was too late," he said. "Something terrible has happened."

I braced myself for the worst.

35

From almost the moment the door flew open, Jena began to wail. She was the first to realize what was happening in the mob scene outside. Aliyah figured it out next. Nabil must have thrown open the door just as his pursuers caught him. Her immense relief at seeing him alive changed instantly to fear for his survival.

Two policemen in blue berets were tugging him backward, one at each arm. Their apparent destination was a blue panel van with a caged windshield, just across the narrow street. And that was the least of Nabil's worries. A mob had converged and was growing by the minute. Angry shouts of "Traitor!" and "Murderer!" flew from every direction, and the policemen could barely make headway. A stone soared above the crowd and landed with a sickening thud against Nabil's back. He gasped and staggered as Jena screamed above the din.

Aliyah fought her way outside just as a chunk of cinder block landed by the doorway. Frightened for the child, she saw the girl squirming in her mother's arms just inside the house. Dust from the maelstrom billowed into the living room like a brown spirit.

The crowd surged, and Aliyah was carried along with it, her chest squeezed so tightly she could barely draw a breath. It was all she could do to keep her footing. Fall now and she would be trampled. She held her balance and turned her head just in time to see Nabil looking right at her from a few feet away. His eyes were wide, but they seemed almost serene, as if he had already resigned himself to whatever was going to happen.

The policemen dragged him the final few feet to the van, where four more officers were wading into the crowd, clubs swinging. She heard the crack of wood against a skull. Several men fell, swallowed by the mob. The policemen gave a great heave, and Nabil ducked in through the rear of the van as his forehead banged against the top of the doorway. A spot below his hairline bloomed red just as the doors slammed shut and took him out of sight. Then the stones rained down in earnest, clattering off the top of the van.

As Aliyah turned to see where all the missiles were coming from, she saw a familiar face, back toward Nabil's house. It was the doctor. He was shouting, "Murderer! Murderer!" as if leading the charge. Aliyah must not have been the only one to recognize him, because she saw the doctor suddenly turn as if to ward off a blow, and then she heard Nabil's wife shrieking.

"You!" the woman said, stepping toward him with a sobbing Jena still in her arms. "It is your doing! You did this to Nabil!"

For a moment the mob seemed uncertain whom to support in this new confrontation. Then a few men opted to protect one of their own, although Jena's presence helped to blunt their fury. Aliyah quickly moved forward to help. She found it maddening that she still didn't know the woman's name. Some of the more levelheaded men in the crowd helped her to chivy mother and child back through the doorway, but Nabil's wife continued to scream at the doctor, who, looking a bit rattled, nodded in a gesture of thanks to his rescuers. Then he saw Aliyah, and smiled. She turned to try and escape, but couldn't push through the mob, and before she knew it he was at her side, aided by his impromptu bodyguards. He placed his hand on her forearm, exactly where he had gripped her in the lobby bar of the hotel, and leaned closer to shout into her ear.

"How fortunate for both of us that I found you here."

Her anger overcame her fear.

"What does she mean?" she shouted back. "What have you done to Nabil?"

"Now, now," he said, in the manner of parent to child. "We are all upset. It has been a long and terrible night, but I am sure now that justice will be done."

He released her forearm but then placed his hand around her shoulder. To everyone else it must have looked like a gesture of help or reassurance, but his grip felt strong enough to bruise.

"Come over here," he said into her ear. "Let's get you out of harm's way. This is not your affair."

Her impulse was to wrench free, maybe even to spit in his face. But she didn't dare, not with emotions running so high. His protectors were still in tow, and the mob might do anything. So she let him steer her to the mouth of an alley, where they found a brief respite from the jostling. She opened her mouth to speak, but he beat her to it, lowering his voice so that only she could hear.

"Surely you shouldn't remain here. Not after who you've been seen with, and who you've been talking to."

"Are you threatening me with the same treatment?"

"I'm offering my help. Please, you look very upset. I will take you to my office. It is safer there, and only a few blocks away."

"No, thank you."

"Please. Why ruin things for your husband?"

Anyone watching might have thought from his expression that he was being as solicitous as possible. But his fingertips dug into her shoulder. She did as she was told. They walked side by side through the streets.

"I don't want to go into your office," she said, turning to speak into his ear.

"But you must, because I have news. Although perhaps you already know."

"What news? Tell me now." She tried to stop, but he dragged her inexorably forward.

"Patience. Just know that even on a day as horrible as this, there has at least been one moment of good fortune."

"What do you mean?"

He stopped, looked her in the eye.

"Have you really not heard?"

She shook her head. The doctor smiled.

"The senator, your husband's patient. He has at last left this world. Your husband's glorious work may now proceed. Come, I will tell you all about it."

The doctor released his grip and resumed his progress. Aliyah stood dumbfounded in his wake, as stunned as if she had been struck by a stone from the mob. The last bit of sanity in her world had just slipped from her grasp, and was now lost in the chaos of the streets.

36

They've taken him away," Omar said slowly, in apparent disbelief. "They think he did it."

"Did he?" I asked.

By then I would have given even odds on a "yes" answer. It wasn't just the warning signs having to do with Nabil—all those dark hints I'd foolishly ignored, mostly because I liked him, true believer or not. It was Omar's bearing that now convinced me. He was slumped in a chair with his head in his hands. His eyes were brimming wells of despair. I knew as acutely as anyone the crushing power of guilt, and I saw clearly the impact it had made on Omar. He had met the blow head-on and was reeling.

"*Did he?*" I repeated.

Omar looked up with a start, as if finally hearing me from across a canyon. His eyes flared with anger.

"How the hell could Nabil have done it? He'd be in a thousand pieces!"

"Not if he planned it. Or supplied it."

Omar shook his head.

"That's crazy."

"Then what about his contacts? The people he's been meeting. I've heard things, you know, here and downtown."

"I've heard them, too. I was even responsible for some of the introductions. But they were all part of a setup. If you think Nabil was capable of doing this to his own people, then you know less about all of us than I thought." He looked up. "Do you truly believe what you're saying? In fact, what *do* you believe anymore? I've been wondering that since the day you arrived."

It was the same question Nabil had asked, when he caught me following him. He certainly hadn't behaved then like a person with something to hide, and I now felt ashamed of the glib answer I'd given, my usual boilerplate of foolishness. Nabil hadn't scorned me for that, either. If anything, he had seemed to pity me, not as an infidel doomed to damnation but as someone still searching for a place to drop his moral anchor.

"I don't know what I believe. About any of this."

"Well, stop believing Nabil was involved. All he's guilty of is associating with some of the wrong people in Bakaa. Or wrong in the eyes of Dr. Hassan. *He's* the one who did in Nabil. And like an idiot, I was helping him along the way; if only I had realized it at the time."

"Dr. Hassan set up the arrest?"

"He's been setting it up for weeks, apparently. He actually seemed proud to tell me all about it. Arranging for certain people downtown to invite Nabil in for a chat—using my name as entrée in some cases—and then having the meeting photographed. Having it arranged for Nabil to play host to some stupid American woman who was up to God knows what. Then whispering all the details into a few key ears on the Eighth Circle. All a part of the usual political vendetta out here. More of the same old Palestinian fratricide. Which I was happy to exploit for my own ends, of course. Thinking I was being so clever by pitting one side against the other. I thought they would both try to outdo each other and that the hospital would reap the rewards. Instead it's the opposite. Everything has been undermined. Then the bombings came along, and Nabil was already at the top of the police list. They were already looking for him, and by the end of the week they probably would have arrested him anyway. That's the way it works with my people. We turn on each other like fools. Then some even bigger fool turns on all of us and blows himself up, and the police go out and start throwing all the wrong people in jail. Just watch—they'll arrest a few hundred by Friday. It's the perfect excuse for getting rid of all the ones nobody likes."

But I was still thinking of what he had said about the American woman.

"I saw her," I said. "The American. Not just with Nabil. With Dr. Hassan, too. And I'm not sure she's so stupid. Maybe they're planning something."

"Maybe."

Then he waved it off, seemingly disinterested. Or maybe he wasn't paying attention. I knew that symptom, too. You became so absorbed in the idea of your own complicity that you refused to contemplate someone else's. He needed a good shock to the system. So I administered one.

"Listen to me, Omar. Dr. Hassan isn't the only one who's been using you. So have I."

He seemed to finally emerge from his stupor.

"What do you mean?"

"Well, for starters, I was over on the Eighth Circle this morning. They sent a car for me. Asked me all kinds of questions about you."

He surprised me by smiling, although it was not a happy smile.

"Fat fellow in a bad suit? Served you tea on a horrible painted tray?"

"Yes."

"His name's Mahmoud, or so I'm told. My personal case officer. Always looking into my business."

"You know about his interest?"

"How could I miss it? He's questioned about half my friends. I think he does it just to put me on notice."

"Why?"

"Because of my work."

I gave him an opportunity to lie, just to see if he would take the bait.

"For the hospital?"

"No. Other work. Things I haven't told you about."

Now we were getting somewhere. If he would level with me, then I would level with him. And as far as I was concerned, then neither the Mossad, the Mukhabarat, nor the CIA need know what passed between us.

"Like helping Basma Shaheed, you mean?"

"Mahmoud told you about her?"

"He wasn't the only one."

Omar raised an eyebrow, and seemed to store that item away before continuing.

"She is a Palestinian who does the good work of helping people keep their houses and their land, so I support her when I can."

"With whose money?"

"My own, mostly. Sometimes I pass along donations from Europe. From people who are more comfortable doing business that way. It isn't always so popular helping Arabs these days, you know." He seemed to detect the wariness in my face. "What? You don't think I'm giving her money from the hospital fund, do you?"

"Mahmoud thinks so. He said you're keeping two sets of books."

"Of course I am. One for the charity and one for, well, whatever it is you want to call this other passion. That doesn't mean I'm stealing from one for the other. But it doesn't surprise me Mahmoud would say that. It's probably his latest way of fighting us. Smear us behind our backs."

"Who's 'us'?"

"You've met most of them. Sami Fayez. Rafi Tuqan. A few others. Then there's our artist friend, Issa Odeh."

"The one who painted the stuff on your living room wall."

"Yes. He got us hooked."

"On what?"

"History, if you strip it to its essentials. Archaeology, if you want to get technical. Staking our claim on the future by finding our past. He took us out in the desert one weekend, one of his little excursions. He puts them together to recruit people to the cause of land preservation. I'm sure he never dreamed it would go over so well. And it probably wouldn't have if I hadn't just seen some news report from Israel. One of those biblical archaeologists who had just dug something up. You know how it goes. They find a few stones and say they belonged to King David. Then everyone oohs and aahs and says, well, it must really be true, then. They really *are* the chosen people, and this is their promised land, so those Arabs should go take a hike.

"Well, a few days later Issa takes us out to the terrace of a big wadi, out in the desert northeast of Amman. It's a Late Bronze Age site, practically virgin. Hardly anyone knows about it. Why? Because no one cares, of course. Because no one is kicking in money for a dig, and no one is saying, 'This was King David's royal outhouse' or 'This was Solomon's mudroom.' But when you pick up an object from the sand, and then hold it in your hands knowing that someone made it over three thousand years ago, and not a soul since then has ever touched it, well, there is a certain power in that experience.

"And that's when it hit me. Why not make those old ghosts work for us, too? Because Arabs have been walking these hills just as long as Jews. Longer, even. The Edomites, the Moabites. All of them built bigger and grander civilizations. If we can raise them from the dead—archaeologically speaking, of course—they'll become part of our army. And that's where Basma Shaheed comes into it. Support her and you save a few Arab houses, a few more dunams of Palestinian land. Hold on to enough land and, who knows, maybe you can get your own diggers in place, legally or otherwise. So that next time you find a site in East Jerusalem, or Nablus, or wherever it might be, then you have another army fighting for you. No need to throw stones anymore, Freeman. You just dig them up and put them behind glass."

Omar's eyes were ablaze. I hadn't seen him this impassioned since our days on patrol.

"But that's the West Bank. Why should anyone on the Eighth Circle care?"

"Because we're doing it here, too. Jordan is untapped, untouched in so many places. That makes it the perfect place for building our body of evidence, establishing our tradition. It's like staking claims in a mine. Of course, land prices being what they are, not everyone wants you to stake a claim. So you start making enemies."

"Jordanian investors?"

"Saudis, too. And Iraqis, Euros, Americans. Probably even a few Israelis. Everybody with money wants in on this boom. Except they want to buy and build, and we want to preserve and protect."

"What does the palace want?"

"Depends on who you ask. Everyone has his patron, and right now everyone with enough money and connections has at least one patron on the Eighth Circle."

"Is that why Mahmoud asked me about Qesir, and the Wadi Terrace Project, and someplace near Madaba?"

"Hesban?"

"That sounds right."

"Three of our resort sites, plus a guesthouse near Wadi Fidan."

"What's a resort got to do with preservation?"

"Our way of footing the bill, paying for more. You preserve the core of the site, then develop the surrounding area. Do it right and you've built both a buffer and a moneymaker to help with more acquisitions. Sami's idea, and it's genius, really. Except it infuriates the competition, which makes it harder to get all the permits and easements."

I thought of the photo Mahmoud had showed me of Omar coming out of the Ministry of Tourism and Antiquities, and the one of Sami with his arm around the king. They must be spending some of their proceeds on bribes and patronage in palace corridors and at various ministries. But between Sami, Rafi, and Omar, they would have lots of valuable connections. No wonder the outsiders were pulling out the stops, even to the point of hiring freelance help from the Mossad once the Eighth Circle failed to produce the desired results. Enemies, indeed.

Now it was my turn to let him know just how deeply those enemies had burrowed beneath his foundation. I wasn't looking forward to it.

"Didn't you say the Mossad was tailing you in Athens?"

"I don't think it was me they were following. They were after a contributor."

"A contributor to the charity, you told me."

He lowered his head and grinned sheepishly.

"A white lie, I'm afraid. I wasn't yet ready to tell you about all this. Why put you in jeopardy when your work was going to free me up for more of this?"

"And this fellow, he's sure it was Mossad?"

"He took down a tag number from the agent's scooter and had someone run it. Apparently the rental agency is a known Mossad supplier."

"And your contributors in Athens. They would be Norbert Krieger and Professor Yiorgos Soukas?"

His jaw dropped.

"Now how did you . . . ?"

"That was me on the scooter. Following Krieger, and following you. Only I didn't know at the time who I was really working for."

I was prepared to have to shout him down in order to explain myself further. Even then I knew I wouldn't have the heart to tell him that Krieger was dead. But Omar's stunned reaction made it clear I wouldn't need to do any yelling. His mouth was agape, and he slumped in his chair. So I began telling him my story before his shock turned to anger. I told him everything, going back all the way to that strange night on Karos when the owls hooted their warning. Then I backtracked further, to the fields of the dead and the dying in Tanzania, because he needed to hear it all—even the parts about Mila, if only because he was the one person who deserved a full explanation.

Then I apologized, not that I expected him to accept.

"At least it was for her, for Mila," he said, hanging his head. "Consolation for you, perhaps. But not so much for me. I must have looked like such a fool a few moments ago, spouting off all about my new passion. Saving the world with a shovel and a little carbon dating. A fool's errand, isn't it, especially with people like you on the loose."

"Believe me, if I had really known who was hiring me . . . ."

"Does it really make any difference which agency? Mossad, CIA,

Mukhabarat. They are all the same kind of people, especially on a night like this, when a few old stones seem pretty silly even to me."

"I went by the Hyatt," I said blankly. "It was horrible. Bodies piled at the curb. People with blood all over them."

"Don't try to pretend you're one of us, Freeman. I know you sympathize, but it's not the same."

"I know."

"But you do like some of our ways, don't you? I suppose you think of this as a form of *taqiyya*, all these things you've been doing. Allowing yourself to lie and betray because you think it's necessary for survival. Even if it's Mila's survival. Yes, *taqiyya*. Just like you told me back in the car in Nablus."

He said it with weary resignation. And that might have been the way the evening ended, with a hollow feeling in my stomach, yet the relief of confession. But I still had a final chore to complete in Bakaa. One last sin to atone for, one last troublesome lead to pursue.

I headed out the door and began walking toward Dr. Hassan's office.

Neither Omar nor I said good-bye.

37

Aliyah's mind was a chaos of urgent questions as she walked robotically alongside Dr. Hassan through the streets of Bakaa. How soon would the airport reopen? Could she arrange another flight home? If so, how could she get away from the doctor? Even if she could, would she be too late? What day was the senator's funeral, and at what time? How far along was the tunnel, and had Abbas yet reached the point of no return—not just in his digging, but in his spiral down a sinkhole of vengeance?

The only images strong enough to penetrate this emotional tangle were unwelcome—flash visions of Nabil's face as he receded into the mob, echoes of his daughter's sharp cries of sorrow. Every time she recalled little Jena sprawled against her on the floor she had trouble swallowing. Jena had reminded her a little of Shereen, her poor lost daughter.

"Please, come inside my office where you can rest."

It was the doctor's voice. Or Dr. Hassan, as she now knew he was called. His name was on the door, and as soon as she saw it she remembered Nabil using the name when they had run into the American at the field office.

"Dr. Hassan is expecting us," Nabil had said, seizing upon it as an excuse to depart. Now it all made a certain sense, especially if the doctor had been in position to betray Nabil to the authorities.

And where did that betrayal leave her? she wondered. Perhaps she was also vulnerable, especially if her name had been put on some list as a result of her dealings here. She might be marooned here indefinitely, unable to return to America. And if Abbas succeeded, then that would close the door forever. She would spend a lifetime on the run in the Middle East, month upon month in teeming places like Bakaa, sleeping beneath sheet-metal rooftops and owing her freedom to the likes of Dr. Hassan.

Enough of this self-pity. She would turn her energies to the task of getting home as soon as possible.

"You will have tea?" Dr. Hassan asked.

He had opened the door onto a gloomy office where all the curtains were drawn. At least here the electricity was working, although all the light seemed to be soaked up by dark paneling and a large brown couch. It must be the waiting room.

"My receptionist has gone for the day, but I will be happy to make you a cup."

"Yes, that would be fine."

"Milk and sugar?"

"Just sugar, please."

"Take a seat in my office. Right through that door. And please, do not even think about leaving. You are now under my protection, and will remain so. I suppose I should be angry with you for nearly getting away from me, but seeing as how things seem to have turned out for the best . . ."

He smiled with a slight shrug, very satisfied with himself, and then stepped into the other room to make tea. She collapsed on a chair by his desk. It must be where his patients sat. She looked at the anatomical charts and file drawers. There was a stethoscope on his desk. She shuddered to think of him pressing it coldly against her skin, then she sat up straighter as he entered with a tea tray. A sprig of fresh mint poked from each steaming china cup.

"We will be happy to provide shelter for you, of course, after your husband has brought his plans to fruition. There are many places where we can keep you out of harm's way."

She didn't like where this was going.

"What do you mean?"

"Well, you can't very well go back now, can you? And unfortunately there may be people here who will want to talk to you about tonight's events."

"But I had nothing to do with anything that happened tonight."

"Of course you didn't. But certain people you have been seen with are now under suspicion, justifiably or not. The authorities will cast a very wide net, I'm afraid. Without our assistance, you might fall into it."

"It's only because of your 'assistance' that I'm vulnerable at all."

He spread his hands and tilted his head, a smug gesture suggesting he was conceding the point. That was the closest he ever came to admitting a mistake, she imagined. It was the arrogance of the lifegiving. The same arrogance, she supposed, that had made Abbas decide that he, too, could be the arbiter of the fate of hundreds, drawing on his balance of human capital as if it were a personal savings account.

Or maybe, between his grief, his medication, and his misguided zeal for vengeance, Abbas had simply lost sight of what was moral. She might never find out for sure unless she got home in time to stop him.

Dr. Hassan was still prattling away, gloating about his little victory over Nabil in whatever silly dispute had existed between them. Then he moved on to a more sensitive topic.

"You must be so proud of your husband," he said, eyes glittering. She detected no hint of sarcasm. He must have convinced himself that she, too, was committed to the cause even if wary of the means.

"Yes," she said, playing along. "I am." She set aside the teacup. The doctor had added far too much sugar. "But I haven't been able to speak with him, of course, due to our precautions. We agreed before I left that it would be too risky to communicate by phone, or even by e-mail."

"Very wise of you."

"It has been a sacrifice, but it is the only way."

"Of course."

The pompous fool.

A sudden bumping noise from another room startled her, and she wondered if his receptionist had returned. Dr. Hassan looked up with a questioning frown.

"Are you sure we're alone?" she asked.

"Quite alone. I regret to say that what you just heard was probably a mouse."

He lowered his head in a gesture of humility, which, as far as Aliyah could tell, was entirely for show.

"They are quite a problem, you know. Yet another threat to the health of the people here."

"All the better, then, that people like you are here to serve them."

"I thank you."

"So tell me where things stand, then, with Abbas and our plans. What have you heard?"

He proceeded to offer the latest news in loving and probably embellished detail. Then he went over the proposed timetable. Aliyah listened closely for any sign of weakness or opportunity, and for the first time all day she perceived the faintest glimmer of hope.

38

I headed straight for Dr. Hassan's in hopes of taking him by surprise. Sneaking up was probably the only suitable way of confronting a slippery character like him.

I had a nagging sense that the doctor possessed information truly worth ferreting out. My original job of keeping tabs on Omar, so important only twenty-four hours ago, had uncovered nothing more consequential than a cell of archaeological zealots, worshippers of yet another deity in a region rife with them. But someone as prideful about his accomplishments as Dr. Hassan might be prodded to offer a genuine revelation, or at least something worth passing along to Carl Cummings on my way out of the country.

That is, if I ever made it out of the country. The radio said that the border had been sealed, meaning that the airport was closed. Even if it reopened tomorrow, there were now plenty of people who might want to keep me here, to keep an eye on me. I hoped Mila had an easier time getting free and clear. If she made her flight as planned, then she would soon be safely high above the Atlantic. Tonight's upheaval in Jordan might even work to her advantage, by distracting an organization like the Mossad long enough to let her slip away unnoticed.

The streets of Bakaa were still seething with emotion. All the women and children seemed to be indoors, and every man who passed wore an intense, purposeful expression, as if he had been jarred out of bed by an earthquake. The police were in evidence everywhere. A few blocks from the doctor's office I witnessed an arrest that gave me a hint of what Nabil must have just gone through. A blue van pulled up at an unmarked door, and five officers carrying truncheons and riot shields barged inside while another five waited outside with automatic weapons locked and loaded. The first bunch emerged with three young men in tow, all with their hands bound behind them. A crowd formed quickly, shouting and tossing stones. A curfew was supposed to be in effect across the country, but out here it hadn't taken hold, and the police were too busy rounding up suspects to care.

A day earlier you might have found sympathy, even support, for the arrested men, just as you would have found plenty of people eager to give lip service to the exploits of Zarqawi in Iraq—he was a Jordanian, after all—or bin Laden in Pakistan. I couldn't help but recall Rafi Tuqan's comment about how there was a little Osama in the heart of every Arab. For tonight at least, those little Osamas were being evicted all across Jordan.

I reached the doctor's office and checked in the back for his car. It was still there. I went around to the front, where I considered knocking. Then I dismissed the idea and tried the knob. It wasn't locked, so I slipped inside and latched it gently behind me. The reception area was empty. I was about to call out the doctor's name as stridently as possible, hoping for the shock value of an intruder. If he objected, then I would wave the gun in his face. Give him a well-deserved scare. Then I heard muffled voices from the rear, and I held my tongue. It was a man and a woman, but I couldn't make out the words.

I ducked under the reception counter and entered a treatment room behind it. It was dark, but the voices were louder. I groped my way around a table toward a door on the left, which, if I remembered correctly, led to the doctor's private office. The top half of the door was smoked glass, so I approached with care, not wanting to cast a shadow. And it was a good thing I was moving slowly, because I nearly tripped on a footstool. I had to grab the back of a chair for support, and it made far too much noise.

The voices stopped. Blood rushed to my fingertips as I waited to be discovered. What the hell would I say if he caught me sneaking around like a thief? Fortunately I never had to answer that question, because they resumed their conversation. Then I heard a skittering noise in the corner and realized it was probably a mouse, some country cousin of the one at my place.

I crept as close as I could to the doorway and paused to listen. It was indeed a man and a woman, both speaking Arabic. The woman had an American accent. It was Aliyah Rahim, the surgeon's wife, still visiting. Good thing for her that none of the bombs had been at the InterContinental.

As my eyes adjusted to the dark I noticed a framed portrait of the king watching me from across the room. I was spying on one of his subjects, but he smiled anyway. The doctor spoke. He seemed to be talking about funeral arrangements, yet his tone was upbeat, even cheerful, and for a moment I assumed he was gloating about Nabil. Maybe the poor fellow had been beaten to death.

Then Dr. Hassan mentioned Washington, and although I couldn't be positive I thought he also made a reference to the Secret Service. In Arabic the translation was imprecise, but it certainly made my ears perk up.

When Aliyah Rahim spoke, the words were clearer, even if the tone was altogether more somber.

"So the president won't be there?"

The doctor's answer was indistinct. A few moments later he said something about a tunnel. Phrases came and went, with too many blanks in between to make total sense of the conversation. By the end I had heard several more references to a funeral, and, incongruously, to a pizzeria. From the general sense of things, this pizza joint seemed to belong to Aliyah's husband, Abbas. But that made little sense if he was a surgeon. Maybe I misheard. Or maybe there was a different Abbas Rahim, married to a different Aliyah. Or, for all I knew, Dr. Hassan and she were merely discussing plans for a late dinner.

The thought made me hungry. I hadn't eaten since breakfast, unless you counted the sweet, milky tea Mahmoud served on the Eighth Circle. So, of course, I was suddenly and absurdly ravenous. Enough of this sneaking around. Why not just burst through the door to confront the doctor then and there? I would demand an immediate accounting of his role in Nabil's demise.

A single word from Dr. Hassan stopped me: "explosives."

He said it clearly, and a few seconds later he said it again. Shortly afterward he repeated the word "tunnel." It convinced me to remain in hiding. I was even a little frightened now, and for the first time I noticed the deepening chill of the darkened room.

The next noise I heard was the scraping of chairs as they stood. They exited toward the waiting room, so I eased back across the floor, where I heard the main door of the clinic open. They must have paused on the threshold, because Dr. Hassan's next words were clearly audible. This time I was able to make out an entire sentence, even though it made little sense.

"I like the idea of your husband, down in his pizza parlor, ready to serve, but with a new kind of delivery," the doctor said. Then he laughed lightly, and somewhat pridefully, as if he had just made a bon mot over cocktails. "It will be grand and glorious, and for me the day cannot come soon enough."

Maybe it was the shock of hearing this that made me cough. Or maybe I had dropped my guard because they were already outside. Whatever the reason, a sudden tickle in my throat burst into a gasping hack.

"Who's there?" Dr. Hassan shouted. "Who is it?"

By the time I heard him throw back the door I was thumbing a lock on the knob of the door to the treatment room, and then running for the rear window. I heard the door behind me rattle violently as the doctor shouted again and I fumbled with the window latch.

"Who is it? The drugs are locked in a safe! I am calling the police!"

I heard him detouring through his own office to get to my room's other entrance, but by then I was vaulting across the windowsill and landing on the packed dirt of a dark alley. I scrambled blindly toward a side street, and the last thing I heard as I rounded the corner was a fearful shout from the open window.

"Stop! I have called the police!"

But the police, of course, had far more to do tonight than respond to a mere break-in, so there was little worry of being apprehended. What did concern me was the sudden sound of footsteps, from just around the corner. They couldn't have been the doctor's—his shout had been too distant—but clearly someone else was running just as fast as I was. I redoubled my effort and sprinted off into the night.

I was exhausted by the time I reached my car, and I knew there would soon be other worries to contend with. Would I be able to make it back to Jebel Amman the same way I had come? Once I reached the main highway I decided to tell the checkpoints that I had been out at Jerash, a popular tourist site to the north, and had been delayed in returning by the uproar over the bombings. I was also in violation of the curfew. But, for a change, having an American passport was likely to be a help rather than a hindrance. Playing the bumbling tourist should help get me back to my house.

I moved with urgency, and not just for my own safety. Whatever Dr. Hassan and Aliyah Rahim had been talking about, it certainly seemed worth reporting, especially given the references to explosives and to Washington. I was assuming the worst possible interpretation, of course, but I supposed that's what a fellow like Carl Cummings would have wanted me to do.

Who knew, maybe now I might even begin to balance the scales a bit. First thing in the morning, I would report for duty at the embassy. Then, having fulfilled that obligation, I would give everyone the slip to join Mila in Massachusetts.

The sooner the better. Today's events had made it all too clear that I was playing among people and forces well out of my league.

39

Aliyah had never been happier to see the Washington Monument, the first landmark she recognized as the plane broke through the clouds. It was 5 p.m. on Friday. The funeral was Saturday at 4 p.m. She had twenty-three hours to stop Abbas.

Luckily, the airport in Amman had reopened the day after the bombings. But her greater stroke of fortune was still a puzzle to her. Someone, or something—a stray animal, perhaps?—must have gotten into Dr. Hassan's clinic while she was trapped with him in his office, sipping his sugary tea.

The doctor, judging from his shouts, had obviously thought it was a thief. And as soon as he rushed inside, Aliyah seized her chance and sprinted away, not stopping until she reached the doorstep of Nabil's neighbor, who was holding her luggage. She spent a restless night on the family's couch, haunted by the day's worst images. Once she heard next morning that the airport would reopen, she was able to phone ahead and reserve a seat for that night on the same connection via Frankfurt.

At the airport she fretted for three hours while awaiting her flight, certain that at any moment a customs official or ticket clerk would alert the authorities or, worse, Dr. Hassan. When the wheels finally left the ground she sagged in exhaustion. Then she fell asleep and didn't wake up until Frankfurt.

Twenty hours later, there was the Washington Monument out her window, rising like a pale periscope from a dusky November sea of browns and grays. Her momentary relief quickly gave way to nervousness as she contemplated the gauntlet of passport and customs officials. She knew better than to expect anything but intense curiosity. Her name alone ensured that.

She picked the fastest-moving passport line, where the clerk was a short, talkative blonde with an easy smile. A family of four just ahead of her breezed through in seconds, nodding and sharing a laugh. Now it was Aliyah's turn.

The clerk flipped open her passport without a word, riffling the pages until she found the exit stamp from Amman.

"Reason for your visit?" No smile this time.

"Vacation."

The woman looked closely at the photo and then studied Aliyah's face, checking twice to make sure.

"You were there quite a while."

"It was a long vacation."

"I'll have to ask you to step over there for a minute."

"Excuse me?"

The woman pointed toward a small booth with gold curtains.

"Routine security check. You were chosen at random."

"Of course."

At the booth, an African American woman told her in a businesslike tone to remove her clothes.

"My clothes?"

"Yes, ma'am. Random check."

Perhaps it stung all the more because this time they truly had reason to be suspicious, had they only known who she had visited, or what her Abbas was doing. But of course they didn't know any of that, nor would they learn it merely by inspecting her naked body and then using a wand to scan her buttocks, just to make sure she hadn't hidden something up there where they couldn't see.

The wand whooped and screeched as the woman nudged Aliyah this way and that.

"Okay," the woman said brusquely. "You're clear."

Red-faced and breathless, Aliyah dressed quickly, and then rolled her bags toward customs, where she was stopped again. Two men spent fifteen minutes unfolding every item of clothing and squirting her toothpaste from its tube.

But for all the humiliations of the strip search and the scrutiny, the low point came a few moments later, after she rode the shuttle to the main terminal and emerged onto the concourse. Following their pre-trip plans to the letter, Aliyah had e-mailed her flight details to Abbas the night before. He was supposed to be waiting to pick her up.

Instead, she saw only the usual assortment of limo drivers holding aloft signs with names, and groups of loved ones with eager, expectant faces. Some people happily cried out as they recognized arrivals. No one called for Aliyah.

She stopped, put down her bags, and scanned the faces a second time, her anxiety growing. Never before had Abbas failed to meet her at the airport when she was returning from out of town, no matter how briefly she had been away.

Maybe he was stuck in traffic. But Abbas always allowed plenty of extra time for that. She could think of only three other explanations, and all were disturbing.

One, he had been caught and arrested. She imagined police hauling him up from a hole in the ground, yet another mug shot for the papers, and this time for more than just the inside page of a tabloid on a slow news day. He would be the villain of the month, the new face of terror, residing alongside shots of would-be shoe bombers and makers of "dirty bombs."

Two, he had come to his senses and decided to call the whole thing off, but had then been kidnapped, detained, or killed by whoever was helping him.

Or, three, and worst of all, if only because it suddenly seemed so likely, so plausible, maybe he was simply too preoccupied with his work, too busy to come. That would mean he was still down there underground, tunneling his way toward infamy beneath the streets of Washington, so obsessed with finishing the job that he couldn't take time out to read his e-mail, much less drive out to Dulles Airport to pick up his wife. Because his wife was now a part of the past, while he had forged ahead into the murky glory of the future.

Aliyah shivered and looked out the front windows of the airport, into the bleak and heavy sky. Funeral weather. Time to get moving. She bustled toward the taxi stand. Outside, it was raw and damp, and then the taxi was too hot, the heater gasping loudly. The smothering warmth made her want to curl up and fall asleep. But even the thought of nodding off on the ride home was alarming. She couldn't afford to lose focus for a moment.

The trip to their house in Chevy Chase seemed to last forever, and not just because of the four-mile backup on the Capital Beltway. When they pulled up out front, she saw both cars in the driveway. It was the first good sign since her return. But the moment she unlocked the door she sensed the house was empty. She called for Abbas. No answer.

Strolling into the kitchen, she saw dirty dishes in the sink. Newspapers were strewn on the dining room table. Several days' worth of mail was piled on the counter, none of it opened. There must have been a recent power outage, because the digital readouts on the oven, the coffeemaker, and the microwave were flashing. No one had reset them.

The answering machine flashed with a bright red "4." Two messages were from her friend Nancy, who was wondering if she had returned. The third was from Annie Felton, asking if Aliyah wanted to reschedule her next appointment. The fourth, from yesterday, was their son, Faris, who asked them to call. He sounded worried. Or maybe that was just the mood she was in. The next time Faris saw his father it might be on CNN, next to some horrible logo, or accompanied by a death toll.

She turned on the television and checked the news channels. Fox was talking about the hottest-selling videos. CNN was previewing tomorrow's college football schedule. She put down the remote and dialed the number for Abbas's office at the hospital. His secretary answered.

"Martha? It's Aliyah. I've just returned from overseas and was looking for Abbas. We must have gotten our wires crossed because he was supposed to pick me up. I thought maybe he was caught up in something there."

"Oh." Martha sounded flustered, even embarrassed. "I, uh, hadn't heard you were traveling. But Abbas is still on his leave, if that's what you're asking."

"Oh, yes, his leave. How stupid of me. I guess I thought he might have stopped by to catch up on things, you know, and lost track of time. But you're right. It's probably the last place he'd be."

"But if he does stop by—"

"Oh, I'm sure he'll be home soon enough."

"Please say hello for me."

"Certainly."

She was about to say good-bye when Martha spoke up again.

"Aliyah?"

"Yes?"

"Is he all right?"

"Abbas? Why do you ask?"

"Well, it's just that this leave request came up so suddenly. And then when I didn't hear from you, I was worried there might be trouble somewhere. Maybe with your son. I mean, after what happened to Shereen and all."

The name struck her heart like a needle.

"Oh, no. Everything is fine. I think he just needed some time. It's been hard for both of us."

"Of course."

"But he'll sort things out. He'll be all right."

"I hope so."

"Thank you, Martha."

"Certainly."

As Aliyah hung up, she saw that the door to his office was open, and for a moment she half hoped to find him in there, sprawled on the small couch where he sometimes napped. But not only was the room empty, it was neat as a pin, an unnerving contrast to the disarray elsewhere.

His desk was open, as if he wanted her to see what was inside. All the papers and bills that had been jumbled so chaotically before were now stacked neatly in a pile on the left. She flipped through the stubs. He had paid them all within the past few days, the work of a man who wanted to put his affairs in order, as if before a long journey, or worse. The pain in her heart grew sharper.

She remembered that Shereen's passport had been here, too, but now it was nowhere to be found, nor was it readily apparent in any of the drawers, which she hurriedly pulled open, one after the other, until the desk was like a pair of trousers with all the pockets pulled out. A framed picture of Shereen that used to hang on an opposite wall was also missing. There was only an empty space, outlined faintly in dust.

A second neat pile of papers on the desk now caught her eye. On top was an opened envelope. The return address was for the law offices of Jack Lindner, a friend of theirs in Bethesda. Below it was a typewritten note with his signature.

"Abbas, please sign and notarize two copies and mail them back to me. Keep the third one for yourself. If there are any other changes you'd like to make, pencil them in and I'll draw up another set."

Attached was a single copy of a last will and testament for Abbas Rahim. He must have already signed and mailed the other two. It was dated from the day after she left for Jordan. Now she was almost nauseous. She stooped over the trash can and steadied herself just in time, swallowing hard. Then she reopened the biggest of the side drawers and began a more careful inspection. That was when she found the lease for the pizza parlor on Cordell Street, with Abbas's signature on the last page. Evidence, she thought. My God, she should probably burn it, but what good would that do?

Paper-clipped to the top was a small brown envelope with the word "Keys" scribbled on the outside. One was still inside. Abbas must have the other one.

As she held it in her hand, her attention was diverted by the sound of the television in the kitchen. The newscaster had just said something about Senator Badgett. She raced out the door just in time to see a shot of the United Baptist Church of God, and heard the newscaster say that the president would not be able to attend because of his trip to Japan. But the vice president and all the top leaders from both houses of Congress would be there, and so would much of the Cabinet. Even a few justices from the Supreme Court were expected, and seats were in great demand. The Secret Service was already securing the location in anticipation of the year's greatest gathering of Washington's power elite outside of Capitol Hill.

So Skip Ellington had been right, she realized. The senator's funeral had become an A-list event. A place to see and be seen. And perhaps also a place to die, if Abbas had his way. Famously so, in a blinding flash, a blast for the ages.

Aliyah felt a sharp pain in her right hand, and realized she was squeezing the spare key. At that moment she knew for certain where Abbas was, and where she now had to go. He was there, right on the scene, probably sitting tight in the dark so the Secret Service agents wouldn't notice anything suspicious when they combed the nearby streets. Even if they peered through the windows, they would see nothing but an abandoned pizzeria. The location wouldn't overly concern them anyway, since none of the windows or doors offered a sniper's vantage point of the church. They might put someone on the roof, but not inside.

She snatched up her purse and retrieved her car keys from a basket on the kitchen counter. On her way out the door she glanced at her suitcases, still sitting where she had dropped them on the way in. She wondered almost wistfully if she would ever be back to unpack.

Almost as soon as she pulled out of the driveway, she decided it would be better to take the Metro, and she realized that Abbas must have had the same thought, which explained why both cars were here. No sense leaving your car parked near the church to attract the attention of some policeman, who might get curious enough to run the numbers on your tag. There was also the practical matter of knowing that by now she probably wouldn't even be allowed to park in the area.

She walked to the Metro stop and caught a train. The whole trip took more than an hour, and by the time she rounded the corner onto Cordell Street it was dark and the air was a few degrees colder.

Every parking meter on the block had been hooded with signs saying, "Special Event. No Parking." No one else seemed to be around, which was fortunate, because she spent several seconds fruitlessly trying her key on the padlock still in place at the front entrance. She put her face to the caged grate across the front window. No sign of life. It looked exactly as it had before, except that the "For Rent" sign was gone.

She remembered there was also a door in the back, facing onto an alley, so she strolled down the block away from the church in case someone was watching, and then turned the corner toward the back. The light of the streetlamps didn't reach into the alley, and she made her way cautiously, jumpy from the stirrings of rats around a Dumpster. She glanced around nervously as she reached the door. Then she tried the key. The scrape of the metal sounded unnaturally loud, but the lock snicked back. She had to lean against the door to open it. Then she pushed it shut behind her.

There was still no sign of Abbas. Inside was barely warmer than outside, and as she stood in the silence her breath vapored into the darkened hallway. Yet there was something else in the air, too, a scent of human occupation with its whiff of sweat and exertion, of old food wrappers. She stepped forward. The soles of her shoes slid on grit, a whispering sound that made her skin crawl.

"Abbas?"

She said it tentatively the first time, and heard the tremble in her voice. Then she spoke it louder, stronger.

"Abbas!"

There was a scrabbling noise not unlike that of the rats, only this time it turned into footsteps approaching from the basement. A faint line of light appeared beneath the doorway that led downstairs. Then her husband's voice called out in a tone almost as timid as her initial effort.

"Aliyah? Is that you?"

"Yes. I am home. I am here to help you."

He opened the door only enough to shine a small flashlight toward her. The beam made it impossible to see him, but she heard him sigh, in either relief or exasperation. She held her breath, wondering what he would say.

"Come down, then. It's too risky waiting here. They've been by three times already, and they'll probably check again in an hour or two."

She assumed he meant the Secret Service or the Metro police, so she did as he asked.

He turned and shut the door behind them, and at the bottom he opened another door to a basement storage room, where the dank smell of turned earth was strong and ominous. A small camp lantern burned in a corner, and when Abbas turned now she saw his face clearly for the first time.

The last thing she wanted to do was alarm him, or somehow turn him against her, but she couldn't help but put a hand to her mouth. It wasn't just the dirt and the grime, which made him resemble a coal miner. It was his eyes, opened wide in manic exhaustion. A bunker mentality, she thought. Abbas against the world.

She looked around the small room. A blue plastic tarpaulin was draped across what must be the mouth of the tunnel. A pair of insulated copper wires emerged from the right of the tarpaulin. They were attached to a small box with a silver toggle switch. So was that it, then? His means of detonation?

Opposite the tunnel was a pile of bricks, which he must have removed from the building's foundation. On the floor he had unrolled a cheap sleeping bag next to an alarm clock and a small Styrofoam cooler, where presumably he stored his food and water. Propped on top were a small radio and the picture of Shereen that had been on the wall of his study. The orange plastic vial of pills was there, too, right next to the radio.

At that moment Aliyah knew that her decision to leave Washington had been a fatal mistake. She had already suspected as much, but the sight of this bleak little room confirmed it. Abbas was now completely captive to his wayward emotions, and no manner of elaborate artifice would stand a chance against him. The only plausible course of action was outright sabotage, but she had never learned how.

The only good news was that he appeared to be alone. Whoever had helped him dig the tunnel and place the charges must have cleared out.

"My God, Abbas. Are you all right?"

He nodded, letting his eyes answer. They might as well have been calling to her from across a canyon, judging from his distant stare. When he finally spoke, his words made it clear that he had misinterpreted the nature of her concern.

"I was too worried about the timer."

"The timer?"

"On the explosives. Ahmad set it when we finished the tunnel. He said it was foolproof, but their real expert on explosives never made it here. He was detained at the border by the Canadians. So I decided to stay here and do it manually. I was too worried it would go off at the wrong time, or not go off at all. And with funerals, it seems like they never start on time anyway. You remember Shereen's."

She did, all too well, and down here in the darkness their daughter's spirit seemed close at hand, grieving and mournful at her father's vengeful folly. This is not what Shereen would have wanted, no matter what Abbas had talked himself into believing.

"So you're going to push the button, then," she asked, trying to muster enough false enthusiasm to keep it from sounding like a challenge, or a dare.

He nodded.

"And I don't need you here for that, you know. It's a one-man job. I don't think there is enough food and water for both of us."

"I doubt we'll need much. It's only another nineteen hours, Abbas."

He glanced at his watch, as if to make sure she wasn't trying to fool him. Then she noted a new look in his eyes, one of worry and concern, and at that moment she realized why. She imagined the blast going off. Not only would the explosion heave up the floor of the church, it would also throw a massive load of concussive energy back down the tunnel. It seemed obvious that whoever was in this room would be killed. The realization must have showed on her face, judging from what Abbas said next.

"There is no guarantee I will survive. That is why I don't think you should stay here."

Her next words spilled out before she could stop herself.

"So you've become a suicide bomber, then. In that case you might as well put on a vest of explosives and go walking up the church steps, holding a copy of the Holy Quran and shouting, 'God is great!' like all the other fanatics."

"It's not like that. Not at all. And there are things I can still do to improve my chances."

"Like what?"

"There's a table upstairs I was going to move down. To put across the opening."

"That won't do it. And you're not going to move it anyway."

"Or I could extend the wiring, once the service starts. Splice on another few feet so I can turn the switch from upstairs. I just won't do it now. It might go off prematurely."

Aliyah shook her head, unconvinced.

"You're not going to do that, either. Not unless I stay here and make you. So I will stay. I won't lose my husband. Not without a fight."

He nodded, as if resigned. Maybe he was too weary to contest the point.

"Stay if you want. But not for me. For Shereen."

How was she supposed to triumph over that kind of passion? And when the appointed hour arrived, how would she defeat him? Or worse: If she couldn't defeat him, what would come next, even if they both survived? It was only then, for a single fleeting instant, that she allowed herself to contemplate the feeling of release that one might experience in carrying out such a horrendous act. Maybe it was her own weariness, her own lingering grief, but she had to admit there was a certain horrible beauty to the whole idea. Why *not* kill all those bastards, after everything they had done? Why *not* awaken all the slumbering fools who thought they could simply bludgeon their way across the globe without regard for any lives but their own? Show them that you could decapitate the leadership here just as easily as in some weaker nation. Show them that they weren't simply putting the poor slobs on subways and in tall towers at risk with their stupidity. Put them on notice that, henceforth, their lives would be on the line as well.

But the moment passed as quickly as it came. And, as with the breaking of a fever, she shivered in its wake. Think of Faris instead, and of how terrible his life would be in the aftermath. And think, as well, of how terrible life would be for all the other sons, daughters, mothers, and fathers of those who would die in the church.

Somehow, despite all the pity and compassion she now felt for her husband and his doomed cause, from this moment forward she had to think of him as the enemy, a threat both to her and to Faris. She must defeat him at all costs.

40

The longer I talked to Carl Cummings, the more he convinced me I was overreacting to what I'd overheard in Dr. Hassan's office.

"You got caught up in the moment," he said. "It's understandable. Yesterday was a bad day for all of us, and you're new to this stuff. Hey, by late last night a ton of people were talking about funerals and explosions, and they will be today, too. So unless you've got something a little more solid, well, you get the idea."

I was lucky to be speaking with him at all, even if only by telephone. A secure line, he assured me. How he knew that about the connection at my end I had no idea, which made me suspect he was bluffing. Earlier I'd been turned away at the embassy gates. I then placed half a dozen calls from my house. Even my old friend Mike Jacoby wouldn't answer. The rejections let me know exactly where I must have stood in Cummings's small constellation of operatives and informants.

But my persistence finally made an impact, because Cummings called back a little before noon. Then he threw cold water all over my story.

"Well, could you at least run the woman's name, this Aliyah Rahim?" I said. "She's from Washington, and—"

"Look, you really wanna know the truth, Fremont?"

"Freeman."

"Sorry. It's been that kind of day. But just save it, okay? I know you want to earn brownie points, but I haven't slept in twenty-eight hours, and right now you're the least of my worries. Sit tight and I'll get back to you in a few days."

"This isn't about 'brownie points.' I was worried. It sounded like a possible threat. How long could it take to just run one name?"

"You know how many Rahims there must be in the network? And right now I've got a fresh kill to worry about—fifty-six of them, in fact—all of them wiped out by a local al-Qaeda faction. Plus the Mukhabarat is breathing down my neck because they find it mighty hard to believe our NSA guys didn't pick up some kind of advance chatter. And frankly, so do I. So unless you've got something better?"

"Fine. Maybe I'll just write a report, and later you can—"

"Whoa, now. Putting it in writing is the *last* thing you wanna do. Start putting stuff like that into the system and God knows where it will end up. I really do have to go now. Many thanks for your concern, but why don't you take a chill pill and then we'll talk next week about your recent employers, if you take my meaning." Secure phone or not, I suppose you didn't dare say "Mossad" over any line in Amman. "That's my interest in you, okay? Stay on topic and we'll get along fine. But no more phone calls. We've got our hands full as it is."

"Yeah, sure, Chris."

"It's *Carl*."

"Sorry. It's been that kind of day."

He didn't get the joke, of course, and we both hung up. So much for due diligence. And after sleeping on it, I had to admit that the few snatches of conversation I'd picked up didn't add up to much, especially when compared to the reality of what had happened at the three hotels. The topic of explosives was indeed on everyone's lips. Maybe I got carried away by the hysteria, as Cummings suggested. Or I took everything in the worst possible light because of my dislike for Dr. Hassan.

Whatever the case, I had done what I could, and would defer to professional judgment. There was a certain relief in that, seeing as how I had been playing the game alone for too long. Cummings had just talked me down from a ledge, in a sense, a dangerous place where I might have made a fool of myself.

Yet part of me was still disconcerted, even if Aliyah Rahim didn't seem to have the necessary zeal or cunning for cooking up some terrible plot. From what little I'd seen, she looked and acted like what she was, a wife from a wealthy suburb, perhaps with a job of her own. But if that were the case, then what the hell was she doing here all alone, meeting shady characters with iffy connections in a bad neighborhood like Bakaa? Maybe she was an emissary for her husband. But the scant info on him didn't add up, either. Was he a surgeon or a pizza maker? And when I thought of these so-called "facts" long enough, my fears did seem overblown, just as Cummings said.

To further ease my mind, I decided to check Mrs. Rahim's latest movements. I punched in the number for the InterContinental. When she answered, I would offer my help, as one expat American to another on this tragic day, in hopes of being able to find out more about her.

"I'm sorry, sir, but Mrs. Rahim has not returned to her room."

"She's checked out?"

"No, sir. In fact, in light of events, we are worried for her safety, and you are not the only one who has inquired of her whereabouts."

"What are you saying?"

"I am saying, sir, that her room is empty and her luggage is gone, but she has not been seen by anyone since she left here yesterday evening. And if you or anyone else has any information that would—"

I hung up. Because *I'd* seen her, of course, or heard her voice, at any rate. But the last thing I wanted to get involved in was some sort of official search, which had been implied by the clerk's mention of others asking her whereabouts.

It made me all the more suspicious of her. Who knows, maybe she had even gone back to America. The thought was unsettling. Why leave so precipitously unless she had urgent business? Then again, maybe Cummings was right, especially when there seemed to be little that I could do about her if she had truly disappeared. Time to move on.

Having reached that conclusion, I was giddy with restlessness. There seemed to be little work left to be done. I had come clean with Omar, gotten Mila out of harm's way, and reported my suspicions about Dr. Hassan to the agency best able to act on them.

As for Black, White, and Gray, I no longer felt any obligation. Even my vow to help Cummings seemed insubstantial now that he was preoccupied with the bombings. If I left now, he could always reach me in Boston. Time to move on before I showed up on someone else's radar. Norbert Krieger's fate had showed me why.

Amman was a changed city, and probably would be for quite a while. The airport had reopened, but plenty of checkpoints were still in place. Although, with the streets virtually empty, it was in some ways easier than ever to move around as long as you had the right credentials. The local news was talking about a late-afternoon demonstration that would protest the bombings, so I decided to pack as lightly and quickly as I could before the streets began to fill. Then I would head for the airport and take the first available flight to the States. I would make it a clean break, swift and certain. Leaving some of my clothes behind seemed like a small price to pay.

In some ways, the timing was ideal. If Carl Cummings was too busy for me, that would go double for the Mukhabarat. Judging from news accounts, the agency was still rounding up suspects by the dozens. My only worry was that good old Mahmoud, true to his warning, had put me on some sort of watch list before all hell had broken loose. There was only one way to find out.

I got my answer two hours later while waiting at a café in the airport's international terminal, biding my time before a 4 p.m. departure. Just about every flight had empty seats, so I chose a route via Zurich on Lufthansa that would land me in Boston tomorrow afternoon.

The ticket transaction went smoothly enough. To my surprise, so did passport control, and I was relaxing with a magazine and a cup of coffee when the PA announcer paged me to the Lufthansa counter.

A smiling woman with a British accent greeted me sheepishly, a bad sign.

"I'm sorry, sir. We are unable to honor your ticket. You will receive a full refund, of course."

"Unable to honor?"

"We can't allow you to board."

"Why?"

She looked down, ashamed for me.

"I'm afraid you don't have clearance to leave the country."

"But here's my exit stamp." I held my passport open. "And I've paid the departure tax."

"Yes, sir. But we have received instructions that—"

"Instructions from who?"

But why ask? I already knew. She must have realized this herself, or seen it in my expression, because she blushed and turned away.

"Please, sir." She lowered her voice. "I really can't tell you anything more."

I angrily headed off to collect my refund. I considered appealing immediately to the embassy, but doubted they would take my call, much less lend a hand. Cummings wanted to keep me around as much as Mahmoud did. Everyone wanted their cut of information before letting me go, and by then the Mossad would be after me. I might be stuck for weeks.

I thought of Mila up in Massachusetts. If her flight was on schedule she would be landing in another eight hours. I pictured late-afternoon sunlight filtering through the white curtains in my mother's kitchen, and Mila and my parents pulling up chairs around the long walnut dinner table, the places set too far apart for any real intimacy. I imagined Mila picking at her New England pot roast, all three of them wondering what to talk about and how they were going to fill the awkward hours until my arrival.

Such thoughts predominated as I rode the taxi back to the city, the desert looking as drab as ever, a pall over everything as the radio droned on with an updated death toll and a new claim of responsibility—expat Iraqis, for the most part, working for some al-Qaeda offshoot run by Zarqawi, the expat Jordanian. At least my mind was now at ease on one point. It wasn't the sort of bunch that either Nabil or Dr. Hassan was part of. A different poison altogether. And that, in turn, made me feel better still about the conversation I'd overheard. I supposed Cummings was right.

But nothing could improve my mood about being stuck in Jordan. Or, at least, not until the taxi reached Othman Bin Affan Street, and I saw Fiona working yet again in her front garden.

I waved quickly and rushed inside before she could say a word. Then I scrounged through my cupboard for the best available bottle of wine—with only three to choose from, it didn't take long—and headed back outdoors.

"There you are," she said, managing a faint smile. "I was worried about you last night until I heard your car pull up. You were out late. Such a terrible evening."

She looked as if she had barely slept. Her face was drawn, with dark semicircles under the eyes. Even her exertions in the midday sun hadn't put any color in her cheeks. It was more than just the standard sorrow that anyone might feel after yesterday's events. She was in mourning not just for the dead and the maimed, but also for her romantic view of her adopted land, and her place in it. Like many Westerners who fell for Jordan, she had convinced herself of its impregnability as an island of sanity. Yet another fellow traveler in search of moats and fortresses. Well, I hate to break it to you, Fiona, but no such place exists. Not here, not on Karos.

"Glad to see you're okay, too. I was stuck in the hinterlands for a while. Otherwise no problem." I held aloft the bottle. "I've come to offer my condolences. It's also a peace offering. For all the ill repute I must have brought to the street yesterday morning. And for, well, the little surprise you found out in the garden."

"You don't have to tell me anything more, you know."

"If it's any comfort, I'm out of that business now. For that employer, anyway."

"I figured as much, or you never would have come back from the Eighth Circle. Unfortunately, visits like that aren't all that rare, even for foreigners sometimes. It's funny. I wouldn't have admitted that yesterday morning. I was even blaming you some for probably bringing it on. Then the bombs went off, the roundups began, and I had to rethink all my assumptions. Last night changed a lot of things, I suppose."

I wondered if she would continue to live here, but didn't have the heart to ask. Instead I uncorked the bottle while she fetched two glasses. We sat on the cool tiles of her porch and talked quietly. When the bottle was half empty I explained my plight and asked for help, while hoping she still had enough faith in her connections to give it a try.

Fiona creased her brow and sipped the wine.

"It's not going to be easy. Not in this climate. But let me make some calls. Who knows, it might be exactly the kind of chore to cheer someone up. A little busywork to soothe the soul. Maybe it will cheer *me* up. Anything to make life seem normal again. I suppose that's how it was for everyone in London after 7/7, or in the States after 9/11. It must have felt just like this."

"I can't really tell you. I was in Africa on 9/11, way out in the bush. Didn't even hear the news for twelve hours, and even then it was on BBC shortwave."

She nodded, seeming to instantly understand all the implications of that remark.

"That's how it is with people like us. We forget how things are back home. The whole point of view. Then something big happens, and instead of drawing closer we get a little more out of touch."

"All the more reason for me to head back."

"I suppose so." She stood. "I'll get on it straightaway. Give me your passport number. They'll need it if we're going to make this work."

Later I saw her leave the house for one of the demos being staged downtown, and when she returned her face was streaked in tears. But early the next morning she knocked on my door with a smile on her face.

"The palace came through," she said. "But we have to hurry. We should get moving before the Mukhabarat has time to react. Do you have a flight?"

"No. But I'm sure I can get one at the airport."

"Then let's go."

My bags were still packed, so we left almost immediately. There was another demo scheduled in a few hours, so we took my car rather than try to flag down a taxi. Omar would have to get someone to collect it from the airport. I left my house key on the kitchen table and took a last look around the place, almost shaking now at how close I had come during my stay to losing everything I held dear. But maybe such prideful folly was the norm for professionals, too. The occupation offers too many mirages to ever know for sure when you have succeeded. A little like the aid business, I suppose. Even when you are serving thousands, there are always thousands more hidden away in places you could never reach. Maybe we were all amateurs, all across the board. Cummings, too. I shut the door for the last time and heaved a great sigh of relief.

"Let's go," I said.

Fiona's efforts had procured a typewritten note on heavy cream-colored stationery with an important letterhead, a gold-embossed royal emblem, and a looping signature of someone I had never heard of. She assured me the name would be quite familiar to anyone who mattered.

She was right. The letter worked wonders for both of us, allowing the ticketless Fiona to steer me past every point where I might have been halted—ticket counter, passport control, customs, and then the lobby for international departures, where she waited patiently at my side, making comfortable small talk until the boarding call.

None of the flights leaving within the next few hours had decent connections to Boston, so I had settled for a route to Washington Dulles, where I would have a four-hour layover before the final leg. But now it was time to say good-bye.

We stood, and I was about to give her a hug and a peck on the cheek, but she was already offering a handshake, again the demure Englishwoman.

I was too keyed up to relax until the plane reached cruising altitude. Then I drank a couple of gins to settle down. It reminded me of my flight from Vienna, on my way down to the intifada, where I first met Omar. That produced a stab of nostalgia and a brief moment of shame over the end of a friendship.

It then began to hit me just how exhausted I was. Handing the dregs of my second drink to the stewardess, I sagged against the plastic window and was soon asleep, not awakening until the wheels bounced against the runway in Paris. I spent most of the two hours before my connecting flight in a stupor, not even bothering to buy anything to read for the long journey across the Atlantic, most of which I also slept through.

We landed at Dulles, and only after I had cleared customs and bought a cup of coffee did I begin returning to my senses. I yawned and stretched like an overindulged dog that has slept away an entire afternoon. Then, feeling expansive and more than a little hungry, I bought a few sugary pastries to go with the coffee. I placed my bags next to me and settled into a café with a burgeoning sense of freedom and well-being. It was the first time in ages I had been able to relax. A new sense of resolve began to bloom, only this time it concerned Mila instead of my work. I had phoned her wearily from Paris, and she had been thrilled I was out of Amman. With any luck we could get away for a drink or two after dinner at my parents' house.

It was about then that a man in a business suit sat down at the next table, which in the cramped café meant he was only a few feet to my left. He opened up Saturday's *Washington Post* and, with nothing of my own to read, I stole a glance at the headlines.

Maybe it was the reference to a funeral that caught my eye, coming so close on the heels of the bombings and the strange conversation I'd overheard at Dr. Hassan's. Or maybe the name mentioned in the second column of text somehow registered in my subconscious and begged for more attention. Whatever the case, I zeroed in on a story at the bottom of the front page with the headline "At Powerful Senator's Funeral, Spouse Takes Center Stage."

I began reading, and in only seconds the name of the late senator's attending physician, Dr. Abbas Rahim, leaped out at me. Between that and the jolt of caffeine, I felt a flutter in my chest. Dr. Rahim was quoted briefly from an interview that had been conducted on the day of the senator's death. He dismissed any speculation that the senator's family had foregone further lifesaving measures for any political reasons, such as giving his successor extra time to settle into the job before the next elections.

The story focused mostly on political machinations, but I was more intrigued by the descriptions of plans for the funeral, which was scheduled for later today. The guest list was illustrious. Even the vice president was coming, meaning the Secret Service would be on hand. With growing apprehension, I found myself again reconstructing the stray pieces of the puzzling conversation between Dr. Hassan and Aliyah Rahim—the word "explosives," the frequent mentions of a funeral, a tunnel, and the doctor's possible reference to the Secret Service, not to mention the many times the name of Aliyah's husband, Abbas, had come up. The only item that still didn't seem to fit was the pizza restaurant.

My earlier suspicion no longer seemed so hysterical, and my cup of coffee, so satisfying a moment ago, now carried a bitter aftertaste that was almost nauseating. The man next to me turned the page, but not before I saw that the funeral was scheduled for 4 p.m. at the United Baptist Church of God, said to be in a lesser neighborhood just beyond the fringes of Capitol Hill.

I checked my watch in a panic. It was 2:57 p.m. Then I drew a deep breath and quickly took stock. Surely if the Secret Service did its job, any threat would be detected. But the possibility of a tunnel made me wonder. Maybe I was again being alarmist, but my oldest and best instincts said that if there was ever a time to risk acting like a fool, this was it. On the other hand, given my uncertain status with at least three of the world's security agencies, sounding the alarm might be a tricky proposition.

Here in the airport, where practically everyone in a security uniform had a shoulder patch for the Department of Homeland Security, blurting out my suspicions would probably only guarantee a sudden commotion, with me at its center. Gates and concourses would close, and I would be spirited away for questioning. There would be skepticism, anger, outright mistrust, and I, not the church, would be the focus. Unless someone did the right thing within an hour, it might be too late.

I decided instead to telephone the authorities in hopes that they would act quickly. But if, like Cummings, they reacted with derision, what then? Then it would be up to me to take action. Amateur or not, I was about to rejoin the game for one final play.

41

The phone call was a disaster.

To begin with, my lack of a cell phone meant I wasted an agonizing four minutes getting change from the café, tracking down a pay phone, and fumbling through the directory's blue pages until I found the main number for the FBI. I considered dialing 911, but figured the operator might not know what to make of someone blurting out a vague warning about tunnels, bombs, and a senator's funeral. And if the Secret Service had already scanned and screened the church, at this late hour they would probably ignore my call as the ravings of a lunatic unless I could name an exact location, which I couldn't.

The number rang three times before a machine answered:

"Hello, you've reached FBI headquarters. If you are calling regarding the fraudulent e-mail from a Victor Kasimir, please contact your local Web provider. All other calls, please hold for the next available operator."

Two more rings. Then an actual human came on the line.

"Duty officer, please. It's urgent."

Three more rings. I'd just wasted another two minutes, and it was 3:05. I'd been trying to think of how to word my warning in a way to get their attention without making them think I was a crackpot.

"FBI."

"Hello. I'm calling to report a potential, no, a *probable* bomb plot in progress at or near the funeral for Senator Badgett."

"A bomb plot in progress?" He sounded calm, routine. I would learn later that all his questions came straight from a bureau script for these things, but at the time the conversation seemed so surreal as to be ludicrous.

"And what is your name and location, sir?"

"Freeman Lockhart. I'm at a pay phone at Dulles Airport and I've just returned from Amman, Jordan. I reported my suspicions yesterday to a Mr. Carl Cummings at the American embassy, and he didn't seem to take them seriously. But since then I've learned more information."

"When is the bomb going to explode?"

"The funeral starts in less than an hour. Anytime after that, I guess."

"Where is it right now?"

"Hell if I know for sure, but there may be some kind of tunnel."

"What will cause it to explode?"

"A detonator? Look, I—"

"Did you place the bomb?"

"Good God, no. I'm reporting it. I'm a citizen. I know the Secret Service is there, but—"

"Slow down, sir, I need to confirm some of your information."

"Slow down? The funeral's at four."

"You said your name was Freeman Lockhart, correct?"

"Yes. And the church is called the United Baptist Church of God. I think it's near Capitol Hill, but I don't have an address."

"That site is covered, sir, as you yourself indicated. But I'll pass along your concerns to the detachment at the scene. Now please give me the name again of your embassy contact in Amman."

"Carl Cummings. I'm not sure that just 'passing it along' is going to cut it."

"And you're presently at Dulles International Airport."

"Yes, but—"

"Please hold, sir."

I waited while the seconds ticked away. At 3:08 I looked around for signs of any security officers rushing my way. Undoubtedly the FBI had caller ID, and he must know exactly where I was standing. If he was phoning someone here, I'd be rounded up shortly and probably held for questioning. Meanwhile, the church would explode. I dropped the receiver and ran for the exit, looking both ways until I spotted the taxi stand. Six people were in line, but I went straight to the front.

"Sorry," I shouted. "Medical emergency!"

I cut in front of a woman in a business suit, pushing away her luggage just as she had rolled it to the curb. The cabdriver looked around uncertainly.

"Move it!"

He obliged, but not before the woman in line gave us both an earful. "We're all in a hurry, asshole!"

It was 3:10. I was twenty-five miles from Capitol Hill, a forty-minute trip if I was lucky, an hour if I wasn't. But maybe even now my phone call was causing agents and police to swarm to the scene. It wasn't rush hour, but as we crossed the Beltway fifteen minutes later the traffic slowed to a crawl.

"We've got to do better than this," I told the driver. "It's an emergency."

If worse came to worst, I suppose I could have him radio his dispatcher and relay a call to 911. Maybe I should have called Metro police instead. They might have cleared the church. Or maybe not. Not if it had already checked out as secure. Perhaps I should have given a specific location and time of an explosion, just to ensure that everyone was evacuated. Maybe I was too vague for my own good. I wished I had a cell phone.

"Driver!" I said. "Tell your dispatcher to call 911. Tell him to say that there may be a bomb at the funeral of Senator Badgett."

The driver looked at me in the mirror like I was crazy.

"Do it!"

He did as I asked, but kept an eye on me in the mirror the whole time, as if I might suddenly reach across the seat and try to take the wheel. He passed along the message in an oddly desultory tone, as if humoring a drunk, and I doubted his supervisor would do anything but roll his eyes. Another nutty fare, indulged for a big tip. It was 3:42, but at least now we were in the District.

At 3:50 we reached Capitol Hill, and I listened for sirens, alarms, or any sign that my warnings had instigated action. Then the driver got stuck in traffic, and by the time we came within sight of the church on Cordell Street it was 3:58.

"There it is," I said. "End of the block."

"Looks like the cops have cordoned off the street."

I threw three twenties onto the seat, scrambled out the door, and took off as fast as I could run. If I alarmed some cop enough to attract attention, all the better. That's when I saw the sign for the pizza place, "Alighieri's," in faded red script above a padlocked door only fifty feet away. It was across an alley from the church. I jolted to a stop, breathing hard, while all the stray words at last clicked into their proper places, particularly Dr. Hassan's little aside just as he and Aliyah Rahim were leaving the office.

Abbas the doctor was down in his pizza parlor, where he had dug a tunnel and set his charges. He was probably there now, awaiting the appointed hour, maybe giving it a few extra minutes to allow for all the arrivals to take their seats. I looked around wildly, wondering how to get in, then I ducked down an alley that took me behind the buildings onto another narrow lane, slick with rotting garbage. Two policemen watched me from the upper end of the alley, near the church. I was too out of breath to shout, but at least now I had their attention. I saw the name again, "Alighieri's," painted shakily on a rear wall, then I nearly tripped on a cardboard box as I skidded into the door.

"Hey, you there!"

It was one of the policemen, running toward me, drawing his sidearm.

"Here!" I said. "Hurry!" He was perhaps thirty yards away.

I turned the knob and shoved for all I was worth, fearing that at any moment the pavement beneath me would shudder and heave, and the glass windows of the church would shatter in an awful roar. Bodies and limbs raining down. More people I had failed to save.

After twenty of the longest hours of her life, Aliyah finally succeeded. Or so she hoped, with a desperation bordering on hysteria. At 3:42 p.m., after urging Abbas to make one last inspection of the wiring down in the tunnel, she watched him crawl out of sight with a small flashlight in his teeth. Then she went to work.

She was exhausted and nauseous, her stomach grumbling constantly and her hands shaking from nervousness and lack of sleep. They had talked their way through much of the night, their conversation a bizarre mix of reminiscence and family trivia. For her part, she dwelled as much as possible on their son, Faris, as if to remind Abbas that besides having a past, they also had a future, which he might still possess if he wished.

Abbas mentioned the mission at hand only once, and even then it was an oblique reference.

"Do you think it will make a difference?" he had asked, his eyes almost pleading with her. She knew exactly what he meant, but she forced him to clarify it all the same, thinking that it might do him good to have to articulate exactly what he was about to do.

"Do I think what will make a difference?"

"This. My work here."

"The bomb?"

He nodded. He might even have flinched. But he still wouldn't say the word, now that the appointed moment was only a few hours away.

"Things like this always make a difference. But maybe not the kind that you want."

He didn't ask for more.

At around 2 p.m. they went upstairs to fetch the table he had mentioned, and they wrestled it down the stairway and finally laid it clumsily in place a few feet in front of the hole. The wires snaked around it. It was such little protection as to be pathetic, and she could read the folly of the gesture in his eyes. Here was a trained surgeon, drilled for years on end to proceed only after every possible contingency to save a life had been followed to the letter, and he was relying on a flimsy wooden table to save him and his wife from certain disaster. They said nothing to each other for the next hour. Then Aliyah began making the case that he should venture inside for one last inspection.

She had already decided what she would do when he was out of sight, and now she set about her work, fingers fumbling at one of the contacts on the back of the detonator box with its toggle switch. She worked at the screw that held one of the wires in place, the metal of the nut biting sharply into her fingertips. It finally loosened, and she twisted it off, then it slipped from her fingers with a small ping. It took a few precious seconds to find it in the dim light. She heard Abbas, still grunting his way forward, and smelled the damp earth more strongly than ever now that the tarp had been pulled back from the opening. By now there must already be people inside the church.

She picked up a rubber band that had been wrapped on a head of celery Abbas had packed in the cooler, along with his other supplies. She placed the band around the terminal and twisted it several times to hold it in place. Then she put the loop of wire back on the contact, taking care that it touched only the rubber band and none of the metal on the terminal. She hoped it would be enough insulation to prevent a complete circuit. When she had first thought of the plan, hours ago, it had seemed foolproof. Maybe that was because she was exhausted. Now it seemed far too flimsy to trust. And once the bomb failed to detonate, what would she do when Abbas discovered the reason why? When he unscrewed the wire to make the repair, she would have to try and wrench the box away from him. She would fight him, if necessary. But now Abbas was coming back. For the moment she would have to trust in her handiwork.

He emerged with a grunt and a shower of dirt. He looked worse than ever, sweating heavily despite the chill of the basement. She had been shivering off and on since she got here.

The event was being covered on C-SPAN radio, and when the announcer mentioned that events were proceeding on schedule, Abbas decided he would act at exactly 4 p.m. The vice president had already arrived. Both of them watched the small digital alarm clock as its red numerals changed to 3:59. Abbas eased closer to the box and rested his hand next to the switch.

She was horrified that he was actually about to do this, even if her sabotage was successful. And who knows, maybe he would see the rubber band even now. She held a screwdriver behind her back, knowing she might have to use it. A teardrop spilled from her right eye and rolled warmly down her cheek, but Abbas kept his eyes on the box, the switch, the looming tunnel.

The numerals switched silently to 4:00.

It was shocking to see him reach out and place his fingers on the toggle. She realized then that, whether the bomb went off or not, if he followed through with this final motion she would never be able to live with him again, even if they made it away free and clear and no one was harmed. One flip of the switch and their marriage—their entire lives together—would be blown to ruins.

Yet she also knew instinctively that if she were to shout, or plead, her action would only goad him to make the final move. The only person who could stop Abbas now was Abbas. So, instead, she merely spoke his name, almost in a whisper. Not since their courtship, so long ago, had she called out to him so tenderly.

"Abbas?"

He paused, his fingers resting on the toggle.

"Abbas?"

He slowly removed his hand, stared at it briefly, and turned toward her. His eyes conveyed a thousand different questions. Then he turned back toward the box and cried out, as if in agony. But it was not her name he called.

"Shereen!"

He doubled over as if someone had punched him in the stomach.

"Shereen! I am sorry, my daughter! I am sorry, but I cannot do it. I cannot!"

Aliyah moved quickly to his side, as much to ensure that he wouldn't change his mind as to console him. But when he collapsed against her the alarm in her brain finally shut down. She knew he was finished. The danger was past.

"It's all right," she said, as sweetly as if they were lovers entwined in bed. "It's all right, my love. It's what she would have wanted."

For a moment or two he did nothing but sob, shaking in her arms, and now her tears fell, too. That was when she heard a door burst open upstairs, and remembered with a sudden chill that in her haste the night before she had never gone back up to lock it.

Someone had come for them.

At the bottom of the basement stairs I looked straight into the eyes of Aliyah Rahim, her face streaked with dirty tears. She was crouched on the chilly floor by the light of a camping lantern and was cradling someone in her lap. I could tell from her expression that she recognized me.

"It's all right," she gasped bitterly. "It is finished. You needn't have come."

From all I could tell, she was right. There was some sort of black box next to her on the floor. Wires led from it to the mouth of a hideous tunnel.

"You're sure?" I asked, still too frightened to let go now that I had come all this way.

She nodded slowly, no hint of urgency in her movements. Then she leaned over to kiss the forehead of the man in her lap, who I realized must be her husband, Abbas. That was when I heard the banging of the upstairs door as it opened and the clatter of footsteps on the stairs behind me.

I realized then what I had just unleashed, and as I stared dumbly at Aliyah I knew that my eyes were probably already begging her forgiveness.

"Don't move!" It was a Metro policeman, gun raised. "Stay right where you are!"

He grabbed my shoulder with his free hand while a second armed man in plainclothes brushed past me toward Aliyah Rahim. All the while she kept her eyes on me, and her expression was that of doomed resignation, as if she had known from the moment we met that I would only bring her harm.

Epilogue

I suppose that when the mourners filed out of the church into the gray dusk, down the marble steps to waiting limos and television cameras, they must have wondered what all the fuss was about at the building next door. Perhaps their hearts beat a little faster as they watched helmeted men scurry into the alley behind an abandoned pizza joint. Reporters undoubtedly asked a few questions.

But to date the world has yet to learn of Washington's near miss at the hands of Abbas Rahim, much less of the heroics of his wife, Aliyah, or the belated arrival of some nameless amateur spy who, still dusty from his seasons abroad, was immediately taken into custody as a material witness.

So here I sit, writing this account at the urging of captors who have yet to tell me which government agencies they represent. They refer to this document as "my statement," and they keep demanding that I finish. Seeing as how they have offered no assurances of my release upon its completion, I am taking my own sweet time.

Mila, at least, finally tracked me down, which speaks volumes about her persistence, her energy, and her commitment to our cause. She even convinced them to let me speak with her, if only for a few minutes on the phone. I learned that for a while she thought I was lost forever. My trail went cold at Dulles Airport, or so the feds wanted her to believe. But she, too, has proven to be an able amateur, and in her usual indomitable fashion she found the cabbie who drove me to the church. Then she reached the first and only Metro cop who made it down into the cellar (until he, too, was hushed up by the Secret Service agents who swooped down in his wake).

Even then, the authorities informed her of my whereabouts and current status only after she phoned a newspaper, two television networks, and a congressman. To my mind, every lie I have told on her behalf has now been repaid in full.

I have reflected quite a bit on Mila and me during the idle hours at my disposal. Much of my focus has been those awful days back in Tanzania. I can easily recall a photo taken of me that week, and in it I look utterly lost. The only comparable image would be one of those old daguerreotypes you've probably seen of defeated generals on the field of battle, standing shell-shocked among their dead and wounded. One look at their eyes convinces you they never again could have led an army into battle. Yet the history books tell us they were back on the warpath within days, even hours.

And here I am as well, ready for the next engagement, come what may. The generals had their staff officers and supply trains. I have only Mila. And in reviewing even the most terrible of my past chapters, any sweetness and redemption hiding among the pages are due to her. Not just from what I endured on her behalf, but for what she endured on mine. For that reason, I have decided I can now live with my past. Not easily, perhaps, but with some measure of grace.

But first the authorities must decide what to do with me.

You may wonder what sort of case they have. Roughly the same one they have against Aliyah Rahim, I suppose. We were amateurs among professionals. Practicing without a license, so to speak. Then we were caught at the scene of a potential catastrophe, one that they don't wish to make public partly because it was us, not them, who prevented it.

But I suspect the deeper problem is that Abbas Rahim is not the kind of scalp they wish to hang on their wall just now. I have learned much about him from my questioners, and it is little wonder they're in such a quandary. If he were truly foreign, or well financed, or, better still, some sort of religious zealot, matters might be different. Instead he is a respected surgeon who has saved the lives of soldiers and statesmen, a very secular and very aggrieved parent from an affluent suburb of our nation's capital, albeit somewhat addled by prescription drugs. Until they find some way to dress him up in a more fitting suit of clothes, his wife and I will likely remain under wraps.

Then again, I may be underestimating Mila's talents as a persuader and agitator. My warders tell me that the journalists she contacted may soon publish their findings. This could explain the recent change in the tenor of my treatment. From the tilt of questions it is becoming clear they are trying to refashion me as some sort of hero, the man who figured things out in the nick of time. If they have their way, you might soon see me celebrated on television as the selfless aid worker who did the right thing for his country.

Freeman Lockhart, patriot at large.

The problem with that version is that I keep insisting on the full truth, warts and all. Minus my one last and best secret, of course.

So here I sit, still waiting, while each passing day makes it a little tougher for them to assemble the pieces in a manner to their liking.

That's what they get for dealing with an amateur.

Acknowledgments

In my travels during the past few decades, I have crossed the paths of aid workers in many countries, and they have almost universally proven to be among the world's most tirelessly dedicated individuals. What little they take from their professions—the adrenaline buzz of excitement or the deep satisfaction of worthwhile labor—they repay many times over with their long and often dangerous days in the field.

Several were a huge help to me in researching this book, and I would like to thank them by name. I owe particular gratitude to MacKay Wolff of the United Nations, whom I first met in Zagreb in 1993. He put me in touch with several helpful colleagues and also spent hours telling me about his life as an UNRWA observer on the West Bank during the intifada. Anything I got right about that period is due to his vivid recollections. Anything I got wrong is my own damn fault. Thanks also to Jenni Wolfson, Mica Polovina, and Bradley Foerster for sharing their experiences.

In Jordan, I'm grateful to architect-artist-botanist Ammar Khammash for enduring my badgering questions and answering them so eloquently and expansively, and also to editor Ayman Safadi of the *Al Ghad* newspaper for providing contacts and sharp observations. Thanks as well to Mamdouh Bisharat, a.k.a. "the Duke of Mukhaibeh," for an afternoon of hospitality, and also for letting me appropriate the essence of his beautiful old house on King Faysal Street as a fictional salon for one of my characters. Matar Saqer, at the Amman office of UNRWA, offered helpful insights on growing up as a refugee, as did the many people I spoke with at the Bakaa refugee camp. And I couldn't have learned how a clinic operates in such a place without having stolen some valuable time from the heroic Dr. Nabeel Heresh.

In Jerusalem, thanks to John Murphy and Rena Singer for several days of hospitality and good advice, to Dr. Eilat Mazar for sharing insights on biblical archaeology, and to Joshua Brilliant for assisting with logistics. An appreciative nod as well to Luis Leon, for recommending an excursion into Hezekiah's Tunnel.

In Athens, thanks to the Nikolaides family for their gracious welcome.

—D. F., April 2007

A NOTE ABOUT THE AUTHOR

Dan Fesperman's travels as a writer have taken him to thirty countries and three war zones. *Lie in the Dark* won the Crime Writers' Association of Britain's John Creasey Memorial Dagger Award for best first crime novel, and *The Small Boat of Great Sorrows* won the association's Ian Fleming Steel Dagger Award for best thriller.

A NOTE ON THE TYPE

This book was set in Janson, a typeface long thought to have been made by the Dutchman Anton Janson, who was a practicing typefounder in Leipzig during the years 1668–1687. However, it has been conclusively demonstrated that these types are actually the work of Nicholas Kis (1650–1702), a Hungarian, who most probably learned his trade from the master Dutch typefounder Dirk Voskens. The type is an excellent example of the influential and sturdy Dutch types that prevailed in England up to the time William Caslon (1692–1766) developed his own incomparable designs from them.

Composed by Creative Graphics, Allentown, Pennsylvania
Printed and bound by Berryville Graphics, Berryville, Virginia
Designed by Virginia Tan

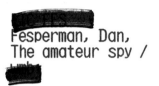